THE WISHING WELL

THE WISHING WELL

Anna Jacobs

This first world edition published in Great Britain 2004 by
SEVERN HOUSE PUBLISHERS LTD of
9–15 High Street, Sutton, Surrey SM1 1DF.
This first world edition published in the USA 2005 by
SEVERN HOUSE PUBLISHERS INC of
595 Madison Avenue, New York, N.Y. 10022.

Copyright © 2004 by Anna Jacobs.

British Library Cataloguing in Publication Data

Jacobs,   Anna
    The wishing well.
    1.   Domestic fiction
    I.   Title
    823.9'14 [F]

    ISBN 0-7278-6147-6 (cased)
    ISBN 0-7278-9141-3 (paper)

Typeset by Palimpsest Book Production Ltd.,
Polmont, Stirlingshire, Scotland.
Printed and bound in Great Britain by
MPG Books Ltd., Bodmin, Cornwall.

One

The doorbell rang twice before Laura realized what the noise was and jerked out of her reverie. She pressed the intercom and called, 'I'm coming!' then walked reluctantly down the stairs to answer it, wishing whoever it was would go away and leave her in peace.

Craig had been gone for a week now. Their marriage was finally over. It had been faltering for a while and she'd tried to tell herself they could patch it up again once he slowed down at work. She should have thrown him out the first time she found he'd been unfaithful, she knew that now. But she'd believed his promise never to stray again, believed he really was working late. How stupid could you get?

The trouble was, she felt disoriented on her own, lacking confidence in her own judgement. Well, she and Craig had been together since she was eighteen and he twenty-two. All her adult life, really. It would mean changing everything about her life now, and she could do it, she was sure she could, but it wasn't going to be easy. So she was taking it slowly. The first step would be to sign up for that advanced course on interior design she'd always wanted to attend. She'd got the information on it from the technical college where she'd studied the beginners' course, and had even started filling in the forms before this happened.

Craig had rung her a couple of times to discuss business matters but had refused point blank to tell her where he was. She had his mobile number if she wanted to contact him. That was enough. So of course she hadn't tried to contact him. What else was there to say anyway? They'd only wind up having another row.

1

She sighed and opened the door, staring through the security screen in shock. Two police officers, a man and a woman, with solemn expressions on their faces.

'We have some bad news for you, I'm afraid, Mrs Wells. May we come in?'

Her first thought was Ryan. She'd read an article saying young men had more car accidents than anyone else. As she fumbled with the lock, she prayed silently: please let him not be dead, please, please, not dead, not my Ryan. Images of him as a boy, a youth, a sometimes defiant but always loving young man, flashed in front of her.

Numbly she led the way to the family room and gestured to a sofa, sitting opposite them. 'Who is it?' she prompted. 'Who's hurt?'

The female officer leaned forward. 'It's your husband, I'm afraid.'

Craig, not Ryan. She closed her eyes for a moment in relief. 'How badly?'

There was a pause. The silence went on and on. She stared at them in shock. 'He's not . . . he can't be . . .' She couldn't get the words out.

'I'm afraid Mr Wells is dead.'

Laura closed her eyes to stop the room spinning. Next thing she knew, the female officer was forcing her head down. She struggled against it. 'I'm not going to faint.'

'Just stay still for a minute, please, Mrs Wells. It really does help.'

'Let me up!'

They did but continued to watch her warily.

She straightened her tee shirt, avoiding their eyes, her thoughts in a tangle. She couldn't imagine not seeing him walk through the door again, just couldn't.

When she looked up again she saw them all reflected in the mirror: two solemn young officers, one forty-four-year-old woman with a white face wearing a shocked expression. Was that really her? 'How?' she managed at last. 'How did he die?'

'Car accident. He was killed instantly. He couldn't have known anything, wouldn't have suffered.'

They were expecting her to weep. The male officer cleared his throat and reached for the box of tissues, pushing it nearer. She *should* be crying, sobbing on someone's shoulder, calling Craig's name—shouldn't she? Only, she didn't feel like weeping, just felt chilled and distant, as if this was happening to someone else.

The male officer cleared his throat again. 'Is there someone we can fetch, Mrs Wells? Someone who can stay with you?'

Her brain seemed not to be working properly, because it took a while to realize who she should send for. 'My children.'

'Are they at school?'

Another moment of blankness then, 'Heavens, no. They're grown-up, at work.'

'Tell us where and we'll get someone to contact them.' The male officer took down the details and went away. She could hear him in the hall talking into his mobile phone, but couldn't make out the words.

The female sat watching her.

'I need a drink.'

'Shall I make you a cup of tea, Mrs Wells?'

'Not tea. Brandy.' Her father always gave people brandy for shock.

'Are you sure that's wise?'

'I'm not sure about anything, but I'm definitely going to have a brandy.' She pushed herself to her feet and made for the bar, sloshing some cognac into a brandy balloon. She sipped it slowly, finding its warmth comforting because she felt cold.

When the male officer came back, he saw what she was drinking and exchanged worried glances with his companion. 'You need to keep a clear head, Mrs Wells.'

Laura shrugged, then caught sight of the framed photo on the mantelpiece—Craig, Ryan and Deb, arm in arm, smiling. Other memories flashed before her eyes, the laughing young Aussie she'd met in Lancashire and fallen madly in love with, the proud father holding their newborn son, the not

3

brilliantly successful business executive skirmishing at office parties, turning on her after they got home for not getting on better terms with the chairman's wife. Why had she remembered that stupid incident, for heaven's sake?

She and Craig had drifted so far apart in the past few years. When had he started being unfaithful? It didn't matter any more—not now.

Yes, it did. It always would. She took another swig of brandy to drown the pain.

'We'll wait with you till your children arrive, shall we?'

Shrugging, she set the empty glass down, feeling suddenly swimmy-headed. When had she last eaten? She couldn't remember. She was on a diet, trying not to eat too much because during their final quarrel Craig had told her she was a fat old cow. She'd intended to lose weight and prove him wrong, but already the diet was faltering. She wasn't fat, just a few pounds overweight, but he only admired scrawny women.

As if all that mattered now!

She turned to the young officer. 'Where was he?'

'Pardon?'

'My husband. Where was he when he was killed?'

'On the freeway heading south.'

'Big pile-up?'

'No.' The woman hesitated, then said, 'Actually, one of his tyres blew and he slammed into a bridge. He was killed instantly.'

Laura tried to picture it. 'Did he have his seat belt on?'

'I couldn't say.'

Craig had hated seat belts. Often drove without. Pretended to be contrite when the police stopped him and gave him a lecture, then unfastened the belt again within minutes. A sudden thought occurred to her. 'Am I supposed to go and identify the body?'

'I'm afraid so.'

'Well, I won't do it.'

The officer blinked in shock.

'I definitely won't. It'd give me nightmares for years.'

4

She couldn't even watch a horror movie without it playing back in her memory regularly. Craig had laughed at her for that, called her a wimp. Well, he wasn't going to have the last laugh now and have his battered corpse haunt her nightmares for ever. No way.

There was a sound of the front door opening and footsteps running down the hall. Deb came in, stopped at the sight of the police officers, then flopped down opposite her mother. 'What's wrong? They told me there was an emergency.'

'Your father's—' Laura hesitated, wanting to soften the blow, but finding no gentler way through the tangle of words in her head than the bare truth, '—he's been killed, Deb.'

'I don't believe you!'

'It was a road accident,' one of the officers said quietly.

Deb stared from one person to another, then wailed, 'Nooooo!' She burst into tears, shrugging her mother's hand off her shoulder and burying her face in a cushion. Laura gestured to the police officers to leave her alone, set the box of tissues on her daughter's lap, and they all waited uncomfortably for the first paroxysm to subside. Deb never cried for long, not about anything. She was the sort who held her sorrows inside her, striking out at those who tried to comfort her.

After a few minutes, Deb grabbed another handful of tissues, wiped her eyes and blew her nose. As she straightened up, she looked at her mother and her expression hardened. 'Had you two been quarrelling again?'

'What on earth has that got to do with it?'

'You *had* been having a row! It's your fault he's dead. He'll have been upset.'

Your fault! The words seemed to echo round the room, then Laura rejected them, stared at her daughter and said very loudly and clearly, 'He'd left me, been gone for a week, so if someone made him angry today, it certainly wasn't me. You were holidaying in Bali with your friends or he'd no doubt have told you what had happened.'

Deb goggled at her. 'He'd been gone for a week?'

'He found someone else. Moved in with her.'

'Caitlin?'

'He didn't tell me her name.'

'He was seeing someone called Caitlin, but it wasn't serious. It *wasn't*!'

'Does that matter now?' Laura watched her daughter frown. Deb looked so like Craig, same dark wavy hair and eyes. His princess, he'd always called her, and spoiled her in every way he could. After she'd left home, Deb and her father had lunched together regularly. Laura had never been invited to join them. Deb came home for lunch sometimes, usually with her brother, rarely on her own.

Ryan came to see his mother much more frequently, eating huge meals and making her laugh. A gentle giant, her son. Everyone liked him. And very mature for his age. He'd been good buddies with his father. They'd gone fishing together and lately started playing golf. And he'd been a protective older brother.

'They want someone to identify the body, Deb.'

'Aren't *you* going to do that?'

Laura shook her head. 'No. I can't face it.'

'It really should be you, Mrs Wells,' the female officer said quietly.

She swung round. 'Well, it's not going to be. What are you going to do about it? Drag me to the hospital screaming all the way, then force my eyes open?'

The officer looked helplessly at Deb, who gulped audibly.

The front door banged, Ryan came rushing in and Laura had to explain it all again.

He sat in frozen shock for a minute or two, then shook his head and wiped his eyes, saying in a thickened voice, 'I can't believe Dad's dead. He was always so—alive. I haven't seen him all week. I wish now I had.'

'I haven't seen him either,' Laura said quietly. 'He left me last week.'

Ryan stared at her. 'Oh, Mum. I'm so sorry. Why didn't you tell me?'

'I couldn't tell anyone. I felt so ashamed.'

'She won't even go and identify the body,' Deb offered once the explanations had tailed away.

6

'God, you're a hard little bitch sometimes!' He looked across at the officers. 'I'll come and identify him. I'd like to say goodbye. Deb? You coming?'

His sister stared at him in shock, then shuddered and shook her head.

'Then how can you blame Mum for not doing it?' He went to put his arm round his mother's shoulders. 'Will you be all right while I'm gone, Mum?'

That act of sympathy was Laura's undoing. She began to sob, clinging to her tall son and shaking with the vehemence of her grief. Because now she and Craig would never patch up their last quarrel. Because so many hopes had died in the past few years. And because no one deserved to be wiped out at the age of forty-seven.

The more she tried to control herself, the harder she sobbed. In the end Deb and the woman officer put her to bed and Ryan sent for a doctor.

He offered her some tablets to make her sleep and she took them, closing her eyes in relief and letting the world tick along without her for a while.

When Ryan went downstairs after seeing his mother sink into sleep, he found Deb curled up on the sofa, sobbing quietly. He went across and put his arms round her, letting her continue to weep against him, knowing she only let down her guard with him and their father.

It was a long time before she stopped, then he had to take her home before he could go and identify his father's body, because she was in no condition to drive.

His own grief ran deep but somehow he managed to control it, because someone in the family had to take charge and there was only him now. Grandpop had taught him that: you did what was necessary to look after your family. Oh, hell, he'd have to phone his grandparents and let them know.

What the hell was going to happen to his mother now, though? How was she going to cope? She hadn't worked outside the home for years.

Two

Bangkok

Kit Mallinder decided to return to the hotel, so dodged down a side street he hoped would lead him to the Patpong Road. Suddenly he'd had it with this place. Heat and humidity, the worst traffic jams on earth, people pushing you to buy cheap tee shirts and silver jewellery. And every alternate shop seemed to be an optician's—did everyone in Bangkok have bad eyes, for goodness' sake? In the distance he could hear the sound of whistles, which the traffic police blew incessantly, though it seemed to make no difference to the snail-slow tangles of vehicles, nor did it alter the fact that crossing a main road was a suicide mission, for when the cars suddenly jerked into movement they seemed to ignore pedestrians completely.

Yeah, he'd really had it with Bangkok. This was to have been his last assignment, an extra investigative fling offered by a friend, a potentially huge story that Kit hadn't been able to resist. Only it had gone sour on him. The inform-ation he needed was scattered to the four winds by now and he couldn't be bothered to chase after it. Someone else could bloody well unravel the scandals and muddles—if they wanted to bother. And he'd throw in his notes free. He was quitting. As of now.

He wasn't desperate for the money this assignment might have earned, because he had quite a nest egg put by. He'd never lived richly and had had a few bits of luck here and there over the years, scooping major stories and selling them to the big syndicates. And he had not only reaped the rich dividends so many freelance journalists never saw, but invested them wisely, making a few killings on the stock market. So why the hell was he wasting his time here?

The thought made him feel better, freer, and maybe that was why he stopped looking over his shoulder before he turned the next corner. Suddenly he was surrounded by a group of anonymous young men in baseball caps and sunglasses. Before he had realized what was happening, a fist rammed into his guts and they began to beat him up. He shouted for help as he tried to weave and dodge, but there was no one close. Someone pinned his arms and more pain jabbed at his body, first in one place, then in another. After a particularly vicious punch to the head, the world began to waver around him and he could feel himself sagging against the strong young bodies.

When a police siren sounded in the distance, hope flickered in him for a moment, then one of his attackers called something and they picked him up bodily. He didn't even have the breath to yell as they rushed round the corner on to the main road and tossed him in front of a big truck.

It was red. That colour was the last thing he saw as he thought what a stupid, messy way this was to die.

Kit stared around, his vision blurring and wavering as he wondered where the hell he was. It looked like—it *was* a hospital bed! He tried to sit up and couldn't. Just as panic was setting in, a nurse bent over him.

'Well, hello there. Awake at last. How are you feeling?'

'Bad.' His voice was croaky, his throat a sandy desert, and he was strapped up like a Christmas turkey with a life monitor beeping gently beside him. 'Bloody hell!' he whispered. Or he might only have thought it.

'Do you remember your name?'

'Mm–Mallin–der.'

'Good, good.' She might have been encouraging a small child to say its first word. 'Don't try to move. Your legs are broken and the rest of you is somewhat battered.'

He was alive, though! Joy welled up inside him. Alive! Whatever had happened to him hadn't finished him off.

9

Within minutes his room was invaded by another nurse and a doctor who prodded and poked at him, asking him irritating questions. Of course it damned well hurt! The two of them kept looking sideways at electronic instruments whose purposes he couldn't fathom and whose dials he couldn't see.

When he felt the darkness descending again he welcomed it with a sigh of relief. He wanted nothing but to sleep. If they'd just leave him in peace and let him sleep, he'd get better in his own time. He always did.

When Kit next awoke he felt clearer in the head and there didn't seem to be as much machinery around. It was night and the lights were low. He'd have liked to lie quietly and try to remember how he'd got there, but the minute he raised his head, some damned alarm started beeping.

'Shut up!' he told it, his voice muffled and hoarse.

A nurse came hurrying through the door and switched the beeper off. She stared down at him, eyes narrowed in professional scrutiny, then felt his forehead. 'Good.'

'What the hell's good about this?'

'It's good that you're awake. What is your name, please?'

'They asked me that last time. Did no one write it down?'

'Your name, please?'

He hadn't the energy to argue. 'Mallinder, Christopher Mallinder, freelance journalist, more commonly known as Kit. What's yours?'

But, of course, she didn't answer, just pressed a buzzer then aimed a thermometer into his ear and slipped another gadget on his fingertip.

A doctor came to join her and when they'd finished prodding him around and confirmed that he was indeed in full possession of his senses, he demanded the right to ask them a few questions.

The doctor glanced quickly at her wristwatch and sat down beside him. 'Very well. But I can't guarantee to answer them all.'

'Where am I?'

'Jamieson Blane Hospital for Foreigners.'

It meant nothing to him. 'Where?'

'Bangkok.'

He hadn't even remembered that he was in Thailand, let alone why. 'How the hell did I get here?'

'You were brought in by ambulance. We were the closest emergency centre—and we had the facilities to save your life. You were very lucky, actually. If you'd been further away, given our wonderful traffic jams, you might have bled to death on the way.'

He tried to remember what he had been doing to get in this state, but his mind was a blank. 'I can't remember anything about the accident.'

'That isn't surprising. You've been unconscious for several days. Your wallet was missing, of course.'

He could only gape at her.

'We found out who you were from your passport. Luckily your travel insurance papers were in your bag with it—' she grinned at him, '—or else you'd have been transferred to a public hospital. Not nearly as comfortable.'

'What happened to me?'

'We were hoping you could tell us that.' She cocked one eyebrow at him and he shook his head. 'Well, it appears you were mugged, then pushed in front of a truck. The driver saw them do it, but didn't see any of their faces. You should have died but you didn't because the truck driver swerved and managed to miss your more vital organs. Unfortunately he couldn't avoid running over your legs.'

In a sudden panic he tried to peer down at his body. 'Have I still got everything, though?'

'Yes. Two arms, two legs.'

'Fingers, toes?'

'Those as well. Ten of each. Though they're not intact, I'm afraid. Lot of smaller bones were broken as well as one or two bigger ones. You'll need quite a long period of rehabilitation when you get out of here, some reconstructive operations and—' she hesitated, then added, '—you'll probably always walk with a limp.'

11

He stared at her in horror.

'Don't waste time on regrets, Mr Mallinder. What has happened cannot un-happen. You're alive and if you hadn't been so fit, you might not have recovered at all.' She sighed and wriggled her shoulders in a discreet stretch. 'I must go now.'

She looked exhausted so he stopped asking questions and, thank heavens, they left him in peace for a while. But the damned nurses still kept peering through the door at regular intervals and he couldn't sleep for long because people kept coming in to take his blood pressure or temperature.

'Is all this necessary?' he snapped the fourth time they woke him. 'I'm trying to get some sleep here.'

'I'm afraid so.' The nurse smiled. 'You're lucky to be alive, Mr Mallinder. Hang on to that and put up with our prying ways.'

She was pretty. Normally, he'd have been chatting her up. Now he felt nothing. Surely he hadn't lost that most essential part of him?

He found out the next day that he was still intact when they pulled the catheter out.

'You swear a lot,' the nurse said disapprovingly afterwards.

'You'd swear too if they did this to you!'

Why? he asked himself when they left him alone. He asked the same question at regular intervals over the next few weeks. Why had someone tried to kill him? What had he been investigating? Or was it just a random mugging?

As soon as Kit was able, he returned to England, needing a nurse to escort him there. The night before he left hospital he woke to find a man in his room.

'Who are you?'

'Reporter. Looking for a story.'

'Well, you won't find one here.'

The man shrugged. 'You never know. What happened to you?'

'Damned if I know. I've no memory of the accident.'

'Ah, it'll come back to you.'

'They think not. If it was going to, I'd have started remembering by now.'

A nurse was passing and stared in shock at the stranger. 'Who are you?'

He shoved her out of the way so violently she crashed into the wall and fell over, by which time he was well down the corridor.

She scrambled to her feet and pressed an alarm button. 'Are you all right, Mr Mallinder?'

'Yes. And you?'

She began to straighten her uniform, keeping a wary eye on the door and breathing an audible sigh of relief when a security guard came rushing in. 'Intruder.'

Kit didn't get much sleep the rest of that night, because, even when the staff left him alone, he couldn't stop going over in his mind what the intruder had said. It must be connected to what he'd been investigating. Only, what the hell was that?

He was relieved when they let him fly back to England, but before he left he got a journo he knew slightly to write an article for the local newspaper, stressing his retirement due to ill health and his complete loss of memory about why he'd been in Bangkok. His friend came and interviewed the doctors and one of them said he'd probably never remember anything now. Kit hoped that would satisfy whoever it was who'd been nosing around, and wondered if he'd had another narrow escape that night.

He was determined about one thing. Even if he did remember something, he'd never admit it to a soul.

He went through a hell of a lot of rehabilitation when he got back to England. Too bloody much. He even sold an article on it to one of the weekend magazines. That tickled his sense of the ridiculous, at least.

It was stubbornness that kept him going, and a determination to prove the doctors wrong. He might never run again, but he was determined to walk without a limp.

Three

The next day Laura got up at her usual time but couldn't settle to anything. When the post arrived she found nothing but bills and a bank statement, which she studied carefully. She usually left this side of things to Craig, not because she couldn't read a bank statement, but because that was the way they'd split the family tasks between them. He was an accountant working in the finance section of his company, after all.

She frowned at the totals. There didn't seem to be as much in their joint account as she'd expected, certainly far less than last month. She'd be all right for money, though, because they'd taken out a big life insurance policy on Craig and renewed it recently. Well, they had a big one on her too. It made sense, after all.

She'd better ring up and find out how to collect the insurance. She sighed. There were so many things to sort out when a man died and what she was dreading most was going through his remaining clothes and personal effects, she didn't know why. The mistress could keep the other stuff.

Picking up the phone, she dialled the insurance company and explained her situation, then sat tapping her fingers impatiently until they put her through to an older-sounding man.

'My husband had a life insurance policy with you—has had for years—and he's just been killed. What do I do about claiming?'

'Do you have the policy number?'

'No. I can't find it, but I know he took one out because there's a payment been made recently through our joint account.' She gave Craig's details and waited again.

'Your name is?'

She could not hold back a snort of angry breath. 'Laura Wells. I'm his wife.'

'Yes. But I'm afraid—'

He hesitated for so long she guessed something was wrong, but not how badly wrong.

'—you're not named as the beneficiary.'

'*What?*'

He repeated it.

'I don't understand. I've always been the beneficiary, just as he's the beneficiary for my own life insurance.'

'He—um—changed that when he renewed recently.'

'Who is the beneficiary, then?'

'I can't divulge that, I'm afraid.'

She slammed the phone down and rang their lawyer, but he wasn't available, so she left word for him to ring her on a matter of urgency, then began pacing the house. Mirror after mirror reflected back her angry face and at last she stopped in front of one and faced the possibility squarely. 'Surely he can't have named his floozy as beneficiary?'

The mirror didn't answer back, and after a minute she moved on, not knowing what to do today, though normally she could find a dozen tasks demanding her attention.

When their lawyer rang back half an hour later she explained the situation briefly.

'Ah.'

'What do you mean by that?'

Silence, then, 'Look, in the circumstances, I need to inform you I'm acting for the other party as of a few days ago; that is, your husband and his—um . . .'

'Mistress.'

'You know about her, then?'

'Yes.'

'I think you should find yourself another lawyer, Mrs Wells. It would be more appropriate now. And I'd better warn you—your husband made a new will. He's left every-thing he could to his new—er, partner, including his shares.'

After he'd put the phone down, Laura held the receiver

15

in her hand for a long time, until the buzzing sound registered, then she set it back in the cradle. She went into the kitchen and couldn't think why she'd gone there.

How could Craig have done that to her? The shares were going to be their superannuation fund.

Later that day the doorbell rang and she hurried to answer it, pleased at the thought of seeing someone.

But a stranger stood there. A young woman.

'Yes?'

'Mrs Wells?'

'Yes.'

'Look, can I come in? It's not the sort of thing we can discuss on the doorstep. It's about Craig. I'm Caitlin Sheedy. He was living with me when he—he . . .' Tears welled in her eyes and one rolled down her cheek.

Laura stared at her, feeling too angry to be sympathetic. Twenty years younger than her, at a guess. Auburn hair, slender figure, pretty face—and reddened, puffy eyes. The woman must have really cared for Craig to have got herself into this state. Taking a deep breath, she ordered herself to be civilized, opened the door wider and gestured to the other to come inside.

She didn't offer any refreshments or small talk but led the way into the formal living room, indicated a sofa and sat down opposite her visitor. Which was as civilized as she could manage.

'I don't know how you're supposed to deal with this sort of thing, but I want to try to be—calm and polite,' Caitlin said as the silence grew too ominous. She gulped and fought for control, wiping her eyes quickly with a tissue. 'Sorry. I was a bit nervous of coming. Craig said you had a temper.'

Laura sighed and pulled the reins even more tightly on her anger. 'Take your time. We're neither of us at our best just now and I'm not going to attack you.' She waited, watched the other woman take a deep, shaky breath.

'He had a new will drawn up after he left you.'

'So the lawyer said.'

'I've made a copy for you. I only knew roughly what it contained until I found it among his things this morning.' Caitlin fumbled in her handbag and pulled out some papers, looking down at them and saying in a wobbly voice. 'I—you see, I'm pregnant. We didn't mean to, but well, it happened. So he decided he'd better make a new will.'

Laura was so stunned she couldn't speak for a moment. *Pregnant!*

Caitlin stared down at her lap, then across at Laura again, her expression pleading. 'I came to ask you if we could sort it all out without—you know, acrimony. You see—I'm going to need money, given the circumstances.'

Laura suddenly realized that Craig had set up his mistress at her expense. 'You've got his life insurance money as well as part of the house and the shares. It seems to me you've taken nearly everything from me.'

'Life insurance money?'

There was no mistaking the other's sincerity. No actress was that good. Caitlin definitely hadn't known about the insurance. Actually, in other circumstances Laura would probably have thought she had an honest, open sort of face. At the moment, however, she wanted the other woman out of the house, hoped she'd never need to see her again. 'Thank you for bringing the will. I'll have to get myself another lawyer and find out where I stand before I can comment further, Miss Sheedy. Apparently our old lawyer is acting for you now.'

'He is?'

'Craig could move fast when he wanted something.' Laura bit off any criticism of her late husband, because if she once started she'd never stop. 'If you'll give me your phone number, I'll get back to you. I agree with you that acrimony won't do either of us much good, but this house—' she gestured around her, '—is the result of a lot of hard work on my part, and the shares were meant to be *my* superannuation too, so I have to warn you that I don't feel good about that.'

Caitlin's face crumpled. 'I didn't mean this to happen. I promise you I didn't. It's—the being pregnant and—'

'Mm.' Laura stood up, not wanting to discuss anything else.

'Um—there's one more thing.'

Laura sat down again, keeping her lips pressed firmly together. She was going to stay polite if it killed her.

'The funeral.'

She'd been avoiding thoughts of that all day. 'What about it?'

'I'd like to—arrange things. But I need to know: do you want to come? If so, we can discuss how we organize it.'

Laura stared at her in horror. The thought of being on public view at a ceremony where Craig's mistress was playing the central role made her feel sick. 'No. I definitely shan't be coming.' This time when she stood up, her visitor did too.

Caitlin pulled out a piece of paper and put it on the table. 'My address and phone number.'

Laura nodded and moved towards the door as quickly as she could, avoiding the temptation to look at the other woman's stomach and estimate how far on the pregnancy was. All she could do was concentrate on being *civilized*. She was giving no one a chance to say she'd lost control and made a scene.

She closed the door quickly, not waiting for Caitlin to drive away, then picked up an ornament she'd always hated, one which Craig's mother had given them just before she died. Carrying it outside into the back garden, she smashed it down as hard as she could on the paved area, then stood there breathing deeply, staring down at the fragments.

That helped.

A little.

Ryan drew up just as Caitlin was getting into her car. As she waved to him and drove away, he gaped after her, then went to ring the doorbell. After a short delay his mother opened it.

'Did Caitlin come and see you, Mum?'

'Yes.'

He let out a long, soft whistle. 'She's the last person I'd have expected to find here. I didn't think you even knew who Dad's—um—friend was.'

'I didn't until Deb told me her name yesterday, though I've known for a while there was someone. How do *you* know her?'

He flushed. 'Oh. Well. I've seen Dad with her a couple of times. He introduced us. I've only said hello to her, though, not spent any time with her.'

'Well, maybe you can go round and comfort her after you've finished here. She is, after all, about to present you with a new brother or sister.' She turned away from his open-mouthed astonishment and went inside, leaving him to follow or not as he chose.

He shut the front door and followed her into the kitchen, clipping her up in a big hug, though she struggled against it for a moment. Then she gave in and clung to him, glad of his support, surprised at how strong he felt. A tall young man, her son, not exactly good-looking with that large nose, but very attractive. Everyone said so, not just her. He had a smile that could melt butter and—much more important to her—a kind, generous nature. Actually, he was rather like her father in many ways.

'Cup of tea?' she asked, knowing what his answer would be.

'Don't you have any coffee?'

'You and your coffee,' she teased.

But he didn't smile back and insist that coffee was the better drink as he would usually have done. Instead he walked round the kitchen, fiddling with things while she put the kettle on and made two mugs of instant.

'We'll have it in here, shall we?'

Ryan nodded and sat down at the table in the family meals area. He studied his mother and sighed. She looked as if the slightest thing would make her burst into tears and who could really blame her after an encounter with her

19

husband's pregnant mistress? 'Mum, I was thinking—what are we going to do about the funeral?' He watched her cradle her mug in her hands and saw how they were shaking.

'*She* is arranging the funeral. She asked me if I wanted to attend.'

He reached out to lay his hand on hers, wishing he knew how to comfort her. 'Oh, Mum, how rotten for you! But you will go, won't you?'

She shook her head. 'No. I can't face it, not with *her* there as well. If he'd been gone a year, no one would expect me to attend and I don't see why it should make any difference that it's only just over a week.'

He sipped his coffee, wondering what to say.

'I shan't mind if you and Deb go.'

'You will, but I think we should anyway.'

'Caitlin left her address and phone number. I'll let you have them before you leave.'

'Thanks.' He took a deep breath, wondering how to give her his other news, but of course she guessed something was wrong.

'Just tell me straight out, whatever it is,' she said quietly.

'I'm being transferred to the Melbourne office. They want me to move over there next month.' Two thousand miles away, a three-hour plane flight. It wouldn't be easy for them to see one another or for him to keep an eye on her, though she'd be all right financially, what with this house and Dad's insurance money. His father had always boasted about how well he'd provided for his family—in case the worst happened. He saw her take an uneven breath, then clamp her mouth shut. 'I'm sorry, Mum. It's rotten timing, I know.'

'Is it a promotion?'

'Sort of. It's part of the management-training programme.'

'Then congratulations.'

'Thanks.' He saw how wobbly her smile was and guilt made him say quickly, 'Look, I'll help you with whatever I can before I leave, only I can't refuse to go. It's a brilliant opportunity to extend my skills.'

'I'm glad for you, really I am.'

'So was I, but now—well, I feel awful. I should be here helping you at a time like this.'

'I appreciate the thought but I can manage. If you'd clear out the clothes and personal possessions your father left here though, I'd be deeply grateful. I'd been dreading doing that. Keep anything you want and send the rest to the Salvos. You can even ask *her* if she wants anything. I truly won't mind.'

Relief brightened his face. 'Right. Can do.' He swirled the remains of his coffee round and round in the mug. 'Has Deb been in touch?'

'No.'

'She promised me she would be.'

'Well, that's her choice. Um—there's something else. Caitlin told me your father had made a new will and that she's a beneficiary. Do you mind if I have a quick glance at it? She gave me a copy.'

'Go ahead.'

Laura read the will in growing indignation, this time making no attempt to rein in her anger. When she'd finished she flung the papers down on the floor, scattering them. 'I can't believe that even Craig would do this to me! He made *her* the beneficiary for his life insurance policy without telling me—and *I* wrote the damned cheque that paid for it! Surely that's enough for her, given the short time she's invested in him? But no. She also gets a third of his half of the house, sharing it with you and Deb, and it sounds like most of his superannuation shares. *That woman* is going to come out of this far richer than me, it seems. I shall contest the will.' Her voice broke on the last statement and she dashed away a tear. Damn! She had promised herself not to break down in front of anyone.

'Oh, Mum, that's awful!' Ryan reached out and took her hand, his expression changing, then changing again as the implications of this for his own future sank in.

She let her hand lie in his for a moment, limp and uncon-nected, the way she felt. 'We'll have to see what my new lawyer says about it—once I find one. Jack Benham is apparently acting for *her* now. When I think of all the work I've put into our various houses...' When he didn't say anything, she realized suddenly that she now had a goal, something to keep her busy. 'I guess you and Deb will want to take your money out, and I certainly don't want to stay here, so I think I'd better sell this place as quickly as I can.'

'Mmm. Probably a good idea. If you don't mind moving out, that is.'

'I do mind having to move out but I can't afford to stay. I shan't have any money coming in and this is a big place to run.' She'd been thinking of starting up her own business, designer decorating; she knew she was good at it but had hesitated to take the plunge. Now, she didn't think she could face the hassles. She felt diminished by what had happened, there was no other word for it. Craig being unfaithful and leaving her was bad enough, but the fact that he'd ripped her off financially made her feel less confident about her ability to deal with the world, somehow.

Ryan nudged her. 'Look—have you actually found yourself a new lawyer yet, Mum?'

She shook her head.

'There's a woman at work who's just been through a rather nasty divorce. She had a lawyer who did well by her. Want me to get his name?'

'I suppose so.'

When Ryan had left, Laura went out into the garden and swept up the crockery shards, then began to deadhead some flowers. She needed to keep active and the house had to look its best if they were going to sell it.

But she kept remembering that Craig was dead and tears continued to escape and drip down her nose. Damn it, he didn't deserve any tears, not after the way he'd treated her! Only she couldn't forget the good times they'd had together. He hadn't always been such a rat. And he'd always been a wonderful father.

What the hell was she going to do with her life afterwards? She wasn't close to her daughter and Ryan was moving away. Most of her friends were couples who'd known them both for years. She'd seen it before when people divorced: singles didn't fit into dinner parties so weren't invited as often and gradually dropped out of the group.

She could feel herself shrivelling inside, growing smaller, less certain of herself and her place in the world. Well, she'd never had Craig's ebullient confidence. She'd always been the quiet one; the supporting act, he used to call her.

The stupid one, she now knew.

She wondered whether she should revert to her maiden name, but that would seem like cutting herself off from her children, as if she didn't belong to them any more. No. She'd been Laura Wells for much longer than she'd been Laura Cleaton, so she'd stick with it.

Joe arrived at the hospital near Manchester where his brother was recovering from the final operation on his left leg, which had been the more badly damaged.

'How are you feeling?'

Kit shrugged. 'All right. At least the end is in sight now.'

Joe fidgeted with the paper bag he was carrying, studying it as if he'd never seen it before, then held it out. 'Grapes and chocolate.'

'Thanks. Put it there.' Kit studied him. A large bear of a man, Joe, not good with words. No need to open the bag: his brother always brought red grapes and dark chocolate. 'Come on. Tell me what's wrong.'

Joe pursed his lips, then shook his head ruefully. 'I wasn't sure whether to say anything yet, but well—Uncle Alf died suddenly yesterday. A heart attack.'

'Oh, no! I was looking forward to seeing him again. He was such a feisty old devil.'

'The funeral's on Saturday, but I asked that sister in charge and she said you couldn't possibly be let out to attend.'

Kit stared at the wall, trying to curb his anger at whoever had done this to him, something he'd had to do many times.

He knew he'd only damage his leg if he disobeyed and went to the funeral, but it was a hard pill to swallow, because he'd been very fond of his Uncle Alf. 'I'm sorry about that,' he managed at last. 'I'd have liked to see him off properly. He phoned me only last week. He never said much, but it was nice to keep in touch. I was supposed to phone him back tomorrow.'

Joe's voice was gentle. 'He enjoyed your phone calls. You need to know—he told me a while ago—that he's left everything to us. There's the house, you know, and there'll be some money, so, it'll be—useful.'

'I'd rather have him around.' Pictures cascaded through Kit's mind. Uncle Alf had brightened up both of their lives as boys, because their parents had cared more about the material side of things than listening to lads' doings. Not that they'd been bad parents, but they'd certainly never been *fun* as Alf had. 'Shall I send some flowers?'

'He didn't want any. Said flowers are for the living and people should drink to his memory instead.'

Kit smiled. It sounded so like Alf.

On the following Monday evening, Joe turned up again and this time proffered a fat letter in a business envelope instead of his standard gift. Kit studied it in puzzlement, noting the name of a firm of lawyers on the envelope. 'What's this?'

'A letter from Uncle Alf about what he's left you.'

'Oh.'

'Go on! Open it.'

Kit found a covering letter from the lawyer, then a letter in Alf's familiar spidery handwriting and a copy of the will. The mere sight of the letter brought tears to his eyes and he had to blink hard before he could read it. He looked up in shock at Joe even before he had finished. 'He's left me his house! That's not fair. Look, I'll share the proceeds from it with you and—'

Joe shook his head and gave his brother a wry smile. 'He's left me enough money to make up for it. He said in

24

my letter that I needed to go out and do something rash or extravagant, not settle down. What did he say in your letter?'

Kit finished reading and his smile echoed his brother's. 'The old devil!' he said softly and fondly. 'He said it was about time I put down roots, so he's leaving me the house, but only on condition that I live in it for at least a year before I sell it.'

'And shall you do that?'

'I don't know.' Kit had never stayed anywhere for a whole year since he left university. Was this gift a pointer from fate as to his future, or a wise old man trying to guide him? He didn't know. Hell, the only thing he knew at the moment was that he wanted out of hospitals and rehabilitation centres.

He'd think about the legacy later.

Four

Ron Cleaton watched his wife stand stock-still and stare round in puzzlement and fear. His heart clenched in anguish. She was becoming more forgetful by the day.

'I'll get the tea, love. You sit down and have a rest.' But he had to guide her to a chair before she did as he suggested. It was as if she didn't understand what he was saying, and she hardly ever spoke now, let alone answered his questions. He still kept talking to her, though.

The tablets had helped for a while but the effects had suddenly begun to fade and the doctors said there was nothing else they could do for her. So, Ron looked after her as best he could, thankful he'd retired and could do this himself. The social workers called him a 'Carer' and offered him respite accommodation for Pat, to give him a break. But he didn't want a break from her. He wanted to make the most of every single minute while she could still recognize him. Only, he wasn't even sure if she did now, on her bad days.

Once, she had never been still for a moment. Now she spent long periods staring aimlessly into space, and when she wasn't staring, she was walking. If she was indoors, she'd pace round and round the table till he thought he'd go mad. He'd made the back yard secure and, on fine days, he let her go outside and walk to her heart's content, keeping an eye on her from the kitchen window as he washed the dishes or did other household chores. There never seemed to be enough hours in the day to keep up with everything and he knew the house was looking run-down.

It was more than time to let Laura know about her mother

and suggest that his younger daughter come back for a visit before it was too late. The Australian grandchildren as well, perhaps. Eh, it'd been hard to keep Pat's condition to himself when Ryan phoned up every month for a chat. Ron had been going to tell Laura about her mother last week, but then Ryan had rung to let him know Craig had been killed, so it'd seemed better to leave it until after the funeral and fuss were over.

His older daughter Sue lived across the other side of town, near enough to visit frequently, but she hadn't come for a while. She wasn't taking her mother's condition very well and had burst into tears on her last visit and left hurriedly. That had upset the new, timid Pat and he'd told Sue not to come again unless she could control herself. He shouldn't have spoken so sharply, though. Regretted that, because Sue hadn't been well either.

Some people just couldn't cope with a loved one having Alzheimer's, he knew that from the books he'd read about the condition. But as far as he was concerned, Pat was still his wife, the woman he loved, the mother of their two daughters.

After they'd had a cup of tea, he left her sitting in front of the television, went into the hall and picked up the phone. This would be a good time to call Australia.

'Laura?'

'Dad, how are you?'

'I'm well. Look, love—' he hesitated, glanced quickly over his shoulder and launched into the speech he'd prepared while lying awake at three o'clock that morning.

'I'll see you as soon as I can, then, Dad.' Laura put down the phone and sniffed away a tear. She couldn't believe that her lively little mother had Alzheimer's, didn't want to believe it. Her own troubles suddenly seemed far less important.

She would book a flight to England as soon as possible and . . . she sighed. And then what? Stay in that small house and watch her mother fade before her eyes? Sit and wonder

27

whether she too was destined to lose her mind? The tendency to Alzheimer's was inherited, wasn't it? She'd have to find out more about it. She really must get better at using computers. Ryan always said you could find out anything you needed to know on the Internet.

Feeling as if she had to start preparing for the trip this very minute, she jerked to her feet, then sank down again on the chair. There were a few problems to solve before she could leave. Major problems. She had an appointment with the new lawyer the next day. Wasn't there a rule about a wife being entitled to a fixed share of a husband's estate? If there was, she'd push for every cent she could. She'd worked damned hard on those houses and all *that woman* had done to get a slice of the profits was sleep with Craig.

And love him. Caitlin must have loved him, to judge from the reddened eyes. It'd be much easier to hate her if she hadn't.

Deb beamed at Ryan when he told her the news about their inheritance. 'Oh, good. That means I can quit work for a while and do some travelling. I should have gone to university like you. Office work sucks. Wasn't it great of Dad to think of us?' She blinked away the tears that threatened every time she talked about her father.

'Great for us, not so great for Mum.'

She pulled a face. 'She didn't deserve him.'

'Hey, that's not fair!'

'Well, look how she's let herself go. She's at least ten pounds overweight and she used to slop around the house all day in *rags*. No wonder he didn't fancy her any more.'

'She wore old clothes because she did all the painting, decorating and gardening on each new house they built. If it hadn't been for her, they'd not have made the fat profits they did. Anyway, that's irrelevant now. I think she's going to contest the will.'

'What? But that'll stop us getting our share.'

'You're a right little bitch, you know that?'

'And you're a—'

The phone rang and she went to pick it up. 'Oh, Mum.

Hi. Must catch up with you soon and—Yes, he's here. Right, yeah! I'll put him on.'

'Hi, Mum.'

'Ryan, can you and Deb come round here—now? I've something to tell you. More bad news, I'm afraid.' Her voice wobbled on the last word.

'We'll come straight away.' He put the phone down and scowled at his sister. 'Mum needs us.'

'But I need to wash my hair. I'm going out clubbing later and . . .' Her voice trailed away at the disgust on his face.

'She was in tears.'

'*Mum was?*'

'Yes. Said there was more bad news. Hell, what else can have happened?'

Deb gave an exaggerated sigh, but picked up her bag and jacket and followed him out. Their mother didn't often cry. She was more likely to fly into a temper.

Laura waved her children to chairs, then said bluntly, 'It's your grandmother, I'm afraid.'

'Gran? She's not dead too?' Deb stared at her in horror.

'No. But she's got Alzheimer's. Dad rang me last night. She's apparently slipping away fast.' Laura had to stop for a moment to pull herself together. 'He says if we want to see her while she still recognizes us, we'd better go to England soon. Very soon.'

Deb burst into noisy tears, suddenly looking younger than her twenty-one years.

Laura knew better than to offer her daughter a hug, but she was sure the grief was genuine. Deb and her grandmother had always got on like a house on fire. Her parents had visited them in Australia three times, longer visits than Craig had wanted, but it was silly to come all that way for two weeks, so they'd stayed for two months each time. And Laura had taken the children back to England one year, though Craig hadn't gone with them. As far as he was concerned, it wasn't his country, he hated the English weather and Laura's parents weren't really his family.

29

He'd made it very plain to her in private that he resented the money their trip had cost and didn't want her to repeat the exercise. She should have done what she'd threatened and got a job, paid her own way from then on. Why hadn't she? Because he always said he didn't want her to go out to work, wanted her at home for the children.

Looking back, she wondered if that was when the coolness had started between them. Had he been unfaithful when she was away? Oh, what did it matter now? Why did she keep going over it? He was dead.

She watched Ryan move across to put an arm round his sister and waited for Deb's sobbing to stop before continuing. 'As soon as I've sorted out the will and made arrangements to sell this house, I'm returning to Lancashire. I'll probably stay until—well, until I'm not needed any more. I'll get a job over there if I can. I'll need to—now. You two will have enough money from your share of your father's will to come for a visit. I think you should, but it's your decision. I can't afford to pay for you, given the circumstances.'

They sat very still, reminding her suddenly of when they were little and in trouble. They'd frozen then in just the same way, sitting or standing side by side to face the music. They'd always got on really well, considering Ryan was two years older and about a hundred years more mature than Deb.

'What are you going to do about Caitlin and the will?' he asked.

'Tell my lawyer to settle matters as quickly as possible. *That woman* is going to get a win out of this, because I haven't time to fight it through the courts. I want to see my mother, spend time with her. And Dad needs help. He's seventy-five, too old to be doing everything for her.'

Ryan hesitated. 'I could speak to Caitlin for you if you like.'

Laura let out a snort. 'To what end? She's not going to give up her share in this house and he's named her as beneficiary for the share portfolio. Why I let him put them in his name, I don't know. I must have been crazy. Then there's the five hundred thousand dollars of life insurance paid for by the wife who gets nothing. This Ms Sheedy will do very well indeed out of all this.'

Deb gaped at her. 'What do you mean?'

Laura explained in quick, terse sentences.

'You're kidding!'

'Nope. Your father not only named her the beneficiary for his life insurance without telling me—he let me write the cheque for the premium.' That really rankled.

'I don't *believe* Daddy would do that to you,' Deb said, scowling at her. 'You've got it all wrong. He used to laugh at the way you made mistakes with the finances all the time and needed his help.'

Ryan tugged at her arm. 'Deb, stop that!'

'Why should I? It's true.'

As if from a distance, Laura heard herself say, 'He was exaggerating. I simply wasn't as quick as he was—but then I didn't train as an accountant. Couples usually split the family jobs between them, you know. It was logical for him to do that one.'

Ryan shook his head at his sister and gave her a warning look.

Laura bit back more angry words. 'Go and see the insurance company if you don't believe me, Deb, or better still, go and see Caitlin. She'll confirm that nearly everything is coming to her. You'll want to wish her well with the baby, too.'

Deb clearly didn't know about this either. She goggled at her mother, then looked at Ryan.

'Caitlin's expecting Dad's child,' he said quietly. 'I didn't want to tell you till you were calmer.'

Deb's mouth formed a 'No!' but no sound came out.

Laura didn't pursue that point, just finished what she had to say. 'Anyway, that's neither here nor there. I'm going to England as quickly as I can. I have to sell this house to pay you two off and I'll be selling the furniture as well, so if you'd let me know whether there's anything you particularly want by tea time tomorrow, I'll summon the estate agents and get the place to display stage as quickly as I can. And if you want to ring your grandfather, well, I think he'd welcome your support. He sounded very upset.'

'I'll ring him tomorrow once I've got my head together,' Deb muttered, standing up and slinging her tote bag across one shoulder. She looked across at her mother. 'You should have split up with Dad years ago, you know. You'd both have been happier.'

'I didn't know about his other women until quite recently or I would have left him.' Laura walked towards the front door, holding on to her self-control—just.

Deb walked out with the merest nod.

Ryan followed, pausing to say, 'She's upset about Dad. She isn't usually so unkind.'

'She is, you know. With me, anyway.' And it always hurt.

'Oh, Mum!' He hugged her. 'I'll be round tomorrow night to go through Dad's things for you.'

When Laura closed the door, she sagged against it for a moment, tears welling in her eyes. Then she sniffed and reminded herself of how her poor father must be feeling. How did you face the slow disintegration of someone you loved? At least she'd no longer loved Craig, hadn't for quite a while if she was honest with herself. And he'd gone quickly.

On the principle that work is the best way to stop yourself brooding, she went round the house figuring out how to make it look its best and taking notes, a task that always gave her great satisfaction. Even Craig had trusted her artistic judgement and her practical flair for decorating.

But, thinking of him, she had to stop and swallow hard. Why had he implied that she was incompetent with money? She wasn't—was she?

Perhaps she was. Perhaps someone more astute would have prevented Craig from taking everything away from her.

Kit waited impatiently for his brother to pick him up from the rehabilitation centre just outside Manchester. He'd had a gutful of hospitals over the past few months, and all he wanted now was to live in a real house again and pull his life together.

He glanced at his watch then clicked his tongue in exasperation. Trust Joe to be late. His brother had a very relaxed idea of time.

Almost quarter of an hour later he saw an ancient red Sierra rattle through the gates and come to a halt at the other side of the car park. Kit stared at it in disgust. Could Joe really not afford a better car than that? He was amazed it'd got through the MOT. He greeted his brother with, 'I thought we said eleven o'clock?'

'Sorry. Got delayed. Had to take a relief class for another teacher.' Joe glanced at his watch. 'As it is, I've just time to get you home, then I must dash back to school. Is this all your luggage?'

'Yes.'

'Looks like you've got more books than clothes.'

'Probably. Careful with the laptop.' Kit swung his crutches into position and followed Joe out of the front door, grimacing as one of the crutches twisted on the uneven surface and he lurched into the wall. 'Damn!'

'Should we have got you a wheelchair?'

'No, we bloody well shouldn't. I'm slow but I can manage.' He hated the ignominy of wheelchairs. The minute you sat in one, people treated you as if you were brain dead. Crutches were marginally better, though not much. And as for his left leg, it disgusted him, all bumps and hollows and scars. He was sure any normal woman would shy away from being made love to by a man with that leg.

He reached the car, slapped Joe's hovering hand away and manoeuvred himself carefully into the front passenger seat, slanting the crutches alongside him. 'What are you grinning about?'

'You're still an independent devil.'

Kit scowled down at his leg. 'As much as I can be.'

Joe's voice grew more gentle. 'Look, I've got a studio couch, so you can sleep in the front room downstairs if you want. Trouble is, the bathroom's upstairs, but I could prob-ably borrow a camp toilet from school and—'

'I'll sleep in a bedroom, thank you very much, and get myself to the toilet like everyone else does.'

'But that leg—'

'Is getting better. Final operation over, pins removed. Just have to take it easy now and wait for everything to mend, then I can get rid of these damned crutches. Besides, I can go up and down the stairs on my arse, if that's all you're worrying about.'

'But the doctor said you should—'

'Sod the doctor.'

Joe pressed his lips together and looked disapproving.

Kit felt marginally better for winning that round. But it wasn't going to do any good to either of them to argue or score points. It was going to be hard enough for two such different people to live together, no need to make it worse. The trouble was, as Kit was only too well aware, he couldn't manage on his own yet. And besides, he had nowhere else to go. Joe was his only close relative now.

He'd been living in a tiny furnished flat in London at the time of the accident, a place he'd rented to store his gear and camp out in between projects. Once he found out he was going to be in and out of rehabilitation centres and hospitals for months and could stay in a hostel nearby, he'd asked an old friend to shut down the flat and put his posses-sions into storage. He trusted Jules, though he hadn't seen her for a while. Once they'd been close, but that hadn't lasted. They were still good friends, however, and she'd done what he wanted with no fuss. He owed her one for that.

He'd chosen to be treated in the north, near his brother. Perhaps he'd settle here permanently now. Who knew? He hadn't got his head round all that yet. But as Joe still lived here in Rochdale, the town where they'd been born and raised, Kit had decided to accept his offer to stay with him for a while. They really should get to know one another better. Joe was seven years younger than he was, had been

34

little more than a child when Kit left home, so he didn't even feel they knew one another well. Which was a shame when they were the only two left.

But these temporary arrangements were just until he could cope physically. Definitely. 'Sorry, bro. I shouldn't take out my irritation on you.'

'It's all right, Kit. It must be very frustrating for someone as active as you to be disabled.'

He gritted his teeth and said nothing. He hated people using *that word* about him, absolutely hated it.

'The doctors say you're doing really well, though, far better than they'd expected.'

'Yeah, I have an extremely elegant limp.'

'A limp isn't the end of the world,' Joe said quietly.

Kit knew that intellectually, but emotionally it felt like the end of the world sometimes when your leg ached if you were on it for more than half an hour, or you woke up feeling like a long run in the peaceful dawn world—then suddenly remembered you'd never run again. Damn! He hadn't meant to let his bitterness show. He'd sworn to himself that he wouldn't complain to anyone, not even to himself. He'd have to work on that.

'When's your first physio appointment?'

'Friday.'

Joe's face fell. 'Oh, dear. I've got lessons all day and it's a bit hard to take time off twice in one week.'

'Look, you don't have to ferry me around. I can get taxis and—'

'That'll cost too much. No, I'll rustle up a lift.'

Kit held himself together with an effort. 'Thank you for the thought, but I'd *rather* take taxis. I'm not short of a bob or two, you know.'

There was silence, then Joe said quietly, 'You should let people help you. We all need help now and then.'

'I'm coming to stay with you, aren't I? If that's not accepting help, what is?' He waited a minute and added quietly, 'Look, we'll see how things go. All right?'

'Yes. Of course.'

They reached Joe's house and stopped outside. It was near the middle of a long straight terrace built in the 1850s for workers at the local mill, which was now a craft centre. All the houses were identical: twelve feet wide, with two rooms upstairs, two down, and minuscule bathrooms squeezed in over the stairs in the 1960s and 70s with government modernization grants. Joe had lived here with his wife till she left him and now he lived here alone. Their divorce had surprised Kit, as had the fact that they hadn't had any children, but his brother had refused to talk about it or explain what had gone wrong, just saying it was an amicable split and for the best.

Ten minutes later Joe went back to work and for the first time in four months Kit was alone, truly alone. Silence washed around him, wonderful in its lightness. No burden of keeping alert or hiding your pain from others. He leaned back on the tired old settee and closed his eyes. He was only staying here until he was well enough to manage without help. He needed his own space. Desperately.

Chalk and cheese, he and Joe, and always had been, so how they'd get on living together, he didn't know. They didn't even look alike, because Joe favoured their mother's side of the family. He was a shambling bear of a man, a phys ed teacher, muscular and radiating good health. Kit was like their father's side, of just over medium height, wiry at the best of times, thin to the point of emaciation now. He stared down at the bony legs outlined by his jeans. Heaven only knew how much of his former strength and energy he'd get back. He'd never play squash again, that was certain.

Don't think about that. *Don't!*

He closed his eyes for a moment and woke an hour later unable to remember where he was. Then it all came back to him and he heaved himself to his feet, stumbling and nearly falling because he tried to move too quickly. A cup of coffee would do him good. Not hospital coffee, which tasted remarkably similar to hospital tea—or to dishwater.

In the kitchen he stared round in distaste. Couldn't Joe

at least decorate and get rid of all this fussy wallpaper? The accent tiles above the scarred green working surface had alternating carrots and apples and tomatoes, and were going to drive him mad.

Everything here would drive him mad.

Tears welled in his eyes and he blinked furiously, then snorted and let them fall. Who said real men didn't cry? He'd wept a few times since his accident, though only in the stillness of the night when no one else could see. But one day he'd get that damned leg functioning better. He was *not* going to go through life limping like a badly engineered robot! He might never run again, but he'd find a way to walk normally, at least. He'd promised himself that.

The doctors said low spirits were quite natural and had suggested putting him on antidepressants, but no one was going to dope him up, thank you very much. They'd also wanted him to have some counselling, but he wasn't baring his soul to any bloody do-gooder of a psychologist. No way!

He'd get through this as he'd got through everything else in his adult life—on his own. He hadn't done too badly and things could only get better from now on. He'd make sure of that.

Five

Laura went to see her new lawyer. His office decor was what she called 'spiky modern' and the chairs were even more uncomfortable than they looked. Knowing that lawyers billed by time spent with the client, she outlined the situation crisply and waited impatiently for his reply.

'Were you joint tenants or tenants in common?'

'I'm not sure. Does it matter?'

'Very much.'

She fumbled among the papers for those connected with the house and pushed them across to him.

'Tenants in common,' he said a few moments later. 'That's not good. If you were joint tenants, you'd automatically inherit the house. As it is, you own your half and that's all.'

'You mean—I can't contest the will?' Her voice came out squeaky with indignation. Well, she had a right to be upset.

'You can, but there's no way of predicting the outcome because there are so many factors to be taken into consideration. That's a risk you'd have to consider. Mind you, I think you'd have a good case for keeping most of the shares, as long as you can prove they were intended for superannuation—though the judge would still have to take the other woman's child into consideration. You could ask for DNA tests after it's born, though.'

If she did all that, this man would be earning nice fat fees from her with the money she recouped, she thought sourly. 'Look, I need to get to England as soon as possible. My mother's terminally ill and I have to be there for Dad. I just want to get this settled. Do what you can for me but sort it out as quickly as possible please.'

'How about arbitration? Will Ms Sheedy accept that?'

'She might. She said she wants to get through this without acrimony, because she's pregnant. I have her details here.' She pushed a piece of paper across the empty desk. It looked scruffy, curled at one edge where she'd stuffed it into her handbag. She felt the same, dog-eared, worn, past her use-by date. Realizing the lawyer was speaking again, she forced herself to concentrate.

'Depending on how the will's phrased, there might have to be a share for the baby if Ms Sheedy can prove it's his.' He looked at the photocopied sheets and pointed. 'There. It just says "my children".' He shook his head as if he didn't approve. 'Until things are settled, how are you off for money?'

'I have some savings of my own. Not much unfortunately, because they've frozen our joint bank account.' She hadn't told Craig about her savings, but what difference did a few thousand dollars make when a luxury home worth $800,000 was going to be shared among three—no four—others! She could understand now why people ran amok. She had felt like screaming and hitting out several times recently.

'If there are bills outstanding, you should be able to get those paid by the estate. Don't spend a cent more of your own money on anything except maintaining the services, like electricity—and keep all the records of payment. I'll contact the mistress re arbitration.'

'Yes. Thank you.'

That evening Ryan came round and started on his father's remaining possessions, clothes, various oddments, golf clubs—heavens, it was years since Craig had played! Ryan worked quickly then insisted on taking his mother out for a late meal, because for once she hadn't prepared anything for them.

Laura sat in the café trying to eat enough to please him.

'You've lost weight, Mum,' he said softly. 'And you've hardly eaten anything tonight.'

'I'm not very hungry these days.'

He leaned back, holding his glass of red wine up to the light and staring at it. 'It's a real mess, isn't it?'

'Yes.'

'Do you miss Dad at all?'

'We hadn't been close for a while. Mainly I feel angry with him—very angry.'

'I miss him.'

'Yes. I realize that. He was a loving father.'

'He didn't ill-treat you, at least,' Ryan said.

'Isn't it ill-treating you to tell your children lies about you and put you down all the time about your weight? It's only now that I'm beginning to realize how subtly he did that and how stupidly docile I was.' She hesitated, then said what she'd been thinking for the past few days. 'I think he was determined to come first with you two.'

Ryan stared down at his plate, brow furrowed as if thinking about this.

Once started she had to let the rest out. 'Craig was not only unfaithful to me, Ryan, he cheated me out of money I was owed morally. I've been checking the deeds for the various houses we've owned.' She'd had to break open the locked drawer of Craig's desk to find them, had been surprised he'd left them behind, but perhaps he'd been so eager to go to his mistress he'd forgotten the previous years' records. 'Your father deliberately changed the terms on this house contract from joint tenants to tenants in common, and without explaining the difference to me. I trusted him and signed without reading it, even though we weren't getting on very well. How stupid can you get?' She felt very stupid, had done since she found out what Craig had done to her. 'He was planning to keep money from me, Ryan, even before he shacked up with this female.'

'Are you sure of this?'

'Yes. I can show you, if you like.'

'Would you mind?'

She did mind. It was as if he doubted her word, but she didn't want to antagonize him, so when they got home she produced the various papers. He looked through them, then pushed them aside and let out a short, impatient sigh. 'Couldn't have been to protect Caitlin, because he didn't know her then. I wonder why he did it?'

'Because he was going to leave me anyway. I think he was just waiting for me to finish doing up this house. I reckon once we'd sold it, he'd have made his move.'

Ryan reached out to clasp her nearest hand in both his. 'I'll come round on Saturday to see if you need any more help, eh?'

'Thanks, but I'd prefer you to come round on Friday evening.' She managed a smile. 'Whoever she is, you'll have to cancel your date. The house will be open for inspection for the first time on Saturday afternoon. I have, if I say so myself, been very efficient in dealing with the real-estate agents.'

He doffed an imaginary hat to her. 'All right, Friday after work it is. And I don't have a steady girlfriend at the moment.' He struck a pose, one hand on his chest. 'I'm resting!'

She forced a smile. 'I'll have a nice tea waiting for you on Friday then. Oh, and I need Deb to come and see what she wants. Soon. Will you tell her? I've left a message with her answering service, but she hasn't got back to me. If she doesn't, I'm throwing all Craig's possessions out, even his books. I just can't face anything of his. Not any more.'

'Ah, Mum.' He hugged her again.

She resisted for a moment, then sagged against him and hugged him back, but after a minute pushed him to arm's length. 'Thanks, Ryan. I really appreciate your support.' She might have gone to pieces without it.

Instead of going to bed when she got back she cleared out the linen cupboard. She'd never have slept anyway. Better to go on working. There was, after all, a great deal to do. Thank goodness. Being busy would help get her through this.

Two days later Laura's lawyer rang up. 'Ms Sheedy refuses to go to arbitration, says there's no need.'

'Oh.'

'However, I don't believe her demands are unreasonable, given the circumstances.'

Laura made a non-committal murmur as she waited to hear the details.

'The good news is that she feels you deserve your husband's superannuation shares, all of them. She intends to keep her share of the house and all the insurance money, though, and won't budge on that. But she doesn't intend to make a claim for a share of the house for her unborn child. Oh, and she agrees to the estate paying the household and selling expenses.'

'I see.'

'Shall I accept those terms on your behalf?'

Laura closed her eyes for a moment, then opened them and faced facts, reminding herself that the main thing you did by going to court was make your lawyer richer. 'Yes. Accept them.'

She put the phone down very gently and sat there for a few minutes before she started work again. She'd made a real mess of her life and didn't think she'd ever trust a man again. Other women remarried, but she wasn't going to, not for anything.

No one was surprised when the house sold the first weekend. Well, it looked beautiful, thanks to Laura's efforts, even if she said so herself—and who else was there to say it now? She was good at interior design, as well as understanding the practicalities of decorating, making curtains and upholstering. Good at cooking and running a house, too. They were the only marketable skills she possessed. She hoped they'd be enough to get her a decent job.

Two weeks after that she sold the last of the household goods she no longer wanted. The things she was keeping were put in storage and she camped out for a few days until the handover date for the house, because it was cheaper than staying in a hotel. She slept on an old studio couch that had lived in the garage, using Ryan's sleeping bag, ate at a rickety garden table and had only an old plastic garden chair to sit on. The empty house seemed to echo around her, an alien landscape now.

She thought twice about every dollar she spent. The shares weren't to be touched. They were to provide for her old age. Her house money had to buy her a new house one day and perhaps set her up in a business. She pushed the thought of all that to the back of her mind. It was her parents who mattered now. They needed her, at least. And she needed to have something to do with her life.

Ryan took her out for a final meal with Deb, but it was an awkward evening and broke up early. The following morning he drove Laura out to the airport in her car, gave her one of his cracking great hugs, then took the car away to sell.

She got on a plane to England feeling shaky and uncertain of herself. Was she doing the right thing? How could you ever be certain?

Six

The first few days of living with his brother, Kit decided gloomily as he bumped down the stairs on his backside, had been worse than he'd expected, with Joe trying to fuss over him like a mother hen. The only times he'd been out of the house had been to go for physiotherapy sessions with a local guy, gentle ones until the last operation had done its work and the bones had knitted together properly. He was desperate to work his body hard and seek the sheer release of letting out some of his pent-up energy, but didn't dare. Even in this mood, he wasn't stupid enough to risk the progress he'd made so painfully.

He hauled himself to his feet and went into the kitchen, still worrying at the problem. Not until they'd cleared the air with a quarrel the other night—or at least, until Kit had done some shouting and threatening while Joe had become increasingly tight-lipped—had his brother backed off a bit from fussing. The two of them were definitely not meant to cohabit. They didn't even talk much, because they couldn't find enough common interests to hold a decent conversation.

His brother wouldn't talk about his marriage, seemed to have no social life any more and had no interests apart from sport—and that was all he wanted to watch on television. Even pulled a face at the news, for heaven's sake!

Kit was starving, absolutely starving for a good, sharp discussion or two about current affairs. He ached for banter, jokes, incisive views of the world and its leaders from thinking people of all nationalities. Ah hell, forget that! It was gone for ever.

He knew this situation couldn't go on but how the hell was he going to get out of the arrangement without hurting Joe? He looked up as his brother came down into the kitchen and dumped two heavy bags of sports gear on the floor.

'I'll be away all day but I'll be back in time to cook tea. Are you sure you'll be all right?'

'Very sure. You enjoy your Saturday matches.' As Joe still hesitated, Kit added in a mock-threatening tone. 'You're not going to start *fussing* again, are you?'

Joe spread out his arms in a gesture of surrender. 'I wouldn't dare.' He hesitated. 'But if this weren't the five-a-side finals, I'd not be leaving you on your own, the mood you're in.'

Thank goodness for junior football! Kit thought, but held back the words when they sprang to his lips. Listening to Joe's badly adjusted car engine throbbing unevenly as the vehicle pulled away from the kerb, he shook his head at the way his brother seemed to think machinery would behave itself without due attention and servicing, yet was obsessive about people looking after their bodies properly.

Blessedly alone, he got out his laptop, set it up in the kitchen and told himself firmly to start work and not play solitaire. But it was no good. He simply couldn't settle. Sunlight was pouring in through the windows, tempting him to go out. Well, why not? He might not be able to drive, but there were taxis, weren't there? He had a mobile phone and he wasn't short of money.

He edged across to Joe's phone directory and looked up taxis. When he picked up the phone, one of the crutches slipped and fell on the floor. Cursing, he rebalanced himself and dialled. 'I'd like a taxi in fifteen minutes, please.'

Feeling like an escaping prisoner of war, he manoeuvred his way back to a chair, used his remaining crutch to hook the fallen one and drag it towards him, then heaved himself to his feet again and made his way slowly upstairs . . .

Fifteen minutes later he slid the crutches down the stairs and bumped slowly after them, dressed for an outing. The taxi arrived promptly and took him across town to the house

Uncle Alf had left him. He hadn't seen it for a while and needed to get the feel of it again. If he thought he could live there, it would solve one of his immediate problems, at least.

Alf's will stipulated that he had to spend a year there. Whatever happened afterwards, that would suit him. And surely by the end of that time he'd have tested his new limits and grown accustomed to them? Would have started to build a future for himself. Yes, of course he would.

His spirits lifted as the taxi took him across town and out towards Wardle.

Laura walked out of Manchester airport, her stomach churning with nerves. She was dreading seeing her mother. The thought of that had hung over her for the whole journey, preventing her from immersing herself in her novel or doing more than doze for a minute or two.

Her sister Sue and niece Angie were waiting for her at the barrier. Sue's smile of greeting faded almost immediately, leaving her with a look of—surely it couldn't be apprehension?

'How was the flight?' Sue clutched a large handbag in front of her like a shield, making no attempt even to air-kiss Laura, let alone hug her.

'Long and boring, as usual. I'm glad to be here.' She turned to her niece. 'You've grown up since I last saw you.'

'I should hope so.' Angie stepped forward and hugged her aunt.

'Don't pester her, Angie!' Sue snapped. 'Not everyone likes your touchy-feely ways.'

Laura blinked at her sister in shock, gave her niece another hug for good measure and said firmly, 'Well, *I* do.'

Sue's expression was that of someone who'd just sucked a lemon. 'I'll drive you over to Dad's, but I can't stop. I have to get back to work ASAP. I'll have you over for a meal soon, then we can really catch up.'

'Surely we can nip in to see Gran and Pop, just for a minute or two, Mum?' Angie protested.

Laura stared from her niece to her sister in surprise, as tension suddenly frosted the air.

'There isn't time. I've already told you that. Now, let's go and retrieve the car.' Sue turned and began walking away, so they could do nothing but follow.

Angie fell in beside her aunt, taking the wheelie suitcase off her. 'She won't go and see Gran any more,' she said in a low voice, scowling at her mother's back, 'and that really hurts Pop.'

Sue stopped walking for a minute to turn and yell, 'I heard that! And it's my choice if I want to remember Mum as she was, not as she is now.'

'Well, I'm going to go in and see them, so I'll catch the bus home.'

'Suit yourself.'

Laura felt too muzzy from lack of sleep to cope with what was obviously an ongoing quarrel, and therefore kept silent. But Angie looked so despondent she couldn't help reaching out and giving her niece's shoulder a quick squeeze in sympathy, which won her a grateful smile.

The car was red. That, at least, was the same. Her sister had always bought red cars. 'I'll have to buy myself a set of wheels,' she said as she buckled the seat belt.

'My boyfriend sells used cars. I can ask him to call you if you like,' Angie said from the back. 'He'll give you a good deal and make sure you're not cheated.'

Sue turned to glare at her. 'For goodness' sake, don't be so pushy. Anyway, your aunt will probably want to buy a new one.'

Laura jumped in quickly. 'I can't afford new. I'm on a tight budget. Ask your boyfriend to give me a call after the weekend, will you, Angie? Perhaps you can help me choose one? The cars look different here, much smaller. I wouldn't have a clue.'

Sue glanced sideways, the frown seeming a permanent fixture. 'How come the tight budget? I'd have thought Craig would have left you well provided for.'

'I'll tell you about it another time.' Laura leaned against

the headrest with a tired sigh, her whole body aching for sleep, but once they left the urban sprawl of Manchester behind, she opened her eyes again to watch the scenery. 'I always feel I'm home again when I see the moors in the distance. Do you know, this is only the second time I've returned to Lancashire since I moved to Australia?'

Again it was her niece who replied. 'You'll probably find things very different, then. And you'll miss the sun. The weather's been awful lately, nothing but rain.'

'It was early spring when I left Perth. Long-sleeve weather still and plenty of rain.' She'd miss the spring, which was the wildflower season, with breathtaking fields of colour outside the city. 'It's only hot in the summer and it gets quite cold there in winter, you know, though not cold enough for snow or frost, but still chilly.'

'I'm going to see for myself one day,' Angie said. 'Australia's definitely on my list of places to visit.'

'Not till you've found yourself a job, you're not,' Sue snapped. 'Trev and I aren't subsidizing you much longer unless you buckle down and do something worthwhile. If you'd stayed at university, you'd nearly have finished your degree by now and have a decent future ahead of you. I never thought a child of mine would drop out.'

'I didn't drop out, I took time off because of Gran.'

'There's nothing you can do to help her!'

Laura let her breath filter out slowly, telling herself not to intervene, but the words came out anyway. 'If I'm back in Australia, you can come and stay with me, Angie.'

'Don't encourage her!' Sue snapped. 'She's full of dreams but hasn't the money to pay for them.'

'I will have, one day.'

'And pigs will fly. You haven't even got a job, except for that part-time thing in the pub.'

More silence, heavy and impenetrable as a granite wall. Laura was relieved when they drew up outside their child-hood home and she could get out.

Sue drove off immediately they'd unloaded the luggage, not attempting to go inside or even wait for her father to answer the door. Laura wheeled her suitcase along the short concrete path, surprised to see weeds choking the usually immaculate flower beds. She rang the doorbell and waited.

Angie came to stand beside her, looking sad. 'Um—about Mum, Auntie Laura. She can't cope with what's happening to Gran and she's ashamed of that, so she gets angry. And she hasn't been well herself, so I try to make allowances for her, I really do, but it's hard when she never stops nagging me. Dad goes out to the pub on his own sometimes to get a break. I don't know how he puts up with her moods lately. She's better with him than with me, though. I seem to cop all the flak, can't do a thing right. I should definitely have stayed at university—' she offered a wavery smile, '—but if I had, I wouldn't have been able to come and see Pop and Gran except in the holidays. And there isn't much time left for Gran. That mattered more to me than the degree. Pop's having a hard time of it and I help him out sometimes. Mum won't. And then—well, I met Rick and that clinched it, so I didn't go back this year. He's a great guy and I want to give us a chance.'

Why had Deb never talked to her like this? Laura wondered. Was she that bad a mother? She smiled at her niece. 'I'm sure Dad's grateful for your company.'

'He is. I sit with Gran sometimes when he needs to visit the doctor or whatever. She's good with me, but I still have to watch her all the time. If she takes a dislike to people, she can be a real terror.' She put out a hand to stop her aunt ringing the doorbell again. 'It takes Pop a minute or two to answer. He has to make sure Gran's OK first.'

The front door opened a few seconds later and Laura's dad stood there. He looked smaller than she remembered, and tired, deep-down tired. He tried to blink tears from his eyes as he stepped forward to hug her, but she could feel the slickness of moisture on the wrinkled cheek that pressed against hers. She burrowed against him for a moment, as she had so many times in her childhood.

When he pulled away, she said softly, 'I'm so glad to be here.'

'It's grand to see you. I've been counting the days. Eh, fancy keeping you standing on the doorstep like this! Come in, love, come in.' He looked beyond them for a minute. 'Sue too busy to stop again?'

''Fraid so.' Angie followed them inside. 'Where's Gran?'

'In the kitchen. We were just having a cup of tea.' He held his daughter back. 'Look, love, Pat may not recognize you. She's getting worse quickly. There's nothing any of us can do about it, so don't—well, don't take it to heart if there are any problems.'

Laura had tried to prepare herself for this meeting, but her heart was thumping in her chest as they went down the narrow hall, past the door into the front room and on into the kitchen. She remembered this house so well from her childhood. Even the woman sitting at the table was familiar and dear—until she looked up. The face was still her mother's, but the expression on it belonged to a stranger. Distant and disinterested, as if not quite part of this world.

'Look. Our Laura's come to see us,' Ron said heartily.

Pat stared at her daughter blankly, then started rocking to and fro, muttering under her breath. When Laura moved towards her, she picked up the nearest thing, a cup half-full of tea, and threw it, yelling, 'Hussy! Keep away from my husband.'

Laura looked down at her soaking jacket in shock and turned to her father in bewilderment.

'It's Laura,' he said loudly to his wife. 'Our daughter.'

But Pat wasn't to be calmed and again reached out, her hand scrabbling around, as if she was looking for something else to throw.

Laura stepped back into the hall and whispered urgently, 'What am I doing wrong?'

'Nothing, love. She sometimes takes against strangers.'

'But I'm not a stranger.'

'You are to her now. She's having one of her bad days, I'm afraid.' While he spoke, he patted his wife's shoulder as if she were an upset child.

Angie went into the kitchen. 'I've come to visit you too,

50

Gran.' She gave the older woman a hug and Pat seemed to forget Laura, smiling and raising one hand to caress her granddaughter's hair.

For a moment she seemed almost her own self, her eyes lighting with affection, then the light faded and she sagged down in her chair again.

Angie immediately stepped away from her. 'Shall I make some more tea, Pop?'

'Yes, love.' He moved across to Laura. 'I'll help you upstairs with your things, shall I, love?'

He took the suitcase and went up the stairs, clearly finding it heavy, but she knew better than to offer to take it from him. Her dad had always had strong views about men doing the physical jobs for women and it was too late to change him now.

He pushed open the second bedroom door and wheeled the case in, panting a little and trying to hide that. 'You're in your old room. Same bed, I'm afraid. I hope it'll be all right.'

'I'm tired enough to sleep on a log.' She could barely hold back a yawn.

'Why don't you have a shower and go to bed, then?'

'When I've just arrived?'

He shrugged. 'Your mum won't notice and I'll understand.' His mouth wobbled and he said in a husky voice, 'I should have rung you about her sooner, only she started going downhill faster than anyone expected.'

'It must be hell for you.' She watched him studying his shoes, something he'd always done when he didn't want to look you in the face. He glanced up at her and teardrops leaked out of the corners of his eyes, zigzagging down the wrinkles. 'Oh, Dad!' She moved to take him in her arms, cradling him against her, amazed at how shrunken he felt, without any spare flesh on his bones.

He wept silently, trying desperately to hold back the grief and failing. She wept with him, for him and for her poor mother—for herself too, because she felt so lost.

After a while, the convulsive sobs stopped and he looked at her shamefacedly. 'I'm sorry.'

'Don't be.' She fumbled in her pocket for some tissues and came out with two crumpled pieces, offering the better one to him. 'It's supposed to be good for you to cry and heaven knows you've got enough to cry about.'

'Life's not been treating you so well lately, either.'

'No. I'll tell you more about that tomorrow.' A yawn took her by surprise and it seemed as if everything was distant and unreal. 'I think I will have a sleep, if you don't mind. I was busy right until the last moment before I left and I didn't sleep much on the plane.' Getting rid of a lifetime of possessions after someone's death was a supremely painful thing, she'd found. If she'd started crying in Australia, she'd never have stopped. Perhaps she'd have time now to grieve for all she'd lost.

'I'll probably run our Angie back home after we've had a bit of a natter. Your mum still likes to go for a ride in the car. Sometimes it's the only thing that'll settle her.'

Laura had the quickest shower possible, standing in the adapted bath and wishing for the rush of hot water she'd had at home instead of this sparse trickle. But at least it washed the aeroplane smell off her.

She crawled into bed, hearing the low hum of voices downstairs as she had in her childhood. It was comforting, though she missed her mother's voice and laughter. Soon exhaustion took over and she gave in to sleep.

Kit got out of the taxi and balanced on his crutches as he adjusted the backpack over his shoulder. The vehicle pulled away behind him and he stood looking at his uncle's house—his house now—with an appreciative eye, instead of rushing heedlessly inside as he'd always done before. He could feel his spirits lifting by the second, because this place brought back so many happy memories.

It was a large, double-fronted, semi-detached residence of three storeys, built in 1884, according to a carved stone, set where the two houses were joined. People usually split this sort of house into flats nowadays, but he had no intention of doing that. It had belonged to his grandfather and, as the elder son, Alf had inherited it, plus enough money to stop working. This had annoyed Kit's father, who felt he should have inherited something more than a modest financial legacy, even though he had never got on with his parents.

Alf's wife Maud had died when she was seventy, which Alf considered young, and from then on, Kit's uncle had lived in the house alone, though it had been far too big for one person, especially as he got older. Kit's parents had often spoken scornfully of how stupid it was for an elderly man to stay on in a great freezing barn of a place when he could have had a centrally heated flat like theirs, with all modern conveniences. But Alf had loved the old place and refused to move out.

He'd outlived Kit's parents by several years, for all their vaunted modern comforts, though the house had grown shabbier with each year that passed. In his letters of the last few years he had reported his friends dying one by one, joking that he was going to be the last skittle standing and get his telegram from the Queen. But he hadn't made a hundred, only ninety.

Smiling at his memories, Kit moved along the path, placing his crutches carefully on the crazy paving. He didn't want to risk a fall, because he was terrified of slowing his progress. In only a few weeks the doctors would let him start driving again, which would be a major step towards independence.

At the front door, he fumbled for the key the lawyers had sent him, and an elderly woman whose hair was dyed an improbably bright orange poked her head over the low wall separating the two properties and stared at him suspiciously.

'Did you want to see someone? Mr Mallinder passed away recently, I'm afraid.'

'Yes, I know. It's Mrs Ramsay, isn't it? I'm his nephew, Kit. I've inherited the house.'

She squinted at him, then nodded and smiled. 'Oh, yes. I recognize you now—you've lost a lot of weight, though, and your hair's a lot longer. Have you been ill?' She didn't wait for an answer. 'Alf was very proud of you. He showed me some of your pieces from the papers. Very hard-hitting stuff. Not that I read that sort of thing usually, I'm more the women's magazine type. Still, it used to make him happy to see your name in print, though he worried about you going to such dangerous places.'

Kit interrupted the gentle monologue. 'Look, it's nice to see you again, Mrs Ramsay, but I can't stand for long on these crutches. I'll catch up with you properly another time.'

When he went inside the house to take possession, he felt as if there should be some sort of ceremony to mark the momentous occasion. After all, he'd never owned a house before. But there was only him surrounded by a few stray rainbow-hued sunbeams which had daringly penetrated the narrow stained-glass windows to either side of the door.

Excitement rose in him. If he found himself a live-in housekeeper, he could move in quite soon. He wasn't ungrateful to Joe, but the cramped little house was driving him mad. He didn't need nursing now, or a personal carer, just someone to relieve him of the housework, shopping and cooking—and to be there in case he had an accident. Even he acknowledged that such a thing was possible.

Slowly he did a tour of the downstairs rooms. Alf had obviously lived in the smaller front room towards the end, and it was very shabby, still littered with the old man's personal effects. Kit wasn't looking forward to clearing them out. It would seem like such an intrusion. Anyway, physically he couldn't do it yet, so it would have to wait until later.

He continued his inspection. The other front room had always been known as the parlour and had a formal dining room behind it. Both seemed long-unused and the old-fashioned furniture was covered in yellowing dust covers. When he lifted them, he found everything in immaculate condition. He stroked the mahogany dining table before he moved on. He'd keep that. But the lounge suite was hard and uncomfortable. That was going, for a start.

The rear room behind the smaller sitting room had been

54

converted into a bedroom for Alf as he grew more infirm, and next to it was a compact modern bathroom with shower cubicle. It would be perfect for Kit's present needs, though, like the rest of the house, it needed a good clean.

The kitchen jutted out at the rear, large and extremely old-fashioned but with a new gas cooker at least, plus an elderly fridge-freezer. There were plenty of cupboards and enough room still for a table and four chairs. To hell with modern houses and their miniature fitted kitchens! Kit had always loved this one and remembered sitting at this table and eating his aunt's home-made scones fresh from the oven, with butter melting from them down his fingers. Maud had died when he was eighteen, had been dead twenty years now, poor thing.

He went across to stand by the window and gaze out at the back garden. A wilderness, and not a pretty one either. Nettles lay in wait for the unwary and brambles looped down one side, while some sort of grass had grown high in the middle area and was laden with seeds. He'd have to get someone in to tidy that up before it spread everywhere.

He scooted himself up and down the stairs, feeling tired now. It irritated the hell out of him that sitting in a taxi and walking slowly round a house could exhaust him!

He explored the five bedrooms in a cursory manner, standing in the doorway of each. Only one bathroom up here, and of the same vintage as the kitchen. It was dominated by a stained bathtub with gigantic clawed feet, a massive, square washbasin whose white surface was crazed with fine lines and whose dripping taps had left green stains below them.

He didn't have the energy to go up to the attics but could remember visiting them when he was a small child and playing treasure hunts up there.

As he bumped his way down the stairs again, he wondered with a wry smile if he was creating extra muscles in his backside from this way of moving around.

When he stood up again at the bottom he felt dizzy. 'Enough, already,' he admonished himself. 'Go home and rest now, Mallinder.'

As he called on his mobile for another taxi, he was already thinking out his advert for a housekeeper and feeling happier than he had for a long time. Tiring or not, the outing had lifted his spirits. He was about to take charge of his own life again and that felt so good.

He turned at the gate to smile at the house. I'll be back soon, he promised it.

Seven

In Western Australia Ryan knocked on the door of the two-storey town house, feeling nervous but determined. When Caitlin opened it, they stared at one another in silence for a moment, then he said the words he'd been rehearsing. 'I'm Ryan Wells. Dad introduced us.'

'Yes. I remember you.'

'Can I speak to you, please?'

'Not if you're here to quarrel about something.'

'I'm not the quarrelsome type.'

She took a long, searching look at his face, as if trying to read the truth of what he was saying, then held the door open. He followed her inside, unable to imagine his luxury-loving father living in a house this small.

'Would you like a coffee?' she asked.

'I'd love one.' He followed her into the kitchen and perched on a stool at the breakfast bar watching her make it. Real coffee. His father had always insisted on that and Ryan had shared that love. Her hands moved surely, very slender, the nails bare of polish. Her hair hung in a tumble of curls to her shoulders, beautiful hair. He'd always been a sucker for natural redheads, though her hair was darker than red, more an auburn shade, really. Over her jeans she was wearing a large, shapeless sweater that he recognized as having once belonged to his father. She didn't seem to be wearing make-up of any sort and she didn't look very pregnant.

When he thought of her and his dad together, he was puzzled. What had a girl of his own age seen in a man so much older?

'Are you keeping well?' he managed as the silence lasted too long. Oh, brilliant opening gambit! She'll think you're an absolute fool.

'Yes, very well, thank you. I've been lucky really. Just some morning sickness.'

'When exactly is the baby due?'

'Still six months to go. I hardly even show.' Her hand went to cradle the gentle curve of her stomach and he found that unbearably poignant, since the baby's father would never be able to see her growing lush with his child.

'It's because of the baby I came,' he said as she perched beside him and waited for the coffee to drip through the filter.

'Oh?'

'It'll be my brother or sister and, well, it seems wrong for us not to know one another. So I wanted to ask you to keep in touch.'

Tears filled her eyes. 'I hadn't expected that. I thought you'd all hate me.'

'Nobody hates you, not even my mother.'

'She has reason to, if anyone does.'

'You weren't the first time my father's strayed, if you'll pardon my saying so. Their marriage had deteriorated in the last few years, we could all see that. My sister and I wondered why they'd stayed together so long. And besides, Mum's got other problems now, so you're sidelined. Gran's got Alzheimer's and Mum's gone to England to help Pop look after her.'

'How terrible! I didn't know about that. Craig never said.'

'Pop didn't tell us until after Dad had died.' The percolator had fallen silent and the aroma of good coffee filled the small room. Ryan breathed it in, enjoying it. He never bothered with real coffee in his tiny flat, just went for instant everything, living mostly on takeaways and bacon sandwiches, or bacon butties as Pop would call them.

Caitlin got up to make their drinks, handing him a mug without asking how he liked it. He stared down at the black liquid. 'Um—I take it with milk.'

Her face crumpled and she gave a muffled sob, pressing one hand against her mouth as if to hold more back. 'I'm sorry. I still do it automatically for Craig.'

He watched her try to stem the tears and, without thinking, because he hated to see anyone hurting, he pulled her into his arms. 'Shh. It's all right. You're bound to do things like that and there's nothing to be ashamed of in crying for Dad.' His mother certainly wasn't weeping for him. She seemed angry at him more than anything, and Ryan didn't blame her. Dad had treated her very badly.

When Caitlin pulled away, he said, 'White with two sugars, please,' in a brisk voice and watched her beautiful hands again as she added milk to his coffee. Then she came back to sit beside him and stare blindly out across the small rear courtyard.

'I'm not sure,' she said at last.

'Not sure of what?' He watched her reflection in the window, but it was too faint to give much clue to what she was thinking, and her hair had curled forward to hide the side view of her face.

'Whether it'd be a good thing for us to keep in touch. I'll have to think about it. Perhaps you could give me your phone number and—'

He fished in his pocket for a card. 'I'm moving to Melbourne next week, so this'll only apply until next Tuesday. I've been transferred, you see.' He scribbled on the back of the card. 'This is the number of head office over there. They'll know where I am if you decide to— well, keep in touch. I'll be coming over to Western Australia occasionally on business, so I could still see you and the baby from time to time.'

She nodded and took another sip of her own weak, milky coffee.

He didn't know what to say so kept quiet, a tactic that had served him well many a time. He just wished his sister would learn it.

'I'm grateful that you came, that you cared,' Caitlin said at last.

'Oh?'

'It was a nice thought.'

He drank his coffee, chatting about trivial things, then left. It *had* been the right thing to do, he was still sure of that, but he didn't think she'd bother to get in touch with him. Pity. He'd have liked to know his new brother or sister.

His mum would throw a blue fit if she knew what he was doing.

So would Deb.

Well, let them! He knew his grandpop would approve.

When he'd gone, Caitlin wandered out to the small court-yard behind the house, caressing the leaves of the bush she'd planted in one corner. It was doing well. She'd intended to plant some annuals, too. Even a few flowers could brighten things up. But now, well, she wasn't sure.

She turned as the doorbell rang again, frowning as she wondered who it was. When she opened the front door and saw her parents standing there, her father grim faced, her mother with an anxious expression, and her cousin Barry behind them wearing his I-am-concerned-about-you look, her heart sank. But she couldn't refuse to let them in, though she wanted to—oh, how she wanted to!

Her mother stood in the hall. 'It took us a while to find out where you were living, Caitlin. With *him*! No wonder you didn't tell us your new address.'

'Come into the lounge room. We can't stand talking in the hall.' Caitlin turned and led the way, a sick feeling settling heavily in her stomach. She gestured to the couch and took Craig's big armchair.

Her father sat next to her mother. Barry took a chair from the dining table, swung it round and sat astride it, studying her.

It was her mother who spoke. 'Where is this man of yours?'

Caitlin looked at them in shock. 'Haven't you heard?'

'Heard what? How can we hear anything when our only child vanishes and doesn't tell us where she's living? If it

60

wasn't for Barry, we wouldn't even have known where you were.'

'You wouldn't leave me alone. I needed time to sort out my feelings and decide about my future.'

Her father scowled at her. 'Without consulting us! You've been brought up to know what's right and wrong. Did you think we'd accept you living in sin? Other people may be lax about morals, but in our church we know right from wrong.'

Her mother nudged him. 'What should we have heard, Caitlin?'

Caitlin looked at Barry. 'Didn't you find that out?'

'Find out what?'

'Craig was killed last week.'

It was her father who broke the heavy silence. 'How?'

'A car accident.'

'So, it's over.' A look of satisfaction crossed her mother's face. 'The Lord's will be done. And we'll have no more of this sort of thing, Caitlin Sheedy. You'll come home again and live modestly, go to church on Sundays and—'

'I'm *not* coming home, Mum. I've told you that before. I'm twenty-five. Old enough to choose my own life and, as I told you when I left, I don't want to belong to your church any more. It's too—extreme for me.' She hesitated, then said it. 'Besides, it's not over. I'm expecting his child.'

Disgust on her father's face, shock followed quickly by eagerness on her mother's, revulsion on her cousin's.

'You'll need our help even more now,' her mother said in satisfaction. 'I'll be able to look after it for you when you go back to work. It's not the child's fault if it's born in sin. It'll still be our first grandchild.'

'I'm *not* coming home,' Caitlin repeated. 'I prefer to live on my own.' She knew better than to tell them about the money or she'd never get rid of them. They'd been dirt-poor all their lives, but had given more than they could afford to their peculiar little church. They would want to do the same with her windfall.

Barry cleared his throat and, when they were all looking

61

at him, said very solemnly, 'I'm still prepared to marry you, Caitlin, though not till after the baby's been born. You know my feelings for you haven't changed.'

'Nor have mine for you. I can never think of you like that.' She stared back at him, refusing to let him outstare her. She had grown up with him and let him boss her around when she was younger, but the thought of him as a husband repelled her. It'd be like marrying a brother, and a stern elder brother at that. She waited till he looked away, then asked, 'Now, would you like a cup of tea before you go?'

Barry followed her into the kitchen area. 'You're not thinking clearly, Caitlin.'

'Am I not?'

He smiled, a confident smile, as if he considered himself in a winning position. 'No. Definitely not. And you'll change your mind about marrying me. You'll have to now if you want to keep the child. I'll give you a week to get used to the idea, then I'll come over and we'll discuss it.'

'Don't bother. I won't change my mind.' She'd not let him through the door next time.

'How long do you think you can hold out against your parents? Your father's a very determined man when he wants something and will probably bring the pastor with him next time. And your mother's been longing for grandchildren.' He paused, then added, 'I too am very determined where you're concerned, Caitlin.'

She hoped she'd hidden her fear of him, of the whole machine that was her devoted, ultra-religious family.

Barry was watching her, still smiling confidently. 'You'll marry me,' he said softly. 'I'll make sure of that.' His smile didn't falter as he sauntered back to sit beside her parents again. And when he looked at her, his gaze was that of a man studying a prized possession.

In your dreams, Barry Donovan! she thought. And in my worst, my very worst nightmares.

Thank God she had the money!

Eight

In the middle of the night, Laura woke to hear footsteps going down the stairs. She slid out of bed and grabbed her dressing gown, wondering if her mother was ill or needed something. But she didn't find her father in the kitchen as she'd expected, only her mother, who had turned on all the gas burners without lighting them and was in the process of putting empty pans on them.

'What are you doing, Mum?'

Pat spun round, saw Laura and cried out, hurling a pan at her, then another. 'Stay away from my husband!' she shrieked.

Footsteps pounded down the stairs and Ron came in, pushing Laura outside into the hall and moving towards his wife, speaking soothingly as he switched off the cooker. It took him a while to get her to sit down, and then he stood beside her as if on guard, calling, 'Are you all right, Laura love? She didn't hurt you, did she?'

One of the pans had hit Laura's arm and no doubt left a bruise, but he didn't need to know that. 'I'm fine.' She went into the kitchen, picking up a pan from the floor, intending to set things to rights, but as soon as she appeared, her mother grew agitated again.

He looked at her in anguish. 'I'm sorry, so very sorry. She's taken against you. It's happened before and for no reason that anyone could tell. They get delusions, you know. She thought the milkman was trying to poison us, so I had to stop having it delivered and use that long-life stuff in paper cartons. Perhaps you should go back to bed till I get her settled?'

'All right.' But it wasn't all right. Laura went upstairs and huddled in bed listening to her father talking soothingly, wondering how her own mother could reject her so violently and absolutely. As her husband had. And her daughter. Why? What was wrong with her? She fell asleep again with tears drying on her cheeks and that gentle, murmuring voice coming from downstairs, unknowingly offering comfort to her as well as her mother.

When she got up the following morning, her father was asleep at the kitchen table, his head pillowed on his arms. Her mother was nowhere to be seen. Sorrow for what he had to endure put a tight band round Laura's chest, and for a moment she couldn't move. What had he ever done to deserve this? Or her mother? It wasn't fair!

She didn't want to wake him but was desperately thirsty, and hungry too. She put the kettle on, then checked the downstairs rooms for her mother. No sign of her. Worried that she might have slipped out of the house, Laura laid a hand on her father's shoulder and shook it gently.

He jerked awake and immediately looked round. 'Pat?'

'I don't know, Dad. She isn't downstairs.'

'I'll check our bedroom. I always lock the front and back doors now, so I don't think she'll have got out. She can't work the locks any more.' He came down almost immediately. 'She's still in bed, fast asleep, thank goodness.'

'Would you like a cup of tea? I've just brewed some.'

He nodded and sat down again.

'You look exhausted.'

'I am. It's getting too much for me, really, but I don't like to put Pat in a home, not till I absolutely have to.' He looked down, fiddling with a spoon as he added quietly, 'When I do that, we'll both be on our own, you see.'

Deeply moved by this admission and the sadness on his face, Laura waited a few moments, then asked, 'Is there any way I can get her to trust me, Dad? I came here to help you, not make things worse.'

'Eh, love, I don't know. We'll have to see how things pan out. Maybe she'll get used to you when she sees you every day.'

She didn't think he sounded optimistic.

He drained his cup of tea, then pushed himself to his feet. 'Look, I'd better go and have a shower while I can. Just help yourself to anything you fancy for breakfast.'

'Can I make some for you?'

'I'm not hungry.'

When he came down, he still looked tired but his face wore the familiar polished look it always had after a wash, and his sparse white hair was neatly parted and arranged, the comb lines showing pink scalp beneath. 'Your mother stirred when I went in for some clean clothes, but she dropped off again. I've been thinking—perhaps you could do some shopping for me later? You can borrow my car and there's a good supermarket just down the road now. That'd be a big help, because I can't take Pat to the shops any more, you see. She gets bewildered and upset.'

'Of course I will. And I'll cook the meals for you as well.'

'That'd be great. It's hard to keep up with everything. And you've got your mother's flair for cooking. I've never really got the hang of it.'

'How do you manage to get out and do the shopping, Dad?'

'Angie comes in sometimes and sits with Pat, and social services have arranged for a carer to come in two afternoons a week to give me a break, but by the time I've bought the groceries and changed my library books, the time's gone. I sometimes manage a few minutes in the park when it's fine, though. They've a lovely display of flowers there this year.' He sighed. 'I can't do our garden these days, because if I take her outside Pat wanders off. Maybe you and I could go to the park together on my next free afternoon, though? If I don't have the shopping to do, I'll have more time. There's a nice café there.'

'I'd love that. I'll buy you a cappuccino.' She had introduced him to them on her parents' last visit to Australia. Such a happy time they'd all had.

'That'd be great. Remember when . . . ?'

Laura let him talk, watching him cheer up. He'd lost a lot of weight since she'd last seen him and his skin was

65

muddy-looking but his smile was still as warm as ever. No one had a smile like her dad's.

At half-past nine Angie rang and said her friend Rick could come and pick Laura up if she wanted and show her some cars.

Her father looked at her questioningly as she set the phone down.

'That was Angie. I need to buy myself a car and her boyfriend sells them. Is it all right if I do your shopping later?'

'Of course. She's found herself a nice lad there. He's lovely with your mum. What sort of car are you looking for?'

Laura looked down at the table, fiddling with the cloth. 'One that's not too expensive. I don't have as much money as I'd expected, Dad. Craig left his share of the house to his mistress, you see, and his insurance policy named her as beneficiary. There are some shares, but I'll need those as a sort of superannuation fund. He moved out to live with his mistress a week before he died.'

He looked at her in shock and it was a minute before he spoke. 'Eh, why didn't you say before?'

'I couldn't talk about it on the phone.'

He reached out to squeeze her shoulder. 'It'll have made a big change in your life. Have you had time yet to make any plans?'

He was a great one for planning, her dad. She tried to summon up a smile and failed. 'Not yet. Perhaps I'll stay in England to be near you?'

'Only if it's the right thing for you, love. I'm seventy-five and I've got a few problems with my heart. By the time your mother goes, I'll not have long left myself, so don't build your life round us.'

The words escaped before she could stop them. When she was young she'd had trouble with runaway words, especially hot, angry ones. 'It's not *fair*! You don't deserve this.'

'Nor does Pat.' He looked up as there was a thud, then footsteps. 'And talk of the devil. I'd better go and make sure she doesn't do anything silly.'

Laura listened to him showering her mother, having to treat

her like a little child as he washed and dressed her. It took much longer than she'd have thought it would. Once she heard him beg Pat to stand still and another time there was a hoarse yell and he had to soothe her before he could continue.

Then she had to wait in the front room while her mother had breakfast in the back. She felt so utterly useless it was a relief when Rick turned up.

He took her to where he worked and showed her one car after the other till she was bewildered. In the end she stopped him moving on and said, 'Just tell me which one to buy, Rick. I need something reliable, that's passed its MOT and won't guzzle petrol. Not too expensive, either.'

'The blue one,' he said at once.

'It's OK, but a little more than I wanted to pay,' she said, automatically falling into bargaining mode.

He grinned. 'You're Angie's aunt—let's say we've agreed a price of two hundred below what my boss is asking. I know he'll not go any lower than that.'

'Thanks. I'll take it, then.'

He looked at her anxiously. 'It's a good one, honest. I don't want you to think I'm foisting something off on you.'

She lowered her voice and looked round as if making sure no one would overhear. 'I'll tell you a secret: I've never cared much about cars. As long as they get me from A to B and have a wheel on each corner, that's all that matters.'

'Wash your mouth out, Mrs Wells!'

They both laughed, then he took her to see the blue car again and they took it for a test drive. Afterwards he drove her home, promising to pick her up the next day when the car would be ready. 'Good thing you brought proof of no-claims insurance and all that stuff. Very efficient.'

'I'm usually quite well organized.' Her dad was right about Rick, she decided. Angie's guy wasn't good-looking and his hair was thinning already, but he had a broad smile and radiated honesty. No wonder her niece cared about him.

Once back inside that small, claustrophobic house, she had to sit in the front room while her father tried to keep her mother calm and happy in the back—an impossible task today, it seemed. Laura being there was adding to the complications, not making life easier for him. She went to stare blindly out of the window.

She went out after lunch and did the shopping, and at least she was able to cook tea while her father sat dozing in the living room with the television on and her mother slumped on the couch beside him.

When Laura peeped in to tell them it was ready, it was almost like old times. He'd always dozed in front of the TV—and invariably denied it. Smiling, she went back to the kitchen. The food could wait a few minutes.

Her smile faded. Dad looked so deep-down tired, it worried her.

As teatime approached, Kit began to prepare the vegetables for a stir-fry, sitting at the table and humming beneath his breath as he chopped and sliced.

Joe came in just before six looking tired but happy. 'Sorry to be late. Some of the parents are very slack about turning up on time to collect their little darlings.'

'Never mind. I've got tea ready to cook.'

Joe stared at the array of vegetables. 'You must have been shopping! How the hell did you manage that?'

'I went to look at Uncle Alf's house, then persuaded the taxi driver to nip into a supermarket for me on the way back.'

'You shouldn't be going out of the house yet, except to the physio's. They told me you were to take things *easy* for a few weeks.'

'Try stopping me.' After yet another exchange of challenging looks, Kit broke the heavy silence with, 'I hope you like stir-fry, because that's what you're having for tea.'

'Oh.'

Kit groaned. 'Don't tell me!'

'It's very kind of you, but I prefer my steak in one piece, actually.'

'Sorry. I'll remember that next time. I've already sliced up the steaks, though, and put them to marinate.'

'Ah. Well, I dare say it'll be all right. You'll have to tell me how to cook it.'

'No way are you getting near it! You'll cook the vegetables to death. I'll prop myself next to the wok and do the cooking while you stand beside me passing things and acting as kitchen slave.' He frowned. 'How on earth did you acquire a wok, if you don't like stir-fries?'

'Lois left it behind. She tried out that sort of cooking at one time, though we neither of us thought much of it.'

'Why did you two break up? I thought you were ideally suited.'

Joe's face froze. 'I'd rather not discuss it.'

'OK. But if you ever want to talk about it . . .'

'I don't.'

Kit ate more than he had for a while, relishing the crunchy vegetables and spicy flavours. He watched Joe pick at his food but didn't comment. Too bad. He was sick of plain steaks, roast lamb with nothing more than a scattering of salt on it, or whole chickens bought from the only take-away place which Joe trusted, a place which seemed as wary as he was of spices and herbs.

While his brother cleared up the dishes, Kit asked idly, 'Don't you usually go down to the pub on a Saturday night?'

Joe hesitated, then shrugged. 'Not any more.'

'Because of me?'

Another shake of the head.

'Why, then?'

'Because I don't.' He hesitated, then said stiffly, 'Look, I'd prefer to drop this.'

'I wouldn't. I shall feel guilty if my being here stops you enjoying your life. Especially after a day of five-a-sides. Surely you're longing for a pint?'

'I'm perfectly happy to have a quiet evening in.'

'Right. Be a bloody martyr. Mind if I work in here on my laptop? I haven't had a chance to pick up my emails today.' The kitchen was the only place with a telephone line.

'You should relax a bit.'

'And do what?'

'Well, watch TV. I don't mind if we have your sort of programme on for a change.'

'Joe, you're the kindest of brothers, but we're chalk and cheese when we try to live together—and it's not just the food and TV programmes.' He sighed and decided to get it over with. 'I may as well tell you—I'm going to live in Uncle Alf's house, but I hope you'll bear with me here a bit longer, because I can't move into it till I find myself a housekeeper. As soon as I do, I'll leave you in peace.'

'I see.'

His brother's stiff expression made Kit feel guilty, but not guilty enough to change his mind about leaving.

As the days passed, Pat continued to get agitated every time she saw her daughter. Several times she threw things at Laura and had to be restrained by her husband.

Her niece saw it happen once and went into the front room, to which Laura had retreated, to find her aunt in tears.

'How can my own mother hate me?'

Angie came over and hugged her. 'She doesn't. This isn't really Gran any more.'

'I try to tell myself that, but it still hurts.' More tears flowed, try as she would to pull herself together, and when Angie gave her a hug, Laura was so grateful for it that she wept again, unable to explain that her own daughter hadn't hugged her for years and she didn't dare offer Deb any open affection.

She stayed in the front room when Angie went back to sit with her grandmother, worrying about the situation. It took a minute or two for her to realize that her father had come in and was about to sit down beside her.

'I don't think your mother's going to change, love,' he said gently. 'Angie tells me you were crying just now.'

She nodded.

'It's what I told you the other day. You have to get on with your own life.'

'But I wanted to *help* you, Dad!'

'The fact that you came all the way to England did help me. It made me feel loved, especially with our Sue being so . . . Well, no use going into that.'

'Did it really mean so much, me coming here?'

'Of course it did.' He took a deep breath. 'But I think you'd better look for a job now and find yourself somewhere else to live. It's not that I want you to leave—heaven knows I don't—but the sad truth is that Pat's easier for me to manage when you're not here. Though I'll miss your cooking.'

'A job.' She summoned up a smile but it wasn't a very good one. 'I haven't worked outside the home for years. Who do you think's going to employ me?'

He thought for a minute, then said slowly, 'Maybe you could get a job *inside* someone's home, then, as a housekeeper or something? Your house always looked so beautiful.'

She'd come to much the same conclusion herself. 'I might try that. I suppose there'd be agencies dealing with that sort of thing.'

'And don't forget the newspaper adverts.' He laid the evening paper down beside her. 'You could even put your own ad in the jobs-wanted column.'

When he'd gone, she sat staring at the paper and it was a while before she could bring herself to open it. Actually, she was scared stiff of applying for jobs and hadn't expected to have to launch herself on the job market quite so soon. But if she had to pay rent and buy furniture, she'd need to find work. She didn't want to erode her capital more than she absolutely had to until she knew where her future lay.

And she didn't want to go back to Australia until she'd sorted herself out. She was in such a muddle internally, going round in circles trying to find a way out of the maze. She seemed to have lost her confidence, feeling hesitant every time she had to make a decision. There was a photo of a confident, laughing teenager in her room, and that photo seemed to accuse her of something, she wasn't sure what.

Nine

Kit's first advert for a housekeeper brought in only two replies. People who wanted live-in jobs were not, it seemed, thick on the ground in this part of the world.

The first woman he interviewed was fifty-something with iron-grey hair and a steely expression to match. As he showed her round, he listened to her laying down the law about what she would or would not do, and what living conditions and wages she expected. He went through the motions but it didn't take him long to decide that he could never live with such a sour-face.

The second woman was his own age, maybe a bit older, and eyed him in a way that suggested she fancied him. He still hadn't regained his libido and that worried him, but even in his prime he'd never have wanted this blowsy female. Besides, he'd specified a non-smoker and she reeked of cigarette smoke. Did she think he wouldn't be able to tell? Smokers never realized how strongly their habit perfumed them—skin, hair, clothes and even breath.

When he got back to Joe's he felt depressed. Very. Drank several stiff gin and tonics, then fell off his crutches when he tried to walk across the room. Got a lecture from Joe about being sensible, then had to let his brother help him up to bed.

Well, to hell with everything! He was sick to death of being sensible.

The leg he'd twisted in the fall woke him in the middle of the night aching furiously. He lay there for a while, willing himself to go to sleep again, but couldn't. He knew that if he got up and went down to find a painkiller, he'd wake Joe, who was a very light sleeper. So he stayed where he was. He didn't need any more lectures.

He wouldn't get drunk again. Too risky. But somehow, he vowed, he was going to find a housekeeper he could get on with and move into that lovely spacious old home. And soon.

To prove his faith in that he arranged to have the electricity and phone switched on, then hired some commercial cleaners to go through the place. It looked so much better with the dust covers removed.

When they'd left he fell asleep on the sofa, waking in the dark as someone hammered on the front door.

Joe. Worrying about him again.

Kit prayed for patience as he got up from the sofa, opened the front door and waited for the lecture to start.

Laura opened the newspaper and explored the situations-vacant columns. She traced her finger past jobs she'd never even heard of, then came to the heading *Domestic*. What they mainly seemed to want was cleaners of all sorts: night-time, early mornings, in private homes, in shops. Not much good to her, because most of them were for a few hours only and anyway, that sort of work definitely wouldn't use her skills.

She found an employment agency in the *Yellow Pages* and went for an interview, coming home thoroughly depressed. They hadn't thought her skills very marketable—that had been all too clear!—and they didn't hold out much hope of finding her a job. People only wanted experienced housekeepers, it seemed.

And yet she knew she was good at running a house, could organize a dinner party in two hours flat, as long as she had her pantry and freezer stocked with her usual standbys, could find and keep an eye on tradesmen—yes, and stop them cheating her, too.

But she wasn't good at interviews, as she proved when the man interviewing her videoed their practice one. She heard her voice wobble, some of her answers sounded foolish, her body language betrayed her nervousness, and she got angry once at something he said. He recommended that she attend their course on interview techniques and naturally that didn't come cheap. She told him she'd think about it and left, muttering angry comments about him and his agency all the way back to her car.

She stopped at the supermarket on the way back and after she'd bought a few things just sat there in her car, unable to summon up the energy to do anything, think anything, plan anything. Only the knowledge that her dad would worry about her if she was late made her start the engine.

After her mother had gone to bed, she and her father watched a holiday show on TV, showing happy people staying in all sorts of sunny places.

'That's what you need,' her father said. 'A holiday.'

'So do you.'

'I can't have one.' He paused and said in a strangled voice, 'It's so unfair. Poor Pat! What did she ever do to deserve this?'

She put her arms round him for a moment and patted his back, and he sighed against her before straightening his shoulders.

'Eh, I'm being silly. I can't change things, but I'd like to see you getting a little holiday, love. I'm sure it'd do you good.'

His words stuck in her mind and she lay there in bed considering her options. After living in a warm country, she didn't feel the longing for the sun that seemed to be sending shoals of Brits across the Channel and south. But she suddenly remembered childhood holidays in Blackpool, building sandcastles, simply walking along the firm sand or paddling in the frilly white edges of the waves. She could drive there in a couple of hours, find a bed and breakfast and just chill out for a day or two. Surely then she'd be able to think about the future, plan something?

The mere thought of getting away lifted her spirits. Her dad was right. She did need a break.

But when she woke in the morning, it didn't seem as easy. She'd never in her whole life been on holiday on her own, except to bring the children to England. And even then her husband had dropped her at one airport and her dad had met her at the other. What if something went wrong?

She caught sight of her face in the mirror and glared at it. I'm turning into a wimp, she thought. I'm afraid of everything. Why? What's happened to me?

So, in a spirit of grim determination, she packed her case, had a cheerful chat with Angie on the phone—well, she hoped she'd sounded cheerful—kissed her father and left.

Maybe, if she was very lucky, she'd find her old self on the beach, or a new one. And if she stuffed up this holiday, hated every minute of it, no one need ever know.

Deb Wells went home from work that Friday feeling lonely. It was beginning to sink in that she had no family left in Perth now. She hadn't realized she'd miss Ryan so much, and the mere thought of her father being dead brought tears to her eyes still. She'd phoned her brother a couple of times, but he sounded busy and excited about his new job. *He* wasn't missing anyone, that was for sure.

She even missed her mother, something she hadn't expected, especially the knowledge that she was there if needed. But she doubted her mother missed her. She hadn't tried to phone, had she? And anyway, Deb knew she'd been unkind to her after Dad died, had been feeling guilty about that.

The two other girls she shared the flat with came home just after her, rushing to get ready for their dates. She didn't have a date, didn't have much luck with men, somehow. She glued a smile to her face, insisted she was perfectly happy to have a quiet night in, and thought she'd fooled them.

But Linda lingered to say, 'You're not happy to stay in on your own, Deb, however much you pretend. Maybe it's time you made a few changes. How about going to see your grandmother?'

'Maybe.'

'And you should make it up with your mother, too.'

'She won't want to.'

Linda looked at her scornfully. 'Of course she will. She's your mother. They're always ready to forgive you. You were never fair to her and actually, I always thought your father was a bit of an old lech. He asked *me* out once, you know.'

Deb gaped at her in shock. 'I don't believe you. He *wouldn't.*'

'Suit yourself. I'm telling the truth, though. As if I'd go out with an old man like him. That sucks. How old was his fancy lady?'

Deb didn't answer. Caitlin wasn't much older than her. What was wrong with that? Her father had been a good-looking man for his age. He'd been over twenty years older than Caitlin, though. And soon Deb would have a brother or sister the same amount younger than herself. The thought of that didn't sit easily with her.

There was nothing worth watching on the telly, she'd finished her novel and she definitely couldn't be fussed with going out, so she did her washing and then phoned Pop in England. And he, at least, was there for her.

'Eh, love, you've just missed your mother. She's gone away for a couple of days. What a pity! I'll get her to call you back when she comes home.'

'Never mind. I'll catch up with her next time. How's Gran?'

Silence, then, 'Failing fast. She doesn't recognize your mother any more.'

And suddenly Deb found herself saying it, though she hadn't intended to. 'I'm coming over to see you. Soon. If you'll have me, that is.'

'Lovely! I can't wait to see you, love. Your mother'll be that pleased when I tell her. She's a bit down in the dumps, needs something to cheer her up. Your dad leaving her will take a while to get over. She's not as confident as she tries to appear. But then, you'll know that better than I do.'

Deb put the phone down. She didn't know much about

76

her mother, actually. She'd always been Daddy's little girl. Tears rolled down her cheeks. She missed him dreadfully, still thought of things to tell him, only to be brought up short by the realization that she'd never see him again.

He couldn't really have invited Linda out. He'd probably just been teasing and Linda had taken it the wrong way. Yeah, that was it.

Only— when she said that to her friend on Monday evening as they were having a drink after work, Linda got really angry. She dragged Deb across the café to two other girls they knew slightly and asked them baldly, 'You've met Deb's father, haven't you? She won't believe he asked me for a date.'

They both laughed loudly.

'She was mistaken. He was just teasing her,' Deb insisted.

They looked at her pityingly, and when she glared at them, one said, 'Sorry. Don't like to speak ill of the dead, but he was known for it. Mind you, those who went out with him said he gave them a good time. But I don't fancy dir—er, older men.'

Deb turned and left the café without a word. *Dirty old men*, the girl had been going to say. Her dad hadn't been the sort of man who chased young girls. He couldn't have been!

She didn't care who saw her crying as she stumbled back towards her car.

Ten

Laura turned westwards, glad of the motorway system, which made travel so easy. She was soon on the M55 heading towards the coast. Cars whizzed past her, driving more quickly than in Australia, but she didn't feel like hurrying. She'd decided not to stay in Blackpool itself. It was too big and brash for her present mood. Seeking somewhere quieter, she turned off north when she got to the Fylde region. After a while she came to a sign saying Tideshall and took a whim to visit it.

The land was very flat now. Home-made signs advertised farm potatoes for sale. Fields stretched in every direction, with low hedges separating them. The older cottages were whitewashed and picturesque. Large modern houses guarded by walls and hedges were succeeded every now and then by rows of small terraced houses with gleaming windows and carefully arranged ornaments displaying the owners' pride in their homes to passers-by.

Tideshall itself consisted mainly of a cluster of three-storey terraced houses backed by rows of small bungalows. It boasted a tiny promenade, a few shops and a beach of reddish sand on which two people were strolling. It looked peaceful, which was the main thing Laura was after. She got out of the car and leaned on the wall that separated the promenade from the beach, breathing in the tangy sea air.

When she went to find a bed and breakfast, however, she found that there were only two places offering accommodation, and both were full. 'We don't get a lot of casuals here, love,' the second woman said. 'I've got mostly regulars in now. Try the Fisherman's Arms at the other end of the prom-

enade. They do B & B for commercial travellers and such.'
She closed the door again before Laura could even thank her.

The pub stood on its own next to a couple of boarded-up shops. It looked very old, huddling under a sprawl of uneven roofs. A new and over-ornate sign said *Fisherman's Arms* in gold against maroon, but the effect was spoiled by the way the sign tilted to the right, as if it had been drinking heavily.

When she went inside, she found the bar empty and had to call out before someone came to attend to her. 'I'm looking for a room for a couple of nights.'

The man stared at her as if suspicious of her reasons for this, then admitted grudgingly that he did have a room available, though the main floor was being refurbished, so there was only the top floor. He showed her up two flights of creaking stairs to an attic room with a shared bathroom next to it. The room was shabby but clean and the price very reasonable, Laura considered, at twenty pounds a night including a cooked breakfast.

She couldn't be bothered to drive on and look elsewhere. After all, a bed was a bed, and if the room was shabby, at least the view was lovely, looking out over the beach. 'I'll take it. I'll just fetch my suitcase in.'

'Breakfast is at half-past eight.' He handed her the room key and shambled off downstairs without another word.

When she went through the bar, there was no sign of him, but a cheerful barmaid nodded a greeting. Laura fetched her suitcase and lugged it upstairs, then couldn't resist walking along the beach. But the tide was coming in fast, so she returned to her car and sat wondering where to spend the rest of the day. She settled on Fleetwood, because she could vaguely remember going there as a child.

The outskirts of the town were busy and very different from her memories, with new factory-shopping outlets and industry of various sorts. But there was enough of the old promenade still for her to walk off her fidgets and fill her lungs with more salty air.

She fell asleep in the car afterwards, waking with a start, not knowing where she was.

Feeling ravenous, she was tempted by Singh's Fish Bar, which was doing a lively trade. It took her back to her childhood again to sit at a plastic-topped table and eat fish and chips with vinegar, accompanied by white bread and butter on the side. Full of fat, not at all healthy, but she enjoyed every mouthful.

As she got into the car, she shivered, suddenly aware that it was getting dark and she was feeling chilly. The wind had turned fresh and she suspected it'd rain before morning. Well, let it. There was always something to do in Blackpool.

But she couldn't help wishing she had someone to go there with. She hadn't yet grown accustomed to being on her own and still turned to share comments about what was happening around her, feeling foolish to find herself talking to thin air.

When she got back, the pub was almost empty and the barmaid greeted her with, 'Eh, I was wondering if you'd get here before closing time. You'll be on your own tonight, love. No one else has booked a room and the owners don't live in.'

Laura was startled. 'On my own?'

'Yes, but don't worry. The outer doors will all be locked, so you'll be quite safe, though you won't be able to get out. Of course, the emergency doors work if there's any trouble—only you can't get back in if you let one shut behind you, so if I were you, I'd not try to get out if you don't have to.'

Laura wondered uneasily how it'd feel to be on her own in a strange building whose layout she didn't even know, apart from the public rooms and the way upstairs. She ordered half a pint of bitter, her first glass of English beer for many years, savouring the taste, which brought back more memories of her youth, when she and her friends had scraped together the price of half a pint of beer or shandy and made it last all night.

Ten minutes later the barmaid called time and came to pick up the empty glasses, clearly in a hurry to get off home. Laura went past the sign saying *Residents Only*, climbing the stairs reluctantly, her footsteps muffled by a thick, garishly coloured carpet. She didn't at all fancy being on her own in a strange place, but it was too late to do anything about it and, anyway, she was probably worrying about nothing.

Her room looked most unwelcoming by the dim light of the single ceiling lamp, which was swinging to and fro as the wind blew in through the open window. She went to use the bathroom and, when she returned, found the wind gusting so strongly that the window had come off its catch and was banging open and shut in a most annoying way.

She went across to fasten the catch. The sea view outside was now nothing but darkness because the moon was hidden behind heavy clouds. As she looked out, she heard a car start up and headlights swung round to one side, then vanished. After the sound of the engine had faded into the distance, she was left with only silence inside and windy darkness outside.

The catch didn't fit very well and within a minute of her closing it, the window had blown open again with a loud bang that made her jump in shock. No amount of fiddling would make the stupid thing stay closed, because the wooden frame had warped so badly. What did they do with it in winter, for heaven's sake? Or was this floor also destined for refurbishment?

Think! she told herself. *No need to panic.*

The wind shrieked at her derisively and the window banged even harder. Tears rose in her eyes and she almost packed her bags and left.

Then she grew angry with herself. She would not give in to this minor setback! She had to learn to stand on her own two feet in all situations. Had to. Would do.

In Melbourne, Ryan strolled along Collins Street, enjoying the sunshine on his face after a morning of meetings in air-conditioned offices. However good the system, canned air never felt quite right to him. He'd always meant to get an outdoor job, but had been pushed into the university stream by the school authorities and had wound up graduating with a degree in commerce.

Melbourne was still new enough to delight him. He loved the statues in the city centre, the old-fashioned arcades with their stained glass and intricate patterns of tiles, the trams, the massive older buildings, the many bookshops—there were so many things to see and enjoy here.

As he turned a corner, he bumped into a woman, stepped back hastily, then gaped at her. 'Caitlin! What are *you* doing over here in the eastern states?'

'I've come to live here.'

'But I thought your family were over in Perth?'

'They are. And they were driving me crazy fussing over me. They—um—belong to a small, very strict, religious sect and they're upset about the baby. They won't stop pestering me to go and live at home, and my cousin Barry has been turning up every day to try to persuade me.' Her voice trailed away and she looked down at her stomach with a grimace.

'Why didn't you tell me you were thinking of coming here when I said I was moving to Melbourne?'

'I hadn't made up my mind then.'

'Have you time for a coffee?'

She hesitated, biting her lower lip, frowning at him. He held his breath, willing her to agree. He didn't know why it seemed important but it did.

'All right. Thank you. That'd be nice.'

He let out a sigh of relief before he could stop himself. 'You're looking well.'

'I'm feeling a lot better. The first three months, I felt sick in the mornings, but I'm getting over that now. Well, most of the time. I still have off days.'

They sat and chatted over two flat whites, both agreeing that cappuccino was vastly overrated, then he looked at his watch. 'I've got to get back to the office now, I'm afraid. Look, let's meet sometime, eh? I don't know many people in Melbourne yet. We could maybe have dinner one night?'

Another of those hesitations, then she looked at him, reluctance showing clearly in her face. 'Why?'

'Why what?'

'Why do you want to keep seeing me?'

He shrugged. 'I feel connected because of the baby. I'd hate not to know my own brother or sister.'

She continued to look at him searchingly for a minute, then gave another of her slight shrugs. 'All right. As long as it's for the baby, not me.'

They exchanged addresses and phone numbers, then he had to rush back to the office, but her words stayed with him all day. Was it for the baby's sake he wanted to see her? Hell, he didn't know. *Just let it flow*, he told himself. See what happens.

And if he still continued to feel attracted to her?

He didn't know. If he had any sense, he'd back off now.

He definitely didn't have any sense. He *wanted* to see her again.

Caitlin watched him vanish into the distance with that long-legged, energetic stride, then sat on in the café, cradling the now cold coffee cup between her hands to stop them clearing it away. She still felt guilty about all the money she'd received from Craig, knowing his poor wife had more right to it than she did. Only, it spelled freedom and security for her and the child, and she couldn't bear to give that up. No way was she ever going to be dependent on her parents. Or Barry.

She hadn't told them she was moving and had taken very elaborate precautions to prevent Barry from finding out where she was, breaking off connections with all her friends in case they betrayed her, though Barry's computer skills worried her. He'd boasted that you could find out anything on the Internet, and for some reason hacking didn't seem to be against his morals. He was as fanatically religious as her parents and had no tolerance of opposing views, social-izing only with other members of their sect, treating women as lesser beings. Though how they could think their sect knew the perfect way to salvation when it was so small and showed no signs of expanding, she had never understood.

As soon as she'd grown old enough to question their ways, she'd stopped believing, which had led to some very unhappy times, till she'd learned to dissemble. Even so, it had taken her till she was twenty-four to pluck up the courage to leave home. She was determined that her child should have a more open upbringing—and a happier one.

People didn't believe it when she told them what it had been like to live in such a family, so she'd stopped telling them. They couldn't understand the crushing weight of love and duty that had been piled on her for as long as she could remember. She was the only child and her mother had been unable to have any more children after her. And it had been all the harder to pull free because they'd not ill-treated her. No, they'd lavished all their love on her, pinned their hopes on her, urged her to marry and give them grandchildren, until she felt she'd suffocate under the weight of their hopes.

Craig had been like a breath of fresh air. Sophisticated yet casual, making her laugh as she'd never laughed before. She'd been temporarily infatuated, ripe for the plucking, and he'd not hesitated to pluck her. The baby had been a cruel jest by fate, a condom that burst at exactly the wrong time of the month. Condoms weren't supposed to do that, but you could hardly take the defective merchandise back to the chemists and ask for your money to be refunded, could you?

She sighed. Well, she'd got away again and this time hoped her family wouldn't find her, She didn't know what she wanted to do with the rest of her life, could only look ahead as far as having the baby. She'd rented a furnished flat, bought a modest second-hand car, and the worst thing she had to contend with now was a little boredom now and then.

She glanced at her watch and went to pay her bill, walking out into a street that seemed to be filled with couples. She envied them. Ryan wasn't the only one who was lonely. But she'd had a lot of practice at coping with that. You could be just as lonely in the middle of a close-knit family whose views you didn't share as on your own in a strange city.

But if she got to know Ryan, if he got to know her, then he might find out how she had really felt about his father once the first flush of infatuation had faded. Then he'd despise her for taking the money, she was sure.

Well, she despised herself. But she wasn't giving it back. That money meant freedom, not only for her but for her child.

Eleven

Laura knew she'd have to do something about the banging window or she'd never sleep. No one was going to rescue her; she had to rescue herself. After staring at it, feeling angry that this was happening to her, she bent her mind to the problem.

Maybe she could find something to hold it shut with. She peered out of the door and the darkness of the corridor nearly made her retreat to her room again. *Stop being such a coward, Laura Wells!* Taking a deep breath, she went out to face her demons.

Switching on the corridor light, she began trying doors. Only two opened. One proved to be a cupboard full of neatly folded towels, and the other a bedroom.

Her heart still pounding with nervousness, she went down to the first floor, stopping halfway to listen. What if someone was lurking in those shadows? *Stop that, you fool!* Tentatively, with many quick glances over her shoulder, she began trying doors that had been stripped of their paint and numbers. But they were all locked.

She went on down to the ground floor, hating the way this flight of stairs creaked and groaned beneath her. Anger helped push her onwards—anger at herself as much as the situation. What was she afraid of, for heaven's sake? The building was empty. It was only shadows. *Pull yourself together, woman!*

If she had to, she decided, she'd search every cupboard in the place till she found something to tie that damned window shut. She would not be beaten!

To her immense relief she found a meter cupboard at the

foot of the stairs, and in it some copper wire. A door banged somewhere in the empty pub. Snatching up the roll, she ran up both flights of stairs again as if all the fiends in hell were after her. She yanked open her bedroom door and was inside within seconds, locking it and leaning against it, panting.

The window banged and she realized it had been that she'd heard.

Fool!

She managed a weak smile. Pulling the window closed yet again, she wired its handle to the other one.

'I did it,' she said aloud, sitting on the nearest bed. 'I coped.' But her moment of triumph was short-lived. The sound of her own voice quavering in this shabby little room was the final straw. Her life was a mess and there was no one to care whether she sorted her problems out or not. And she certainly wasn't going to confide in her dad how depressed she was feeling, because he had enough on his plate.

When tears began to trickle down her cheeks, she let them flow, lying down and burying her face in her arms. She didn't know how long she wept, but when she felt sleep overtaking her she gave in to it with a sigh of relief.

In the middle of the night she woke shivering, crawled under the duvet and lay there for a moment or two. To her surprise she felt better, as if the tears had been a necessary catharsis. 'It *will* get better,' she said aloud as sleep tugged at her again. 'I'll *make* it get better.'

Morning brought a beautiful sunny day. 'There, what did I say?' She smiled out at the view as she got dressed.

In the dining room, she enjoyed every mouthful of her 'full English breakfast' of bacon, sausage, half a tomato, mushroom and egg, then went up to her room to stand by the window and consider her options. She'd stay here a second night on the principle of better the devil you knew. And she'd go into Blackpool today.

A long walk along the promenade there cheered her up

further. She bought pink candyfloss and ate it like a child, licking her sticky fingers clean. Then she found some Blackpool rock to take back for her father and Angie. She'd always loved the way the tiny letters spelling Blackpool went all the way along the stick of candy. Later she went into town and bought a novel that looked interesting, then strolled round the shops.

What she didn't do was work out any practical plans for her future. Well, to hell with that! Everyone deserved a holiday, didn't they? And today she felt better than she had at any time since Craig's death. It was as if her successful overcoming of her own fears the night before had acted as a catalyst for change. She smiled. Such a small problem to most people, but it had seemed big to her at the time.

When she got back to her room at the pub, she cut off a piece of the wire she'd used to hold the window closed and put it into her purse to remind her that she could cope. Strange sort of lucky talisman that was! But it was a symbol of what she hoped would be a turning point in her new life. No, not *hoped*, she'd start taking control of her future from now on.

The following day, when she got back to Rochdale, her father greeted her with, 'Our Deb rang while you were away, love. She's coming over to see us. Now won't that be grand? You'll have missed her. Pity Ryan can't come too, then we could all be together.'

Laura pinned a smile to her face and agreed with him that it was wonderful news. But she wasn't so sure about that. How would she and Deb get on without Ryan to mediate? She couldn't see Deb changing her sharp ways.

Well, she wasn't the first person not to get on with her own daughter and she wouldn't be the last. She'd cope with that as well.

She looked at her reflection in the mirror and squared her shoulders. The first thing you need, she told it, is a job. And she would find one, by hook or by crook.

But first she had a personal pilgrimage to make, to a

place she'd often visited as a girl. She'd been meaning to go there since she got back.

Kit phoned a couple of employment agencies, both of which seemed inordinately suspicious of his reasons for wanting a live-in housekeeper and insisted he come in to their office to register. They offered to send him some literature about their services, but when pressed didn't sound at all hopeful about finding the sort of person he needed.

That afternoon, as the walls of Joe's tiny house seemed to be closing in on him more tightly than ever, he went out to the park to think things over. He'd been there a couple of times and could just make it on his crutches from the gates where the taxi dropped him to the Rotunda Café, where there were usually plenty of people for him to sit and watch.

That day a woman of his own age and an elderly man took the table next to his and he began his usual guessing game about their relationship. When she called the man 'Dad', Kit felt inordinately pleased that he'd interpreted the situation correctly. It was a journalist's skill, he'd always told himself, to analyse a scene and its players. Not that he needed that skill any longer, but still, it was nice to know he hadn't completely lost his touch.

After a while the elderly man looked at his wristwatch and stood up. 'Will you be all right, love?'

'Of course I will, Dad. I can easily walk back from here. In fact, I'll enjoy it.'

When her father had gone, however, the woman's smile vanished and she sat frowning into the distance.

Kit was intrigued. Maybe she had a problem she didn't want to trouble the old man with. She was about his age, he'd guess, quite attractive in an understated way, with gleaming brown hair that bounced around her face, and clear skin with a residual tan. She hadn't got that tan in England, so where had she been or come from?

And she was woman-shaped, not one of these scrawny females who looked like human safety-pins, all bones and skin. They'd never turned him on. She did, for some reason. It was the first time he'd found a woman attractive since the accident, and that really pleased him, another sign that he was continuing to get better.

A waitress came up to ask the woman if she wanted anything else and when she said no, began to clear the table.

Nothing like a broad hint, thought Kit, sorry to see the woman leave. She walked away slowly, as if she had nowhere urgent to go. *Know that feeling*, he thought.

He wondered if she came here regularly. Half hoped so.

Laura looked up at the sky as she left the café, and decided she'd just have time to visit the old wishing well before it began to rain. She'd been meaning to go there ever since she got back.

It was still there, unchanged since her girlhood, till she looked inside and saw that they'd filled it in and the water was now only about a foot deep. There was heavy wire mesh padlocked firmly across the top, presumably to stop people from pinching the coins that gleamed silver and bronze beneath the ruffled surface of the water. In the old days, you tossed your coin in and that was that. It vanished from view. It really did feel as if you'd made an offering to the gods. Now, a small sign announced that proceeds from the well were given to the Karen Drake Hospice.

She fished in her purse and pulled out a two-pound coin, tossing it in and making her wish as it splashed and sank. It'd been sixpences she'd tossed in when she was a girl, or she'd blown the seeds off dandelions and made wishes as they floated away. But her wishes then had been no less fervent than today's: to find a job, and soon.

She didn't know why she was bothering with the wishing well, really, except that she'd always felt it brought her luck.

Raindrops began plopping into the water, setting up ripples that were so pretty she spent a minute or two watching them before turning to leave. Her father would start to fuss if she got wet. Maybe she should find shelter and see if this was only a passing shower?

She remembered the old bandstand and turned towards it, grinning as she walked briskly along. She'd had her first kiss there—and snogged several other boyfriends there as well. It had been a favourite rendezvous for her generation.

The waitress moved to Kit's table and began the same routine of 'Can I get you anything else, sir?' He'd have stayed and outfaced her but the afternoon was sliding towards teatime and he needed to get back. Standing up, he settled his crutches in place and moved outside.

When a few drops of rain hit his face, he looked up in surprise. Damn! Where had those clouds come from? They seemed heavy enough to dump a good dose of rain on him and he had to get to the gates before he could call a taxi, because only parks department vehicles were allowed to drive inside the park. There was a metal pole across the gateway, sporting a big padlock.

He tried to take a short cut along one of the narrower paths that led past the bandstand. It was all right at first, then it changed suddenly to crazy paving, one of his bugbears these days. Taking infinite care, he moved slowly on, but for all his efforts one of his crutches slipped and he could feel himself falling.

He let out a yell as he hit the ground, and lay there for a moment, winded and feeling furious at his own incapacities.

Footsteps came running and someone asked, 'Are you all right?'

'Yes. Thanks.' He looked up to see the woman from the café bending over him, and felt pleased with fate. If he had to be rescued, then this was the person he'd have chosen to do the deed. 'Well, I will be all right once I get to my feet. It's my own fault. I shouldn't have taken a side path. Crazy paving is hell on crutches, especially when it's raining.'

As if to prove that the weather was definitely not on his side today, the rain grew heavier.

'The bandstand's just round the corner. We could shelter there till it eases off. The weather report said "a few showers".' She helped him to his feet.

'You've dealt with someone on crutches before,' he guessed.

'My son. He broke his leg a few years ago. Can you manage now? Right. This way.'

She walked in front of him, turning occasionally to check that he was all right, and they soon reached the bandstand. It was dilapidated and much in need of a coat of paint, but the roof was still sound enough to keep the rain off, and the wooden benches in the centre were still dry. He sank down on one with a sigh of relief, then looked down at himself ruefully. 'I'm soaked—and I've made you get wetter than you would have been. Sorry about that.'

'It's only water.'

'Is that an Aussie accent?'

She nodded. 'You've been there?'

'Several times. Whereabouts are you from?'

'Perth. That's in Western Australia.'

'I know it. Lovely city. I'm going back there one day.'

Rain beat down relentlessly, bouncing up from the path and blowing on to the seats at the edges of the bandstand. It made such a noise they both stopped speaking to stare out at it in amazement.

'It was sunny an hour ago,' she said. 'I'd never have expected it to change so much.'

'This is Lancashire! Rain is the natural state of affairs. Mind you, I'm still getting used to that again myself. Haven't lived here for ages.'

She chuckled, a warm musical gurgle of sound. 'I should have remembered it and brought an umbrella.'

'I saw you in the café. With your father, I think? I wasn't being nosey—' He stopped and grimaced, then admitted, 'Yes, I was. I love watching people and trying to guess what they're doing. Comes of being a journo.'

'I watch people too. I noticed you when you came into the café. How did you hurt your leg?'

That brought him back to reality with a thump. 'Road accident in Bangkok.'

'Sounds very glamorous.'

91

He shook his head. 'No. Painful. And will leave me with a permanent limp.'

She could hear the frustration ringing in his voice and, without thinking, put her hand on his. 'I'm sorry. That must be hard. I'd guess you were an active person before.'

Without thinking, he grasped her hand, staring down at it. Well cared for, but her skin wasn't as soft as he'd expected. 'Yes.' He let go, relieved when she didn't pursue the point or offer gushing sympathy as some people tried to. 'What about you? You spoke of a son . . . is there a husband in the background? I have to tell you, you don't look married.'

'My husband died a couple of months ago.'

'Oh, hell, I'm sorry! I've really put my foot in it now.'

She liked his crooked, rueful smile and his dark, untidy hair, which he'd pushed back impatiently from his forehead. It needed cutting. She paused mentally on that thought. Strange. She hadn't really looked at a man for months and now a gorgeous one had literally landed at her feet. She became aware that he was still staring at her anxiously. 'It's all right. My husband and I were separated.'

'Ah.' After another pause, he asked, 'What are you doing in England? Or is that too private? Just tell me to mind my own business if it is. I can't seem to help asking questions.'

For some unfathomable reason, she felt comfortable enough with him to explain about her mother and her search for a job.

He nodded, not commenting, just listening with quiet concentration.

'There's nothing you can do,' he said when she fell silent. 'I did research once for an article on a celebrity with Alzheimer's. It's a cruel disease, so hard on the relatives. I'm sure your mother's reaction to you isn't meaningful if you'd always got on with her before.'

Somehow, having a stranger say that made things feel better, because he could have no personal interest in lying to her. 'Thanks.' She smiled at him.

'What for?'

'Listening. Saying what I've been trying to persuade myself to believe.'

It was he who reached out to clasp her hand this time. 'Believe it. I'm not making it up. And it's nice to know I'm still a good listener, even though I've retired now.'

She stared down at their hands, not knowing what to say or do next, and after a moment he let go. She looked outside. 'The rain's easing, I think.' But she wished it wasn't, because she'd have liked to get to know him better.

'You really are looking for a job as a housekeeper?' he asked suddenly.

'Yes. It's all I can think of to do. But I'm pretty bad at interviews and the agency I went to suggested I do a course before they took me on—a very expensive course. I thought it a real rip-off, so I refused.'

His smiled broadened till it lit up his whole face. 'Why don't you come and work for me, then? I'm absolutely desperate to find a housekeeper.'

She could only gape at him. 'Do you mean that?'

'Yes.' He stuck out one hand. 'Kit Mallinder.'

She took his hand again. 'Laura Wells. Tell me more.'

She didn't believe in the old wishing well, of course she didn't, but this was the most amazing coincidence, and if the job was at all suitable, she'd snap his hand off.

And make a thank-you offering into that well! Just in case.

Twelve

A ngie was waiting for Laura when she got home. 'Mum wants you to come to tea tonight.'

She was half-inclined to say no, given such short notice. Her sister hadn't been in touch since her arrival and she'd been upset by that. It felt as though this invitation was a spur of the moment thing only, as though seeing her wasn't important enough to make a fuss about. Or, just as bad, that Sue only needed to beckon and she'd come running.

'You go round to our Sue's, love,' her father said. 'Me and your mother will be fine.'

She knew it'd upset him if she refused, so she gave in. 'All right. But let me tell you my news before I get ready. I may have found myself a job.'

'But you've only been to the park! How can you . . . ? Surely you're not going to work at the café? You get some strange characters there.'

She explained what had happened and was surprised when he pursed his lips and frowned. 'What's wrong, Dad?'

'Well, this man could be anyone, couldn't he? A serial killer, even.'

She managed not to laugh. Impossible to think of Kit Mallinder as a criminal. 'He's not got a shifty sort of face.'

'You can't always tell.'

'Well, he's on crutches, so I can run faster than him.' She saw that her father was in no mood for jokes, back in his old protect-my-daughters mode in fact, and stifled a sigh. 'I've arranged to meet him tomorrow to look over the house, so I'll make sure I find out more about him then.'

'Take our Angie with you, just to be safe.'

'Dad . . .'

'It never hurts to be careful, love.'

She didn't say that she was forty-four not fourteen, or ask what being careful had done for her so far. In fact, now she thought about it, she didn't want to be careful any more, wanted to spread her wings—just a little. Ever since her brief holiday, the desire to do something had been bubbling up inside her, quietly insistent. Strange sort of catalyst, two days in a run-down pub near Blackpool.

She still had that piece of wire, though.

'We'd better be going, Auntie Laura,' Angie said. 'Mum's a real stickler for serving meals on time.'

'She always was. It used to drive me mad when we were kids and she wanted to organize everything we did, including my half of our bedroom.' She laughed at the memories that evoked, though the two of them had had some pretty fierce quarrels about the division of their space and the privacy of their possessions over the years.

Angie got into the car with her aunt and sat in silence, which was unlike her.

'Something wrong?' Laura asked gently as she navigated her way through the teatime traffic.

'Oh, just Mum. She's been nagging me again. I'd move out, only I can't afford a place of my own. And Rick lives with his family, so I can't move in with him. Anyway, it's too soon for that sort of thing, though I'm hoping . . .'

Her voice trailed away and she sighed. When she didn't say anything else, Laura said gently, 'It can be one of the hardest things there is, dealing with families. I don't get on all that brilliantly with Deb, though I've never understood why.'

Angie looked at her in surprise. 'She doesn't know when she's well off, then.'

'What a lovely compliment!' When her niece didn't offer any more confidences, she changed the subject. 'Look, you don't have to come with me tomorrow if you don't want. Dad's always been a bit too careful where his womenfolk are concerned.'

'I don't mind. I think Pop's right, actually. After all, this man is a total stranger and it's not as if anyone introduced you. I'll sit in the car outside, so if you need help, you only have to scream and I'll come running.'

'All right.' But Laura wanted to sort things out for herself. Needed to. And she couldn't imagine Kit Mallinder being a criminal, or even a sexual harasser. She had taken an instant liking to him.

From the front, her sister's house hadn't changed since her last visit. It was a small detached bungalow set in the middle of a row of others which were almost identical to one another. The garden was rigidly neat. Laura would have put in some bedding plants and softened up the stiff clumps of greenery, but her sister had never liked things to be 'messy'.

Sue came to stand in the front doorway, watching with folded arms as Laura parked. She nodded a greeting but once again didn't offer a kiss or hug. 'We're sitting in the conservatory.'

Laura followed her through the house to where a small conservatory stuck out backwards from the dining area next to the kitchen, neatly bisecting the tiny rear garden. The cane chairs in it were arranged with geometric precision round a low table, and two plants in pots graced the far end. 'It's very—um—pretty.'

'I know this isn't in your league for houses, but we like living here and it's easy to keep clean.'

Laura bit back a sharp response at this undeserved dig. You just had to ignore Sue's prickly remarks or you'd be quarrelling with her all the time. She could see Angie rolling her eyes heavenwards, but thank goodness her niece didn't make things worse by intervening. At least Trev hadn't changed much, except to lose most of his hair. He came towards her with arms outstretched, beaming as he pulled her into a hug.

'You're looking well, Laura love. It's just a pity you had to come over here in such sad circumstances. I'm really sorry about your loss.' He glanced at his wife as he said that and she sniffed audibly, turning away to polish the already sparkling glasses which were set out on an ornate, silver-plated tray ready for drinks.

'I lost Craig long before he died, long before he actually left me,' Laura said, determined not to pretend about anything. 'So, I'm not exactly sunk in grief.'

'Yes, Sue told me. But him dying must still have upset you. I mean, you were together for over twenty years. That has to count for something.'

Her throat tightened. 'Yes, and you're right, it does upset me. No one deserves to die so young. But that didn't stop me being angry when I found out he'd left his share of everything we built together to his mistress.'

'Women who go after married men should be taken out and shot.'

Sue's tone was so vicious Laura wondered for a moment if Trev had been unfaithful, but she couldn't see that. He was such a straightforward, warm-hearted man you couldn't imagine him cheating on anyone. 'Can we change the subject now, please? I'm trying to put all that behind me. I may even have found myself a job.'

The conversation limped along. They moved to the dining end of the L-shaped living room to eat food which was plain but tasty. The wine was unexpectedly good and she complimented them on it.

Angie beamed at her. 'I chose it. That's one benefit of working at a pub. You can buy your wines at cost. I asked my boss which one would be best to go with casseroled steak.'

Sue looked across at her sourly. 'You were wasting your money. We're not in the gourmet wines class here.'

Laura couldn't believe that her sister would be so spiteful, and hated to see how hurt Angie was by this remark. 'Pity I can only have one glass, because it's lovely, but I like to be careful when I drive.' Taking tiny sips, she heard herself muttering platitudes, making bland statements, murmuring agreement to her sister's staccato comments. Why she should always feel uncomfortable in Sue's house, she had never been able to work out, but this time she felt worse than on previous visits and was thankful when enough time had passed for her to leave.

But it was no relief to go back to her father's, either. Laura drove slowly through the dark streets with the windscreen wipers beating out a rhythm behind her troubled thoughts.

One thing was certain: if the job Kit Mallinder had offered her was at all bearable, she was going to grab it with both hands.

The following morning Laura took her car keys out of her handbag and called, 'I'm off now, Dad.'

He came to the door of the kitchen, glancing back quickly to make sure his wife wasn't following. 'You look nice, love. Blue always did suit you. And I'm glad you're not going on your own.'

She picked Angie up then headed towards Wardle, where Kit Mallinder lived. Laura remembered cycling out there as a teenager and picnicking near the reservoir. She hoped the village hadn't changed too much.

They found the short side street quite easily and Angie called, 'There it is!'

Laura parked and they sat looking at the house.

'Not bad,' Angie said. 'He can't be short of money, then.'

'He's definitely not short of money if he's employing a full-time housekeeper.' She took a deep breath and opened the car door. 'I'll try not to keep you waiting too long.'

Angie grinned and brandished a battered paperback at her. 'Just got some new reading supplies from the charity shop. I'll be fine.'

Laura felt nervous as she walked along the path to the front door. Crazy paving again. The poor man was bedevilled by it. And these worn pieces of elderly grey stone didn't make for an attractive entrance path, either. It'd have looked better if it had curved slightly, instead of bisecting the rectangular garden so precisely. By the time she reached the front door, she'd mentally rearranged the garden.

The door opened before she got there, and he stood smiling at her. 'I was watching for you, afraid you wouldn't turn up.'

'Why should you think that?'

He shrugged and had to grab a crutch that started to slip. 'Well, you only met me once in the park, so I could be anybody, a mass murderer even.'

She chuckled and pointed in the direction of her car. 'My father's already thought of that, so he insisted I bring my own insurance with me—my niece Angie is riding shotgun. He doesn't realize I'm grown-up and is still trying to look after me.'

'You're lucky to have him to care about you.'

'I know.'

'Why am I keeping you standing at the door? Come inside and I'll show you round the ground floor, but I'll have to leave you to go upstairs on your own.' He grimaced down at his crutches.

'It's a lovely house,' she said as they returned to the hall after their downstairs tour. 'I could do a lot with this.'

'Pardon?'

'Oh, sorry. I've done a lot of renovating. I was going to start my own designer-decor business in Australia. I may still do that later. Now, I'll just go and have a quick look round upstairs, shall I?'

He called after her, 'If you're going to accept the job, you may as well choose a bedroom for yourself while you're up there. I'm sleeping down here, since it'll be a while before I'm able to get up and down stairs easily.'

She turned to look back at him and admitted, 'I'm feeling very positive about the position at the moment.'

He beamed up at her. 'The big bedroom at the front is rather nice.'

The smile warmed her as she inspected rooms full of old-fashioned furniture, with unmade beds and bare mattresses. Someone had cleaned up here fairly recently, though there was a faint covering of dust again. There were vacuuming marks on the carpets and the windows had been cleaned, but the curtains were faded, elderly things and the furniture looked sad and neglected. The bedroom Kit had suggested was furnished as spartanly as the others but had lovely views down the main street of the village, and you could see across some fields to the moors through a gap in the houses.

She decided to sleep in this one. Which meant she was definitely taking the job. Smiling at herself in the mirror, she tried her new title out on her reflection, 'Mr Mallinder's Housekeeper,' and nodded approval.

When she ventured up the narrower stairs to the attics, she found two much smaller bedrooms and a large open space containing piles of old, discarded furniture and trunks. She lifted the lid of a couple of trunks, feeling guilty but unable to resist peeking. They were full of old clothes, some at least a hundred years old, giving off a strong smell of both lavender and camphor. Those things really should be aired and stored properly. They were probably worth a lot of money now.

When she went downstairs, Kit called out from the kitchen and she found him making mugs of coffee. 'Here, let me do that,' she said instinctively.

'I can manage!'

His voice was just that bit sharper, so she stood back and left him to finish on his own.

He slipped the crutches in place under his arms and smiled at her. 'I'll let you carry the mugs to the table, though.'

She looked out at the back garden while he manoeuvred himself into a chair, because she was beginning to understand how very much he hated his disability. Only after he'd eased himself down did she take the coffee across to the table. 'Pity about the garden. I bet there are some lovely plants hidden in that jungle.'

'I'm getting some contractors in to clear it.'

'Oh, don't! You'll lose everything if you do that. Get a jobbing gardener instead and I'll help him. In Australia I belonged to a group which rescued old plant species and saved the seeds, though I could only do annuals, because we moved house so often. I had to turn my collection over to another member when I left Australia. I bet you anything you like we'll find some interesting old plants under the tangles. I must buy some books so that I can identify them.'

'Aha! That sounds as if you've definitely decided to work for me.'

She felt suddenly shy. Had she assumed too much? 'Well, yes. If you still want me to.'

He reached out to shake her nearest hand, pumping it up and down, then keeping hold of it for much longer than was necessary. 'Of course I do! I can't tell you how happy that makes me. How soon can you start? Tomorrow?'

She was startled. 'Are you in such a hurry to move in?'

'In a hurry to move out of Joe's house, more like. I'm fond of my brother but his house is tiny and he's driving me crazy fussing over me.'

'I'll remember that and neglect you shamefully when I come here, Mr Mallinder.'

He leaned back, still smiling. 'Kit. I'm not big on being called mister.'

'OK. And I'm Laura. We're not big on formality in Australia, either.' It had surprised her that her dad still called the neighbours Mrs Bayton and Mrs Gleed, after living next door to them for nearly forty years.

'I'm sure we're going to get on brilliantly.'

She was a bit taken back by the warmth in his tone. Did he always make such rapid decisions about people? And no two people living together ever got on 'brilliantly' after the first few careful weeks, she was sure, unless they had love to blind them to the other's faults—and even then you didn't stay blind for nearly long enough. 'Wait till we've lived together for a month or two before you say that. I'm a bit of a perfectionist about some things and I'll probably drive you as crazy as your brother does.'

'I'd welcome some order and domestic comfort, actually. I seem to have been living out of suitcases for years. And a hostel attached to a rehabilitation centre isn't exactly a home from home.'

His eyes took on a distant look, as if memories were surfacing, so she waited a minute or two before saying, 'It's going to take a lot of organizing for us to move in tomorrow.'

'I don't care if we have to camp out for the first few days! If it's at all possible, let's do it.'

For a moment she hesitated, the doubts that had filled her lately trying to creep out again, but she pushed them back resolutely. 'All right. You're on.' If nothing else, it'd stop her brooding about her mother.

They discussed details, he gave her some money, then saw her to the front door. 'Until tomorrow.'

'I'll look forward to it.'

As she got back into the car, still lost in her thoughts, Angie had to prompt her for information. 'Well?'

'I'm starting tomorrow, going shopping for him this afternoon, then bringing the stuff round here. He's given me a key already. I'll air some sheets and make up the beds when I come back.'

Angie's voice was hesitant. 'I could help you if you like. I've nothing on today and I don't start work until seven tonight.' Her smile faded a little. 'And I'd like to come and see you sometimes—if I'll not be a nuisance, that is?'

'You'll be very welcome indeed.'

'That's great. I can cycle over, because it's not all that far from home.'

'I'm to have my own sitting room and TV, so we'll be perfectly private, though I doubt Kit will care who comes and goes. He's very laid back. I suppose that comes of living all over the world in primitive conditions. It's Dad I worry about.'

'He'll be sorry you're moving out but Gran will be easier for him to manage on his own,' Angie said softly. 'I go round and help him sometimes, and you can still do things for him like shopping, cooking and stuff.'

'Yes. And Deb's coming over soon. Maybe she'll be able to help him, too.'

'Depends on how Gran takes to her, doesn't it? Is she good at toileting old ladies and helping them get undressed?'

'I can't imagine her doing it,' Laura said frankly. 'Though

she did always get on with Mum when they visited us in Australia.'

'We'll have to wait and see. It's rotten for Pop, isn't it? But I can granny-sit for him sometimes, so that he can come and visit you here.' She hesitated, then added, 'I don't mind helping him out, but I'd go mad if I had to live like he does, tied to the house, always watching over Gran. I don't know how he stands it.'

'He's always been a very loyal and caring person, the best dad a girl could have had.' Her voice thickened as she said that, and she had to blink away the tears that threatened to spill from her eyes.

'Gran's lucky to have him. Heaven knows what she'd be like if she was in one of those homes. He can still settle her down better than anyone else can. It's as if she recognizes subconsciously who he is and knows instinctively that he loves her.'

Laura decided that this conversation wasn't cheering either of them up. 'Right, then. I accept your help gratefully. Let's go shopping and afterwards I'll buy you lunch.' She didn't have to feign enthusiasm, the words burst out of her, 'Oh, I *am* looking forward to this!'

It felt absolutely wonderful to have something to do with her time again, and to be earning money instead of eating into her savings. It was amazing sometimes how quickly life could change—for better as well as for worse. She'd have to get her national insurance number sorted out. She'd found her old number when she'd cleared out the house in Australia, and presumed she'd still be using that.

She smiled at a sudden thought that the wishing well had brought her exactly what she'd wished for. Good thing she hadn't been wishing for romance and a man to love, as she always had when she was much younger!

Maybe she should go back and do that. Ha! No way. She'd finished with marriage and wasn't putting her head into that trap again.

She paused. Ever? She didn't know. Maybe once she'd got herself sorted out she'd think about it.

Thirteen

Kit called a taxi and on the way home asked the driver to stop at an off-licence and get him a bottle of wine for tonight, plus a bottle of the good whisky that Joe particularly liked, as a thank-you present for having him.

When his brother came home he broke the news that he'd be leaving the next day and, as he'd foreseen, Joe wasn't pleased.

'It's all a bit of a rush, isn't it? Are you sure this woman will be reliable?'

Some imp of mischief made Kit say, 'Oh, yes. She's a very motherly type. I shall be spoiled outrageously, I'm sure. And you'll have your house to yourself again, which I'm sure you'll appreciate.'

'I was happy to have you here.'

'I know. And I'm truly grateful for your help. Now, let me pour you a glass of wine. Or do you want to open the whisky?'

'Wine please. I'll just nip up to the bathroom.'

The doorbell rang as soon as the bathroom door had closed on Joe, so Kit went to answer it.

The guy on the doorstep looked at him with narrowed eyes, then said, 'You can't be the brother, surely? You don't look at all like him.'

'You must be a friend of Joe's. And I'm definitely the brother. Kit Mallinder at your service.'

'I'm Gil. I won't shake hands or I might knock you off the crutches.'

'Come in. He'll be down in a minute.'

Gil hesitated, then followed Kit into the living room.

Footsteps clattered down the stairs before he'd had a chance to sit down.

'Did I hear the doorbell?'

Joe stopped dead as he saw who the visitor was, and for a moment Kit thought he saw an expression of panic on his face.

'I asked you to give me some space, Gil,' he said sharply.

The visitor shrugged. 'You know me, always turning up like a bad penny.'

'Well, I'm busy, so I'm afraid you can't stay.'

Kit was intrigued. What the hell was going on here? He couldn't help noticing the slight sibilance in the visitor's speech and the fact that the man had an almost girlish prettiness. 'Look, if you two need to talk privately, I can go into the kitchen and work on my laptop.'

Tight-lipped Joe turned to the front door. 'No need. My friend's just leaving.'

Gil didn't move. 'You haven't told him, have you?'

'There's nothing to tell. And I want you to leave *now*, please.'

Gil spread his hands and rolled his eyes to heaven, as if giving up, then turned away. From the doorway, he looked back at Joe, his expression sad, then, with an almost imperceptible shrug, he left. Joe slammed the door shut behind him.

'What was that all about?' Kit asked.

'Nothing.'

'Oh, I think there was something happening.'

'Nothing important. Now, I'm tired. I think I must have picked up a cold, so I'm going to bed and I'll give the wine a miss. In my opinion you're wrong to move out, it's far too early, but you never would be told about anything once you'd made up your mind.'

When Joe had gone, Kit put the bottle of wine aside and got himself something to eat. He cleared up as well as he could afterwards, then packed his laptop into its travelling case. He listened at the foot of the stairs but could hear nothing, so heaved himself slowly up on his backside. It was too early to sleep, but he wanted to do the packing tonight and get an early start in the morning. He had packing down to a fine art after all these years of globetrotting and had never been a collector of possessions, so it didn't take long.

Afterwards he tried reading but couldn't concentrate on the story, so put out the light and let his thoughts roam where they would. To Joe and his strange behaviour. To Laura Wells and her pretty face, one minute with a vulnerable expression, the next with a managing, capable expression. He was looking forward to getting to know her. Looking forward to having his own house and leading the sort of life he wanted.

Thanks, Uncle Alf!

From the creaking of the bed in the next room, Joe didn't get to sleep for a long time, either.

In the morning Kit was woken by Joe getting up. He blinked at the clock. Half-past five. Turning over, he tried to get back to sleep again, but only managed a short doze.

When he went downstairs at six, his brother had already left, a full two hours earlier than usual. There was a note propped up on the kitchen table, wishing him well, and that was all. He could have done with help getting his bags downstairs, but he'd manage somehow.

He still didn't understand exactly what had happened the previous night, though there were several possibilities he couldn't help considering. Why would Joe not discuss whatever it was with him and trust him, for heaven's sake? And why was he avoiding Kit this morning?

Surely Joe couldn't be gay? No, not Joe. There must be some other explanation.

Only, Gil was definitely gay—and had looked so sad when Joe asked him to leave.

Fed up of sitting in the kitchen, Kit called a taxi earlier than he had planned, and set off for what would, he hoped, be a more congenial way of life. He smiled wryly at how his horizons and ambitions had narrowed since the accident. Now his main ambitions were to make a home for himself, start driving a car again and learn to walk properly. Maybe, after that was all in place, he'd finish writing the book of foreign-correspondent memoirs a publisher was interested in. He hadn't been able to settle properly to that at Joe's place, and it had been even more difficult to write in the rehabilitation centre, with all the exercising to do. But now he'd have the freedom of his own space and timetable.

Those modest aims would do him for the time being. After that, who knew? He was living proof that you could never be truly certain what would happen next.

He did hope something would happen. Hated the thought of living quietly for the rest of his days.

That made him grin. Be careful what you wish for!

Sue looked at her daughter, who had just rocked in well after the time they always served tea, with the excuse that she'd been helping her aunt. Angie was flushed and happy, talking of going across to help Laura again the following day, and that annoyed Sue, because her daughter was never like that with her. 'If you're into helping people, how about helping me for a change? Goodness knows there's enough to do here.'

'I've tried helping you and you only complain that you don't like the way I've done things, then you do them all over again.'

'Well, you should be more careful how you work. I like to keep my home clean. Some germs can be very dangerous to health, you know.'

Angie was definitely not going down that road again. 'Yes, Mum. I know. Is there any food left?'

'I don't like your tone of voice, young lady. And I've finished serving tea in this café for tonight. You know what time meals are served. You've not been at work, so there's *no* excuse for not getting back on time.'

Angie breathed in deeply. Her mother was in one of her excitable moods again. She knew from experience that they'd not be able to discuss this rationally, that if she even tried, her mother would wind up screaming at her. 'Fine.

I'll get something at work. They'll let me have the leftovers for nothing.'

Trev stepped forward hastily. 'You go up and get changed for work then, Angie love, or else you'll be late. Your mother's—' he hesitated, then finished, '—not feeling well.' He waited until his daughter had gone upstairs before saying quietly, 'You're being unfair to the girl, Sue. Why send her out hungry, for heaven's sake, when there's food cooked?'

'I don't think it's unreasonable to expect her to be on time for meals. And I might know *you* would take her side. You always do.'

'It's starting again, isn't it? Please go and see the doctor, love. I'll come with you if you like.'

'There's nothing starting! I'm just a bit stressed, that's all. And that doctor doesn't know what he's talking about. There's a medical conspiracy to get women on tranquillizers and keep them calm and docile, you know. Well, they're not turning *me* into a zombie again.'

'You need help. And they didn't turn you into a zombie last time. They made you feel happier and—'

'Excuse me, but I think I remember how I felt better than you do. At the moment I need help with the housework, because Angie is always messing things up. But I don't need help with anything else, thank you *very* much!'

When Angie had left, he went to get his jacket.

Sue confronted him in the hall. 'Where do you think you're going?'

'Out.'

'With *her*, I suppose.'

'I keep telling you there is no "her". I'm simply going down to the pub for a bit of peace because I can no longer find it in my own home.'

'Why don't I believe you? You weren't in the Hare and Hounds last time you went out, because I checked.'

'And I shan't be there tonight, either. If I want some time on my own and a bit of peace, I go to a pub where I'm not known and where *you* can't find me. Heaven knows, I deserve a break from all this.' He waved a hand at the house.

When he'd left, Sue turned round and scowled at the kitchen, which she'd already tidied up after their meal. 'It's filthy!' she said out loud. 'I can't *bear* to live in such filth.'

She was still cleaning it, wiping the surface again and again, when Trev came home, and an hour later, Angie.

Each of them peeped into the kitchen, saw what was happening and went quietly to bed. Trev lay awake for a long time trying to figure out how he could persuade Sue to see the doctor, but finding no magic arguments, only the same old reasons she'd rejected out of hand several times lately. Tiredness finally overcame him.

Angie was exhausted after a busy shift serving at the pub. She wedged a chair under her door handle so that her mother couldn't erupt into the room and start scolding her about her untidiness, which had happened more than once lately in the middle of the night. Her mother might not need much sleep, but she did.

Her father had begged her to keep their problems in the family, but Angie didn't think she could keep silent much longer. She needed to talk to someone about this.

Pop had enough on his plate but perhaps she could talk to her aunt? That would keep the problem in the family, wouldn't it? She'd give Auntie Laura a day or two to settle in to her new job, then go and see her.

She couldn't continue like this, she just couldn't!

Kit arrived at his new home as most people were heading off to work. The taxi driver obligingly carried his luggage inside, after which Kit stood in the hall and simply soaked up the feel of the house. Something inside him seemed to settle and change, and a warm feeling rose in every part of him. *Home.* He had a home of his own, hadn't realized how much he'd needed that.

'Alf, you old devil, how did you know to leave me the house?' he whispered, and could have sworn he felt gleeful laughter swirling round him.

He began a slow tour of the ground floor, delighted to find his bed already made up and a vase of flowers on his sitting-room table, which smelled faintly of polish. How had Laura managed to do so much so quickly?

In the kitchen he found basic food supplies in the pantry, fresh food in the fridge and a coffee plunger set out temptingly on the surface near the sink, together with a packet of ground coffee and one of the new mugs. He hadn't felt hungry before but was suddenly ravenous, so made himself a mug of real coffee, closing his eyes in bliss as he took his first sip. Then he prepared two slices of toast and honey, putting them on the little serving trolley she'd unearthed from somewhere and set ready. How had she known he'd need it to carry his food and drink across to the table? Oh yes, her son had broken his leg once. He ate the toast with relish, licking the honey drips off his fingers. Strange how simple things could please you.

When he heard a key in the front door, he called, 'I'm in the kitchen.'

Laura poked her head through the doorway. 'Hi. Won't be a minute. I'll just unload my car.'

He put the kettle on and got out another mug, but didn't know whether to make tea or coffee for her, so left it at that.

She came and went a couple of times, then the front door closed and she took her luggage upstairs. It irritated the hell out of him that he couldn't help her do that, but he knew she wouldn't mind. She wasn't the sort of person to get into hassles and stiff silences, he was sure. He'd offered her the job out of sheer instinct, the same instinct that had saved his life once or twice, and he already suspected he'd found a treasure in Laura Wells—or even a friend.

When she joined him, he waved a hand towards the mug. 'I don't know your preferences, so I didn't make you a cuppa.'

'I like coffee too.' Laura made herself some and joined him at the table. 'What do you want me to do first?' She watched him look at her blankly for a moment and hid a smile as he frowned and ran a hand through his hair, making it even more untidy than before.

110

'Hell, I haven't a clue what you should do. Do you need daily orders? Can't I just leave you to get on with things?'

'You can once I'm settled, but I'll have to keep checking with you until I know how you like things done. Some starting information would be helpful, though. Food, for instance—what sort of meals do you prefer?'

'Interesting or spicy food, preferably not plain cooking, but I'm not a fussy eater. Apart from regular meals, what I mostly want is to make this place feel like a home.' He tried to gather his thoughts, which seemed to be flying in every direction. 'I'd like to use the dining room as my office. I—um—have a publisher interested in a book I'm writing.'

'How wonderful!'

'It will be if I ever get it written. It's very dark and gloomy in there, though, so if you can think of any way of brightening it up, let me know. And that suite in my sitting room is hard and uncomfortable, always was, so I need better seating for the evenings. Do you know anything about choosing furniture?'

'Quite a bit, actually.'

'And thank you for the flowers. They were a lovely thought.'

'I like flowers. Let's go and look at the rooms properly.' She led the way out, holding doors open for him, but otherwise leaving him to fend for himself.

As they stood in the living room, he grimaced. 'Look at those chairs. They just about bristle at you!'

'How about a recliner-rocker? Then you can put your feet up if you need it.'

'Great idea. You're on. But you must get something similar for your sitting room too. My uncle had plenty of money, but he didn't spend much on the house, did he? He left the money to my brother and told him to go out and do something more adventurous, but he left me the house because he thought it was time I settled down. I'm beginning to suspect he was right.' He eyed her sideways. 'And once it's all set up, can we visit one another sometimes in the evenings? Just for a bit of company? I won't pester you and of course you're welcome to have your family come and visit, and I won't intrude then, but I don't want to spend every evening sitting in solitary state in one room while you do the same in another.'

'Don't you think we'd better—keep our interactions businesslike?'

'Nope. I haven't a formal bone in my body and I'm incurably friendly. I like to be around people.'

'Oh. Well, that's fine by me. And as soon as you feel up to going shopping, let me know and I'll drive you into town. There's a rather nice furniture shop in that new shopping centre. Quality but not ridiculously priced.'

His voice was wistful. 'I'd go shopping today, but I think it'd be too much for me. I still need the odd nap in the afternoon, so if I'm in my bedroom with the door closed after lunch, leave me be—though I'm a lot better than I was about that.'

'It'd be too much for me today as well. Angie's coming over to lend me a hand, if that's OK. She's not getting on with her mother and needs to get out of the house. My sister can be very—' she searched for a word to describe Sue and could only come up with, '—difficult.'

'If Angie's helping you, I'd prefer to pay her.'

'There's no need.'

'Oh, but there is! I'm a firm believer in the labourer being worthy of her hire. And if Angie's coming speeds up our settling-in period, I'll be delighted. You can hire her for as many days as you like.' He studied her face. 'I'm not short of money, you know.'

'Very well.' She could see that he was looking tired. 'Let's go and sit down again while we talk.' She didn't wait for an answer but walked through into the kitchen.

There he lowered himself carefully into what she was coming to think of as his chair, cocked his head on one side, as if considering, then said, 'I'll be out three times a week at physiotherapy—'

'Do you want me to drive you there?'

'I usually take a taxi.'

112

'Waste of money. I can drop you, do the shopping nearby and pick you up afterwards. Go on.' She saw his look of surprise and realized what she'd said. 'Oh, sorry, didn't mean to boss you around—boss.'

He grinned. 'I don't mind. You're right, of course. Anyway, it's only for a short time. I hope to be driving myself within a month or so, which will be a great relief.' He heaved himself to his feet. 'I think I need to lie down for half an hour.' He stopped in the doorway as another thought occurred to him. 'I wouldn't mind getting in a few bottles of wine and spirits. I'm not a drunk, but I do like a drink occasionally. Maybe we can visit a supermarket together tomorrow? If you drop me near the door, I can manage a few circuits of the shelves with you pushing the trolley. I'm not totally incapacitated now.'

'You should get yourself a temporary disabled sticker for the car.'

His expression became icy, his voice cut like a knife. *'Never!'*

Before she could say anything, he'd gone into his room, and she didn't hear a sound from him for over an hour. She was nonetheless very conscious of his presence in the house as she sorted out the kitchen, making a list of the cooking equipment she needed. She'd no experience of working for others, but it seemed to her she'd landed on her feet—as long as she kept away from using the word 'disabled'. She really liked Kit Mallinder, and his casual approach to her being his housekeeper suited her down to the ground. She didn't think she could have behaved in a stiff, formal manner, or acted subserviently. She was fairly Australianized now.

Her main worry now was her parents. It hadn't felt right to ask Kit about time off before she'd even started, but she wanted to do her father's weekly shopping and maybe cook him some casseroles and other easy-to-reheat meals. At least that way she'd feel she was helping him.

She realized that the doorbell had just rung for the second time and rushed off to let Angie in.

113

Fourteen

Ryan offered to meet Caitlin at a café on Lygon Street, but she suggested one nearer her flat, saying she didn't like crowds. It was almost fifteen minutes after the time appointed, however, before she came hurrying up, her face glowing with exertion.

'Sorry I'm late! I couldn't find a parking place that seemed safe.'

He pulled a chair out for her, feeling suddenly happy. 'It doesn't matter. You're here now. I should have come and picked you up. Walking the streets at night can be scary for a woman, I know. My mother was mugged once.' He paused as he remembered suddenly how angry his father had been—*at her*! For *letting* herself get mugged. His mother had been nervous of going out after dark for a long time after the incident, and his father had mocked her for that and told her to get over it, for heaven's sake.

He hadn't liked it, but hadn't spoken up for his mother, regretted that now. Why not? Because his father had had a forceful personality, strong enough to dazzle a girl half his age, and a great deal of charm—when he bothered to use it. Which he hadn't towards his wife for a long time.

He saw Caitlin turn her head to look at him in puzzlement, and pulled himself together to push her chair in. 'Sorry. Just remembering something.' He'd better not share that memory of his father being a prize bastard, so summoned up a smile. 'Now you're here, can I order you a drink?'

'I'd die for a glass of white wine, just one. People say you're not supposed to drink while you're pregnant, but I sometimes have one glass. I'm sure that can't do any harm.'

114

'Of course not.'

The waiter came back with her wine and she sipped it, closing her eyes and sighing with pleasure as she savoured the taste. 'Ah, that's so good. And it's lovely to get out. I usually watch television or a movie at night.'

'It must be hard for you living alone. Are you going to get a job?'

'No.' She shrugged. 'I hated being a secretary, shut up in an office all day. I wanted to go to university, but my parents wouldn't let me, could only see it as a waste of time and effort, when all I'd do was get married and have children.' She grimaced. 'They're stuck in a time warp in that sect of theirs and still believe in chaining women to hearth and home.'

'You could go to university now. You can afford it.'

She flushed. 'I'm thinking about it, actually. In the meantime I'm reading a lot, watching a lot of DVDs, going for walks. How about you? Are you making friends in Melbourne?'

In other words, he thought, change the topic, so he obliged. 'It takes time to make real friends, don't you think? The guys at work are mostly older than me and married, so, although we get on OK, they're not likely to become close friends.' It was his turn to grimace. 'I was invited to a barbecue at my supervisor's house, but I was the only unattached male there and they were all watching to see how I'd get on with the woman they've paired me with. That irritated me so much I vowed to take someone along next time, even if I had to hire a woman.'

She laughed. 'I don't think you'd have to hire anyone. You're attractive, intelligent and single. I'm sure you'll have no trouble getting dates.'

He was pleased she thought him attractive. 'I'm a bit picky. Comes of watching my father chase anything in skirts.' He realized what he'd said. 'Oh, hell, sorry! That wasn't a dig at you.'

She stared down at her glass. 'I knew what Craig was like.'

'Surely he didn't—not after you . . .' He broke off.

115

'I don't think so, but he never stopped *studying the market*, as he put it.'

He could see the hurt in her eyes, hear it in her voice, wanted to ask why she'd shacked up with his old man in the first place. Didn't dare.

Luckily the waiter brought their order just then and Ryan was able to turn the talk to food. The meal was all right, but nothing special, and he noticed she didn't eat much. 'I thought you were supposed to be eating for two?'

'I don't feel all that hungry these days.'

'I always have a good appetite. I'm not the world's best cook, so I eat out a lot or get takeaways. Actually, I'm thinking of going to cookery classes. It sounds corny but I miss Mum's cooking. She used to invite me round at least once a week and feed me royally.'

'They ought to run survival courses for unattached males whose mothers didn't teach them to cook and wash.'

He looked at her, frowning as another memory surfaced. 'She did try to teach me, but Dad made fun of us—so after a while we both stopped trying. Do you know, I'd forgotten that. Dad said no man needed to learn to cook while there were willing women around. I remember them quarrelling about him saying that.'

'Well, he certainly never lifted a finger in the house during the one week *we* lived together.'

Her tone was so sharp he looked at her in surprise.

'I wasn't blind to your father's faults, and if I hadn't been so stupidly sick and tearful, I'd have put my foot down from the beginning about sharing the housework. Pregnancy plays havoc with your assertiveness as well as your hormones, you know.'

'I doubt it'd have done much good. Dad always went his own sweet way.'

'Tell me about it. Have you seen that film they're all talking about . . . ?'

He let her change the subject again and they found they had similar tastes in films and television shows, but not so similar that they couldn't disagree about a few.

As he was walking her to her car, however, she said hesitantly, 'I could teach you to cook a few basic dishes if you like, Ryan. I love cooking. But I shan't be offended if you—don't want.'

But he did want. It saved him the trouble of finding an excuse to see her again. 'Would you really? I'd be enormously grateful.'

'How about next Friday?'

'Great.' He watched her drive away, then strolled back to his own car.

He couldn't stop wondering what Caitlin had seen in his father, given that she seemed well aware of his faults. It was such an unlikely pairing. He'd loved his dad, who had always made a lot of effort to spend time with him, not to mention going to school cricket matches and functions, but as he grew older Ryan hadn't been able to avoid noticing the old man's faults. Unlike Deb, who could see none.

And he'd hated the way his dad had been cheating on his mother, making Ryan a sort of accomplice because he had often boasted of his extra-marital triumphs to his son. 'Man to man talks', he'd jokingly called them.

Deb drummed her fingers on the table as she waited for Ryan to answer her call, but he didn't seem to be in. She tried again an hour later. '*There* you are! Where have you been all evening?'

'Out with friends. Why? Is something wrong?'

'No. But I'm dying to tell you my news.'

'Go on, then.'

'I'm resigning from work and going to England to see Gran.'

'This is a bit sudden, isn't it, Deb?'

'I like acting on impulse and I can afford to now! Anyway, I rang Pop and he was telling me that Gran doesn't recognize many people now, except for him and Angie, so if I don't go soon, she may never know me again.'

'Is she that bad already?'

'Yeah. It makes me feel awful even to think of it.'

117

'Where are you going to stay?'

'With Pop.' She wasn't sure how that would work out, but she could go there for a week or so, then play it by ear.

'Is there room? I thought Mum was staying there.'

'She's just moved out. Apparently Gran has taken a dislike to her and gets agitated if Mum so much as comes into the same room.'

'There's no need to sound smug about it.'

'I'm not.'

'This is Ryan, not some stranger. I can tell when you're feeling smug. And actually, I don't understand why you've taken against Mum lately. She had a lot to put up with from Dad and *she* wasn't the unfaithful one in this mess.'

'No, but he wouldn't have done it if she hadn't let herself go and got so fat. That really mattered to Dad. If she'd had any wits at all, she'd have realized she'd lose him.'

'She's not fat! And Deb . . .'

'What?'

'. . . you won't bring him back by bad-mouthing Mum.'

'I'm not. I'm just—'

'You are and I'm sick of it. Don't ring me again until you can speak civilly about her.' He slammed the phone down and when it rang, he let it ring. Mum wasn't fat, she just wasn't scrawny like Deb. In fact, now he came to think of it, his sister had got a lot thinner lately. She couldn't be anorexic, surely? No, not Deb, who enjoyed her food as much as anyone he'd ever met.

But did she? Now he came to think of it, he hadn't seen her finish a meal for a while. She just picked at the food then pushed the plate away. Oh, hell, he wasn't his sister's keeper. If she wanted to be scrawny, nothing he said or did would change her mind.

He made himself a cup of hot chocolate and sat down with a book, but couldn't concentrate, so put it down again. He hadn't realized Gran was so bad. Should he apply for special leave from his employer to go to England? He knew the company didn't like management trainees interrupting their scheduled work experience programme, but maybe this

118

was something that couldn't wait. How quickly did Alzheimer's destroy people's minds? He didn't know, would have to look it up on the Web.

Only—if he went to England, that'd mean leaving Caitlin, and he didn't want to do that either, wanted to get to know her better before she had the baby and was too busy to go out with him.

He froze on that thought. Hell, what was he thinking of? She'd been his dad's girlfriend and had made it very plain she wasn't looking for another involvement.

Trouble was, he liked her a lot.

It seemed suddenly that his father had left a mess behind him—in more ways than one. They were all struggling to come to terms with the new situation, himself, Deb and Mum.

And Caitlin was involved as much as any of the family, because she'd been left holding the baby.

Fifteen

At five o'clock the doorbell rang. Laura knew Kit was fiddling with his computer, so hurried through to answer it.

'Is Kit in? I'm his brother.'

'You must be Joe. Do come in.' She held the door open and then called down the hall, 'Kit, it's your brother.'

'He knows the way,' Kit called back.

She smiled at Joe, who didn't return the smile. 'Would you like a cup of coffee?'

'No, thank you. I'm just popping in on my way home.'

Kit looked up as his brother came in, and gestured to a chair. 'Come to check up on me?'

Joe shrugged. 'I'll feel better if I know you're OK.'

'I'm fine, as you can see. Laura's worked miracles of organization. I even had an afternoon nap today.'

'You said she was motherly.'

Kit couldn't hold back a chuckle. 'Just teasing. Couldn't resist it. Oh, lighten up, bro!'

Joe stared down at the table, then said in a low voice, 'I also wanted to apologize for leaving you to get your bags downstairs yourself this morning.'

'I managed.'

'I let you down.'

'I'm a grown-up. I manage my own life—even now.'

'Well, as long as you're all right, I'd better get off home.'

'Why don't you stay for a coffee?'

'No. Got a lot of lesson preparation to do tonight.' Joe stood up. 'I can see myself out.'

120

When the front door had shut, Laura came through to the dining room. 'Everything OK?'

'Damned if I know.'

'Dinner at six, or later?'

'Six. I'm famished.'

They sat down together in the kitchen to a dinner of chilli chicken stir-fry. She had offered to serve him separately in the dining room, and he'd made a rude noise.

'What, me sit somewhere in state while you sit eating in the kitchen like a servant? Don't be daft, woman. This is the twenty-first century, not the nineteenth.'

'Perhaps you'd prefer us both to use the dining room, then? Only, you've got your stuff spread out over the table.'

He laughed again. 'I like eating in the kitchen. We always did when we came to visit Uncle Alf and Auntie Maud. What's more, if you'd seen some of the places I've eaten in, you'd know why I'm not bothered about fuss and fancy ways of serving. But I do enjoy my food and I love the smell of your cooking, so don't be surprised if you find me hovering behind you as you cook. In fact, when I'm off these damned crutches, I'll do some of the cooking. I really enjoy it, and I do a mean curry.'

He insisted on opening a bottle of Australian chardonnay to celebrate their first night, and raised his glass. 'To us!'

She clinked glasses, though it seemed a strange thing for two near-strangers to drink to. After that, he began to eat and she watched anxiously, unable to enjoy her own food until she was sure he was pleased with what she'd cooked.

He closed his eyes with an expression of bliss. 'Mmm. Wonderful stuff. I can do stir-fries, but not as well as you. This is a very authentic taste.'

'Thank you.' She dug her fork in, feeling happier. 'We should be using chopsticks, really.'

'I have some in my stored belongings. They'll be here in a day or two.'

When he'd cleared his plate, he looked at the cooker, then back at her. 'There wouldn't be any left in that wok, would there?'

'Yes.' She served him, delighted to have her efforts appreciated. 'I love cooking. You should have seen my dinner parties.'

'Elaborate, were they?'

'Not enough to daunt people.' She smiled. 'Or to half kill myself preparing them. But I like to have everything balanced and perfect, and to offer people a little treat—the first asparagus, choice sun-ripened tomatoes. It makes such a difference to buy quality produce.'

'Don't change your habits at all, then. I love that sort of thing.' He consumed a couple more mouthfuls, eating in a leisurely fashion now, as if savouring each bite. 'Did you ever go out to work?'

'Oh, yes. Before I met Craig, I was a typist, and a good one, too, though I was only nineteen when we married, and already pregnant with Ryan, so that didn't last long. Soon after he was born, Craig said he'd had enough of working overseas and wanted to go home, so we moved to Australia.'

'Did you want to emigrate?'

She nodded. 'It seemed an exciting thing to do. You know what teenagers are like. I looked down on Lancashire in those days, and thought anyone with sense should leave it. It was ten years before I came back, and that was only to see my parents.'

'Do you still feel like that about Lancashire?'

'No, of course not. I soon grew out of that, because I was pretty homesick at first, though I tried not to let Craig see. This time I'm enjoying being here, or I would be if it weren't for Mum. I spent a couple of days near Fleetwood and I intend to revisit quite a few places I went to as a child. Some of those villages on the edge of the moors are so pretty.' She realized she'd been going on about herself. 'Sorry to bore you.'

'You weren't. Far from it.'

'Oh, well. That's all right, then.' She felt flustered again. He did that to her sometimes. It was as if he could see more deeply into her mind and thoughts than other people.

122

Heavens, she was getting too fanciful here. Lighten up, Laura, she ordered herself.

'I'm a bit the same, actually, want to revisit my past haunts.' He grimaced at his leg. 'When I can.' Then he brightened and said, 'Maybe you could drive me out to some of them?'

'Yes, of course.' She decided the conversation was getting too personal. 'I'd like to make some arrangement about phone calls. I'll need to call my children in Australia occasionally.'

He waved one hand. 'Go ahead and phone them. You can pay me back for the foreign calls when we get the bills. They itemize such things nowadays. And don't worry about local calls. Call them a perk of the job.'

'All right. Thanks. Now, how about a little dessert—just fruit salad and ice cream. I haven't had time to do any baking.'

He beamed at her. 'Please. How did you guess I love ice cream?'

After the meal, he finished his wine and set the glass down carefully. 'That was absolutely delicious. I made a pig of myself. I can see I'm going to put on weight with your cooking.'

'You don't look as if you'd ever put on a kilo.'

'I haven't until now, but I've never been so inactive before.'

It must be hard for him. She'd wondered, but hadn't dared ask, how badly he would be disabled in the long run.

He yawned and stretched. 'I'm going to sit and read for a while, then I'll go to bed.'

'I'll just clear up in here, then I'll go and sort my bedroom out.'

But although she hung up the rest of her clothes, she didn't rearrange the room as she'd intended. On a sudden impulse, she switched the light off, drew back the curtains and stood looking down the main road through the village. A solitary car went past, its headlights illuminating the footpath for a few moments, then all was still again. By the light of an almost full moon, she could see plants swaying in gardens and hear the wind rising. It rattled her window panes slightly, setting the branches of a tree near the gate dipping in homage to its superior force. Out here in the village it felt peaceful. She'd only ever lived with urban streetscapes when she was growing up, and this was a different Lancashire, although Wardle was only a few miles away from her old home.

When she went down to make herself a cup of hot milk and honey, having a sudden fancy for that childhood favourite, the light was still on in what Kit insisted on calling his 'parlour'. She wondered whether to ask if he wanted something to drink, then shook her head. No. He could manage cups of coffee or whatever on his own, and push them where he wanted on the trolley. She wasn't on duty twenty-four hours, and she was exhausted after her busy day.

But she dreamed of Kit that night, dreamed they were walking together along a beach. His stride was free and easy, and at one stage he set his hands on her waist, lifting her in the air and laughing exultantly. Then they kissed. When she remembered that kiss in the morning, she blushed. She'd had erotic dreams before—what normal woman hadn't, especially one whose husband hadn't touched her for a while?—but this was different, so real she could still taste his lips.

Oh, you're being utterly stupid, Laura Wells! she told herself, and got up that very minute to start work in the kitchen.

Only, Kit was there before her, sitting at the table with a weary, shadowed look to him, so unlike the exuberant man of her dreams, that her heart went out to him.

'Bad night?'

He nodded.

She spoke bracingly, sure he'd resent sympathy. 'You're bound to get them. We all do. And you probably did too much yesterday. Would you like a cup of coffee? And how about some orange juice first? Raise your blood sugar.'

A smile slowly lifted the corners of his mouth. 'Will that cure everything else? If so, I'll live on the damned stuff.'

She put her hand on his shoulder as she passed, and gave it a quick squeeze, intending to move on. But he seized her hand and held it for a minute, looking up into her eyes, his expression very solemn.

'Sometimes there's nothing as welcome or comforting as a human touch after wrestling with the demons of the night,' he said softly. 'Thanks, Laura.'

Kit let Laura drive him to the physiotherapist's, but insisted on coming home by taxi, because it was an assessment session, which would take longer. On the way back, he decided to call on Joe and issue an invitation to visit properly. His brother would have finished school by now.

Joe's car was there, but no one answered the taxi driver's knock on the door. Perhaps Joe had gone out? Kit decided to phone later, after he'd had a rest.

What must Laura think of him, unable even to look after himself, needing naps and rests, for heaven's sake?

Why did it matter so much what she thought of him?

He smiled ruefully. Easy to answer that one. Because for the first time since his accident he fancied a woman. Only— it might complicate matters if he made a play for her. He might lose his housekeeper if things went wrong, and he couldn't bear the thought of searching for another one. He had already realized that he'd found a domestic treasure.

It would be better to keep his feelings to himself. He wished he'd met her in other circumstances, though, he really did.

When he got home, she greeted him with that warm, open smile and said, 'I had a quick look at chairs while I was out. If you're up to coming with me tomorrow, I can show you one I think would suit you.'

He couldn't help it. He dropped the crutches and pulled her into his arms, kissing her on each cheek. 'You're wonderful, Laura Wells, a complete treasure.'

Then he stared at her shocked face, almost on a level

with his. 'Oh. I'm sorry. I forgot—I mean, I'm used to being demonstrative and—well . . .' He gave her a wry smile. 'I'm sorry, but I can't let go of you till I've something else to hold on to. I'm not trying to sexually harass you, honest!'

'I was just—surprised.' And shocked by how she'd reacted to his kisses, which had only been an exuberant expression of his delight. 'Here, you lean on this chair back and I'll—um—pick up your crutches.'

She did so, settling them under his arms, then moving quickly away.

'You still look upset,' he said bluntly.

'I'm not used to people being so demonstrative. It's been a while since . . . I didn't mind, honestly, and I'd rather I changed my habits than you changed yours.'

'You're sure about that?'

She nodded. 'Very sure. It's so refreshing to be open about things, not to have to second-guess someone and . . .'

Her voice trailed away, but she'd said enough to give him another hint as to what her life must have been like in the past few years. He'd like to punch her bloody ex in the face. Only, it was too late to bring the fellow to account now. He tried to keep the conversation light. 'Phew! Thank goodness for that. I doubt I *can* change my personality.'

He didn't tell her that it had been a long time since his old self had resurfaced, and months since he'd felt bubbles of happiness floating through his veins like today. And it wasn't because of a damned chair but because of her. It seemed as if, since he'd met her, life had suddenly started getting better again.

Careful, Kit! he warned himself.

Only, he didn't want to be careful, that was the trouble.

Sixteen

Deb flew out of Perth on a sunny spring day. It wasn't until the taxi dropped her at the airport and she walked up to the counter to check in her luggage that it really hit her what she had done: quit her job, given up her flat, put her possessions in storage, all without knowing what she was going to do with herself after this visit. She wasn't used to doing this on her own, especially not such a long trip, had always had friends and her father to support her before—above all her father.

Last year she'd had Darren too, but that relationship had broken up and she didn't miss him. Well, not much. But it'd been nice to be a couple.

Her mother was coming to meet her at Manchester airport, which felt strange, but Deb had to admit it would be a relief not to have to cope on her own over there. She wasn't sure how she'd get on with her mother now. Ryan said she'd been unfair to her, and perhaps she had, just a little bit. But her mother was so . . . she tried to work out what irritated her so much about her . . . she was overweight and didn't dress well, but that wasn't a crime, was it?

For the first time, Deb wondered if she'd overreacted after her father's death. After all, it wasn't her mother's fault he'd died—and he shouldn't have left everything to Caitlin like that. It was definitely unfair. Perhaps he'd been in love with her, but even so . . .

There seemed to be no easy answers, so Deb pushed these disturbing thoughts away and concentrated on finding her seat.

Things got rapidly worse when she realized her seat was

in the middle of the central block of four. It hadn't even occurred to her to ask for an aisle seat. She turned to smile at the young man beside her. 'I wonder if you'd mind changing places with me? I get a bit claustrophobic when I'm hemmed in, I'm afraid.'

'Sorry. I asked specially for an aisle seat because of my height. My legs don't fit into those middle seats.'

She scowled at him.

He shrugged.

She'd make sure she asked for an aisle seat next time, she vowed, feeling uncomfortably trapped as she sat down.

The first leg of the trip passed slowly. She decided she'd been a fool to bring only magazines. She'd see if she could buy a book in Singapore airport. In the meantime the old lady on one side of her had dozed off and the selfish sod next to her was immersed in his book.

'Excuse me, but could I get out?' she asked him coldly.

'Sure.' He slid out and let her through. Wow, he was tall, towering over her, but he didn't have that look of admiration in his eyes she'd come to expect from guys of her own age. He was probably gay, and if not he was undersexed.

When she got back he wasn't there, so she sat in his seat, enjoying being able to stretch out her legs. She looked round to see the meals trolley heading slowly towards her.

'I'm back now. Can you move over, please?'

She looked up at him pleadingly.

He looked right back and, when she didn't move, said, 'I need to sit down so they can serve the meal.'

Feeling aggrieved, she slid across to her own place.

'It's no use sulking, you know,' he said suddenly.

'I am *not* sulking!'

'You've got the same look on your face as my sister gets when she's sulking.'

'I'm just uncomfortable in this seat.'

'OK. Whatever.' He got out the book again.

She waited for the trolley to reach them. But they'd only got fried chicken left and some greasy potatoes for the main

128

course. She stared down at her tray. If she ate that, she'd get fat.

'Something wrong with it?' her neighbour asked when she poked it uncertainly with her fork.

'It's fattening.'

He looked at her incredulously. 'I'm sure *you* don't have to worry about that. If anything, you're too skinny.'

'*Skinny!* How dare you be so personal?'

He rolled his eyes. 'Pardon me for breathing. And I take back my previous remark—you're *far* worse than my sister.'

He didn't say another word until they reached Singapore.

She tried to change her seat, but it was too late. On the next plane *he* was still sitting beside her. The old woman had gone, but a mother and small child were occupying the two seats on Deb's other side now.

After about an hour they hit turbulence. Seat-belt signs flashed, an announcement was made for everyone to stay in their seats, and the attendants were instructed to sit down as well. Deb felt petrified as the plane lurched, jerked and dropped, while her stomach did the same. On one particularly bad drop, she couldn't hold back a squeak of terror.

A warm hand took hold of hers. 'It's all right.'

She looked sideways at the guy next to her. 'Is it always this bad?'

'Not usually. Haven't you ever experienced turbulence before?'

'No. I haven't flown much, really.' Another sudden drop sent her stomach into her throat and she let out a moan and clung on to his hand for dear life.

'This isn't nice, but it really isn't dangerous.'

She could only nod and tense up against the next surge.

When the turbulence eased, she let go of his hand, feeling embarrassed. 'Thanks.'

'You're welcome.' He gave her a smile that made him suddenly seem more attractive. 'I'm Alex, by the way.'

'I'm Deb. And I'm sorry I was so silly about the seat. I think I was more nervous than I realized about this flight. I've never been so far on my own.'

'Going to Manchester, or further?'

'Rochdale, actually, to stay with my granddad.'

'You look upset about that. Don't you want to go?'

'Yes. Well, sort of. Only, Gran's got Alzheimer's and I'm a bit nervous about how to deal with it.'

'That's rotten. One of my great-aunts had it.'

'Are you going to visit your family?'

'I'm going to work over there for a while, but I'll stay with my aunt and uncle first while I look around a bit. They live in Rochdale too, actually. I've just finished uni, you see, but I don't want to settle down yet.'

They chatted for a while, then Alex fell asleep. Deb wished she could. She was so tired after partying with her friends the night before. But, try as she might, her body stayed obstinately awake.

When they disembarked, Alex helped her to find the luggage-retrieval area and shared a trolley with her. As they wheeled it out, she saw her mother in the distance and groaned.

'There's my mother. She's *so* overweight!'

Alex looked at the woman and back at Deb. 'What's with you and weight? She's not fat. Pretty good figure for a woman her age, actually.'

All the rapport they'd built up vanished in an instant. 'Thank you *very* much!' She snatched her case off the trolley and marched across to her mother, kissing the air beside her face and stepping back quickly out of the embrace.

'How was the flight?'

Deb shrugged. 'Boring. I'd forgotten how it seems to go on for ever.'

'I know. We have to go this way. Do you want me to help with your luggage?'

Deb handed over her cabin bag and they walked along in silence. When Alex passed them, pushing the trolley, she looked in the other direction. How dare he speak to her like that? She wasn't too thin! Her dad had always said she was just right.

130

Laura realized Deb was angry about something—well, you couldn't mistake that stormy look—so said nothing as she led the way out to the car.

'Is this a hire car?' Deb asked.

'No, I bought it.'

'It's a bit old. Dad wouldn't have been seen dead in—' She broke off and tears filled her eyes.

Laura said gently, 'It'd be silly to buy a better one when I don't know how long I'll be here for. Anyway, I can't afford to be extravagant now.'

'I suppose not.' Deb looked at her sideways. 'But you got half the price of the house, at least, didn't you? And the shares?'

'Yes. But I have to save enough to buy myself another house when I go back to Australia, while the shares are my superannuation.'

'Oh.'

Laura drove carefully through the busy streets, relieved when they reached the motorway. 'We'll be about an hour getting there.'

'Right.' Deb looked round, wide-eyed. 'Are the roads always this busy? I mean, it isn't rush hour, is it?'

'They get much busier than this, which is why I'm glad I don't live in a big city here.' She made no attempt to break the silence, letting Deb set the pace.

'How's Gran?'

'Not doing very well. Dad's really tired. It's a heavy burden for a man of his age, caring for someone so difficult. I'd been hoping to help with her, but she won't let me go near her. She seems to think I'm trying to steal her husband. Delusions are common apparently, but it doesn't stop it hurting.' Laura felt her eyes fill up with tears and concentrated on her driving.

Deb looked sideways, not missing the tears. It suddenly occurred to her how she'd have felt if her dad had been the one to have Alzheimer's and had refused to have her near him. 'That's horrible.'

'Yes.'

'Who's the guy you're working for?'

'He's quite a well-known war correspondent, Kit Mallinder. Only, he had an accident and is still on crutches, which is why he needs a live-in housekeeper. He's retired now, though.'

Great! She was going to be surrounded by wrinklies.

When they got to Pop's house, Deb stared at it in amazement. 'I'd forgotten how tiny it was.'

'Yes. But don't say that. He's very proud that he bought it and paid off his mortgage before he retired.'

'I'm not *that* stupid!'

Pop looked so much older, it took Deb a minute to drag a smile back on her face and give him a hug. He smelled the same, though, of shaving soap and peppermint.

Her mother waved her on before disappearing into the front room.

Deb followed Pop into the back room, where Gran was sitting at the table, cradling a cup of tea in her hands and looking almost the same as before.

'Here's our Debbie,' Pop said.

Gran looked up and the illusion was shattered. Her face seemed empty of something that had been there before. Deb gulped and took a step forward.

'Just sit down on the other side of the table,' Pop whispered. 'I'll get you a cup of tea. We've just made a pot. Milk and sugar?'

'Just a tiny splash of milk. No sugar.' She sat down and watched as Gran began to run her finger to and fro on the table, ignoring them completely as she repeated the same action again and again.

He came back with a mug and set it down in front of Deb. 'I'll just take one through to our Laura.'

Deb sat petrified as she was left alone with the old woman. This was far worse than she'd expected. It was Gran's body without Gran inside it. Gross! She wanted to get up and run out, but couldn't. Let alone she was exhausted, she was in a strange country and had to stay here for a few days, at least, till she got her bearings.

When she'd drunk the tea, she yawned and couldn't seem to stop.

Pop grinned at her. 'Our Laura was just the same when she arrived. Out on her feet. Didn't you sleep on the plane, either?'

'No. I couldn't.'

'Why don't you get a shower and have a lie down, then?'

'Would you mind?'

'Of course not, love. But it'd be best if you locked your door. I've put a bolt on the inside. Pat wanders around in the middle of the night sometimes.' He raised his voice. 'Will you show Debbie where to go, Laura love?'

'Sure.'

Upstairs, Deb stared round the room, which contained two narrow single beds, a wardrobe and chest of drawers and not much else. 'It's very small, isn't it?'

'Yes. And when we were children, Sue and I had to share it. We had some right royal quarrels.' She looked at Deb and fumbled in her pocket for a piece of paper. 'I've written down the details of where I am and how to contact me. I can get out in the evenings, though I'm a bit busy in the daytime. Or you could come over to see me. I have my own sitting room. And your cousin Angie has promised to come over and see you once you've had time to recover from the journey. She's your age and she's a lovely girl.'

'Yes. Um—thanks for picking me up today.'

'My pleasure. If I can do anything else, just let me know.'

As Deb listened to the footsteps going down the stairs, she realized suddenly that it was a comfort to know her mother was nearby.

She hadn't realized how *alone* she'd feel over here. Staring at herself in the mirror, she squared her shoulders, tried to smile, couldn't. Felt as if she was Alice in Wonderland, lost in a world where nothing felt right.

She yawned again and told herself she'd feel better once she'd had a sleep. After the quickest shower on record, she crawled into bed. But she couldn't stop remembering Gran and how empty her face had looked. She scrubbed her eyes, but the tears still kept coming. She'd so wanted Gran to recognize her, talk to her, as they used to.

Laura waited in the hall to say goodbye to her father and gave him a big hug.

'What's that for?' he teased.

'Just to say I love you. You're looking tired, though. Don't you think it might be wise to put Mum into respite care for a few days and have a proper rest?'

'I can't do it. Not while she's got any understanding of who I am. And I think she still has.'

He shook his head, his eyes unfocused, his whole body sagging in sad lines, then suddenly burst out, 'It's so unfair! I can't bear it sometimes, seeing her, knowing she'll not get better, having to do *everything*! I get so tired and—' He stopped and fought for control, then gave her a shamefaced smile. 'Eh, it's not like me to go on about it. Sorry.'

'You've every right to get upset sometimes. I don't know how you cope.'

'What other choice do I have?' He stared down at his feet, sighing.

She gave him another hug and was rewarded with one of his tender, loving smiles.

As she drove back, she smiled at the memory of how happy he'd looked when she'd said she loved him. Even if she couldn't help with her mother, she'd done the right thing coming back—for both Dad and herself. There was nothing like moving somewhere different for giving you a new slant on the world and your place in it.

Angie got home from a midday shift and went straight down the hall to dump her things in her bedroom, only to find it in chaos. She stopped at the door and gaped at the mess.

She heard a noise in the kitchen and picked up her old rounders bat to protect herself with, in case it was burglars. But it was her mother, not an intruder. She was crouched down, hauling everything out of the cupboards and hurling it behind her.

'What's the matter, Mum?'

'It's all so dirty! I'm not having it. I just couldn't go to work and leave this mess. I've done our bedroom and I've started on yours, but this needs sorting out first.' She turned her back and began pulling the rest of the things out of the immaculate cupboards.

Angie backed out and her mother didn't even seem to notice. She had that wild look on her face that she'd had once before, only, it seemed worse this time. Very quickly Angie went into her room and locked the door. Pulling out her mobile phone, she dialled her dad's work number.

'It's Mum. She's acting really weird and she seems worse than last time, much worse.' She explained what was happening and he promised to come home straight away.

When she'd hung up, she sat down and put her head in her hands, praying her mother would stay in the kitchen.

Not until she heard her father's car in the drive did she open the bedroom door. She rushed out, relieved to see him. But things got worse before they got better. He wasn't able to persuade her mother to stop what she was doing, couldn't get her to listen to reason, could hardly get her to listen to him at all. She was scrubbing the kitchen cupboards out now, scrubbing and scrubbing, going over the same surface a dozen or more times, then carefully changing the water and doing it all over again.

Angie listened to her father pleading, then heard his voice stop and footsteps come along to her bedroom.

'I need to call the doctor out, love. He'll have to sedate her or even take her in for a day or two. They said last time she shouldn't stop taking those tablets, that it could recur if she did, but she wouldn't listen.'

'She won't go in willingly.'

'No, but it's for her own good.'

They looked at one another, then he held out his arms and she rushed into them. She tried not to cry, because he had enough to put up with, so they just held one another close. Then he put his hands on her shoulders, pushed her to arm's length and looked at her sadly. 'All right. I'll go and phone from our bedroom.'

He got through to the doctor's surgery, had to talk his way past the receptionist, whose main purpose in life seemed to be to keep patients away from the doctors, then explained the state Sue was in.

It was over an hour before a community psychiatric nurse arrived. He went to talk to Sue, came back and phoned the doctor, who arrived shortly afterwards.

Sue fought against the sedative injection and it took longer than they expected for it to work.

'We'll soon have her out of hospital again,' the nurse said to Trev as he left. 'They'll just need to stabilize her medication and start her on the counselling.'

'What if she refuses to take the pills again? She's been pretty difficult to live with.'

'I'll be coming round regularly to check on her and I won't let her off the hook this time.'

As the nurse drove away, Trev looked at his daughter. 'I have to go with her. Can you sort things out a bit here? We'll maybe have a takeaway tonight.'

'Sure, Dad.' She went into the kitchen, groaning at the sight of all the pans and bowls and dishes tumbled carelessly on to the floor. The bottle of washing-up liquid had fallen over, leaking a puddle of sticky green on to the vinyl floor tiles. It filled the sink with bubbles when she wiped it up and she had to rinse out the cloth again and again.

What next? she wondered. First Gran, now Mum. Her Gran used to say that bad things always happened in threes. It couldn't get much worse than this, surely?

Seventeen

Ryan stirred the Bolognese sauce and tasted it, rolling his eyes at Caitlin and making appreciative noises. 'Delicious! And I can't believe how easy it is to make. This is far nicer than the stuff at the local restaurant.'

'Because I'm fussy about the ingredients. Fresh basil makes a big difference and using top-quality minced steak, not cheap stuff. You'll need to check the pasta now.'

He fished out a bit of spaghetti and tasted it. 'Not sure. Need my teacher's advice on this one.'

She came and tasted some. 'Another minute or so.'

She was standing so close he could have kissed her without moving more than his head, but he knew he mustn't do that. She'd been in love with his father until a few weeks ago, for heaven's sake. He swallowed hard and went to pour himself some wine, forcing himself to speak cheerfully. 'It should have breathed properly now. Want a glass?'

'Just a half.' She looked down at her stomach as if to remind him.

That gesture further stiffened his spine. He began to tell her about work and the amazingly silly things some customers complained about, which soon had her laughing.

Only, that made him want to kiss her again. She had such a delightful laugh, low and musical.

When he got home, he lay awake for a long time, unable to get the thought of Caitlin out of his mind, which leaped from one image of her to the other like a drunken grasshopper. He not only found her attractive—correction, *very attractive*—but he liked her too. She was kind and gentle and quirky about some things. Even her clothes were not fashion statements, something he hated. Which made it even more difficult to understand how she could have fallen for his father, or his father for her, because his father usually went with girls who attracted attention by the way they dressed.

Ryan told himself for the hundredth time to find himself another girlfriend and stop seeing so much of Caitlin. Only, when he looked around, he didn't find other girls attractive.

A couple of days later, Caitlin rang to say a neighbour had been fishing and given her some fish. Did he want to help her eat it and, if so, why didn't he come round after work and she'd show him how to cook it?

He'd said yes before his brain clicked into gear. And he didn't even consider changing his mind, because he wanted to see her, spend another evening in her company.

He was in real trouble now! And the worst thing about it all was that he had no idea whatsoever what *she* thought of him, whether she'd ever be able to see him in that way. She never talked about his father if she could help it. But was that because the grief ran too deep or for some other reason?

And what would his mother say if he got together with his father's ex-mistress? She'd freak out.

No, it wouldn't work and he'd have to back off. Definitely. This was the last time he was going to spend an evening with her.

When Caitlin put the phone down, she clapped both hands across her mouth and groaned aloud. Why had she done that? She'd decided after Ryan's last visit that they had to stop seeing one another, and had promised herself to issue no more invitations to him.

But today she'd seen the fish in a shop just down the road, looking so fresh and tempting, and before she could prevent herself, she'd bought enough for two and rung him at work. She loved cooking, but it was no fun cooking for yourself.

Craig had enjoyed her cooking too, said she was the only woman he'd met who was as good as his wife.

Ryan wasn't at all like his father. Both men were warm and generous, but Ryan had a much quieter personality. She loved his sense of humour—Craig hadn't had much sense of humour—and she and Ryan shared a lot of interests. Best of all, she felt utterly safe with him. Not that she hadn't felt physically safe with Craig—she had. The minute he'd found out she was expecting his child, he'd taken charge, wrapping her in luxury at a time when she'd been very tearful and unlike her usual sensible self. He'd been really good to her in the only way he knew how, materially, and had been delighted at the thought of having another child. That had surprised her.

But with Ryan, she felt emotionally safe, which was much more important, she now knew.

Tears brimmed in her eyes. She tried to keep up her spirits, but she knew no one in Melbourne except Ryan, and didn't dare join anything in case one of her family found out where she was. She wouldn't put anything past Barry, knew that it was he who'd found out where she was in Perth.

Her family would never let her go if they could help it. Her father truly believed women should be under the control of their menfolk. Her mother—well, she'd never stood up to her husband in her whole life. Once the baby was born, Caitlin would have to find a more secure place to hide.

Only, where? She'd have to register to vote and she'd bet that as soon as she was on the electoral rolls, Barry would find her again.

Would that mean she had to leave Ryan behind, as she'd left her friends in Perth? She hated the thought of that, absolutely hated it.

What did he really think of her? Was she just his father's mistress, or did he like her for herself?

Was anything possible between them? Did she dare hope?

The following morning Angie rang Laura up just as she was going out to take Kit to his physio appointment.

139

'Can't stop, love. Can I call you back later?' She heard what sounded suspiciously like a sob. 'Angie? What's wrong?'

'They took Mum into hospital last night.'

'*What?*'

'She's mentally ill, has been for a while, and—and I need to talk to you about it, because I need your help in telling Pop. He's got the carer coming in this afternoon. Weren't you going to take him out? Can we go together and tell him then?'

'All right. I'll pick you up in about half an hour.' She went to find Kit.

'I'm ready, ma'am,' he began, then saw her expression. 'What's wrong?'

'My sister's in hospital. She's mentally ill, apparently, and—well, I don't know much more than that. But Angie needs my help to tell my father. Will it be all right if I go out earlier than planned this afternoon? She was crying.'

'Of course it will.' He glanced quickly at his watch. 'It's too late for me to get a taxi, but I can catch one back. Just drop me at the physio's, then go and see what Angie needs.'

'You're sure?'

'Of course I am.'

'Thanks.'

Laura drove up to the neat little bungalow, where everything looked so normal from the outside that it was hard to believe there was a major family crisis going on. Sue's little red car was parked neatly on the drive, the plants were still standing to attention in their stiffly regimented rows and the terylene nets were as crisply white as ever, veiling the family from the world.

Angie opened the door before Laura even got there, and flung herself into her aunt's arms, weeping.

Putting one arm round her shoulders, Laura drew her back inside the house, then simply cuddled her close. 'Shh, now. Shh. It's all right. Just tell me what's happened, then we'll work out what to do.'

When Angie had finished her tale, Laura was so shocked she couldn't at first speak. 'Why did no one tell me before?'

'Dad's been trying to keep the whole thing a secret for Mum's sake. They're used to her at work. As long as they let her follow her little routines, she does a great job for them. It's an advantage for a stores clerk to want everything just so, you see. And because she doesn't eat there, she doesn't get as paranoid. It's food that seems to set her off—and untidiness. I try to be tidier, but I seem to irritate her all the time. I not only have to put things away, but put them away just so. If I change anything, she goes ballistic.

'She's been getting worse and worse and she wouldn't admit anything was wrong, even though she'd been treated for this once already. Only, she stopped seeing the doctor before the treatment was complete. They have to stabilize her medication rather carefully, you see.'

'Where's your father now?'

'At the hospital with her. He didn't want me to tell you, but I *can't* keep it secret any more, Auntie Laura, I just can't. I need someone to talk to.'

'You're coming back with me, then. You're not staying here on your own. You'll only brood.'

'Dad asked me to clear up and I've done the kitchen, sort of. But I'm supposed to be seeing Deb today as well.'

'Oh, hell! I'd forgotten about that.'

'Maybe she can help us tell Pop?'

'Deb?' Laura bit off an adverse comment. She couldn't imagine Deb helping anyone but herself. 'I don't think so. She'll—er—still be jet-lagged.'

'Then what are we going to *do*?'

'We'll pick her up and tell her your mother's ill, then drop her in town. She can go shopping—she loves shopping—then catch a taxi back to Dad's. In the meantime we'll get Dad on his own and tell him.'

Deb was watching for them. She hurried out of the house the minute they pulled up, then saw Angie's tear-stained face. 'What's wrong?'

'We'll go somewhere quiet and tell you.' Laura drove to the park and stopped there to explain what had happened.

Deb stared from one to the other, then spread her hands helplessly. 'I don't know what to say.'

'I'm sorry to let you down,' Angie said. 'I'm just not feeling sociable at the moment.'

'That doesn't matter. What can I do to help?'

Laura hoped her surprise at this hadn't shown. She was pleased to see Deb reacting more normally with other people. Perhaps it was just her that Deb didn't like, hard as that was to face. 'Angie and I need to get Dad on his own, so we thought we'd all grab a quick lunch, then I'll drop you in town. You can go shopping, then catch a taxi back about five o'clock. Will that be all right?'

'Sure.'

'We could go home and grab a sandwich there,' Angie said. 'I'm not in a fit state to be seen in public. I don't know how I'm going to go to work tonight with eyes so swollen, only, I don't like to let them down at the pub.'

Deb looked at her critically. 'I'm pretty good at make-up. I can show you how to hide the worst, and if you just tell them your mother is ill, they'll be kind to you. People were really kind to me at work when Dad died.'

'Thanks, Deb.' Laura smiled at her and for once her daughter smiled back, a smile with no edge to it.

They all worked together to get the kitchen straight, then grabbed corned-beef sandwiches.

'I'm not sure we've got everything back in what she considers the right places,' Angie worried.

'Then you can help her rearrange it when she gets out.'

Angie shook her head. 'No way. I always make matters worse. She seems to have taken against me lately, keeps telling me things are my fault for dropping out of university and being so untidy.'

'No more tears!' Deb said quickly, putting an arm round her cousin's shoulders. 'You have to work, remember.'

Laura watched in chagrin. Why was her daughter never like this with her? Deb was being lovely with poor Angie.

When they went to collect her father after lunch, he came out of the house beaming with pleasure at seeing them. The smile faded as soon as he saw Angie's reddened eyes.

'What's wrong, love?'

Laura intervened before Angie started crying again. 'Get in and we'll go somewhere quiet and tell you, Dad.'

He sat in the back of the car, listening to the story of his daughter's strange and obsessive behaviour, his face racked with sadness.

'Eh, I can't rightly take it in,' he said when they'd finished. He pulled out a spray and squirted it under his tongue.

'What's that for, Dad?'

He shrugged. 'Just a touch of angina. It helps a bit.'

Laura didn't dare state the obvious: that if he had a heart problem, he shouldn't be working so hard. She looked at her watch. 'We'd better see to your shopping and then I have to get back. I've neglected my duties shamefully.'

'I never thought!' Angie exclaimed in dismay. 'And you've only just started working for Mr Mallinder, too.'

'It's all right. Kit's very understanding.'

It was a subdued group who went round the supermarket. As well as Kit's supplies, Laura bought the makings of a beef casserole and promised to take it round to her father's the next day in time for tea.

'Thanks, love.' He gave her a hug and looked from one to the other. 'It's grand to see our family sticking together when there's a problem. I'm proud of you all.'

Kit was in the kitchen drinking one of his endless cups of coffee when Laura got back.

'Sorry I'm so late.'

He cocked one eye at her. 'You look upset. Want to tell me about it?'

She hesitated, wondering if it might be bad tactics to confide in her employer, then got angry with herself. Craig had always thought like that and tried to teach her to speak only about impersonal things at company functions, but it was alien to her nature and she'd often irritated him by her frankness. Besides, Kit wasn't like other people. He was very much his own person. She sat down and explained briefly.

'Poor you. It's been one thing after another lately, hasn't it?'

'It's other people who're having the real problems this time. I'm just—involved. And you haven't had the best few months of your life, either. Thanks for listening, though. It was good to get things off my chest. Now, what shall we have for tea tonight?'

'Takeaway.'

She stared at him in surprise. 'I shall feel I've let you down if I do that.'

'Don't talk daft! You're a human being like any other and I bet you're feeling wrung out.'

'Well, I am a bit tired.'

'So, we'll have takeaway. There's an Indian place in the village I'd like to try. I got the taxi driver to stop and pick me up a menu.' He flourished it at her. 'Ta-da!'

'You're a lovely person, Kit Mallinder,' she said before she could stop herself.

He roared with laughter. 'You give me a compliment, then look at me apprehensively.'

'Well, you're my employer and I shouldn't be so personal and—'

'Do you think I'm going to complain about being compli-mented?' He leaned forward and placed his hand on hers. 'Laura, I told you I'm not into formality. Say what you think, for heaven's sake. I think of you more as a friend than an employee, and I really value honesty in a friend. Get angry at me if I do something that upsets you. And if your family has a crisis, like today, go and help them. Ah, hell, what have I said now?'

144

She sniffed and gulped, but the tears wouldn't stay back. 'You've been kind, so very kind. I'm not used to it—lately.'

He stood up, hands resting on the table. 'Come here, Laura Wells. You definitely need a hug.'

She moved towards him as if it were a dream, walking straight into his open arms. As she rested her head against the side of his with a sigh, she could feel the strength of his wiry body against hers, but more important, the warmth of his innate kindness wrapping her round.

He hugged her close, then said huskily, 'Look at me, Laura.'

When she raised her eyes to his, he bent forward to kiss her. They were almost the same height, fitted together perfectly. His lips were warm, soft, tender, teasing. She didn't want him to stop.

He didn't. He kissed her so thoroughly that she melted like chocolate against him, cuddling up against him when his lips left hers. She'd forgotten what it was like to be held in a man's arms and kissed tenderly. Wanted more.

'Look, Laura,' he said in her ear, 'I know this isn't sensible, given our situation, but if we don't choose to be sensible, who are we hurting? We're both adults, no emotional ties.'

'I feel I'm using you, leaning on you, when I should be helping you.'

'We're using one another. Isn't that what friends do? And to tell you the truth, you're the first woman I've fancied since the accident. I was worried sick about my—um—masculinity. I'm not any more.'

She could feel the proof of that and it made her feel good to know that such an attractive man fancied her. She leaned her head back just a little to study his face, loving that wry smile he had, the way he said exactly what he thought. 'Well, then.'

'What does that mean?'

'I don't know. Perhaps it means we should see how things

go between us, not rush things, though definitely not insist on being sensible.'

His gaze was briefly bitter as he looked down at his leg. 'I can't rush anything at the moment, can't even hold you properly.'

'I don't care about that. Appearances are nothing. What I care about is what you're like inside. And actually—' she paused and grinned at him, '—I fancy you something rotten too.'

He let out a shout of laughter, planting a quick kiss on the tip of her nose before reaching for the chair back to steady himself. 'Then we'll stop denying the attraction we're both feeling?'

She nodded.

'Thank goodness for that. Now, pass me those damned crutches.'

She did as he asked, making sure he was properly balanced before she stepped away.

'It's very unromantic, but I've got to confess I'm ravenous. Let's order that takeaway.'

'I'm a bit hungry myself.' She hadn't been. Was now. Nerved herself to say, 'I'll go and pick it up,' though going out alone after dark still made her nervous.

'I'll come with you.'

'No need.'

He waggled one finger at her. 'Yes, there is, and you know it. I may not be able to drive you there, or hobble in and out of the restaurant with you, but my presence in the car will make you feel safer.'

She stopped pretending. 'Thanks. I was mugged once and it's left me a bit nervous at night.'

'They tell me I was mugged and thrown in front of a truck in Bangkok. They say it's common to have memory lapses after such a bad accident. I didn't remember a thing.'

'Kit, how terrible!'

'Annoys the hell out of me not to know *why*, but that's all water under the bridge now. Come on, woman! Stop talking and let's decide what we want to eat. And we'll

146

open that bottle of champagne when we get back. I want to celebrate.' He gave her one of his quirky smiles. 'Don't you think we've got something to celebrate?'

Joy bubbled up in her. 'Yes, I do.'

But in the middle of the night he woke up, as he sometimes did, and lay there letting his thoughts drift idly. And suddenly another memory came back. It was Shaun Nolan who'd offered him the assignment. Shaun had come to visit him once in hospital early on, but had said nothing about what he'd been doing in Bangkok.

Try as he might, he could remember no more details, either about the assignment or about the mugging. Well, the doctors had told him any memory lost might be patchy and not to push it if bits came back to him, just let things happen.

He really must get down to unpacking his boxes. There might be something in there to give him a clue. It still galled him to have even a small slice removed from his life.

Eighteen

Two days later Deb was nearly back to normal again after the jet lag. She'd woken in the middle of each night, lying in the darkness unable to recognize where she was, then realizing she was at Pop's and snuggling down again. It felt strange to be living here, but he was so easy to be with that it'd gone better than she'd expected. Gran seemed to be in a world of her own most of the time, though, on a couple of occasions, Deb had seen her look across the room and smile in the old way, once at Pop, once at her. But each time the smile had soon faded. She listened to Pop shower and dress his wife each morning, watching him coaxing her to eat, because Gran didn't seem interested in food any more.

It nearly broke her heart, because it was all too obvious that she'd come too late to spend time with the real Gran. She'd cried a couple of times about that, but hadn't let on to Pop, who had enough troubles to bear.

'She's slipping away from us so fast,' Pop said once in a low voice. 'Last month she still talked to me, now she doesn't say much at all. I should have told our Laura about her sooner.'

'You weren't to know.' After a few minutes, he took Gran out into the yard, where she immediately began walking around. He glanced out of the window and began to clear up the kitchen. When Deb went to help him, he gave her one of his gentle smiles. No one smiled like her Pop.

'Eh, it's lovely to see your fresh young face around the house. You and Angie really cheer me up. We'll go out this afternoon, shall we, just you and me? The carer is coming and I usually go down to the park or—I know, we could drive out to Hollingworth Lake. Would you like that? Good, so would I.'

He made it so easy for her to fit in, Deb thought wonderingly. He had no expectations but that they'd enjoy one another's company, so they did. She couldn't remember anyone as easy to be with—except for Ryan. And found herself noticing similarities between her brother and Pop. Ryan had grown up a lot since he left university. He seemed to have left her behind somehow and had said she was being childish a couple of times. She'd not believed him then, but now, well, it made you think, seeing Gran like that.

'You can ring your mother later,' Pop said. 'It's wrong of me to monopolize you like this, only, I thought, with the carer being here today, it'd be a good chance to catch up with one another.'

The only time they disagreed was over meals. He was very disapproving of how little she ate.

'But I'll get fat if I eat too much, Pop. Like Mum!'

He looked at her sternly. 'I don't ever want to hear you saying things like that about your mother. Our Laura isn't fat and never has been. She has a lovely shape, just the sort a normal man likes. And even if she was fat, what would it matter? She'd still be Laura, the best daughter a man could have.'

Deb blinked at him. He couldn't mean all that about what normal men liked, surely?

'You know, love, you're far too thin. You've not got this anorexia thing, have you?'

'Anorexia? No, I just watch my weight.'

'Then you should watch that you put a bit *on*. A man likes a cosy armful, not a bag of bones, and that hasn't changed, whatever those silly fools who design the fashions think.'

She didn't believe him, but then remembered suddenly the guy on the plane. He'd also said she was too thin. And he wasn't Pop's generation.

A little later, she went to study herself in the full-length hall mirror, putting the light on and twisting to and fro, trying to see herself as others saw her, and because it wasn't a mirror she normally used, it seemed to show her differently somehow. Her cheeks were hollow—were they too hollow?—and her arms were very bony. As for breasts, she hardly had any. She couldn't see her legs, because she was wearing jeans, but this hall mirror was merciless in revealing that her backside didn't make the jeans curve as she'd expected it to when she twisted her body round. She moved her face closer to the mirror and frowned. Was Pop right? Could you actually be too thin?

She didn't have anorexia, though, definitely not.

When she turned round, he was standing in the doorway, looking at her sympathetically. 'You've let yourself go, love, grieving for your father, but we'll soon feed you up with good Lancashire grub. Eh, now!'

She hurled herself at him as a wave of grief for her father hit her, weeping and needing comforting as if she were still the child she'd been on their last visit. He held her in his thin old arms, patting her back and making soft sympathetic noises in her ear until the sobs faded.

'I'm sorry,' she muttered as she pulled away.

'What for? I'm just glad you weren't on your own, that you had someone to give you a cuddle when you needed it. It's good to cry out your grief.'

She plonked a quick kiss on his cheek, still embarrassed by her own outburst, but loving him to pieces. She couldn't have had a better father or grandfather. And her mother was all right, really, in her own way.

When they went back into the kitchen, Gran was playing with her food, pushing it round and round the plate with her fingers, clearly fascinated by this activity. Deb saw the deep sadness come back to his face.

'Eh, look at her. She's like a babby again. Sometimes I just let her play.'

'You've two babies to deal with tonight, I think,' Deb said, tearing off a piece of kitchen roll and using it to mop her face and blow her nose.

'Nay, you're just a lass who's recently lost her father.'
He sat down next to his wife. 'If *you* can't cry for him,
who can?'

'I don't think Mum has.'

'Well, he didn't treat her well, did he, towards the end?
They'd not loved each other for a while, so it's different
for her. She probably did her crying a while ago, when they
first drifted apart. But never doubt that she's grieving for
what she's lost, and that includes him. Eh, they loved each
other so much when they were young.'

'Did they really?'

He nodded. 'Definitely. But sometimes that fades. Still,
don't let that affect your memories. Craig might have
stopped being a good husband, but he was always a good
father. On our last visit, Mum and I could see that *you* were
his favourite and he kept getting impatient with her. We
didn't think much of that, but we didn't say anything.
Sometimes you have to bite your tongue.' He picked up his
mug. 'This is stone cold. Would you make me another cup
of tea, love?'

'Of course. Will I make one for Gran as well?'

'Just half a cup.'

Deb felt better than she had for a while, and to please
Pop she ate a chocolate biscuit. You couldn't get fat on one
self-indulgence, after all. She could still be careful of what
she ate the rest of the time, just eat a little bit more.

And whatever Alex had said, she definitely wasn't
anorexic.

Angie phoned her granddad after tea, as she did most days,
and asked to speak to Deb afterwards. 'Do you want to
come out with me and Rick for a drink tonight?'

'Won't I be in the way?'

'Not at all. Actually, his cousin's just arrived from
Australia, so I daresay the two guys will be nattering away,
and I want someone to talk to on my night off.'

Deb looked across at her grandfather. 'All right if I go
out with Angie tonight?'

151

'Yes, love. Of course it is.'

She smiled at him, wishing she'd lived closer to him as a child and had more time with him, then turned back to the phone. 'I'd love to come out with you, Angie.'

'We'll pick you up at eight, then.'

Pop smiled at her as she put the phone down. 'I like to see you young ones going out and enjoying yourselves.'

'You sure you'll be all right?' Her eyes went to her grandmother.

'Of course I will, love. Me and Pat usually watch television together in the evening.' He chuckled. 'I'll probably doze in front of it and she'll sit holding my hand. She still does that, you know, just like we did when we were young 'uns, and she still likes programmes with music best. I look forward to the evenings.'

It nearly broke her heart to see how determinedly cheerful he was and how unresponsive Gran was.

Deb piled into the back of Rick's car and only as they were setting off did she really notice his cousin, gasping in shock when she recognized him.

'This is Alex,' Angie said. 'Alex, meet Deb.'

'Actually, we met on the plane. We were sitting next to one another.' He gave Deb a quizzical look, as if to ask whether they were speaking now.

She managed a smile, but her heart sank. Oh, no! Of all the people to be Rick's cousin, it had to be *him*. She wished she hadn't come out tonight.

As they crammed round a tiny table in the pub where Angie worked, Deb remembered to ask, 'How's your mother?'

'Calmer. She'll be coming home again in a day or two, but they don't think she should go back to work, and we have to make sure she takes her tablets. Trouble is, she hates taking them.' She pulled a face. 'Let's not talk about *her.* Let's just enjoy ourselves. It's been a bit full-on lately at home.'

When the men were buying another round, Angie whispered, 'He's nice, isn't he?'

'Rick? He's a teddy bear.'

'Yes he is, but I meant his cousin.' She nudged Deb. 'I'd fancy him if I didn't already fancy Rick.'

'Um—actually, I don't fancy him. We had a couple of disagreements on the plane.'

Angie gazed at her in shock. 'Oh, no! You're not the—' She broke off.

'What? What did he say about me?'

'Nothing.'

'You might as well tell me. I know it won't be flattering.'

Angie shrugged. 'He just said he was sitting next to a spoiled brat who didn't eat anything, even though she was too thin already.'

Deb looked down at her beer mat. 'Pop said I was too thin tonight as well. Do *you* think I am?'

'I thought that's how you were. I mean, you don't get much choice about the body type you're born with, do you? I'm definitely on the plumper side of things.'

'You *do* think I'm too thin, then!'

'Well, you are if you don't need to be. I read somewhere that normal guys really prefer girls with curves.' She grinned down at herself. 'In which case, I'm all right. I'm nothing but curves.'

Deb forced a smile to her face, then looked round the pub. It was clearly a popular hangout for people her age. Nearly all the girls were fatter than she was—well, not fat exactly, but more curvy—and most of them had fellows fussing over them. She didn't have anyone, hadn't had for a while, had worried about that. 'My dad always said I had a perfect figure.'

'Look, Deb, I didn't mean—'

The guys came back just then with another round of drinks. Deb thanked them for her glass of white wine and sat quietly, listening to the two cousins talk. When she went to the ladies', Angie went with her.

'I'm sorry if I've upset you,' she said bluntly.

Deb pursed her lips, not knowing what to say, then caught sight of herself unexpectedly in a big wall mirror. She walked past her cousin to stare at herself. 'It's not you. I'm just—not sure of anything at the moment.'

Angie suddenly stepped forward and gave her a hug. 'Well, forget all that. Let's just enjoy ourselves tonight. You're still my favourite cousin whether you're fat or scrawny.'

'You've only got two cousins.'

'Well, you're my favourite.'

Deb found herself smiling, really smiling, at the other girl. It felt strange to have a relative of nearly her own age. Nice though. Her dad's parents had died when she was small, and he was an only son, so there hadn't been any cousins in Australia. But she'd always had Ryan. You weren't supposed to get on with your brother. Most girls she knew complained about theirs. But hers was special.

'I wish Ryan was here with us,' she said suddenly. 'He'd love this family stuff. I do too. Even when things aren't going well, you feel connected, don't you?'

Angie nodded solemnly. 'And I think your mum is the greatest. I couldn't ask for a nicer aunt. She's been really kind to me.'

Deb swallowed a sharp comment. It seemed that everyone liked her mother but her. Well, she didn't dislike her, exactly. Just—didn't feel she knew her very well these days. Didn't feel sure of how to deal with her.

Didn't feel sure of anything since Dad died.

Nineteen

After three more meals prepared together, Ryan raised his glass of wine to Caitlin. 'Here's to the cook!'

She raised her wine diluted with fizzy mineral water in response. 'And here's to the assistant cook! I think we make an excellent team.' She wished the words unsaid as soon as she'd spoken. It sounded so corny and obvious. What would he think of her? She stole a quick glance across the table and saw him frowning down at his glass.

As if he'd felt her gaze on him, he asked suddenly, 'What did you see in Dad? He was so much older than you. I just can't get my head around it.'

She couldn't think what to say, how to answer that. It sounded such a simple question and yet the answer was complicated.

He made a dismissive gesture with his right hand. 'Forget it. You're still grieving for him. I was out of order. I think I'd better go home before I put my foot in it again. You have that effect on me, I'm afraid. I keep wanting to know more about you, to understand. It's not just the child now. You must realize that by now, so, if you don't want me to come again . . .'

She watched him run one hand through his hair, and knew suddenly that she couldn't hope for anything longer-term if their friendship was based on misunderstandings. She'd been terrified of this moment, but now it'd come, she felt strangely calm. 'I do want to keep seeing you. Come and sit down. I'll tell you how I met Craig, why we—got together. It's about time.'

He followed her across to the sitting area, gesturing to

her to take the couch and sitting at right angles to her on a chair.

'Just a minute.' She went and switched off the lights in the dining alcove, leaving only one lamp glowing softly in the corner.

'I met Craig at the office party,' she began in a low voice. 'Sounds corny, doesn't it? Well, it was corny. Some people were a bit the worse for wear and this guy was pestering me. I didn't know what to do. It's not easy to fend off a drunk when he's also your boss. Craig intervened, told him to leave me alone.' She wrapped her arms round her knees and was relieved when Ryan didn't interrupt as she tried to get her thoughts into order. 'I was flattered as well as relieved when your dad stayed beside me for a while chatting.'

'Did he come on to you then?'

'Heavens, no. He was seeing someone from the IT section. No, from then on he just said hello sometimes and stopped to ask how things were. I think he sensed I was a bit overwhelmed by working for a large company. I'd moved up from the country the year before and my leaving home was very much against my parents' wishes, even at twenty-four. Silly, isn't it? Most people would laugh at that.'

'I wouldn't.'

'They belong to a fundamentalist religious sect, you see, and they didn't see why I needed to leave, didn't like the idea of me mixing with outsiders. They were good parents in their own way. I never doubted they loved me. I just— couldn't follow their beliefs. When I came to Perth, I was a bit lonely and I think it showed. Craig was just being kind.'

The silence went on for so long, Ryan prompted, 'And then?'

'Then my cousin Barry turned up one day. He'd moved up to Perth too, and my parents had told him where I worked and suggested he keep an eye on me, though I'd asked them not to. He was hassling me to have dinner with him, insisting he wouldn't take no for an answer, when your father came

156

down to reception, saw what was happening and took my arm, apologizing for being late for our date. We walked out together. Only, I was so upset, Craig really did take me out for a meal. He was so kind.'

'Yeah. He could be kind.' Especially to pretty young women. Ryan had seen it before, hated to think of his dad playing those games with Caitlin.

'Barry shouted after us that he'd see me another time, and I blurted out to Craig that I was going to resign and move to the Eastern States. I meant it, too. Your dad took me on to a party after the meal, and somehow I found myself smoking pot. I'd never done it before and I shan't do it again. It was a gesture of defiance, I suppose. I don't think he realized I'd never tried it, and I didn't want to show how naïve I was, but afterwards I felt strange, unreal and floaty, as if everything was at a distance.'

'I don't like the stuff. It makes me feel irritable. Go on.'

'When we drove back to my flat, I saw Barry parked outside and got upset again. So, Craig took me back to his place for the night. He said I could have the spare room. Only, I wound up in his bed instead. It was my first time and he was very gentle, but the condom burst.' She stole a quick glance sideways and saw how darkly he was frowning. 'Shall I go on?'

When he nodded, she took a deep breath. 'I was terrified but he said we'd be very unlucky for me to get pregnant from just doing it once. Only, we didn't do it just once. I stayed with him all weekend and we had fun.'

'I didn't realize my father had a flat even before he moved out of home.'

'Yes. He'd had it for a while, I think.'

'Mum didn't know about it.'

'So I gather. I felt awful sleeping with a married man, but he said she didn't want him any more.' She let out a bitter snort that was meant to be a laugh but failed. 'I told you I was naïve. I actually believed that.'

'Go on.'

'Craig said I should take a restraining order out against

157

Barry. Only, what reason could I have given for that? He wasn't sexually stalking me or anything. He was my cousin, trying to keep in touch because my parents had asked him to. Only—once we grew up, he changed and he made me feel nervous sometimes.' She shivered and stopped talking for a moment, then took a deep breath and went on. 'As soon as I left school, Barry said he was going to marry me one day. I told him it'd never happen, but he just used to smile and say he'd find a way to change my mind. I don't think he'd force sex on me or be violent or anything like that, but he's implacable when he wants something. Like the way he insisted on taking me to my graduation ball when I wanted to go with a guy in my class. He told the guy I'd changed my mind, got my parents on side, and they refused to buy me a dress unless I went with him. I was so embarrassed. He would only do the slow dances, stopped me dancing with my friends, and wouldn't let me drink any alcohol.'

She sighed. 'My parents think Barry's wonderful, and they kept going on at me to see more of him.' She sighed and looked at Ryan. 'I didn't give them my address, though I did phone them every now and then. Mum desperately wants me to give them grandchildren, you see, and I'd like a family too—though not like this.'

She sobbed suddenly and wished he'd hold her, but he sat there without moving, stony-faced now and not looking like the warm, friendly Ryan she knew and liked so much. She made a huge effort and managed not to cry. If she was going to disgust him, make him stop seeing her, better it happened sooner rather than later.

'I told Craig I didn't think we should go on meeting, and he was very sweet about it, though he called me a couple of times. But I refused to go out with him again. Then a month or so later I realized I was pregnant and so I had to tell him. I couldn't even consider an abortion, you see.' She gave Ryan a wavery smile. 'I thought Craig would be furious but he was delighted. He really wanted the baby. I was all tearful and I felt rotten, so I let him take over. He made plans for the baby, for us being together. Sold his flat and bought the house in Perth. He was so happy. At least I made him happy. He never knew I . . .' She broke off and avoided his eyes.

'That you didn't love him?'

She looked up again, drawing in a long shuddering breath. 'Yes. I definitely didn't love him and I'm not sure he loved me, either. I think he simply loved the situation, felt it showed him in a good light, still virile enough to father a child. He hated growing old.'

Ryan's voice was a rough scrape of sound. 'Yeah, he was a great father—but a rotten husband. Go on.'

'Craig and I moved in together—well, at first I moved in and he spent a lot of time with me. I'd stopped work and was letting him keep me. I knew it was wrong, but I felt so stupidly weak and helpless, and I felt so sick all the time. I'd have done anything rather than go to my parents for help, because it'd have meant my moving back home, and then I'd be trapped. I didn't want them bringing up my child, you see, smothering it as they'd smothered me. Everything is black and white to them, with no shades of grey, no tolerance of human frailty.' She fell silent, staring into space.

'Did you know about the will?'

'Sort of. Craig said he'd changed it to include me and the baby. He laughed about it, said he intended to be around for many years to come, but it was always wise to do your paperwork, just in case.'

'I've often heard him say that.'

'I didn't know about the insurance money, but when Craig was killed, I couldn't refuse to take it, because it meant freedom for me and the child. I'm sorry if I've hurt your mother and I'm sorry if you think worse of me for taking it, but I still intend to keep it. Once the baby's born, I have to find somewhere to live where my family won't find me, you see.'

'You're safe here in Melbourne, surely?'

'Barry will find me here sooner or later, I know he will.'

159

'But he still can't force you to do anything against your will.'

'You don't know my cousin. He's like one of those big machines they use for flattening the ground when they're making roads. You just—can't stop him rolling over you. And I'm not—' her voice wobbled, '—in the best condition to stand up for myself. I'm always weeping or dithering, not myself at all lately.'

She watched anxiously as Ryan got up, went to stare out of the window, then turned back to her, his expression giving nothing of his feelings away.

'Do you hate me?' she blurted out, unable to stand the suspense.

'No, of course not. But I don't know how I feel. I thought you loved him, you see. I thought at least you'd loved my father and that explained everything.' His voice broke on the last words.

'He was kind. I liked him. But I was never in love with him. I couldn't pretend about that—not to you.'

'I need to think about it.' He went to pick up his car keys and turned at the door. 'I'll give you a call.'

She didn't move, let him see himself out. Not until the outer door made the snicking sound that said the lock had caught, did she bow her head and weep.

She knew Ryan wouldn't call her, just knew it, and she could hardly blame him.

She only wished she'd met him before she'd met his father.

Which was a futile thing to wish for. You couldn't change the past, much as you'd like to. You had to live with your mistakes. She put one hand on her stomach. She'd never make her child feel unwanted, though. Never. If she did nothing else right in her life, she was going to bring it up knowing it was loved, but able to be itself.

And at least she wouldn't be on her own after it was born.

Twenty

Kit was delighted when the physio said he could stop using the crutches for a half-hour, beginning the next day and adding half an hour each day. The following morning he walked into the kitchen, where Laura was preparing their breakfast, and when she didn't turn round he called, 'Look at me!' and struck a pose.

She turned, saw him without crutches for the first time and, without thinking, ran across to give him a hug. 'How does it feel?'

He hugged her back. 'It feels wonderful to be standing on my own feet. I've had to be so strict with myself when I've been *itching* to walk and drive.'

'You'll still be careful, though? You won't overdo it?'

'No, I won't overdo it. But it makes it much easier to do this.' He kissed her, made an appreciative noise in his throat, then kissed her again.

'I can't think straight when you do that.'

'Who needs to think?' He saw the hint of panic in her eyes and stepped back. 'Now, can you stop doing that for an hour or so and drive me over to my brother's? He isn't returning my phone calls and, as it's Sunday, I thought I might stand a chance of catching him in.'

'Of course.' She covered the vegetables with a damp cloth and ran upstairs to check her appearance. As she came downstairs the phone rang and she heard Kit's voice. She hesitated at the kitchen door, not wanting to interrupt him if it was his brother, but he beckoned her across and gestured to the phone. 'Your mother's here now, Deb.'

She took the phone from him. 'Hello, darling.'

'Hi, Mum. I just thought I'd—um—give you a call to see how you are.'

'I'm fine. And you?'

'Fine. Pop's looking after me very well. He's trying to feed me up.'

She heard the sound of her dad's laughter in the background and wished she could relate so easily to her daughter.

'I wondered if I could come and see you sometime?'

'I'd love you to come and visit me.'

Kit tapped her on the arm.

'Just a minute.'

'We could pick her up after we've called on Joe.'

'Deb? We could pick you up in about an hour. I'm taking Kit to see his brother and we could swing round by Pop's afterwards for you.'

'That'd be nice.'

When she'd put the phone down, Laura asked, 'Sure you don't mind?'

'Of course not. Tell me to butt out if you want, but you didn't seem very comfortable with her.'

'No. She was very much Daddy's Little Princess and she's always been a bit edgy with me. Since he died I don't know how to deal with her.'

'She'll be hurting.' His tone was matter of fact.

'Yes. But I'm getting a little tired of being the butt of her pain. Anyway, enough about my problems, I'm ready to leave now. Don't forget your crutches. You can't walk around for too long today.'

'I know. I'm not going to undo all the good the operations have done.' He pulled a wry face but went to get them, trying not to limp too markedly.

They drew up outside Joe's house just as the door opened and he came out. He stopped dead and Kit was certain this time that it was a look of panic on his face. He took a step forward, saying in a teasing voice, 'If the mountain won't come to Mohammed . . .'

Another man came hurrying out of the door, saying, 'It

162

was on the bedside table all the time and—' He broke off and looked from Kit to Joe, then said in quite another tone of voice, 'I'm not going to be sent away like a naughty schoolboy again.'

Kit stepped forward. 'Hi, Gil. Nice to see you.' He waited.

They all waited, then Joe said in a gruff voice, 'You'd better come in.'

Kit turned to look questioningly at Laura, who waved one hand as if to shoo him into the house.

Only then did Joe notice. 'You're off your crutches! Should you be?'

'Yes. I'm allowed half an hour off them for the first time today, increasing gradually. I'll be driving again soon.'

'Good.' He shut the door. 'You'd—um—better sit down.'

Gil took a seat and folded his arms, not saying anything.

Joe sat down and stared at his feet.

As the silence lengthened, Kit said gently, 'I'd guessed.' He winked at Gil.

Joe looked at him in shock, drawing in a long breath that was almost a sob. '*How* did you guess? Is it so obvious?'

'No. Not at all. It was seeing your panic when Gil turned up the evening before I left.' He smiled apologetically at the other man. 'It's a bit more obvious with you.'

Gil shrugged, flapped one hand mockingly and said in an ultra-camp voice, 'Once a queen, always a queen.'

Joe's voice came out sounding half-strangled as he tried to explain. 'I didn't want this, you know, and—'

Kit couldn't bear to see his suffering. 'You don't have to explain anything to me, Joe. You're my brother whatever you do or are, and I'll still love you. And besides, what's wrong with being gay? I've got several gay friends.'

'He can't forgive himself,' Gil said bitterly. 'It's that damned mother of yours, stuffing him full of her prejudices. How come it didn't hit you the same way? You seem much more a free spirit.'

'I was the rebel while Joe always tried to conform. And in my job, I've seen so many filthy things happen to nice, ordinary people, that whether a man is gay or not doesn't seem to matter that much as long as he's a decent human being.'

Joe burst into tears and sat there, making strangled sobbing noises.

Kit looked questioningly at Gil, who gestured to him to go to Joe, and left the room.

It took quite a while for Joe to calm down, and even then Kit guessed that his brother was tormented internally. 'Have you sought counselling?'

Joe nodded. 'There's a counselling service at church.'

'Let me guess: they advised you to fight against this?'

'How did you know?'

'Mum's church is ultra-conservative. Other churches understand that you don't *choose* to be gay—you're born that way.'

'But I don't *want* to be.'

Kit sighed. 'Some things you can't change. Do you think I want this, just when I've met someone special?' He slapped his thigh and scowled down at this leg.

Joe stared at him. *'You*—someone special? Aren't you the one who was never going to marry?'

'Yeah. And I'm glad I didn't before. Being a foreign correspondent isn't a good basis for marriage. I've seen quite a few marriages break up, however much they loved one another at first. Now—well, maybe I'm ready to settle down.'

'Who is she?'

'It's Laura, my housekeeper, and—Oh, hell, she's been waiting outside all this time!' He looked at his brother. 'I won't bring her in now, but why don't you and Gil come to tea one night?'

'I'll think about it.'

'He seems a really nice guy and he obviously cares about you.'

'He is. The nicest. That's why it's been so difficult. I can't just—repudiate him. I don't want to, anyway.'

'I think love is precious wherever it comes from.' Kit

stood up. 'I'll have to go.' He bent to grasp Joe's hand. 'Just accept it and get on with your life, bro.'

Laura smiled a greeting as Kit came across the pavement.

'Sorry to keep you waiting for so long. Family crisis.'

'That's all right. It's nice to sit and do nothing sometimes.'

'You're a very special lady, Laura Wells. Thanks for not getting impatient with me. It was—rather traumatic in there.'

'Anything I can help with?'

'Not really. It's Joe, who won't accept something.'

'That he's gay?'

He nodded. 'Is it so obvious?'

'I'd guessed from what you'd said, but when I saw his friend today, I felt pretty certain.' She pulled a wry face. 'We humans are a mixed-up bunch, aren't we?'

'Yes. But that's what makes us so interesting.'

'It's not always interesting to live through things.'

'No. I know.'

'How's your leg?'

'I've been sitting down most of the time.' He began to feel more cheerful. 'I'm only counting that as five minutes off my half-hour of freedom. Now, let's go and pick up your daughter. I'm looking forward to meeting her.'

Laura wasn't. She was really nervous of spending time on her own with Deb.

Deb opened the door before Laura had time to knock. 'I'm ready.'

'I'll just say hello to Dad first.'

He came out of the kitchen and gave her a quick hug. 'You're looking well, lass.'

'I'm feeling well. Can you come out and meet Kit, just for a moment?'

He looked at Deb. 'Will you keep an eye on your gran for me, love?'

She nodded.

Kit got out of the car and shook Ron's hand. 'I'm

165

delighted to meet you, Mr Cleaton. I have to tell you your daughter's a treasure. I've never met anyone as efficient in a house, and she's a brilliant cook.'

Ron beamed. 'It's nice to hear that. I gather you've been in the wars lately.'

Kit looked at Laura in puzzlement and she laughed. 'It means in trouble or hurt. Lancashire speak.'

'Ah yes, I remember now.' He looked down. 'Yes. Unfortunately.'

He could never hide his unhappiness with his disability, Laura thought. She thought her father had sensed that unhappiness, because he patted Kit's arm.

'There's not many don't have summat wrong with them, lad, as they get older.'

Kit chuckled. 'Lad! I'll have you know I'm thirty-eight. That's not exactly a lad.'

'It is to me. Well, I'd better get back to my Pat or she'll start fretting.'

As if to prove his point, Deb suddenly called, 'Pop!' and when they turned they saw her struggling to hold her grand-mother back.

Ron ran down the path and Kit followed. Between them the two men got her inside again.

Laura watched as her mother accepted Kit's help. 'Why won't she let *me* near her?' she muttered.

Deb looked at her. 'She doesn't know what she's doing.' She frowned. 'I thought you were looking after an old man.'

'Kit old?' Laura laughed. 'No. He was injured and is still convalescing, but he's hardly old.'

'He's very attractive.' The way she said it was almost an accusation.

'I suppose so.'

Once they got back to Wardle, Kit went for a rest and Laura took Deb through to the kitchen. 'I thought I'd make a Caesar salad for lunch. With chicken. That way Kit can have his whenever it suits him.' She knew it was one of her daughter's favourites.

'Oh, good! And I'll watch carefully how you do it this

time. Mine never tastes as good as yours.'

Laura was astonished to receive a compliment from her daughter, but didn't comment. She started putting the ingredients together. 'How are you getting on at Dad's?'

Deb shrugged. 'All right. But it's a very small house, isn't it? How on earth did four of you manage all those years?'

'We managed because it was all we had.'

'Was your sister always—strange?'

Laura pursed her lips. 'Well, she was always a bit rigid about her possessions. They had to be arranged just so.'

'Angie hates living at home. Do you know, her mother even wakes her in the middle of the night sometimes and insists on cleaning her room there and then, saying it's dirty.'

'Poor Sue.'

'Poor Angie.'

'Yes, poor Angie too. I like her, don't you?'

'Yeah. She's fun to be with, and Rick's nice, but I don't like his cousin. I met him on the plane and he was very rude to me. Ah, that's how you do the dressing!' She leaned forward and pinched a bit of lettuce leaf, dipping it in the dressing and making an appreciative sound in her throat as she ate.

'How long are you staying in England?'

'I don't know.'

'If you want a break any time, I'm sure Kit would let you stay overnight here.'

'Thanks. I'll remember that.' She looked at her mother, hesitated, then said, 'Sorry if I was a bit rude to you after Dad died. I wasn't coping.'

A bit rude! thought Laura. *You were appallingly rude and hurtful.* But what was the use in going back over all that and breaking this fragile rapport? 'I know. It was hard for us all.'

They ate lunch together and, though Deb refused the French bread with her salad, she ate better than Laura had seen her doing for a while.

'Is there a bus from here to Angie's?' Deb asked afterwards. 'She said I could go over there this afternoon.'

'I'll drive you over. It's not far.'

'Won't he mind?'

'Won't who mind what?' Kit asked from the doorway.

Deb blushed. 'My mother taking me across to my cousin's house later.'

'Hey, I'm not her gaoler.'

Laura gestured to the table. 'If you'll be seated, sir, I'll serve you.'

He grinned. 'Good. I'm ravenous again. What gourmet treat am I having today?'

'Just a Caesar salad.'

He rolled his eyes. 'I'm definitely going to put on weight, and I'll enjoy every minute of it.'

'We'll leave you in peace to eat.'

'You haven't finished your food. Unless you two need to be private? In which case, I'll eat in my room.'

'No. I just—didn't want to disturb you.'

He gave a mock sigh. 'You're doing it again, woman—worrying.'

Deb gaped at the way they smiled at one another, and said hastily, 'I think I'd better buy myself a car if I'm going to stay for a while.'

'Rick found me a good one.'

'Yes. I'll definitely ask him once I've made my mind up.'

When Laura got back forty minutes later, Kit was still in the kitchen, sitting with a cup of coffee and reading a book. He put it down. 'Come and join me. Tell me how it went.'

'Better than I'd expected. We're not really at ease with one another, but at least she doesn't seem as hostile as she was. She even apologized for being a bit rude after Craig died. *A bit rude!* She treated me like a leper—even before he died.'

'Give her time. She'll come round.'

'I suppose so.'

'Is there any chance of us nipping out to look at those armchairs tomorrow? Once we know what colours they come in, you can advise me on how to improve that front room.'

'I'd planned to give the place a thorough cleaning tomorrow. You'll think I'm very slovenly if I don't keep things nice.'

'Hell, we can get the contract cleaners in for that.'

'But I'm employed to cook and clean.'

'I think your duties are changing already. Don't you?' He raised one eyebrow at her, smiling when she flushed. 'It's much more important to me to get the place comfortable, and I don't see why we shouldn't enjoy ourselves, either. I've had months of not doing anything for fun, and that's a lot of time to make up for.' When she didn't say anything, he added gently, 'And I don't think you've been happy for a while, either.'

'As long as you think I'm earning my money.'

He patted his stomach and grinned. 'I most definitely do.' He got as far as the door, then turned to face her. 'Hey, let's go and buy a car tomorrow as well. I'll soon be able to drive again and I want to be prepared the minute they give me permission.'

'Just—go out and buy a car?'

'Sure. Why not? I've some money earmarked for it and I'm pretty sure of what sort I want.'

She smiled as she began to clear up the kitchen. He'd said he enjoyed doing things with her. Well, she enjoyed being with him. Too much. Then she frowned, remembering the morning's conversation with her father. Kit was only thirty-eight, six years younger than she was. She hadn't realized that. Perhaps suffering had made him look older. She'd assumed they were about the same age. Did it matter that she was older than him? It might. He had no children, was young enough to start a family, while her children were grown-up. She couldn't imagine life without Ryan and Deb. Surely he'd want children too?

So she'd better not get into this too deeply, for both their sakes. They would just have a fling and then go their own ways.

169

Why did that thought make her feel sad? She really had to get out of the marriage and permanency attitude. Things had changed since she was young.

The next morning they went round a couple of car show-rooms—no second-hand car for Kit. Laura watched in amazement as he looked at some quite expensive cars and eventually settled on a BMW with every extra you could imagine.

'You're very quiet,' he said as she drove him home again.

'I'm still getting my breath after watching you spend so much money without even blinking.'

'I'm not reckless with my money, but I've never had a brand-new car and I promised myself when I was having all those months of operations and therapy that I'd get one this time.' He stared into the distance. 'I think a car will be much more important to me now I've got this.' He slapped his leg.

'I didn't mean to criticize.'

'I know. And once it arrives, you can drive me around in it. We might as well enjoy the luxury.'

'Me? I wouldn't dare.'

'Of course you would. You're a very capable driver. Anyway, I'll put you on my insurance, so if there's any trouble, it won't matter.'

She shook her head. 'Craig hit the roof if there was the tiniest scratch on his car, and he wouldn't let me drive the last one.'

'Your ex-husband, Laura, sounds to have been a prize idiot.' He grinned. 'You'll note how carefully I'm tempering my language here.'

She couldn't help laughing. And agreeing with him. In some ways Craig had been an idiot. She now knew why he had been such a penny-pincher—to save money for his little diversions. Had been angry when she realized that. Found herself laughing again and wondering what words Kit would have used if he hadn't been treading carefully.

Suddenly she felt more carefree. Kit had that effect on her.

*　　*　　*

That afternoon, they went out and chose armchairs and a new sofa, which Kit cajoled the salesman into delivering the next day, since they had plenty in stock. He was very sure of what he wanted, comfort-wise, though he left the colours to Laura.

When they got home, there was a message on the answering service that the car was ready, and he insisted they take a taxi to the showroom and Laura drive him back. He was bubbling with enthusiasm, couldn't stop talking about the car, the new chairs, his plans for the house. He seemed to be changing before her eyes, becoming a different and much happier person than the tense man who'd hired her.

She'd always found him attractive, but he was dangerously so in this mood.

Twenty-One

Ryan let a few days go by without contacting Caitlin. He wanted to phone her, knew he ought to phone her, but didn't know what to say. His feelings for her were in a tangle. Hell, the whole situation was crazy. She was, after all, carrying his father's child.

Where did that leave him? He didn't know.

But he missed her! Thought about her. Worried about her. How stupid could you get, falling in love with your father's former mistress?

One evening he sat watching the seven o'clock news on TV, not making any sense of the pictures and voices, and suddenly the longing to see Caitlin was so intense he snatched up his car keys and left his flat before he could change his mind.

He couldn't find a parking spot nearby, so left his car round the corner and walked along towards her block of flats. He could see that her car was missing but rang the doorbell anyway, just in case she was there. When there was no answer, he went back to sit in his car and worry about her. She didn't sound like she had any friends in Melbourne, so where was she?

He couldn't bring himself to go home. Was that stupid or what? But her block of flats was on a cul-de-sac, so she'd have to pass him to get home, and he knew her car by now.

It was an hour before she turned up, driving past without noticing him. He'd recognize her anywhere, though, with that beautiful tumbled mass of hair. Getting out of the car, he walked along the street as another vehicle passed him. Someone pulled out of a parking space just as the second car got near the flats, and the driver pulled into it quickly. A big beefy man got out and ran across to Caitlin. Ryan hurried forward, worried that the guy might be intending to mug her, but it was quickly obvious that she knew him, so Ryan stopped in the shadows to listen. Perhaps this wasn't a good time to interrupt. Perhaps she'd met someone else.

Her voice rang out clearly, sharp with irritation. 'Barry, I'm *not* inviting you in. We agreed to go out for dinner, that was all.'

It was her cousin from Perth! How the hell had he found her?

The guy's voice was deep and calm. 'We need to talk, Caitlin, come to some agreement.' He reached out to grasp her arm.

'I've said all I intend to, and I don't want you pestering me any more. It upsets me and that's not good for the baby.'

Ryan heard her voice wobble on the last phrase and that was it. He strode across to her, seeing, even by the poor light of the security lamp in the car park, the utter relief on her face when she realized who it was. Her cousin let go of her arm and took a step backward, staring at the newcomer.

'Hi, Caitlin. The meeting ended sooner than expected, so I came over on the off-chance you'd be in.' Ryan put an arm round her shoulders and felt her tension, so pulled her closer as he turned to face the other guy.

'Who's this?' the cousin asked.

Ryan said only, 'A friend.'

'I'm Barry Sheedy, Caitlin's cousin. And you're. . . ?' He stuck out one hand and looked questioningly at the younger man.

Ryan didn't take the hand, didn't want to. 'Like I said, a friend.' He could imagine what her family would think about her seeing her dead lover's son, so didn't intend to reveal who he was.

'I prefer to know who I'm talking to,' Barry insisted.

'My name is my own business.'

173

'Well, whoever you are, my cousin Caitlin and I were having an important discussion about *family* matters, so I'm afraid it's not a good night for you to see her.'

His air of calm superiority irritated the hell out of Ryan, and he turned to look at Caitlin. Their eyes met and the look she gave him was desperate, pleading.

She turned to her cousin. 'I don't need you to speak for me or make decisions for me, Barry. I've already told you I consider our discussion finished, and I don't know why you followed me home. Come on up, Ryan. I'm tired and need to sit down.'

For a moment he thought Barry was going to punch him, then the other man breathed deeply, unclenched his fists and stepped backwards. 'I'll drop round tomorrow, then, Caitlin.'

'No, don't do that,' she said quickly. 'I'll be out all day.'

'We still need to talk.'

'*You* want to talk. I don't.'

'How can you let your parents worry about you like this? And how can it possibly be good for you to be on your own at such a time?'

'She isn't on her own,' Ryan said as mildly as he could. 'She has me.'

Barry looked at Caitlin. 'Does he know?'

Ryan wasn't going to be ignored like that. 'About the baby? Of course I do. You don't think Caitlin would conceal something like that from *me*, do you? After all, we're seeing one another.'

Barry looked from one to the other, his expression suddenly ugly.

'Let's go inside now.' Ryan tugged Caitlin towards the front door of the complex and stood behind her, keeping an eye on Barry as she unlocked it. He heard her fingers fumble, then a faint mutter of exasperation when she dropped the keys. But he let her pick them up herself, because he didn't trust her cousin, didn't like the guy's attitude at all.

When they were inside the hall, Caitlin quickly shut the

174

front door and groaned in relief. 'Let's go up the stairs. It'll be quicker than the lift. I want another lock between me and him.'

'I won't let him hurt you.'

'He doesn't attack people physically, but a verbal battering can be as bad when he's playing on your feelings of guilt.'

'You have nothing to feel guilty for.'

She didn't answer, but threw him a look that spoke her disagreement with this statement.

Once they were inside her flat, Ryan murmured, 'Don't switch the lights on yet!' and went to look out of the front window. Barry had gone back across the street to his car and was leaning against it, arms folded, watching the flats. 'He's still there. Hasn't even got into his car.'

She came to stand beside him. 'And if I know him, he won't go away till he sees you leave. He may even try to get in to see me after you've gone. What am I going to *do*?'

'We'll think of something. How the hell did he find you this time?'

'I don't know. He smiled when I asked that—he has such a knowing, superior smile, it makes me sick. It'll be something to do with computers. It always is. He boasts he can find out anything he wants to know on the Internet or by hacking into government web sites.'

Ryan felt her shiver and put his arm round her again. 'Great moral principles that shows!'

'Barry's morals have always been very flexible. My parents would never believe he could be like that, though. I think he stays in the sect because he can dominate people that way. He's a real control freak.' She sighed. 'I just wish he'd leave me alone.'

'Well, let's sit in the dark and make him wonder what's happening up here. He won't be able to control that.'

She was betrayed into a sound that echoed with both surprise and laughter. 'It won't make any difference. If he's decided to persuade me to go home, he won't go back to Perth until he's done just that.'

175

'Implacable, you said. Like a steamroller.'

'Yes.' She swung round to face him. 'Never mind him. You came back.'

'Good thing I did.'

'You don't—hate me then?'

'Of course I don't. I never did. It's just the circumstances that are—difficult.'

'Tell me about it.'

'Let's sit down. You sound tired.'

'I'm absolutely exhausted, and angry with myself, too. I was so surprised to hear his voice on the intercom that I let him in—well, he said he had a message from my parents. Then he wouldn't leave, so I said I was hungry, and he persuaded me to go out for a meal. I insisted on going in my own car, though. Only, I couldn't eat anything with him sitting opposite me. I know now what they mean by someone *devouring* you with their eyes.' She shivered. 'He talked and talked at me till my head ached, using that measured, I-know-better voice of his. I wanted to scream at him to shut up and go away, but it'd have done no good. He'd only have smiled and told me it was no use getting hysterical. He used my parents to make me feel guilty tonight. And I *do* feel guilty for running away, Ryan, but not guilty enough, or stupid enough, to go back to them.'

Suddenly she was weeping in his arms. 'If he found me so quickly this time, where can I hide next? I can't stay in Melbourne, obviously. He's over here for a week! I can't stay inside my flat for a whole week. And why should I have to?'

He held her gently, loving the way her soft hair tickled his cheek, then pushed her to arm's length and said firmly, 'Don't cry, Caitlin. Or, if you have to, wait until later. We need to work out how to get you away from him.'

She fumbled for a tissue and mopped her eyes. 'Sorry. I weep so easily at the moment.'

'You can weep as much as you like once we get you away. I'll even provide you with a free box of tissues. Expense is no object when I care about someone.' That

176

brought a smile to her face, at least, but he thought she was looking drawn and tired. 'Is there a back way out of these flats?'

'Yes. There's a rear door which leads to the rubbish bins, and there are double padlocked gates on the side street, for when the bins are emptied. All the tenants have keys to the padlock as well.'

He made up his mind to do it and to hell with complications. 'My flat is smaller than yours, but if you want to come and stay with me for the rest of the week, you're welcome.'

There was enough light from the street lamps for him to see the way her mouth fell open and her eyes widened in shock. 'I do have a spare bed, Caitlin. You won't need to share mine.'

'I could go to a hotel if you'd help me get away—'

'He'd be able to trace you to a hotel, but he won't have any idea where I live, because he doesn't know my name. Isn't it lucky I couldn't find a parking place and had to leave my car round the corner? He won't even see the number plate. How much time do you need to pack?'

'A few minutes. Thanks, Ryan.'

When they'd drawn the curtains, she put the lights on and turned efficient, packing her things rapidly and setting her laptop computer out ready to take with her.

Just before they left, he grinned at her and switched the living room light off, leaving only the bedroom light on. 'That should upset him and keep him watching the flat.'

She smiled as they took the lift downstairs and crept out of the back entrance. She was still smiling when they arrived at Ryan's flat.

He couldn't help kissing her.

And she kissed him right back.

They didn't sleep together, though. He didn't want to do that while she was still carrying the child. One day they would find a better way than this to be together, he hoped. Until then he'd continue to play the friend and avoid the lover role. Though it was going to be hard.

Twenty-Two

Angie's father got back from the hospital late that afternoon. 'Your mother can come out tomorrow morning, but we have to watch her carefully to make sure she takes the pills. You know how she hates taking tablets of any sort, and she's already claiming that these are making her dopey.'

'All right. I'll do my best. Though she never listens to me.'

'That's all either of us can do: our best.'

His expression was sad. She wondered if he still loved her mother, but didn't think it possible. How could you go on loving someone who made your life so uncomfortable? She caught sight of the clock. 'I've got our dinner ready, Dad. I can put yours to keep warm in the oven if you don't want to eat yet, but it'd be better if you had it now or it'll dry out. I've got to get off to work soon.'

'You shouldn't have bothered. I could have picked up some fish and chips.'

'Too fatty. You know you're watching your cholesterol.' She went to serve the food.

He dumped his coat in the hall cupboard and sat at the table with a weary sigh. 'Thanks, love. I'll have to clean our bedroom tonight. You know what she's like if the slightest thing is out of place.' He ate a few mouthfuls, then looked at her. 'I was wondering . . .'

When he didn't finish, she asked, 'Well? Wondering what?'

'Wondering if you could go and stay at your granddad's for a few days. Sue's embarrassed about what's happened, and the therapist says it'll be easier for her if she only has to worry about facing me at first.'

178

Angie put down her knife and fork. 'But Deb's staying there.'

'I know, love, but there are two beds and I'm sure Pop wouldn't mind, just for a few days, given the circumstances. I'll ring and ask him as soon as I've finished this, shall I?'

She opened her mouth to protest, then shut it again. She and her mother didn't get on, but she felt Pop had enough on his plate with Gran and Deb. Only, her dad wasn't having an easy time of it lately, either. 'I'll ring him.' She pushed her plate to one side. 'I'm not hungry.'

When she got back, her dad had pushed his plate aside as well, half the food uneaten. 'Pop says it's OK. Will you drop my things over there for me when you've finished? I still have to go to work.'

'I'll drop you at work and then take your things over. Thanks, love.'

She tried not to let her hurt show, but she did feel upset. This was the only home she had and now, it seemed, she wasn't welcome here.

When she finished work, Rick came to pick her up, as usual. She was exhausted after a busy night's work and wished she were going home to her own bedroom.

Her grandparents were in bed but Deb was waiting up for her.

'I'm sorry to crowd you,' Angie said, kicking her shoes off as soon as the front door was shut behind her and setting them on the stairs to take up later.

'It'll be crowded, but if you've nowhere else to go, that can't be helped.'

Angie looked at Deb. 'Something wrong?'

Deb shrugged. 'Mum and Kit.'

'Pardon?'

'I'm sure they've got something going.'

'I hope they do have. He seems really nice.'

'My father's only just died, for heaven's sake. How *can* she fall into bed with someone else so soon?'

'Your mum and dad hadn't been together in that way for a long time, from what I've heard, and *he's* the one who shacked up with someone else first—a girl young enough to be his daughter—*and* he put her up the duff. So, how can you possibly get upset about what your mother does?'

'Because Mum and Dad had been married for over twenty years. Doesn't she *care* that he's dead?'

Angie rolled her eyes and went to pick up her shoes. 'It's not worth arguing about. You've got your head in the sand about your precious father.'

Deb glared at her. 'Oh, and what about your precious mother? Nutty as a fruitcake, she is. *You've* no room to badmouth anyone else.'

'What is it with you, Deb Wells? Do you *like* causing trouble? You treat your mother like shit, then you turn on me. Well, let me tell you, I'm not impressed with that, and if you can't be nice to people, the sooner you go back to Australia, the better for us all.'

'Stop this at once, girls!'

They both swung round to see Pop standing at the foot of the stairs, wrapped in his checked woollen dressing gown, with the striped, faded pyjamas showing beneath it and his scraggy ankles looking vulnerable above his slippers.

He came over and put one arm round Angie, the other round Deb, guiding them into the front room. There he swung them round so that they were facing one another and said severely, in a tone of voice neither girl had heard from him before, 'I'm not having quarrelling and name-calling in my house.'

After a pause during which neither girl said a word, he went on, still speaking sharply, 'You started this, our Deb! And don't deny it, because I heard every word.'

She opened her mouth, then shut it again, shooting an angry glance at Angie.

'I'm ashamed to hear you complain about your mother like that,' he went on. 'Hasn't she a right to her own life? If you want to build a shrine to your father in your mind, that's up to you, but normal people get on with their lives when someone's died, however much they miss that person. One day I'll die, your Gran too, but I'd be sad beyond bearing if I thought you'd start quarrelling about us before we were cold in our graves. If I've learned one thing in my seventy-five years, it's to live and let live.'

The girls exchanged shamefaced glances.

'And how could you call our Sue names like that? No one gets ill on purpose, and it's hard enough on the family when they do.' He looked from one to the other and the tone of his voice changed. 'Eh, my dear lasses, haven't we enough trouble in this family without you adding to it?'

Angie could feel tears welling in her eyes. She hated to think of Pop being upset with her.

He stepped back. 'You're not to come to bed till you've made up your differences. And if I hear any more quarrelling between you two, I shall be sorely disappointed.'

He left them standing there and made his way up the stairs. And the very slowness of his movements, the way he set one foot on a step and brought the other up to join it, because he had a bad hip as well as angina, seemed to underline what he'd said more than mere words could ever have done.

When the bedroom door had closed, Angie turned back to her cousin. For a moment the two girls eyed one another, then she stretched out one hand. Deb took it but somehow didn't want to let go and wound up throwing her arms round her cousin and bursting into tears.

By the time they'd made cups of drinking chocolate and sat talking for a while, it was one o'clock.

Deb yawned. 'I can't stay awake any longer.'

'I hope we haven't kept Pop awake.'

'I've never seen him like that.'

Angie gave her a faint smile. 'I think his disappointment is worse than someone else's anger.'

Deb nodded. Her parents had quarrelled many a time, and both her mother and her father had shouted at her, but nothing had hit home like Pop's disappointment tonight. As she snuggled down in the narrow bed, she prayed that she wouldn't disappoint him again.

* * *

The phone rang at about nine o'clock and Kit took it in his new office. He limped through into the kitchen. 'It's your son, calling from Australia.'

Laura swung round, her expression anxious. 'He's all right?'

He smiled. 'Pick up the phone and ask him yourself.' He left her to it.

'Hello? Ryan?'

'Hi, Mum.'

'There's nothing wrong, is there?'

'No, of course not. I just wondered how everything was going. How's Gran? Has Deb settled in all right?'

They chatted for a while, then she put down the phone and stood staring at it. It was lovely to speak to him, but there seemed to be no reason for his call. And though he'd talked about his job, he hadn't said anything about making friends or taking up tennis again. In fact, it had just seemed like a call from an acquaintance keeping in touch.

He hadn't said anything about how he was coping with his father's death—or asked about her feelings, either.

She knew there was something wrong, she just knew it.

Twenty-Three

Deb went into town on the bus. She really had to get herself a set of wheels, though the public transport here was better than at home. She was at a loose end, not knowing what to do with herself. Angie had gone out to see a friend, the nurse had called round to see Gran and check her progress with Pop's help, so it had seemed better to get out of the house.

But she didn't want to go and see her mother and *that man*. Whatever Pop said, it was indecently soon for her mother to have another relationship, and you wouldn't convince Deb otherwise. Though she'd keep her mouth shut about it from now on, because she didn't want to upset Pop. And she shouldn't have had a go at Angie's mother. She'd been out of order there.

She saw a sign saying *Park and Rotunda*, so followed it. Maybe she could get a really good walk in. Exercise toned you up. Although it was a crisp morning and she was glad of the warmer coat she'd bought, the weak sunlight was bright enough to lift her spirits.

An hour later she found the wishing well and stopped to peer into it. People had thrown coins in. A thing like this couldn't really make your wishes come true, of course, but the coins went to a good cause and she took a fancy to make a wish, smiling at her own stupidity. As if!

She tossed in a pound coin, closed her eyes and wished hard. Then, feeling a bit foolish, she decided to have a good strong coffee, and went back to the Rotunda Café. She felt hungry, too, though she shouldn't be, because she'd eaten a good breakfast, a whole slice of toast and then an apple.

Still, she remembered that merciless mirror in the hall and went to look at the display cabinet, choosing a slice of carrot cake, because it looked to have the least fat and calories.

Only as she was turning back did she notice Alex sitting in a corner watching her. She hesitated, then raised one hand in greeting, wondering if she should go over to say hi. He beckoned, so she did. They'd probably quarrel again, but it'd be nice to have someone to speak to, especially someone who wasn't family. 'Hi.'

'Hi, yourself. If you're not meeting someone, why don't you come and join me? It's not much fun talking to yourself.'

'All right.' She sat down, feeling unaccountably shy. When the waitress brought her cake, he looked at it approvingly but didn't comment, thank goodness, because, after all, it wasn't his business how thin or fat she was, and so she'd have told him. 'So, what are you doing with yourself, Alex?'

'Looking at flats. Only, everything I've seen so far has been about two feet square, with sagging furniture. Not to worry. I'll find something. I've got a car now, so it'll be a lot easier.'

'I'm thinking of buying a car—only, I still don't know how long I'll be staying. Maybe I should rent one, just a cheapie. It's a drag having to use public transport all the time.'

He watched her eat the piece of cake, and his voice was gentle, not aggro, as he said, 'It's nice to see you eating properly. Don't be like my sister. She nearly killed herself, looked like a walking skeleton.'

'That must have been hard for the rest of the family.'

'Yeah. Very.'

She stared down at the crumbs on her plate, picking them up with her fingertip one by one and licking them off it carefully. 'I'm trying to get my head round it all, which size I want to be, I mean. My dad always said I looked great, but here everyone says I'm too thin.'

'Maybe he liked scrawny women.'

'He was always going on at Mum about being too fat.'

'She didn't look fat to me.'

'She's a size fourteen, which is bigger than I ever intend to be.'

He didn't comment on that, and the silence went on for such a long time that she wondered whether she should get up and go—but go where?

'Would you like to come for a ride in my new car? I need to take it out for a spin, and thought I'd go up on the moors. It'll be cold, though. Do you want to go back and get something warmer to wear?'

'I've only got this.'

'Well, we don't have to get out of the car.' He grinned. 'Unless it breaks down. You pays your money and you takes your chance on that.'

'I'll risk it.' She smiled and they walked out of the park together at a brisk pace.

'It's good that you walk fast. I hate it when girls dawdle along. My legs aren't made for small steps.'

'I enjoy exercise.'

He didn't say much as he drove, so she didn't either. It was kind of nice sitting in silence and looking out at miles of rolling countryside. He pulled into a lay-by on the tops and they got out, leaning on the car and staring down at the patchwork landscape and doll-sized houses below.

'I like Lancashire, but I want to go back to Australia when I settle down,' he said after a while. 'What do you want to do after this trip?'

And she couldn't answer, couldn't think of a single thing she wanted to do. She looked at him in near panic. 'I don't know.'

'You're lost, aren't you?'

She nodded.

He held out his arms. 'Well, a good hug never goes amiss.'

She walked into them and stayed there for ages. It felt good. When he stirred, she felt shy. When he lifted her chin and kissed her, she felt as if the world had turned dreamy around them. He didn't spoil it with talk, just gave her another hug, then drove her home.

'You really do need to start making plans,' he said as he pulled up. 'Everyone should have a goal in life.'

185

She waited for him to ask her out, but he didn't. So, what had the kiss been about, then?

It didn't matter how carefully she watched her weight, how well she dressed—she still couldn't pull the guys, she thought as she watched him drive away, hoping the smile she'd pasted on her face looked genuine.

The doorbell rang just as Laura was finishing putting the top crust on an apple pie. She grabbed a tea towel and hurried to answer it, wiping flour off her hands and hoping whoever it was hadn't woken Kit up. He'd walked round the shopping centre with her that morning, still with a limp which she knew he tried hard to minimize, but at least managing without the crutches he hated so much.

When they got back, he'd admitted, with one of those wry smiles, that he needed a lie down, since when there'd been absolute silence from his room.

She opened the door to see two men and a woman, the woman and one of the men very tanned, the other man pale, as if he didn't go outdoors much, and with very chill grey eyes. They didn't look as if they were there to sell religion, Laura thought as she waited for them to state their business.

It was the woman who spoke. 'Does Kit live here? Kit Mallinder?'

'Yes.'

There was the sound of a door opening behind her and she turned to see him standing in the doorway of his bedroom, balancing on the crutches.

The woman pushed past Laura and ran to throw her arms round Kit, nearly knocking him off balance.

Laura dived across to support him and shoved the newcomer out of the way. 'Don't you know better than to knock people around when they're on crutches?'

The woman threw back her head and laughed, ignoring her as she said to Kit, 'Don't tell me. She's your nurse.'

His face was expressionless. 'Laura's my housekeeper, and if you can't speak about her and *to* her politely, you can leave, Jules.'

186

She pulled a face at him, tossing a casual 'Sorry!' at Laura.

One of the men came across. 'You always were good at putting your foot in it, you fool.' He hauled Jules aside and held out his hand to Kit. 'You're looking a hell of a lot better than when I visited you in hospital.'

Kit shook the hand, his expression softening into a smile. 'I see you've been sunbathing again, Andy, but you're still as ugly as ever.' He turned to the other guy. 'Well, Shaun, still working in management, I see. What on earth's dragged *you* out of London?'

Shaun shrugged. 'A meeting.'

'We bumped into him in Manchester, so hauled him along,' the woman said. 'After all, you used to be one of his top correspondents.'

'It's great to see you all.'

Laura, watching with interest, decided that Kit wasn't as close to the pale guy as to the two others.

He turned to her. 'These ruffians are Jules, Andy and Shaun, former colleagues of mine. They don't deserve it, but could we find them a cup of coffee and maybe a piece of your wonderful cake?'

'Certainly.' As she slipped into the kitchen, she heard Kit shepherding the visitors into the lounge, then clicked her tongue in annoyance at herself for feeling left out. It was no business of hers who came to visit him. She was just the hired help around here and she'd do better to remember that. Not that Kit had ever made her feel like a servant. But still, that's what she was.

After putting some coffee on to percolate, she set a tray with one of the hand-embroidered mats she'd found in the linen cupboard and got out the good crockery. It was like old times, when she'd entertained people from Craig's work and made things as stylish as she could. As she worked, her thoughts were still on the visitors. What did they want with Kit? This was such an out-of-the-way place that they couldn't just have been passing through.

And why would someone who clearly wasn't a close friend tag along?

When the coffee was ready she carried the tray through into the hall, set it down on the table there and knocked on the door of the living room.

Kit called, 'Come in!' and she carried the things in, not looking directly at anyone. 'I'll just fetch the coffee.'

When she'd brought the coffee pot, she asked in a deliberately neutral voice, 'Shall I pour?'

Jules leaned forward. 'Oh, I think we can manage that for ourselves.'

'Thanks, Laura.' Kit smiled at her.

She felt bereft as she walked back to the kitchen and mechanically set about finishing the apple pie. *You're so stupid!* she told herself. When she looked at the clock, she realized it was time to be starting dinner. Only, how many would she be catering for?

She worked on some general preparations and checked her emergency stocks, just in case they stayed, working to an accompaniment of voices, shouts of laughter, arguments at times. She couldn't hear what they were saying but she could hear the tone of voice. For the first time, she heard Kit roar with laughter, and later she heard him speaking loudly and emphatically. It was like listening to a man coming alive after a long sleep. This was his milieu.

It wasn't hers.

There was a knock on the kitchen door and the suntanned guy poked his head inside. 'Kit says I have to smoke outside the house. Can you point me in the right direction, please?'

'This way.' She opened the back door. 'There's a bench there, and I'll bring you out an ashtray.'

'Kit never did like smoking, and says the whole of this house is a smoke-free zone.' The guy pulled a face. 'I'm Andy, by the way. How long have you been working for Kit?'

'A few weeks.'

'He says you're a brilliant cook.'

'I'm not bad. He's a brilliant eater. Loves anything.' Then she realized that Andy was pumping her for information, and wondered why. 'You're journalists as well?'

'For our sins.'

'Where did you get the tan?'

He grimaced. 'Middle East. Things are getting worse not better out there. I got shot, just a flesh wound, but they pulled me back home for a while to recover.'

He seemed in a mood to chat, but she had work to do. 'I'm afraid I must get back to the cooking now. I've an apple pie ready to take out of the oven.'

There was the sound of the kitchen door and Kit came in. 'We'll go and get a meal out tonight, Laura, so there's no need for you to cook anything for me.'

She looked at his face, knowing how tired he had been after their outing, seeing weariness and pain under the excitement. 'I could easily provide a meal for you all if you don't mind something simple.'

'I don't want to trouble you. That's above and beyond the call of duty.'

'I told you at my interview: I can always put a dinner together.' She turned to see Andy standing just outside the door, smoking cigarette in hand, shamelessly eavesdropping.

Kit hesitated.

'I'm happy to do it.'

'As long as you eat with us, Laura.'

She shook her head. 'No, Kit. Not this time. I'd be in the way. You all know one another.'

He grimaced. 'I feel awful, leaving you to do the extra work, then eat on your own.'

'It's a chance to show you what I can do.'

'Thanks. Um—is there any wine chilled?'

'Yes. I'll open a red and white and bring them through. Do you want beer as well?'

'No, just wine. You're a marvel.'

As he went out, she turned to see Andy studying them. He gave her a mocking salute with one raised hand and wandered off again. No doubt curious about their relationship. Well, she was, too. Did she and Kit really have the possibility of a relationship? She was not only older than

189

him, but, as today had shown, not part of his world. Look at how confident that Jules was! No, Laura decided, she'd been fooling herself to build up her hopes. Must stop that. Definitely.

She served them minestrone soup to start off with. Not her best minestrone, but her emergency one. It wasn't bad, if she said so herself.

After that came steak, whipped out of the freezer, sliced very thinly and made into a boeuf bourguignon, accompanied by boiled potato slices in parsley butter, and every last vegetable in the place. The apple pie with ice cream provided a dessert.

After each course the two male visitors carried the dishes out to the kitchen, but the woman didn't lift a finger.

I don't like her, Laura thought. I definitely don't. She's got her eye on Kit.

As for the men, they were pleasant enough to her. The pale one, Shaun, was quieter and older, but very complimentary about the way she'd provided a meal at such short notice.

'Why don't you join us now?' he asked.

She shook her head. 'I'd stop the conversation flowing. But I wonder—could you please not press Kit to drink too much. He's still quite unsteady, and if he has a fall, it could put him back on crutches again full-time. He's off them for some time each day now and that means a lot to him.'

'I'll keep my eye on him.'

As she was finishing her own meal, Kit came into the kitchen. She could see how happy he was, his eyes fairly sparkling with life, in spite of the tiredness.

'Is there any chance we can put them up for the night? They're all used to sleeping rough, but have we enough blankets for the Lancashire autumn?'

'We do, as long as they don't mind the smell of moth-balls. I'll make up some beds afterwards.'

'No. Just put out the bedding and let them make up their own beds.'

'It won't take me a minute.'

'No, Laura. You've done enough. And I'm grateful.'

'It's nice to see you enjoying yourself.'

'I enjoy myself with you, too.'

It was very kind of him to say so, she thought, but she had never brought that vividly alive look to his face.

She might have been living in a fool's paradise, but she wasn't going to let herself stay there.

When Andy began yawning, Kit glanced at the clock, astonished to see that it was well past midnight. 'Why don't you go up to bed? There are three bedrooms, doesn't matter which you take, except, not the front one on the right, which is Laura's. You'll have to make up the beds yourselves, though. I told Laura just to put out the bedding.'

Andy nodded and ambled off.

Jules exchanged glances with Shaun and followed him.

Kit had been going to seek his own bed, but clearly Shaun wanted to speak to him. 'Say it quickly and I'll refuse your offer, then we can both go to bed.'

'What do you mean, refuse?'

'I don't want a job. I'm not an office wallah and I never will be.'

Shaun stared at him, then shrugged slightly. 'Pity. It can be interesting in its own way, and it pays well.'

Kit shrugged. 'I've enough money for my needs. And I'm enjoying my freedom.' He yawned and rubbed his aching leg.

Shaun watched him. 'All right if I stay another day? There's something else I need to discuss, but it's a bit late now and I'm not thinking clearly enough.'

'Sure. I've always got room for old friends.' But he wasn't sure how much of a friend Shaun was. The other man had always been fairly reserved, and if Kit wasn't mistaken, he'd fancied Jules. But he'd always dealt fairly with Kit and had given him some interesting assignments.

But no way was Kit taking an office job, or trying to turn back the clock. He'd retired from globe-hopping, both mentally and physically, and that was that.

191

Twenty-Four

Ryan woke in the night to hear Caitlin moving around. He lay for a moment, but the light in the living area stayed on, so it obviously wasn't just a visit to the bathroom. He got up, grabbed his towelling beach robe and went out to join her, yawning as he belted it up.

She was sitting on the sofa, staring into space and looking worried. She didn't notice him come in, and jumped visibly when she saw him. 'Sorry, Ryan. I didn't mean to wake you.'

'Can't you sleep?'

She hesitated, then said, 'It's more than that. I'm spotting blood and having the occasional cramp. I don't know whether to go to the hospital or not.'

Immediately he came fully awake. 'How do you feel?'

'Not well. Just generally—lousy. I have done for a couple of days. And I've a grumbling pain in my stomach.' She looked at him with tears in her eyes. 'I don't want to lose the baby.'

He went across and gathered her into his arms, cuddling her close. When he felt a tear plop on to his bare neck, he pulled her even closer. 'Shh, now. You've got to stay calm. I'll sling some clothes on, then I'll be with you.'

'I can get a taxi.'

'You bloody well can't! If you think I'm letting you go on your own, you can think again.' He held her at arm's length for a minute and they looked at each other with great solemnity, as if their bodies were saying things their mouths didn't dare to yet.

Then she sagged back against the couch. 'Thank you.'

He kissed her forehead, which was the only part of her face not wet with tears, then brushed her hair back and kissed her damp cheek for good measure. 'Two minutes and I'm at your service.'

'I'd better get dressed too.'

'Don't. You'll only have to get undressed again. And it's not as if it's a cold night.'

As they drove to the hospital, she gasped and bent forward.

'Pain?'

'Mmm.'

He couldn't help her, so concentrated on driving carefully through the warm spring night, pulling into the emergency area with a feeling of great relief. Quickly he explained what was happening and the porter took Caitlin away in a wheelchair, telling him to park over to the left and then report to reception.

Grudging every second it took, Ryan did so, then ran back into the hospital. 'Caitlin Sheedy. I just brought her in.'

The receptionist looked at a list. 'Please take a seat. Miss Sheedy is being examined at the moment.'

He wanted to be with her, but he had no right.

And he didn't want her to lose the baby.

A nurse came through the transparent plastic doors and spoke to the woman on reception, who beckoned to Ryan.

'Miss Sheedy wants to see you, Mr Wells.'

He followed her along a corridor and into a cubicle-like room divided from others by nothing more than green curtains. She pulled the front curtain aside and he saw Caitlin lying on a high, narrow bed, her face white, her hair darkened by sweat. One arm was thrown across her eyes and she didn't lift it when she heard them come in.

'Mr Wells is here,' the nurse said. 'I'll leave you for a minute or two.' She turned to Ryan and added in an undertone, 'Fetch me at once if it gets worse. I'm just down the corridor at the nursing station.'

He hesitated at the foot of the bed, not sure what to do. 'Um—how are you feeling, Caitlin?'

She lowered her arm, her eyes searching his face anxiously, then glanced beyond him, as if to make sure they were alone, and beckoned him forward. Her voice was a mere thread of sound. 'I told them—you were the father. I didn't want—to be alone.' Tears welled in her eyes. 'Please don't leave me alone, Ryan.'

He moved forward and took hold of her hand. 'Of course I won't. Do you want me to contact anyone? Your family?'

She shook her head. 'No. They'll send Barry to see me and he'll say it's the Lord's will and all for the best. I can't face him. Or that.'

'Then I'll stay. Willingly, I promise you.'

'Thank you.' She closed her eyes as if the lids were too heavy to hold open, and let out a long, trailing sigh. 'You're so kind.'

When she grimaced, he watched her anxiously. She gasped and drew her knees up. 'It's starting again.'

'I'll fetch the nurse.'

'You'll come back with her? Please.'

'Of course.'

'Promise.'

'If they'll let me.'

But the nurse examined Caitlin quickly and expertly, then shepherded Ryan out.

'I want to be with her,' he protested. 'I'm the father.' But in vain.

'Not now, Mr Wells. We'll take her somewhere more private and call you as soon as we're sure what's happening.'

But he could hear Caitlin sobbing as he walked away. He took a seat in the waiting room, the one nearest to where she was. This was a nightmare. That poor girl had no one— except him.

He gave a wry smile. He had no one in Melbourne, either—except her.

And anyway, this night had shown him one thing: he loved her deeply and surely. As his father hadn't, he was quite certain. His father seemed only to love his children in that way.

194

But did she love him? Could they be happy together after all that had happened? He'd be willing to give it a try. Would she?

Which inevitably led him to wonder what his mother would say if he wanted to marry Caitlin. He paused on that thought. *Marry?* Then he smiled. Yes, of course. He felt so right with her, just like all the romantic clichés he'd once laughed at. But his mother would chuck a fit, he was sure, and you couldn't blame her.

When he'd phoned his mother the other night, he'd planned to tell her he was seeing Caitlin, but something had prevented him. He didn't want to hurt her as his father had done, but when you loved someone as he loved Caitlin, you had to put them first. Why hadn't he let himself admit the depth of his feelings before now?

Because of his father, always because of *him*. Craig Wells might be dead but he was still affecting everyone.

It seemed a long time until the nurse came back for him.

'I'm sorry, Mr Wells, but she's lost the baby. We'll keep her in overnight and let her come home in the morning.' She looked at him severely. 'Your partner will need looking after carefully for a while. No heavy lifting. Lots of cosseting. And she'll be very emotional. It plays havoc with the hormones.'

'I'll look after her properly, I promise. Can I see her for a minute?'

'She's drowsy now. You can have a peep at her, but it'd be better if she got some sleep now. Really, you'd be better going home to bed, then coming back for her in the morning.'

He hesitated, then shook his head. 'I'll stay, I think. One of her cousins is in Melbourne and has been upsetting her. I don't want him getting near her in that condition.' It might have been his imagination, but the nurse seemed to look at him a little more warmly when he said that.

She took him to see Caitlin, who opened her eyes and gave him a tired smile, then drifted off into sleep again.

The night seemed very long and the chairs designed for

discomfort, so he couldn't do more than occasionally doze off, but he was grateful for that when he saw Barry walk into the hospital just as it was getting light. How the *hell* had the fellow known she was here? Ryan stood up, grimly determined to keep him away from Caitlin.

Barry's confident smile when he saw Ryan only reinforced that decision.

Ryan arrived at the reception desk in time to hear Barry ask for Caitlin. He moved forward. 'She doesn't want to see you.'

The other man barely spared him a glance, continuing to speak to the receptionist. 'I'm her cousin, her closest relative in Melbourne. She'll need my help when she comes out of hospital.'

The nurse who'd been attending Caitlin during the night was behind the desk, where she'd been talking to the woman on duty. She pointed to Ryan and said to her colleague, 'Actually, this man is the father, and Ms Sheedy said she didn't want to see anyone but him.'

Barry breathed in audibly and seemed to swell up like a bullfrog, glaring at Ryan, then turning back to the two women. 'He's *not* the father. The father of that baby is dead.'

The nurse smiled. 'I'd think *she* would know better than you who the father is.' Someone called and she waved one hand, mouthing, 'Coming.' Turning to the receptionist, she said loudly, 'I've put Ms Sheedy's request on her notes: no visitors except Ryan Wells. I have to go now or I'll miss my lift. See you tomorrow.' She walked off.

The receptionist gave Barry a cool professional smile. 'If you'll take a seat, sir, I'll just check what Ms Sheedy's wishes are.'

'I'll wait right here.' Barry folded his arms.

Ryan moved to one side. His body had been screaming for sleep a few moments ago, but now he felt wide awake and alert. The receptionist came back and he heard her tell Barry that Ms Sheedy didn't want to see anyone but her partner.

Barry spoke calmly, but there was fury behind his words. 'Has she lost the baby?'

Ryan moved forward again. 'Yes. And she's in a very fragile state, so leave her alone.'

He spun round. 'I'm glad she's lost the child, though if the Lord had given me that burden, I'd have adopted it, but now Caitlin and I can start from scratch.' He raked his eyes up and down Ryan scornfully. 'Wells! You even look like *him*. You surely don't think she cares about you for yourself? And once she recovers, she'll marry me as her parents want.'

'I don't think *she* wants to, though, and that's surely the most important thing where a marriage is concerned.'

'We'll see about that. I'll have no trouble finding out where you live, now that I know your name, and I'll be round to see Caitlin without all these interfering busybodies. She needs protecting from you and your family, and I intend to do just that.'

Ryan watched him walk away. Not a word spoken angrily, but he could understand why Caitlin feared this man. He didn't suppose Barry was certifiable, but Ryan was quite sure he was obsessed where his cousin was concerned.

How the hell was he going to protect her? He had to go to work every day, and soon he'd have to go to England to say goodbye to his grandmother.

It was ten o'clock before they let Caitlin leave hospital. She was pale and looked sad, but her expression brightened when she saw Ryan appear at the door of her room.

'We have to wait for the nurse to bring the final papers, then we can leave. I shall feel a real fool going home in my nightclothes.'

'I need to tell you something: Barry turned up early this morning at the hospital, trying to tell them he was your only relative and would be taking you home.' Ryan wouldn't have believed she could go any paler, but she did. 'Luckily, the nurse had put in your notes that you didn't want to see anyone except me.'

'Does he know who you are?'

'Yes. Unfortunately the receptionist gave away my name.'

'He'll find me, then.' She shook her head blindly, her hands clenched into fists. 'What am I going to *do*?'

'I'll book us into a hotel under false names.'

'They ask to see identification these days.'

He stared at her, wondering how to protect her from that weirdo. 'The trouble is, I can't stay off work too long. I'll ring and tell them my partner has arrived from Western Australia and had a miscarriage, so they'll give me a day or two. But they'll still expect me to go back as soon as I can.'

'Maybe I'll fly out to Bali or somewhere to recover.'

'What if he followed you there? You'd be in an even worse situation in a foreign country with no one to turn to.'

She sighed and shook her head. 'I can't believe this is happening. I thought, when I went to live with your father, that'd be the end of it with Barry. Then when I came to Melbourne, I thought that would show him I meant what I said. But it didn't. Will *nothing* make him leave me alone?'

Twenty-Five

The following morning, Laura got up before it was fully light and tiptoed down the stairs, determined to have the house in order before the guests came down. As she was passing Kit's room, however, she heard voices and couldn't help stopping for a moment—long enough to realize it was Jules who was in there.

Furious, she went into the kitchen, finding the coffee percolator already warm. She got herself a cup of tea, but didn't indulge in her usual morning ritual of gazing out into the garden and watching the birds as she sipped it. She was too angry. Kit had just made use of her because she was handy. The minute his old girlfriend turned up, they'd got together again.

It was Craig all over again, hopping into bed with any woman who tempted him.

Well, she wasn't going to act like a stupid doormat for a second time. Definitely not!

A few minutes later, she turned round and jumped in shock as she saw Jules standing in the doorway.

'Kit would like another cup of coffee. Shall I—?'

'I'll pour it for you.' Laura could hear how stiff her voice was, but there was no law that said you had to be warm and friendly to the woman who'd been sleeping with the man you fancied.

Jules gave her a slow smile, as if she understood exactly how she was feeling. 'We've known each other a long time, Kit and I.'

'Have you? That's nice.'

'I've seen the way you look at him. Don't waste your

199

time. He's not the settling-down type and you obviously are.'

Laura managed a questioning look, as if she didn't understand the implications.

Jules laughed. 'Don't say you haven't been warned.'

Laura maintained the smile until Jules walked out, then closed her eyes tightly to hold in the tears she wanted to shed.

She wasn't taking out part shares in a man again!

Jules went to sit on the end of Kit's bed as he drank his second cup of coffee. 'Has Shaun spoken to you yet?'

'About what?'

'A job.'

'He skirted around it, but I told him flat: I don't like office work and I'm not coming back to live in London.'

'What are you doing now but office work?'

'I may not be very active, but I'm living to my own timetable, doing what I want when I want. That's quite different from following someone else's rules.' He stared at her, eyes narrowed. 'What's all this about? Why does it matter to you what I do?'

She put one hand on his thigh. 'Because we had something good going between us, you and I. Could have again if you lived in London.' She began to stroke the hand up and down his thigh.

He removed her hand from his leg. 'I'm not interested, either in Shaun's offer or yours.'

'You *can't* be involved with that mouse of a woman!'

'Can't I? I'm sure you know best.'

'But we're still friends, surely, you and I? You can't ignore the past.'

'Friends as long as you don't try to push it any further.'

For a minute, she stared at him, as if trying to read his mind, make sure he meant what he had said. 'OK. Have it your own way. You usually do.'

Her voice had a sharp edge to it now that she wasn't using her coaxing tone. He smiled. He wasn't falling into her net again. She was a devil to live with, unlike Laura.

'Is it OK if I stay on for a day or two and go back to

London with Shaun? Andy's driving up to Edinburgh to see his aunt.'

He hesitated, not wanting her to stay, sure she had some hidden agenda.

'Oh, come on, Kit. For old times' sake. You can't say you don't have room for us, and it's great to get a few of us together for a while. I do think you might listen to what Shaun can offer you.'

He'd already told Shaun he could stay a little longer, and now wished he hadn't. If Jules was going back with him, he could hardly turn her out. 'OK. You can stay. But don't get up your hopes. Whatever was between us is dead.' He gave her a long, hard look.

She held up her hands in mock surrender. 'OK. OK. Whatever you say. I must have misread your signals last night.'

'I was just enjoying the company—the company of you *all*, not to mention the gossip and news.' He only hoped Laura would understand that—and she damned well wasn't staying in the kitchen tonight, either, like a drudge.

He wanted her with him. Jules's visit had made him realize that. Laura wasn't a two-faced schemer. She was the person with whom he wanted to spend the rest of his life. This visit had only emphasized that.

He grinned. He was famous for making rapid decisions. He hoped it wouldn't take Laura too long to admit how good they were together.

Shaun wandered into Kit's office, where he was fiddling with papers, unable to settle. 'Got time for a chat?'

'Sure. But if you're going to try to persuade me to take that job . . .'

'No. It's something else that needs clearing up.' Shaun hesitated. 'Look, surely you must have remembered what happened before the accident?'

'No. It's a complete blank. Probably it always will be, or so the doctors tell me.'

'Hmm.'

Kit leaned back in his chair. 'What's all this in aid of?'

Shaun perched on the edge of the table. 'I didn't say anything before, because you weren't well, and even when you were in rehab, your brother said you shouldn't be upset.'

'Oh, did he?'

'The thing is—I'm the one who sent you to Bangkok, and I do know something about the project you were on. I had a few leads, we discussed it and you got interested.'

'Oh?'

'Surely you remember?'

'Sorry, I don't. Not a thing. Why did you wait so long to talk to me? The real reason.'

Shaun shrugged. 'The people you were researching had been warned. I wanted to give them time to cool off—and you time to recover.' His gaze held sympathy. 'That was a rough deal, being mugged like that. But now, well, I thought you might like to finish off what you started.'

Kit shrugged. Once this conversation would have fired his blood, sent him off investigating again; now he didn't have the faintest desire to pick up the dropped threads. 'I've retired from that sort of thing. Permanently.'

'I don't believe it. Not you.'

'Doesn't matter what you believe. My life, my decision.'

'You *can't* just drop everything. You're one of the best investigative reporters in the business. We need people like you.'

Kit smiled. 'That's over. It was time, even if this hadn't happened.' He looked down at his leg, 'I really have quit, Shaun.'

'That's only a limp. Won't even slow you down much. Give you another couple of months and you'll be raring to go off on an assignment again.'

'I won't. And if that's what you wanted to stay on for, to persuade me to work for you again, I suggest you reconsider and leave today. I'm not even faintly tempted to turn the clock back. I've got a new life now.'

When Shaun had gone, Kit stared thoughtfully into the distance. He hadn't been even remotely tempted. He smiled. Not only had he changed, but he'd found Laura. That made all the difference to his life and happiness.

Twenty-Six

That afternoon, as her cousin was getting ready to go to work, Deb went into the bedroom and flung herself down on her bed. 'I'm getting cabin fever here.'

'Why don't you go and see your mother, then?'

'Why don't *you* go and see yours?'

Angie glared at her. 'You know why. She doesn't want to see me, doesn't want anyone except Dad at the moment. But *your* mother's great and she'd love it if you went over to see her.'

'How do you know? I might be interrupting something.'

Angie rolled her eyes. 'Honestly, you're paranoid about her. What if she is shacking up with Kit—though I don't think she is, personally—why would that matter?'

'I'm not in the mood to see her tonight. All right?' Deb started to get up.

'Just a minute.' Angie closed the door and went to sit on her bed, three feet away from Deb's. 'I'm a bit worried about Pop. He doesn't look well.'

'He's not looked well ever since I got here. Did he look better before?'

'Yes. Much better. But during the past month or two his skin's gone sort of yellowish-white, as if he's exhausted all the time. The social services people would take Gran in for a couple of weeks to give him a respite, and I've tried to persuade him to do that, only he won't, says it'd upset Gran.'

Both girls stared down at their feet.

'I'd hate anything to happen to him,' Deb said at last.

'Me too. He's the best.'

'Isn't he just!'

203

After Angie had left for work, Deb went down to see if she could help Pop with the tea.

He gave her one of his wide smiles. 'There's not much to do, love. Your mum's cooked a few casseroles, and I pulled one out of the freezer this morning. She's been a big help to me with the cooking. It was mostly chops or sausages before she came, or those frozen meals. I never was much of a cook. Pat did all that.'

'Well, I'll get the meal ready tonight. You go and watch TV with Gran. I'll call you when it's ready.'

She hummed as she worked. She wasn't in her mother's league as a cook, but she did enjoy making meals for people—sometimes. It'd be awful to go out to work all day and then come home at night and have to cook for a family, not to mention doing the washing and all that stuff. But every now and then it was nice to cook. 'It's ready, Pop!'

There was no answer from the front room, so she called again, more loudly this time. 'Pop, the food's ready!'

Still no reply, no movement, nothing. They must have the television on loud, only, if so, why couldn't she hear it? She went into the front room and saw Pop asleep on the sofa with Gran sitting holding his hand beside him, staring in the direction of the television. Deb hesitated for a minute, but the food was going cold, so she went to shake his shoulder. 'Pop! Wake up.'

He fell slowly sideways, to lie with his head in the angle of the sofa back and arm, his mouth slightly open, his eyes staring at nothing. He didn't move, not a fingertip.

She guessed then what had happened and put up one hand to stifle a scream. She mustn't panic or it'd upset Gran. Perhaps he'd just had a stroke or something. She tried to remember the first-aid course she'd done at school, but it was all hazy, so she felt on his neck for a pulse—only, there was nothing. His skin was still warm, all wrinkled and leathery beneath her trembling fingertips, but he didn't even twitch.

On the mantelpiece there was a crinolined lady ornament standing on a mirror mat, so she got the mat and held it in front of his mouth, because she'd seen someone do that on TV. She bent over to watch, praying there'd be some sign. But there wasn't even the slightest misting of breath on the mirror.

Panic pulsed through her, but somehow she held it in check. When she heard a noise, she saw Gran trying to peer round her at the television, showing no sign of understanding what had happened to Pop. Moving carefully, Deb edged backwards and out into the hall, leaving Gran sitting there.

Reaction hit her suddenly and she sagged against the wall, pressing her hands to her mouth, moaning under her breath. *He was dead! Pop was dead!*

She didn't know how long she stood there in a sort of paralysis till she realized she had to call somebody. She went into the kitchen and took the phone off the wall with a hand that felt as if it belonged to someone else. What was her mother's number? Where had she put it? Then she saw the bit of paper tucked into the edge of the little noticeboard. *Laura*, it said, with a phone number.

Praying that it was her mother's place, she dialled. It rang twice—three times . . . *Please pick it up, someone pick it up*, she prayed. And at the sixth ring someone did.

'Hello?'

It was Kit. Deb found herself sobbing as she tried to tell him what had happened.

'Calm down, love. I can't understand you.'

She took a deep breath. 'It's Deb. Is my mother there?'

'Yes. I'll fetch her.'

'Please. But, Mr Mallinder, can you stay nearby, please? I think Pop's just died. She'll be upset.' Tears were rolling down Deb's own cheeks and pouring out of her eyes. The pain of what had happened was cramping her breathing. When she heard her mother's voice on the phone, she gulped, and all that came out was another sob.

'Calm down and tell me what's wrong, Deb darling.'

'I think Pop's just died. I don't know what to do. Can you come over?'

There was dead silence, then, 'I'm on my way. See if you can find his doctor's number. And if they don't have someone on night call, dial nine-nine-nine and ask for an ambulance.'

The phone buzzed in Deb's ear and she stood holding it for a minute, still finding it hard to think or act. Then she put it down and fumbled in the drawer for Pop's phone book. *Doctor*, it said. She dialled the number, listened to the answering service and scribbled down the number of the night service and called them. It seemed to be taking for ever to get help.

The woman at the other end was very kind when she started crying again, and promised to get a doctor out straight away.

Laura put down the phone and turned towards Kit. 'She says—' She couldn't get the words out, the dreadful words, and began weeping. Her daughter needed her, but the shock of this news was so terrible . . .

He dropped his crutches and came to take her into his arms. 'She told me.'

Laura leaned against him and let the tears flow, feeling the strength of his arms holding her, the comforting warmth of his body. After a minute or two she managed to pull back a little, but it felt as if the whole world had changed, grown darker, more frightening.

She had to force words out. 'I have to—go over there. Will you come with me? Please?'

'Try to stop me.'

Jules appeared in the sitting room doorway and stopped dead. 'Something wrong?'

'We think Laura's father has just died.'

'Oh, hell. I'm sorry. Anything I can do to help?'

Laura shook her head and looked pleadingly at Kit. 'Can we go now? Deb's on her own there.'

'Of course. And I'll drive you,' he said firmly.

'You shouldn't be driving. But I don't think—I'd be very safe.'

'I'm damned sure you shouldn't drive. And I'm very close to getting permission to drive, only another week or so, the physio said, so I'll be all right.' He grabbed his coat from the hallstand and picked up his crutches. 'Come on.'

Jules watched them leave then turned to look at Shaun, who'd just come down the stairs.

'What's up?'

'The father of Kit's lady friend has just died. From his reaction it looks like she's got more than a foot in the door with him.'

'I told you before we came that he never revisits a relationship. I know you were together for a while, but he hasn't contacted you since you broke off with him, has he? And anyway, he and I had a conversation earlier. He told me he was getting married. He didn't say who to, but it can only be her.'

'Why didn't you tell me? Why didn't they say something, instead of pretending he's just her employer?'

'I gather he hasn't asked her yet.'

'She'll snap his hand off when he does.' Jules thumped the flat of her hand down on the nearest surface. 'What the hell does he see in her?'

'His future, obviously.' Shaun put an arm round her shoulder and gave her a quick hug.

She let him for a minute, then shook him off. 'Do I smell burning?'

'Yeah.'

They both headed towards the kitchen, where Jules switched the burners and oven off. 'I'd better sort this out if we want any food tonight.'

'You? Cook?'

She let out a snort of laughter and studied the contents of the various pans. 'I'm still a disaster in the kitchen.' And in relationships, too. Why had she finished with Kit? Ambition, that's what. Overseas assignments had slowed down when people saw her in a relationship, or at least, that's how it had seemed to her. They'd speeded up since, so maybe she'd been right.

Shaun grinned at her. Jules's hatred of cooking was well known to her friends. 'Maybe we can make ourselves a sandwich. And we'll leave first thing tomorrow. We found out what we came for.'

'Yeah. We should have gone today, really. You're right. I shouldn't try to flog a dead horse.'

He looked thoughtful, then said slowly, 'I have a better idea. I wouldn't mind booking into a hotel somewhere for tonight, just the two of us, and getting a decent meal.'

She looked at him and a half-smile crossed her face. 'You never stop trying, do you?'

'Nope.'

'All right. Let's get the hell out of here. You write Kit a farewell note.' Funny how she'd never really fancied Shaun. There was something very cold about him. But he had the power to give her good future assignments and she'd known him for years. So what if she didn't burn for him? Sex could be fun anyway.

Just as they were about to leave, there was a ring at the door. Shaun opened it to see two men standing there. 'Yes?'

'I'm Kit's brother. Is he in?'

Shaun explained quickly what had happened, ending, 'We're just leaving.'

'I think we'll come in and wait. We may be able to help them.'

'You can clear up the kitchen,' Jules said, meaning it as a joke. 'They forgot to turn the pans off and everything burned.'

Gil turned to Joe. 'Show me the way. I'm a better cook than you.'

As they walked out, Jules exchanged glances with Shaun. 'Didn't know he had a brother who bats for the other side.'

'No. Neither did I.'

Laura and Kit arrived at Pop's before the doctor. The door opened as she raised her hand to knock and Deb stood there, her face tear-streaked. Laura put her arms round her daughter and gave her a hug, for once feeling no resistance. Guiding her inside, she left Kit to follow at his own speed.

But when Laura went into the front room to see her father, her mother got agitated.

Deb moved forward. 'I'll take Gran into the kitchen. You'd better check that I'm right about Pop.'

When they'd gone, Laura went across to her father. She'd never seen a dead person before, but you could tell that this was just the body, that the spirit had gone somewhere else. And somehow, she wasn't frightened of seeing her father's body, like she had been of seeing Craig's. 'Oh, Dad,' she said softly, 'I'm going to miss you so.'

There was the sound of the front door closing and Kit came to join her. 'Shall I check that Deb's right? I know a bit about first aid.'

She nodded and moved back, but she didn't need to be told.

He bent over her father and after a short time moved away. 'Sorry.'

'You can see he's dead, can't you?'

Kit nodded. 'I'm afraid so.'

She looked at her dad and brushed away a tear. 'I don't know what to do.'

'There's nothing we *can* do until the doctor certifies that he's died of natural causes. I don't think we should move him, even.'

He went to hold her close, but after a moment she pulled away, not daring to give in to her need for comfort, because, as she had to remember, he had been with Jules the night before. She saw him frowning at her as if he could sense something was wrong between them, but he didn't ask what it was, thank goodness.

A couple of minutes later, headlights shone outside and they heard a car pull up, then the sound of its door closing.

Kit looked at Laura, who was standing looking down at her father. 'I'll answer the door.'

Yet again someone confirmed that Pop was dead. The doctor looked at Laura, who was standing with her arms wrapped round herself. 'He can't have felt anything. Look how peaceful his face is. Um—has he seen the doctor lately?'

She nodded. 'Yes. Dr Sampson, I think.'

He pulled out a mobile phone. 'I'll have to call him. If your father had something wrong with him that might have caused this, I can sign a death certificate and there'll be no need for an autopsy.'

'Dad went for a check-up a couple of weeks ago. He's got—he had—a heart problem, nothing serious, he said, but he squirted something under his tongue if he had to walk far.' Why had she believed her father when he said it wasn't serious? Why hadn't she persuaded him to take things easy and let others care for her mother?

The doctor nodded and began dialling, walking out into the hall and speaking into his mobile phone in a hushed voice. When he came back he said, still in the same quiet tones, 'Dr Sampson has been his doctor for years. I won't go into details now, but he says this could have happened at any time, so I can sign the death certificate for you.'

'Do we need to call the ambulance afterwards?'

'No. A funeral director. Let me do this first, then I'll not intrude on your grief further.'

While that was being dealt with, Kit went into the back room to tell Deb what they were doing. Laura's mother was sitting fiddling with some food.

There was the sound of the front door closing and Laura came to stand just outside the kitchen, where her mother couldn't see her.

'The doctor's left. I need to phone Sue now,' she said in a voice that sounded too controlled to Kit. 'Perhaps Dad had made plans—he did about everything else—so she might know who to call.'

'Perhaps we should drive over and tell them in person?' he suggested. 'It's hard to give such news over the phone.' He'd had to do it once or twice, had hated it.

'I can't leave Deb here on her own?'

'Do you want me to go and tell them for you, then?'

She considered this, then shook her head. 'No. Better if it comes from me. I'll phone her. Deb, can you hand me the phone?'

210

Gran was getting restless and had started walking round the kitchen table, so Deb stayed in the doorway after she'd given her mother the receiver. She watched the old woman's restless circling. Was Gran looking for Pop? Did she even notice who was with her now? Yes, of course she did, or she wouldn't get so agitated when Mum was around.

Not for the first time, she wondered how you'd feel if your own mother rejected you like that.

Or your daughter?

On that thought, she glanced sideways at her mother, who was watching Gran from the hall, her face ravaged with sorrow. Without thinking, Deb moved to put an arm round her, and Laura put up one hand to clasp the hand on her shoulder, giving her a very sad smile as they stood there together.

'Better phone Sue, get it over with.' Laura moved out into the hall again. To her enormous relief, it was Trev who answered, and she managed to tell him what had happened without breaking down.

His voice was even more gentle than usual. 'I'm so sorry, Laura love. I'll tell Sue, then I'll be round as soon as I can. I—um—don't know whether Sue will come with me.'

'Can you contact Angie as well?'

'Yes. I'll fetch her from the pub on my way over there. Eh, she's going to miss the old man. We all are.'

She was about to put the phone down when he added, 'Don't do anything about a funeral director until I get there. Your dad's already arranged that. I have all the details.'

Laura held the buzzing phone for a minute, then took a deep breath. She'd better contact Ryan next. She looked at her watch. He'd be at work now. She rang his number there and they told her he wasn't in today, because his partner wasn't well.

Partner? What partner? Ryan didn't have a steady girl-friend, let alone a live-in one, or he'd have told her. Anyway, he'd only recently moved to Melbourne.

She rang his home number, and when a woman's voice answered, said curtly, 'I was trying to contact Ryan Wells.'

211

'Just a minute. I'll fetch him.'

Ryan came on the phone a minute later. 'Yep.'

'It's me.'

'Mum? Hi. How are you?'

'I'm all right, Ryan, but I've got more bad news, I'm afraid.' She explained.

There was dead silence at the other end.

'Ryan? Are you still there?'

'Yes.'

'Will you be able to come over for the funeral?'

'Yes, of course. But there are a few complications. Now's not the time to explain. I'll get back to you tomorrow morning your time. Will you still be at Pop's?'

'No. I'll be back where I work. Just a minute. Don't hang up. Who's the girlfriend? They said at your work that your partner had been ill. *You've got a live-in partner?*'

'That's the complication. I will tell you about it later, I promise.'

He hung up the minute he'd said that. Kit had to take the phone out of Laura's hand and set it back in its cradle, because she just stood there staring at it, listening to it buzz.

This time Laura let him put his arms round her and hold her close for a few minutes. Then they went to sit on the stairs and wait for Trev to arrive, while Deb kept watch over Gran in the kitchen.

Twenty-Seven

Ryan turned to Caitlin, who was watching him anxiously. 'My granddad's just died and I have to go to England for the funeral. Mum'll need me. I doubt Deb will be much use in a crisis.'

She went and put her arms round him. 'Oh, Ryan, I'm so sorry. You were very fond of him, weren't you?'

'Yeah. He was a wonderful granddad. I phoned him every month and we chatted. I can't tell you how many times I've confided in him, asked his advice—and taken it. He was wise and kind. I try to be like him, but I know I'll never be as good.' He looked at her with tears welling in his eyes. 'He always made more sense than Dad when it came to dealing with people, though I knew if I were in trouble, I could turn to Dad for help, of course.'

She couldn't think what to do but hold him, and then, as he began to sob, she cuddled him even closer, rocking him slightly, letting him weep for his grandfather.

After a while the tears stopped, but he stayed where he was, sighing once, still holding on to her tightly. 'I can't seem to think,' he muttered. He could feel his breath warming the space between their cheeks, his tears still damp on her soft skin. He had never felt so close to anyone in his life.

Her voice was low, her words for him only. 'Then don't try to think. Wait till you've come to terms with it.'

His voice was muffled by her hair. 'Thanks.'

'It's good that I can help you in return for all you've done for me.'

That made him sit up suddenly. 'Oh, hell, I *can't* go to

England and leave you here! Barry knows where you're living.'

'I'll manage. I'll see if I can take out a restraining order against him. Or I'll just head off and find a hotel somewhere. If I get some money out of the bank before I start, he won't be able to chase me electronically. Don't worry about me, Ryan. Your mother needs you.'

But he shook his head. 'No. You both need me.' He sat frowning at her, then took her hand again, looking deep into her eyes, searching, trying to understand her feelings. And it seemed to him that there was that special warmth in them, so he took a risk. 'Look, I have to be blunt because there isn't time to let things develop naturally between us. How do you feel about me, Caitlin? Am I just a substitute for my father, or a friend to help you out in this bad patch? Which I'm happy to do, whatever your answer. Or else—could there be more?'

Her eyes met his steadily and she didn't hesitate for even a second. 'I've been hoping for a while there could be more—wishing I'd met you before I met Craig. And in case you're wondering, I think you're very different from him and I love you for yourself. Can you forgive me?' Her tone became bitter as she added, 'A lonely naïve girl falls for the oldest, corniest line on earth! How stupid can you get?'

Relief coursed through him and he had no need to consider his answer, because she'd spoken from the heart. For all her natural elegance, she seemed to him a typical country girl, open and honest. It was one of the things he liked most about her. 'There's nothing to forgive, Caitlin. We all make mistakes, and what happened brought us together, so how can I regret that? And you made Dad happy, so I can't regret that, either, not now that I know how short a time he had to live.'

'Oh, Ryan, I—'

Her voice choked up and he pulled her towards him, kissing her very gently on the lips. 'No one is perfect. Not you, not me. I look back and feel I didn't support Mum like I should have done. At uni it was full on—work, play, freedom. When I look back, I can see I was high on it all. Then when I got a job, it was great having money for a change. I was enjoying life so much I didn't want to rock the boat by getting serious about anything or anyone. So what right do I have to throw bricks at you?'

'You don't *need* to throw any. I've told myself enough times how stupid I was—even before Craig died.'

He looked at her searchingly. 'I really do care about you, Caitlin. When we're apart, I look forward to seeing you, when we're together I feel comfortable. I worry about you and that cousin of yours . . . This isn't a good time, but I want to pursue our relationship very seriously.'

Her answer came without hesitation. 'So do I.'

'And I'm sorry you lost the baby.'

'Yes.' She stared down at their clasped hands. 'I'm sorry too. It deserved a chance of life.'

He waited a moment, then asked, 'Do you think you're well enough to fly to England with me?'

She stared at him in shock. 'How can I intrude on your family at a time like this?'

'It's the only way. I have to go. I'll never forgive myself if I'm not there for Pop's funeral, and I have to see Mum, make sure she's all right now. Deb says she's shacked up with this guy, you see. I can't believe that. Mum isn't the sort to have a casual relationship. But if she is seeing someone, I want to meet him.'

'That's all very well, but this definitely isn't a good time to tell her about us!'

'We don't have much choice. I'd have told her soon anyway. I tried to do it a few nights ago and chickened out. I won't deceive the people I care about. Pop wouldn't have done that and neither will I. I loved Dad but I'm *never* going to follow his example. So I intend to phone Mum and tell her about us before we leave.'

'But she must hate me!'

'I don't think she's the hating sort.'

'Any woman would resent me, though.'

'Mum may be stiff at first, but that'll change when she

gets to know you, I know it will. Besides, you can't get much further from your cousin than England. You'll be safe if you come with me.' He smiled as he said the all-important words for the first time. 'I love you, Caitlin.'

'I love you too, Ryan.'

'So, you're coming?'

'I suppose so. What about your job, though?'

'They can either give me some leave or dismiss me. I can always find another job, but I can't find another family—or another partner like you.' He gave her a faint smile. 'Hey, if we can make it after such an unpromising start, there has to be something really good going for us, don't you think?'

She found herself smiling back. 'Yes, I do.'

He planted a kiss on her cheek, then went to the phone. 'I'll see if I can contact someone from personnel, then I'm going to visit a travel agent. You'd better come with me. Oh! You have got a current passport, haven't you?'

'Yes, but it's never been used. I was going to Bali, then I started the baby and wasn't well enough. You're a lovely man, Ryan Wells!' She planted a kiss on his cheek, then went to get dressed properly. It had happened quickly, but she loved him so much. She just hoped he loved her enough to stay with her. And that his mother would be able to come to terms with it all. She couldn't bear to come between them, would rather give him up.

What's more, she'd give the money back. Definitely. She didn't need it now, whatever happened.

Ryan turned as she went back into the living room. 'Ready? Good. Let's go.'

But when they got to the door, they found Barry standing there, looking grimly determined, and behind him a couple who could only be Caitlin's parents, because the woman looked so like her.

Trev put the phone down and turned to Sue. 'It's bad news, love. Come and sit down.'

For once she didn't argue but followed him into the

living room and sat without a word, her expression apprehensive.

When he hesitated, she asked, 'What is it? Just tell me and get it over. Is it Mum?'

'No, it's your dad, I'm afraid. He's had a heart attack. He's—dead.'

She stared at him in horror. '*Dad?* Not Mum?'

'I'm afraid so.' He watched her carefully.

Her hands fluttered up to cover her mouth, one on top of the other, as if it took all her strength to hold in the pain, then she spread them helplessly. 'I can't seem to take it in. I can't—think straight.'

He put an arm round her. 'It's shocked me too. It seems so unfair after all he's been through this past year or two.'

'How did it happen?'

'He was sitting watching television with your mother, and when Deb went in to say the meal was ready, he was dead. Looked very peaceful, they said.'

She began to rock to and fro, weeping in great gulping outbursts of grief now. When he pulled her into his arms, she let him, something she hadn't done for a long time.

But Sue never wept for long and soon she was pulling away from him, wiping her eyes, trying to straighten her hair.

He let go. 'I'll do what's necessary, Sue. You stay here, rest, come to terms with it.'

She stared down at her lap, tearing tiny pieces off the sodden tissues, then her hands stilled and she looked up at him again. 'I have to go and see him.'

'Are you sure?'

'Yes.'

'What about your mother? What's going to happen to her now?'

Sue shook her head and a tear rolled down her cheek. 'I don't know. I can't look after her, Trev, I just—*can't.*'

He patted her shoulder. 'I know. Anyway, you've enough on at the moment looking after yourself. But the pills *are* helping, you know they are.'

She nodded.

'Don't stop taking them this time. I want my wife back.'

She gave him a tremulous smile. 'I don't know why. I've been an absolute shrew. And I still keep wanting to clean up, again and again . . .'

'Shh, love. Don't dwell on it. They told you to try to think of something else. Now, get your coat. We have to go and tell Angie, then go to your dad's. Laura's there.'

A hint of bitterness crept into Sue's voice. 'She'll be coping brilliantly. She always does.'

'She's not on her own. Deb's with her, and that fellow she works for is there too.'

'Angie says he's nice. I wonder if he's screwing her.'

'Sue, don't! There's no need to be jealous of Laura, especially not now.'

'I'm a rotten cow. I've got you, and *her* husband left her, but still I feel jealous that she copes with everything so much better than I do.'

'We do the best we can. That's all anyone can ever manage.' He looked at his watch. 'I still think you should stay here.'

She stood up. 'No, I'm coming with you.'

'Are you sure?'

'I'm not sure about anything—except that I don't want to stay here on my own. And I do want to see Dad.'

Laura sat on the stairs with Kit beside her. They seemed to have been there for a long time and she couldn't think of anything to say, was grateful that he didn't try to force conversation out of her.

Waiting. There was a lot of that to do when someone died. 'Do I hear a car?'

As she went to open the front door, Deb came out of the kitchen to join her.

'I'll keep an eye on your mother,' Kit said quietly.

'Thanks.'

Angie came hurrying down the path towards them, but Sue was still standing by the car and Trev had his arm round her protectively as she stared at the house.

The two cousins fell into each other's arms, Angie weeping uncontrollably, Deb patting her back, trying to offer comfort and shedding more tears with her.

Laura wished she could fall into someone's arms and weep herself senseless. Kit's face sprang immediately to mind, but she banished it sternly. She had to remember that he wasn't the faithful sort. She wasn't going to make the same mistake again. Only . . . she'd turned to him instinctively for help this evening and he'd immediately been there for her. And he was very kind, caring . . . Well, Craig hadn't been all bad, either.

Sue and Trev walked slowly along the path, standing in the doorway, now that the two weeping girls had moved on into the hall. Laura thought her sister's face looked haggard, and didn't know whether to go and hug her or not. She turned round. The two girls couldn't go on crying like that. 'Shh now,' she said, putting a hand on each of their shoulders. 'You'll upset Mum.'

She turned back to Sue.

Her sister's face crumpled. 'I haven't seen Dad for weeks. I deliberately didn't come to see him. And I didn't help him enough. He might still be alive if . . .'

Laura put an arm round her and they hugged as convulsively as their daughters had. 'There are always regrets when someone dies. You think of things you wish you'd done differently. I was the same with Craig.' She saw Deb turn to stare at her, surprise written on her face, and asked bluntly, 'Did you think I didn't care about your father, wasn't sorry he'd died so young?'

Deb opened her mouth, closed it again and made a helpless gesture. Laura turned back to Sue and for a moment longer the two sisters stood together, arms round one another's shoulders, then Sue disentangled herself from the embrace and moved back to Trev's side.

'Mum's in the kitchen and Dad—' Laura's voice broke for a moment, then she finished what she'd been saying, '—is in the front room.'

'I want to see him,' Sue said.

'So do I.' Angie came to stand beside her mother and tentatively put an arm round her.

Her father watched them anxiously, but Sue clutched her daughter's arm and they went into the front room together.

'He looks peaceful,' Sue said. 'So very peaceful. Oh, I'm so glad I've seen him! It's as if he's gone to sleep.'

'Pop's been tired for a long time,' Angie said quietly.

'I wish—' Sue's voice broke, '—I'd been in a state to realize that.'

'Pop knew you couldn't help it, Mum. He always seemed to understand.'

Trev stood in the doorway and said in a low voice to Laura, 'We need to talk, make arrangements. Can we go into the kitchen now?'

'I can't. Mum gets agitated if I go near her.'

'Perhaps the girls could get her to bed? Angie?'

She nodded and went with Deb into the kitchen.

Laura watched as the two girls coaxed her mother upstairs, then went to put the kettle on. 'I'm thirsty. I keep thinking I shouldn't be, but that's silly. We'd better wait till the girls come down before we decide anything—what to do about Mum and how to run Dad's funeral.'

'Shall I wait in the front room?' Kit asked. 'Or I can go out and wait in my car?'

Laura turned to him and for a minute they seemed to be the only people in the room. 'You don't need to leave. You've been such a help. And I doubt we'll be saying anything particularly private.'

Kit and Trev managed to keep a conversation of sorts going about his life as a foreign correspondent, but it seemed a long time before the girls rejoined them.

'Now,' said Laura once everyone was seated. 'About Mum . . .'

'I think social services will find her a place in a nursing home,' Sue said. 'They probably have an emergency line.'

Angie spoke hesitantly, 'It'd seem wrong to send her away until after the funeral, don't you think? Moving to a new place is bound to upset her and she might not be in any state to attend the funeral.'

Laura nodded. 'I think Dad would want her to be there for him. I think she *should* be there.'

'I could look after her for a few days, with Deb's help and the carer's,' Angie said. 'Gran's used to me being here.'

'Will she even know what's happening?' Trev asked gently. 'And will she behave herself? Look at the way she reacts to Laura. What if she creates a scene?'

'That doesn't matter,' Angie insisted. 'She *should* be there. And we'd only have to look after her for a day or two.'

Deb couldn't hide her apprehension. 'I'll do my best, but I'm not as good with her as you are.'

'I'll provide meals for you all. I wish I could help in other ways, but I'm very proud of you two for volunteering.' Once again Laura saw the surprise on her daughter's face, but she'd meant what she said and even managed a quick smile at her.

Sue looked up and cleared her throat. 'I can come and sit with Mum for an hour or two to give the girls a break— if she'll let me. I haven't seen her for a few months, but I'll try.'

'You have enough on, getting yourself better, love,' Trev said quietly.

Sue shook her head. 'I need to do *something* or I'll never forgive myself.'

Trev didn't look convinced but didn't press the point. 'About the funeral. Your dad's made all the arrangements and paid for it in advance. He said he didn't want to be a trouble to anyone and gave me all the details. I can ring the funeral director now, if you like.' When everyone nodded, he went and picked up the phone.

Laura's voice wobbled. 'Isn't that just like Dad? Oh, and Ryan's coming to England for the funeral. I rang him to explain what had happened and he said he was definitely coming, but there were complications. So he's going to ring me again in the morning to tell me the details.'

*   *   *

By the time the funeral people had taken Ron Cleaton's body away, everyone was exhausted as well as sad.

Laura let Kit drive her home and immediately moved towards the stairs. 'I'm too tired to speak coherently. Thank you for being there for me tonight.'

She didn't meet his eyes as she spoke. He watched her go up and made no attempt to detain her, because he was as tired as she was. Something was definitely wrong, though, and he intended to get to the bottom of it in the morning. But you didn't talk well when you were exhausted.

When he went into the kitchen, he stopped dead at the sight of Joe and Gil sitting there. What now?

Joe stood up, glanced at Gil and rushed into speech. 'We arrived to see you just as your friends were leaving. They told us about Laura's father and said they'd decided to leave early. They've left you a note.'

'Oh. Right.'

'But I still wanted to see you. I hope you don't mind us staying? We cleared up the kitchen—some things had burnt—and there's some food ready if you need it.'

Kit hauled himself across to a kitchen chair, feeling unutterably weary, but from the expression on Joe's face, this was important, so he forced a smile. 'If someone will get me a beer and a sandwich, I'd be hugely grateful.'

'I'll do it,' Gil said. 'I'm a much better cook than he is.'

Joe sat down and began to fiddle with a mug, turning it round slowly and carefully, aligning it with a second mug, then moving them both. 'I wanted you to be the first to know. Gil's moving in with me and—I'm coming out, letting people know I'm—gay.'

Gil came across to put one hand on Joe's shoulder. 'He's still embarrassed by it all, though. I hope you'll understand that we love one another.'

'I do understand and I'm glad for you.'

Joe looked at him in such utter relief, Kit leaned across and clasped his brother's hand. 'You silly bugger, did you think I'd mind? All I want is for you to be happy.'

They sat there for a minute, still clasping one another's

hands, then Kit extended one hand to Gil as well. 'Welcome to the family.'

'Oh, sorry! Am I interrupting something? Only, I was too hungry and thirsty to sleep.'

He turned to see Laura standing there in her dressing gown. 'Not at all. Come and hear the good news. Joe and Gil are moving in together.'

She looked from the large, blushing man to the smaller one, who rolled his eyes, then winked at her. 'I'm glad for you both.'

'That's just what Kit said,' Gil told her. He looked at Joe. 'I told you most folk won't have a fit about it.'

Laura watched them exchange loving glances. It was good to see such happiness after the sadness of today.

Gil clicked his tongue. 'You sit down, Laura, and I'll get you a sandwich. I know it's your kitchen, but I won't make a mess and you look tired out.'

As she sat down, Joe suddenly looked horrified. 'I forgot. I'm sorry about your father. We shouldn't be flaunting our good news at you.'

'It's great to hear something positive. This has been a very sad day, but it's nice to know that life goes on.'

Gil put a mug in front of her and another in front of Kit. 'Hot chocolate. It's much too late for coffee or beer. Joe, come and help me with this, then we'll go and leave these two in peace. No, don't get up, we can let ourselves out.'

Laura was too hungry to go back to the safety of her bedroom, so she ate and drank quickly, then stood up.

Kit put out one hand to stop her. 'I know something's upsetting you. I was going to sort it out in the morning, but I think we'd better do it now.'

She didn't want to discuss anything just now, most definitely not. 'I'm too tired.'

He stood up, a look of determination on his face, so she fled up the stairs.

'Laura! Laura, come back.'

But she didn't.

He stood at the bottom for a moment, then shook his

head and went to bed, lying awake for a long time, worrying about her. It was since his friends' visit, so it must be to do with that. Had Jules been stirring up mischief? He wouldn't put it past her. But surely Laura wouldn't believe anything without checking with him first?

And you couldn't pressure someone about their feelings when they'd just lost a beloved father.

No, he'd have to be patient for a while.

Twenty-Eight

B arry smiled at Caitlin, an insufferably smug expression that made Ryan want to punch him in the face.

'Aren't you going to invite us in, Caitlin dear?' Mrs Sheedy asked.

'It's not my place to invite you into someone else's house.'

As Ryan put his arm round her, he saw the parents exchange glances. 'Why don't you all come in? We have to be somewhere in half an hour's time, but we can spare you fifteen minutes now.'

'Don't let us keep you,' Barry said. 'It's Caitlin we've come to see.'

'We *both* need to be somewhere, I'm afraid.'

'Caitlin's going nowhere with you,' Mr Sheedy rasped in a voice hoarse with anger.

'I think that's up to her.' Ryan led the way into the living area and gestured to the chairs. The parents took the sofa and Barry the only easy chair, so he turned two of the dining chairs round for himself and Caitlin, managing to wink at her as he did so. She looked as if she was struggling to keep calm, but whether this was from fear of her parents or from anger, he couldn't tell. He sat down and took hold of her hand while they waited for the others to speak.

Barry looked sideways at Mr and Mrs Sheedy, as if silently urging them to speak.

Mrs Sheedy pulled out a handkerchief and dabbed at her eyes.

Mr Sheedy focused his angry gaze on his daughter. 'What do you think you're doing, living with a man? And that man's son, too! Did you learn nothing from your association with his father?'

'Caitlin, don't do this,' her mother begged. 'Don't shame us. Remember how we brought you up. Remember we love you, you're our only child.' She began to sob into the handkerchief.

Ryan felt Caitlin's hand jerk in his and saw her biting her lip. He took it upon himself to reply. 'Do you know why she's living here?' He was surprised at how relaxed his voice sounded, because he felt angry at the way they were treating their daughter—and him. If looks could kill, he'd have died instantly he opened the door, and her father was still glaring at him as if he were a criminal. There was no love in the way the father looked at their daughter, either, though the mother was upset rather than angry. 'It's not because we're sleeping together, because actually, we're not.'

'Why else would she move out of her own place?' Mr Sheedy asked. 'Don't take us for fools!'

'Your daughter's staying here,' Ryan continued, 'because her cousin kept harassing her. It was either take out a restraining order against him or move out of her own flat.'

Mrs Sheedy stared at him in shock. 'Barry wouldn't! He loves you, we all do.'

'It's not harassing to care about your cousin, to want to help her,' Barry declared in that flat, heavy tone.

Ryan scowled at him. 'You've been harassing her for a while now, Donovan. She left Western Australia because of you. You turned up to pester her when she'd just lost the baby and was in a fragile state, and even that didn't stop you.'

Her husband gave Ryan one scornful glance. 'It was the Lord's will that she lost it. Who are we to question that? And as for your lies about my nephew, you're wasting your time. I'd not believe anything *that man's son* said. I'm here to take my daughter back to where she's loved and cared for, where she can be forgiven and brought back into the fold.'

Caitlin stood up so suddenly she took everyone by surprise. 'I'm not going with you *now or ever.* There's nothing to forgive and I've told you several times I no longer believe as you do. Why will you not leave me alone?'

'Because you're our daughter.'

'That doesn't give you the right to dictate to me what I do. I'm twenty-five, not a child. I make my own choices in life. And what's more, Barry, if you don't leave me alone, I *will* take out a restraining order against you.'

He said nothing, just let out a sniff that sounded scornful to Ryan.

Caitlin paused for a moment, then said loudly, 'I know you're not really listening to me, Barry, because you only ever hear what you want to. It's no use continuing this discussion, so will you please leave? As Ryan said, we have an appointment elsewhere.'

'I'm going nowhere till you come with me.' Mr Sheedy folded his arms. 'I've prayed for guidance on this, Caitlin, and I know my duty.'

'In that case, we'll have to ring the police and ask them to get you out.' Caitlin turned to Ryan. 'This is the sort of emotional bullying I've lived with all my life. It wasn't till I moved out that I realized how differently other families lived—how much happier other girls were. So, I'm never moving back, and as for having anything to do with *him*,' she jabbed a finger in Barry's direction, 'I hope I never see him again as long as I live.'

'You heard your daughter. Please leave now,' Ryan said quietly into the shocked silence.

Mrs Sheedy, who was weeping into her handkerchief, half stood up, but her husband shook his head at her and she subsided into the seat again. Barry glared at Ryan.

There was the sound of someone moving about in the flat next door. Ryan stood up. 'I'll just be a minute.' He came back with a man who looked as if he'd just finished a hard night's work. 'Will you witness what I'm going to say, Tom?' He turned to his unwanted visitors. 'Please leave my flat now, all three of you.'

By this time, Mrs Sheedy was looking scared, but the two men still shook their heads and stayed where they were.

'Can Caitlin come and sit in your flat while I call the police?' Ryan asked. 'I know it's a lot to ask when you've just come off shift, Tom, but she's not well. She's just lost a baby, and they're bullying her.'

'Sure.'

Barry moved quickly to block the door. 'She's going nowhere. We're her family. She belongs with us.'

Tom gaped at him, then turned to Ryan. 'Glad you came for me. Phone the police. I'll stay here till they come.'

Ryan picked up the phone.

'No!' Mrs Sheedy stood up. 'Don't. We're leaving.' She turned to her husband. 'Dennis, you're taking things too far.'

'Do you want to lose your daughter, Sandra?'

She looked at Caitlin sadly. 'We've lost her already. But you know you'll always be welcome at home, always.'

Barry's gaze burned across the room. 'I'm not finished with you, Caitlin. You'll find out just how tenacious I am when there's a soul to be saved—especially *your* soul.'

'You see, Mrs Sheedy. He *is* harassing her,' Ryan said.

Caitlin's mother shook her head, weeping quietly as they all three walked out.

Ryan watched them leave, let out his breath in a long gust of relief and turned to Tom, who was grinning now. 'Thanks, mate.' They shook hands, and when Tom had gone, Ryan turned to Caitlin, expecting to find her in tears. But she wasn't. Instead, her eyes were sparkling with anger.

'Barry is crazy. And I've been crazy too for worrying about hurting my parents. My mother's played that trick too often, weeping piteously. It's sucked me in before—but not any more. They don't worry about hurting me, do they? They don't even *listen*! It's sad to cut yourself off from your family, but that's what I'll have to do if I want a life of my own. And I do.'

Ryan put his arm round her. 'I'll help in any way I can.'

She sighed and sagged against him for a moment. 'You're a lovely man, Ryan Wells.'

'You're not half bad yourself, Caitlin Sheedy.'

They walked out of the building together, to see Barry sitting in his car outside.

'I don't need this,' Caitlin muttered. 'At this rate he'll be flying to England with us.'

Ryan grinned at her. 'Don't worry. There's an underground car park at work and it has two entrances. They're at opposite sides, so he can't watch them both. We'll lose him there.'

'Good. I'm sorry you had to be involved in this, though.'

'I'm not. If we're together, then we're there to help one another through thick and thin.'

'Oh, Ryan.' She kissed him, then squared her shoulders. 'Let's go and sort things out, then. The sooner we leave, the happier I'll be.'

Deb lay in the darkness, unable to sleep, listening in case Gran got up. She heard Angie turn over and sigh, so whispered, 'Are you awake?'

'Yes. I was trying not to wake you.'

'I can't sleep. I'm a bit nervous—of looking after Gran, I mean.'

'So am I.'

'You seemed so confident.'

'Well, what else could we do? Don't *you* think Pop would want us to keep her here till after the funeral? I'm absolutely certain of that.'

'Yes. But still . . .'

'We'll manage. And Deb . . . it was good to see you on better terms with your mother tonight.'

'And you with yours.'

'Yeah. Families aren't always easy, are they?'

They both sighed at exactly the same moment, then giggled.

'We'll be no good tomorrow if we don't get some sleep.' Angie yawned and turned over. Soon she was breathing deeply.

But Deb slept only fitfully. She was more than nervous,

she was plain scared of the responsibility—and wasn't looking forward to physically caring for an old woman, either. Her father would have paid someone to do it, she was sure, but no one here had even hesitated to dob her and Angie in to do the job. And she'd found she couldn't say no, not with everyone looking at her like that. Besides, Pop would have wanted it. She *was* sure of that.

It was all too hard for her lately. She didn't know where she stood about anything.

Ryan picked up the phone. He was dreading making this call, but was determined to do it before he left Australia. It'd be about eight thirty in the morning in the UK, which should be a good time to catch his mother, who was an inveterate early riser.

'Hello? Oh, it's you, Mum. Good.'

'Ryan. How are you?'

'Fine. We fly out later today, so I'll be with you in a day and a half.'

'We?'

'Yes. That's the complication I had to talk to you about. Mum, you're not going to like this, but I've got together with Caitlin.' He waited.

'Caitlin. Do I know—Ryan, you can't mean *her*?'

'Yes. I do mean Caitlin Sheedy.' The silence at the other end went on and on. 'Mum?'

'I can't believe what I'm hearing. She was your father's *mistress*, for heaven's sake! And she's carrying his child.'

'No, not now. She lost it a couple of days ago.'

Silence, then, 'Is that supposed to make it any better? I still don't want to see her. She broke up my marriage.'

'She didn't. Dad did that long before he met her. Anyway, I can't leave her behind, so it's either come with her or not come. She's in a fragile state and her family are giving her hell. Now isn't the time to explain her and Dad, but we will once we're there in person. And Mum, when you hear what happened between them, you'll understand it better, I promise you.'

'Will I?'

'Yes. Definitely. Mum, please. Give her a chance. For my sake.'

'Leave her behind, Ryan. I don't *need* this.'

'I can't. Her sicko cousin is pestering her and she's in no state to be left alone. Mum, I love her. *Really* love her. And she loves me.'

Another silence. He tried desperately to think of some way of softening her attitude towards Caitlin. 'I'm so sorry. I knew this would hurt you, Mum, but I couldn't deceive you about it, or about anything else. I'm *not* like Dad.'

'I'll see you at the funeral.'

She gave him the details, then slammed the phone down.

Taking a deep breath, he went into the bedroom, where Caitlin was waiting for him.

She turned round, saw his face and said, 'Oh, Ryan!'

He walked over to take her in his arms and rock her to and fro for the sheer comfort of it. 'I've never heard my mother sound so bitter.'

'You can't really blame her. I should stay in Australia and—'

'No! If you stay here, so do I.' He looked down at her. 'I won't back down on this. You're the most important thing in my life now, so if Mum rejects you, she rejects me as well. Only . . . I hope we can sort it out, because I love her very much. I think she'll come round when she understands, hope she will . . .'

'I hope so too.'

'Right then. Soon as I've sat on my suitcase, we'll go across and get the rest of your things.'

Laura turned away from the phone and burst into tears, weeping so loudly that Kit came hurrying in from his office, where he'd been trying to settle down to writing—trying and failing, because he kept worrying about Laura instead.

'What's happened? I heard the phone.' He took her in his arms and she sobbed against him. When she made no attempt to speak, just continued to weep, he shook her a little. 'Laura, tell me what's wrong. I can't help if you don't tell me.'

'You can't help with this. No one can.'

He took her through to the sitting room in the end, and sat down with her on the new sofa, letting her sob against him until the tears gradually stopped. 'What is it?'

She mopped her eyes with a tissue and, in broken phrases, told him Ryan's news.

'What the hell's got into him?'

'*She* has!'

'Is she some sort of sex goddess?'

Laura bent her head, picturing Caitlin Sheedy, tumbling red hair, unfashionably cut, eyes swollen with weeping, slender and vulnerable-looking. 'No. I wish she were. It'd be easier to hate her then. She seemed—vulnerable. When I saw her, at least. I still can't understand why Craig left me for her. She wasn't his usual type. And now Ryan . . .'

'Does your son fall in love regularly? Is this likely to be a temporary infatuation?'

She shook her head. 'No, he's never been in love before— at least, not that I know of, and I think he'd have told me.'

'Then it must be serious.'

She nodded. 'I told him not to bring her near me.'

It was Kit's turn to fall silent, then he said slowly, 'You'll have to see her eventually.'

'Why?'

'Because he's your son and you love him.'

Her voice was savage. 'Not if he stays with her, I don't.'

'You're overreacting, Laura.'

'I've a lot to overreact about, don't you think?'

The phone rang again. She pulled herself away from him. 'I'll go. It might be Deb.'

It was. 'How are things going with Gran, Deb?'

'We're managing, but it's gross, Mum. She can't even go to the toilet on her own. Auntie Sue's coming over later this morning, so I wondered if you'd come and help me with the shopping and stuff. It's a bit hard without a car.'

'Yes.'

'Mum? Are you all right?'

'Not exactly. I'll tell you about it when I see you. About eleven?'

When Kit appeared in the doorway, Laura was still holding the phone, standing there like a lost soul.

'Like a bit of company?'

She shook her head. 'No. What I'd really like—if you don't mind—is to have some quiet time to think about—things. Oh, and I need to go out and get some food for Angie and Deb later this morning. Will that be all right?'

'Of course it will. You know you don't have to ask.'

'I don't feel as if I know anything any more.' She turned to stack some dishes into the dishwasher, relieved when he returned to his office. Found herself standing there some time later, still holding the dishes, her thoughts churning round and round.

Ryan couldn't do this to her, he just couldn't!

Craig's death had left them with a nest of adders, it seemed, and one after the other was rearing its head and biting deep.

What was Deb going to say to it all when she heard?

Twenty-Nine

Sue sat in her immaculate house and itched to clean it. But she didn't let herself start or she'd never stop. It was stupid to have your whole life ruled by an obsession. Stupid!

She got up and went to stare out of the window. The garden was immaculate too. That was the word the counsellor had told her to hang on to. *Immaculate.* It helped a bit. The pills helped a bit. And Trev was helping most of all. She didn't know what it'd be like when Angie came back to live here. Her daughter was as innately untidy as she herself was tidy.

Untidy isn't the same as dirty. Another of the catchphrases. Only that one was harder to believe in.

She went to look in the mirror, but there wasn't a hair out of place. She hadn't put on any make-up today, didn't want to.

Sighing, she went and switched on the television, wondering if she'd be better off going back to work, but knowing she couldn't cope yet.

By ten thirty she could bear it no longer. Putting on her coat, she picked up her car keys and set off for her dad's house. Trev had offered to take time off work and drive her over there later, but she knew she had to do this on her own. It would show she was getting control of herself again. At least she hoped she was.

She parked the car in front of the house, just behind her father's car. Oh heavens, they'd have to do something about the car as well. Slowly, feeling as if her legs were made of wood, she walked down the little path to the front door.

Deb opened it. 'Thank goodness you've come, Auntie Sue! Angie isn't well and I can't cope with Gran on my own.'

'What's wrong with Angie?'

'The usual monthly stuff. Is she always this bad?'

'Yes. Always has been.'

'She should take extra magnesium. It might help. Do you have any painkillers on you? She took the last one after you'd gone yesterday.'

'No. Do you drive? Right then, go and get some painkillers—and you may as well get her some magnesium too.' Sue gave directions to the nearest chemist's, fished a twenty-pound note out of her purse and held out the car keys.

Deb took them and hesitated. 'You'll be all right on your own with Gran?'

'Yes.'

Sue waited till Deb had driven away, then walked down the narrow hall towards the kitchen. Her mother appeared, ignoring her completely and walking into the front room. She wandered round it for a minute then went back, to wander round the kitchen in the same way, as if looking for something.

'Mum?'

For a moment her mother looked at her, then she pushed past Sue and went upstairs, where she wandered from one bedroom to the other.

Sue followed her and found Angie lying on the bed clutching a hot-water bottle to her stomach. 'Need anything? I've sent Deb out for some painkillers.'

'Thanks.'

'Why is Mum wandering about like this? Does she always do this?'

'No. I think she's looking for Pop.'

'Oh.'

'She won't eat, hits our hands away if we try to persuade her, and it was like dealing with a naughty child trying to get her dressed this morning.' She hesitated. 'Can you manage her for a bit? I know it upsets you but . . .'

235

'I don't know if I can, but I'll try. You stay in bed till this passes.'

Angie groaned and curled up in a ball.

There was the sound of footsteps going slowly downstairs.

Sue took a deep breath. 'Right, then.'

'Call if you need me, Mum.'

Sue ran down and caught her mother in the kitchen. 'Let's have a cup of tea, eh?'

To her enormous relief, her mother sat down and drank the cup of tea when it was set in front of her. She spilled some, but Sue wiped it up quickly. She looked round. This house was anything but immaculate. She could do a bit of cleaning and tidying while she was here, surely? That wouldn't be unreasonable.

By the time the doorbell rang, she'd persuaded her mother to drink another cup of tea and eat a piece of toast, and was starting on the washing-up. She went to answer the door and found Laura there.

'How's Mum?'

'Driving everyone crazy. Angie thinks she's looking for Dad.'

'And you? You look a lot better today.'

Sue caught a glimpse of herself in the mirror. 'Do I? I look a mess to me.' She froze and listened. 'She's turned on the gas burners again. I don't know how Pop coped with her on his own. You can't turn your back for a minute.' She ran into the kitchen to switch the gas off.

Laura went to stand in the doorway, ready to hide in the front room. But today her mother ignored her, seeming agitated about something else.

They exchanged glances.

'She *is* missing Dad,' Sue said. 'It's the only possible explanation.'

'I am too. And—I've had some bad news from Australia.' She explained quickly.

Sue looked shocked. 'You've had enough to bear. It isn't fair of Ryan to bring her.'

There was the sound of the front door, and Deb came in, gave her mother a quick, absent-minded hug and dumped a bag of shopping in the kitchen. 'I'll just take the painkillers up to Angie, shall I?'

Laura could hear the two girls chatting, then Deb came down to join them.

'I picked up some food while I was out, just enough to see us through, so I needn't have bothered you, Mum. But it's—um—nice to see you anyway.'

'It's nice to see you, too. I'm afraid I've got something to tell you, something better said face to face. Come into the front room. Sue, can you keep Mum away from us?'

'Shut the door. I'll do my best.'

Looking apprehensive, Deb followed her mother into the front room.

'It's about Ryan—' Laura began.

'Not about you and Kit?'

'What do you mean?'

'I've been watching the way you look at each other. It's a bit soon to shack up with someone, don't you think?'

Laura drew herself up. 'It's up to me if I want to shack up with someone, and since your father hadn't been near me for months, I don't intend to measure things by the date of his death, thank you very much!'

'Oh.' Deb fiddled with the braid on the sofa arm, then muttered, 'What about Ryan? Can't he come?'

'Yes, he can. But he's—bringing someone with him.' Laura hesitated, but there was no getting out of saying it. 'It's Caitlin.'

'Who? There was a long pause, then, 'Not Dad's Caitlin?'

'Yes. Apparently she and Ryan are an item now.'

Deb gaped at her. 'I don't believe you.'

Laura shrugged. 'Believe what you want, but he's bringing her. She's lost the baby and he says she's being harassed by a cousin. He says he's in love with her and she with him.'

Deb swallowed hard. 'She can't have loved Dad then.'

'No. I don't think so, either. I'm not having anything to

237

do with her, but you must make your own decision. I just wanted to—warn you.' She stood up. 'If I'm not needed, I'll get back. I do have a job to go to.'

Deb sat there for a while, then went into the kitchen again. 'Auntie Sue, I need to use the phone.'

But Ryan's phone in Australia rang on until the answering service cut in. She put the receiver down and looked at her aunt. 'I can't believe Ryan's shacked up with Dad's ex-mistress. Is that sick or what?'

Sue shook her head. 'It's amazing.'

'Is it all right if I go out for a couple of hours? I need to get my head together about this.'

'Yes. You go. Angie can help me at a pinch.'

'Gran seems better with you than she is with me. It's as if she recognizes you.'

After she'd gone, Sue stood looking at her mother. What had she been afraid of? This was just Mum, or the shell of Mum. It must all have been part of Sue's own illness to refuse to see her parents. She looked round. The kitchen wasn't immaculate, but it looked a lot better. She would sit down and have a rest for a minute or two before she got on with things.

It made her twitchy to leave things unfinished even for a few minutes, but she could cope with that.

When Laura returned, still looking furiously angry, Kit followed her into the kitchen. 'You look upset. Anything I can do to help?'

Her tone was icily polite. 'No, thank you.'

He went back into his office, angry at the way she was shutting him out, but couldn't settle to work. From the kitchen came banging of pans and clattering of crockery. He looked at the clock. Nearly lunchtime. Perhaps they'd be able to talk then.

There was a knock on his door and Laura poked her head through. 'All right if I bring your lunch in here on a tray? I'm behind on everything and it'll be easier if I don't have to work round you.'

What could he do but agree?

When she brought the tray, she dumped it on the table and whisked out again without saying anything beyond, 'There you are.' He let out a long, low whistle. He hadn't realized she had such a temper, but if ever he'd seen a furious woman, this was one.

The food was as good as usual, though, and when the smell of baking wafted out from the kitchen, he inhaled blissfully. Being in a bad mood clearly didn't affect her cooking.

She came to fetch the tray, stony-faced, wearing a *leave me alone* expression, so he thanked her for the meal and went on the Internet, reading newspapers from around the world, but listening with half an ear to the noises Laura was making. Feet going upstairs at a run. Back door banging open and shut again. Hoovering in the hall, kitchen and his bedroom.

She didn't stop working. He couldn't start. Whatever was wrong was building a wall between them, a wall that had begun to rise when his friends visited. But he didn't feel he could press her for explanations until she'd buried her father.

It seemed a very long afternoon.

Deb went to what was rapidly becoming her favourite place, the wishing well. How stupid could you get, falling for that stuff? Only, for some reason it soothed her to go there, and she always tossed in a coin and wished for something. Not that her wishes came true, but it helped focus her thoughts on what she wanted.

This time she wished Ryan would leave Caitlin Sheedy behind in Australia.

She found a park bench nearby and sat down, hands thrust deep into her pockets, because she'd forgotten her gloves. How *could* Ryan shack up with Caitlin? Deb felt at one with her mother on this. It just wasn't *decent*.

'Mind if I join you?'

She looked up to see Alex standing beside her. She hadn't

even noticed him coming. 'If you want. I won't be good company, though.'

He shrugged and slouched down beside her, not saying anything.

She didn't answer, but after a while looked sideways at him. 'I thought you were flat-hunting.'

'I was. I have an hour between viewings. I often come here. The place has a good feel to it.'

'Yeah. I like it here too.'

'I'm sorry about your granddad.'

'Thanks. It was a shock. We're all going to miss him.' She sighed. 'It's my brother I'm upset about today, though.'

'I've been told I'm a good listener.'

She couldn't help it, because she desperately needed to talk to someone about it, so told him about Ryan and her father's mistress.

There was a long silence, then he said thoughtfully, 'You've not heard the whole story yet, though, have you?'

'I've heard enough!'

'Yeah, but from what you've said about your brother, he wouldn't do something like that lightly. Maybe you should wait to hear her side.'

Deb thought this over. 'Ryan said her cousin was pestering her. But surely that's no reason to bring her here at a time like this.'

Alex shrugged. 'Who knows? The older I get, the more I try to hold back on making judgements.' He contemplated his feet, stretched out halfway across the path. 'I broke up with my long-time girlfriend just before I left Australia— partly because I listened to what other people said instead of asking her. I regret that now. She was going to come with me. Instead she went off with a group of friends to India. I miss her.'

Deb stared at her own feet. 'At least you had a girlfriend. No one seems to want to date me.'

'Don't take this the wrong way, because the last thing I want to do is hurt you, but perhaps you've been too preoc- cupied with your father.'

'What?'

He held up one hand, palm in a halt position. 'Let me finish, then you can give me your side. From what you've said, it's because of your father's influence you're so thin, and you clearly cared more about him than you did about your mother. There's nothing wrong with loving him, but the pair of you sound like you've shut her out. Perhaps you shut other people out too.'

The Deb who'd got on the plane in Australia would have flounced away in a huff. The Deb who'd seen her grandfather die and tried to look after her grandmother looked at Alex through a blur of tears and didn't know what to say.

'Oh, hell! I didn't mean to make you cry.' He pulled her into his arms. 'I'm sorry. Of all the stupid timing, lecturing you when you're grieving.'

She pulled back a little. 'I'm not crying, just getting emotional and—I suppose you're right. To some extent. Only, I loved Dad so much and I miss him dreadfully. I always will.' After a pause, she added quietly, 'But he wasn't fair to Mum, was he? And we did shut her out. I don't even know how to talk to her, what to say, what not to say. I don't feel I know anything any more.'

'Join the club. I offended my aunt yesterday with my swearing. I tried to tell her swearing doesn't mean as much to Aussies, but she got all stiff and starchy with me. I really do need to move out. I'm not used to being treated as a child, asked where I'm going, told what time to be in by . . .' He pulled a wry face at her, then looked at his watch. 'If you've nothing better to do, why don't you come and help me look at this flat?'

It was quite a nice flat, small but comfortable, and the living room had a view down the street instead of across back yards, which pleased Alex. The furniture was old-fashioned but clean and comfortable. Deb went to stand by the window while he signed an agreement with the agent and paid a deposit.

'Come and have a pub lunch with me?' he suggested. 'I feel like celebrating.'

241

'I wish I could, but I have to get back and take my turn with Gran. Another time perhaps?'

'Yeah. Great. I'll drive you back to where you parked the car.' He beamed round the room. 'Can't wait to move in.'

Pop's house looked cleaner than it had before, and Gran was sitting quietly in the kitchen, rubbing the table top again.

'She won't stop doing that,' Sue worried.

'Pop used to just let her do what she wanted if it wasn't damaging anything.'

They both watched Gran for a minute or two, then Sue said, 'Trev rang to say the funeral's set for the day after tomorrow.'

'I'll have to see if I've got any black clothes.'

A voice behind them said, 'I can probably lend you something.'

Deb turned to see her cousin standing in the doorway, still pale, but looking much better. 'Did you get a nap?'

'Yes.' Angie looked at her mother. 'You've been clearing up.'

Sue stiffened. 'It needed clearing up. I haven't gone overboard. It really did need it.'

'Sorry. I didn't mean to criticize.' She looked at her grandmother. 'She behaves better for you than for me.'

They all looked at the old woman and there was one of those rare moments where Pat smiled back at them, briefly looking her old self. Then the smile faded.

Sue moved over to them and said in a low voice, 'Your father rang social services and they're arranging somewhere for Mum—for after the funeral.' She folded the dishcloth up with great precision and laid it on the draining board. Then she picked the cloth up again to wipe the nearby surface, before putting it down and muttering, 'Immaculate. This part is now immaculate. Look girls, I'd better get back now. It's time for my next pill. Will you two be all right? Good. Trev said he'd pop round to see you on his way home from work.'

When she'd gone, the two girls looked at one another.

'I don't know what I'll do after the funeral,' Angie said. 'I've been lying there worrying about it. I definitely don't want to go home and I know Mum's better off without me around.'

'We'll think of something. I'm going to be homeless soon as well.' Deb gestured around her. 'Never thought I'd want to stay on here, but where else can I go?' Then she paused and stared at Angie. 'How about . . . ?'

'How about what?'

'We could share a flat, if you liked.'

Angie beamed at her, then her smile faded. 'I don't have enough money saved up for a deposit and there are other setting-up expenses.'

'I have plenty of money. You can pay me back later. Or will you be going back to university now?'

'Not yet. I've taken the whole year off. I don't go back till next September. If then.' She sighed. 'It all depends on Rick, really. I like him a lot.'

'Yeah, he's a nice guy. But you still should get your degree. Marriages can break up, then you'd need qualifications. Anything is better than being a clerk, believe me. I should have gone to uni or something.'

'Well, it's not too late.'

Deb looked at her and said slowly, 'No, it isn't, is it? And I can afford it with the money Dad left me. You *are* going to finish your degree, aren't you?'

'I suppose so. I always wanted to be a primary-school teacher. I love little kids.'

'Then go for it. If Rick's worth anything, he'll want you to, and will wait for you.' Deb grimaced. 'Listen to me doling out advice! What do I know about anything?' She stared down at herself. 'I don't even know what weight I want my body to be, and I still worry if I eat more than a tiny meal.'

'You were well on your way to anorexia, I reckon.'

'Yeah. That's what my last boyfriend said. He couldn't bear to see me picking at food, said I was no fun to take out.'

'And were you?'

'What, fun or picky?'

'On your way to anorexia?'

Deb stared at her, then nodded.

Angie gave her a hug, her voice gentle. 'Everyone has some problem or other, you know.'

'Look—if you'd rather not share a flat, I won't be offended. Honestly. Maybe I'm pushing you too hard.

Angie smiled at Deb. 'I want to. Truly I do. But only if you promise to eat more—and regularly. And not to get mad at me if I'm untidy.'

'I promise.' She chuckled. 'Actually, I'll need the same promise from you. I'm not very tidy either.'

Ryan and Caitlin got off the plane in Manchester. 'You look exhausted,' he worried as they went to pick up their luggage. 'I'm going to take you to a hotel, then I'll go and see Mum on my own.'

He picked up the hire car and asked directions to a hotel. When they parked outside the one which had been recommended, he didn't get out straight away, but asked, 'Are we sharing a room? We can do whatever you're most comfortable with. I won't be offended, I promise you.'

'I'd expected to share. Though I'm not able to . . .' Her voice trailed away and she blushed furiously.

'It'll be nice to be together. I hope you don't snore, though.' He was pleased to draw a faint smile from her at that. 'After I've got you settled in, I need to go and see Mum.'

But he hadn't slept much on the plane, and was so tired he couldn't stop yawning as they inspected their room. When he sat down 'just for a minute', he nodded off in the chair.

Caitlin watched him, then shook his shoulder. 'Give your mum a quick phone call, Ryan. You're too tired to drive. I'll use the bathroom while you phone her.'

He picked up the receiver and dialled.

A man's voice said, 'Hello?'

'Is that Mr Mallinder?'

'Yes.'

'This is Laura's son, Ryan. I've just arrived in England. Could I speak to Mum, please?'

'Of course. I'll go and fetch her.' Kit limped along to the kitchen and poked his head inside. 'Your son's on the phone.'

'Thanks.' Laura turned round from the sink, stripped off her rubber gloves and picked up the wall phone.

Kit went back to his office, hating the way she was shutting him out. But he didn't intend to let this stand-off continue for much longer.

'Ryan?' She couldn't stop her voice from wobbling, wanted so much to see him—but only him.

'Hi, Mum. We just got here, but I'm falling asleep on my feet, so I can't come to see you yet. I'd be a menace on the road.'

'When you come, don't bring *her* with you.'

'Mum, we're a couple now.'

'*You're getting married?*'

'No, we're living together. Neither of us wants to leap into anything, just take things gently. And it wouldn't hurt if you did the same. I've been honest with you. Now give us a fair go. I'll tell you the rest when I see you face to face. I think that'll help you understand her better. Until then, please trust me.'

She could feel the anger simmering inside her again. Wouldn't hurt to take things gently, indeed! She could write a book about what would and wouldn't hurt. It hurt when your husband started playing around, it hurt when he left you for a girl young enough to be his daughter—but it hurt most of all when your son took up with the same girl. Just as she was about to open the floodgates to her anger, she heard Ryan yawn, then a woman's voice in the background, and she snapped her lips shut. *That woman* wasn't going to hear her lose her rag.

Neither spoke for a few seconds, then she asked in a

voice which sounded more like her sister's, 'Where are you?'

He told her the name of the hotel and the phone number.

She told him the place and time of Pop's funeral.

They agreed to meet the following day.

Then they said goodbye.

They could have been total strangers, polite but with nothing in common.

She put the phone down and leaned her head against the nearest cupboard, felt herself being turned round, and sagged for a moment into Kit's arms. Then remembered that he too had betrayed her, and wrenched herself away.

'Laura, come and talk about it. You're upset and—'

'It's none of your business how I feel! And I don't *want* to talk about it, to you or anyone else! Now let me get my work done or I'll not feel as if I'm earning my money.'

As he stepped back, she saw his expression grow tight and angry too, nearly reached out to him to say she did want to be with him. Remembered Jules's voice coming from his bedroom, and couldn't.

'I'll have dinner in my office tonight then, Laura, and leave you to wallow in self-pity and take out your anger on the housework.'

After which, she made sure she worked very quietly indeed.

Self-pity! How dare he accuse her of that?

She wasn't in self-pity mode—was she?

Thirty

On the day of the funeral, Laura overslept. She'd had a bad night, alternating between anger and grief, lying awake for hours, at first listening to the odd car drive past, then the faint sound of the wind, swishing the bare branches of the trees, rattling small things. It was the wind that had lulled her to sleep eventually.

It wasn't till Kit came into the bedroom and shook her awake that she came out of the very heavy sleep into which she'd fallen at nearly five o'clock.

'What? What's the matter?'

'Laura, I think you need to get up. You said the funeral was at eleven, and it's nine now.'

She stared at him in shock. 'It can't be!'

'It is. I've made some coffee. Shall I do you some toast?'

'Please. And—thanks, Kit. I'm sorry I was so—abrupt yesterday.'

His smile was warm again. 'You were downright rude, but I forgive you. Now, get yourself ready.'

She raced around like a madwoman, hesitating only when she picked up the black dress she usually wore for dinner parties, and donned it together with the new black jacket she'd found in a shop near the supermarket. She'd be cold, but never mind. She wanted to do things properly for her dad.

When she went down, Kit had some breakfast ready. She nibbled at the fruit and tried to eat the toast, but gave it up, looking across the table at him apologetically. 'I'm sorry. It was kind of you. But I'm not hungry.'

'Well, you've eaten a little. It'll have to do. Don't go fainting on everyone.'

'No, of course not. I'm not the fainting type.'

'Know where you're going?'

She nodded and went up to finish getting ready, coming down just as he was crossing the hall.

'You look very elegant, but don't you have a coat?'

'Only an anorak. I'm *not* going to Dad's funeral in an anorak.'

'No. Of course not.' He walked with her to the door. 'Drive carefully.'

She nodded.

Several minutes later she got out of her car and gave in to the temptation to kick it! When she turned, she saw Kit coming out of the door, wearing a dark overcoat.

'It won't start?' he asked.

'No. Do you know anything about cars?'

'A little. But I think it'd be better if I drove you there in mine. I won't intrude, but I don't think you're in the right frame of mind to drive safely.'

She opened her mouth to say she was perfectly capable of driving, then looked down at the ground and admitted to herself that he was right. What with a sleepless night and her grief for her father, she felt as if everything was unreal. 'Thank you.'

'Come on then.'

It wasn't till they got to his new car that she realized he was holding her hand.

He looked down at their joined hands and then sideways at her. 'I'd like to come to the funeral with you—just in case you need someone. Would that upset your family?'

'I don't know. But I'm feeling in need of a friend. I'm sorry I shut you out before, but I was so *angry*! Ryan's intending to bring *her* to the funeral, says they're a couple now, and if we reject her, we reject him. I'm having a hard time facing that.'

'I'm not surprised.'

'I keep telling myself he's still my son, so I can't give in to my feelings or I might alienate him for ever, but I don't know if I can hold them back, not if I have to be with her. I feel *furious* every time I think of them being together.'

There was a short silence, then he asked, 'Has he explained how she can change so quickly from one man to another?'

'No. He says I'll feel differently once I understand.'

'Is he a reasonable sort of guy?'

She shrugged. 'I suppose so. He's always been mature for his age, and he's settled down still further since he left university. He was very supportive towards me when Craig died.'

'Then perhaps you should withhold judgement and give them a chance to explain?'

'I don't know if I'm that self-controlled.'

'You don't want to lose him, though.'

She looked down at her clasped hands. No, she didn't. She'd lost too many people lately.

The remainder of the drive to the chapel of rest, where Ron Cleaton's body was waiting for them, passed in near silence. She was grateful that Kit didn't try to make small talk.

He parked the car and escorted her inside, where a quiet-voiced man in sombre clothing showed them where to sit. When Kit took hold of her hand, she let him, turning sideways to look at him and return his encouraging smile with a faint smile of her own.

At the sight of her father's coffin, the anger began to fade a little. Such a lovely man. The best father a girl could have had. He'd always told her to control her temper. She'd do it now, somehow, for him.

Sue got up early that day, forced herself not to clean the kitchen beyond a quick wipe over the surfaces, and made a pot of tea, sitting down to enjoy her first cup of the day. Trev joined her soon afterwards, yawning and stretching in his usual noisy way.

'You all right, love?'

She nodded.

'I'll be beside you today.'

'Thanks.'

'You're doing really well, you know. I'd never have believed you could change so quickly.'

'It's still a struggle, Trev. I have to keep telling myself everything's already immaculate. That's my key word. And the tablets do help calm me down.'

'Immaculate is a good word to describe the way you keep the house. I've always appreciated the cleanliness—till it got out of hand.'

She smiled, and when he reached out to give her hand a squeeze, she pressed his in response and they sat for a moment looking at one another.

'Thanks for putting up with me.'

He flushed and spoke gruffly, 'I love you, you see.'

'And I love you too.'

They sat smiling at one another, then she stood up. 'Better get our breakfast now. I won't get dressed till afterwards.'

When they were ready to leave, Sue went to give herself a final inspection in the full-length mirror. 'The black doesn't feel like me.'

'It looks like you. The old you. The one who can smile at me.'

Which made her feel almost shy.

Together they went out to the car to drive to the chapel of rest.

Angie and Deb woke up early, as they'd planned, got themselves ready and then roused their grandmother and took her to the bathroom. She seemed shrunken today, as if she'd retreated into herself and wanted nothing to do with the world. After breakfast, she let them wash her, seeming not to notice what they were doing. When they'd dressed her, they took her to sit in the front room.

'It feels strange to be wearing black,' Deb muttered.

'It suits you.'

'Suits you too. But it makes Gran look sort of faded.'

'I've never seen her so placid for a long time,' Angie whispered. 'It's almost as if she knows.'

'How can she?'

'I don't know. But she's definitely been missing him.'

'Have you packed her things?'

'Yes. I'll go and bring them down.'

In one way it was a relief when the funeral limousine stopped in front of the house. In another way, it made the purpose of the day all too real.

'Thank goodness Gran likes going in cars,' Angie whispered as they all got in. 'She used to get in herself, now you have to shove her into place.'

'I don't like the darkened glass,' Deb said as she settled back. 'It makes the whole world seem dull and unhappy. Angie?'

'Yes?'

'I've only ever been to Dad's funeral before. You'll have to tell me what to do. It might be different here in England.'

'Keep your eye on Mum. She's buried several relatives lately, not just old ones, but two cousins, and she knows the ropes. Dad and I wondered if that was what had upset her, losing so many of her relatives in the past year. And now Pop. I feel sorry for her.'

At the chapel of rest, the girls joined Laura and Angie's parents. Kit was sitting behind them. But Gran wouldn't settle, so the girls took her outside to walk up and down, something she seemed happier to do.

'Isn't Kit coming to the funeral?' Angie whispered as everyone came outside and got into the two limousines, waiting for the hearse to drive in front of them to the cemetery.

'Yes. He's going to follow us in his car.' Laura turned round to see Kit getting into his vehicle. 'Mine wouldn't start this morning, so he drove me here. He's been very kind to me. Oh!'

They fell silent as the hearse pulled slowly round the side of the building with its flower-piled coffin.

'Pop would have loved the flowers,' Angie said softly.

After a moment's hesitation, Laura reached out for Deb's hand.

In the other limousine Sue reached out for Trev's.

Their vehicles started up and fell into place behind the hearse.

'Mum, what about Ryan?' Deb asked suddenly. 'Why isn't he here with us?'

'I told him to make his own way to the cemetery!' Laura snapped.

'Did he say—is he bringing Caitlin?'

'Yes, he is. I told him there wouldn't be room for her in the limousine.'

Ryan and Caitlin both woke early. They'd slept in the same bed, he'd held her in his arms, but that was as far as it could go until she recovered from the miscarriage.

'Are you sure I should be going with you today?' she worried. 'It seems wrong.'

His expression grew determined. 'I'm starting off as I mean to go on—openly. We're together and I'm not hiding it.'

'I still think . . .'

He put one arm round her. 'I love you, Caitlin. If Mum can't at least be polite to you, then she's rejecting me too.'

She was too weary to argue, didn't feel at all well, if truth be told, but didn't want to tell Ryan and add further worries to this sad day.

So they ate breakfast—or rather Ryan ate and Caitlin fiddled around with the food on her plate—then they dressed in the black clothes they'd brought with them.

'You look pale,' he worried. 'You should have tried to eat more.'

'I did try, but I'm really not hungry. I'm too nervous, I think.'

He kissed her cheek gently. 'Let's go, then.'

Thirty-One

At the cemetery, everyone gathered outside the chapel. Some of the Cleatons' neighbours and old friends were waiting there.

Angie walked her grandmother up and down, helped by Deb, not intending to take the old lady inside until the last minute.

'She's frightened,' she said quietly. 'It's all strange to her.'

'Do you think she'll be quiet for the service?'

'I don't know. If not, we'll bring her out and walk her again.'

Trev seemed to recognize all the mourners, leading his wife and sister-in-law round to speak to them.

'How do you know them?' Sue asked her husband.

'I used to visit Ron sometimes in the evenings. I'd see them as I drove up. Sometimes one of them would come in for a few minutes.'

Sue stared at him in shock. 'You never told me.'

'You assumed otherwise.'

Tears filled her eyes. 'Oh, Trev, I'm so sorry.'

'It doesn't matter now, love. You're on the way to recovery, and that's what I most care about.'

Laura stared at the ground while this exchange was going on, understanding that it was important and wishing she could fade away to let them talk. Trev moved on again, and after a moment, Sue followed and she trailed behind.

When Kit arrived, he stood quietly at the edge of the group until Laura noticed him and beckoned him across. She didn't take his arm, but wished she could, because she was very conscious of being on her own today.

When Trev went across to help Angie with her grand-mother, Deb moved to stand beside Laura and link arms with her. She looked at her daughter in surprise, because this was unusual.

'It's hard hanging around, isn't it?' Deb muttered, avoiding her mother's eye. 'I wish they'd just get on with it.'

Then Ryan arrived, with Caitlin on his arm.

Laura was astonished at how much weight Caitlin seemed to have lost. She was thin and pale, even her auburn hair seeming subdued and limp. She was clinging to Ryan's arm as if without it she'd have collapsed, while at the same time looking apprehensively across at the family group.

Ryan walked slowly forward, stopping to introduce Caitlin to his aunt and uncle and leave her with them for a moment before moving up to his mother and Deb. He imme-diately pulled his sister into a big hug, then held her at arm's length. 'You've put some weight on. It suits you.'

She glanced towards Caitlin. 'Why did you bring *her*?'

'Because she's part of me now. And because she has nowhere else to go, no one else to look after her. She's still not recovered from losing the baby, you know. Be kind to her.'

He turned to his mother. 'I'm not going to be the one to break up this family,' he said quietly. 'And you look to me like you need a hug.'

For a moment she resisted, then she let him pull her close. 'Oh, Ryan, why?'

'Because I love her and she loves me. We'll explain about Dad later. It wasn't actually a big deal.'

'Well, it seemed like one to me!'

'I know this is a bad time for you, but don't take it out on her. She's not well.' He beckoned to Caitlin.

Laura took a deep breath and willed herself to be civi-lized, as she had the first time she'd met her husband's mistress, because that was still as much as she could manage. The skin on her face felt suddenly tight, as if she couldn't move any of the muscles, let alone smile, but with a great deal of effort she managed a quick nod. She was pleased when Deb also greeted Caitlin coolly.

Before the silence could last too long, Trev came across to them, with his arm round Sue's shoulders, leaving Angie and Rick on either side of Pat Cleaton.

'Now that Ryan's here, shall we go inside?' He led the way and everyone followed. Deb stayed by her mother's side.

Only when the rest of the family had gone inside did Angie and Rick walk in with Pat. For once she went quietly, seeming soothed by the gentle organ music playing in the background.

Kit went in last, studying the young woman who had upset Laura so greatly, trying to see her objectively. She had a quiet beauty but everything about her seemed faded today. Ryan's love for her was obvious in his every gesture, the protective arm round her shoulders, the way his head bent towards her, the way he murmured something for her ears only.

She didn't look like anyone's mistress, Kit decided, let alone one who'd found a new man so rapidly after the old one died. He'd expected her to be brazen—and she wasn't. She looked gentle—more than that, subdued, as if life had taught her not to put herself forward.

He'd seen similar situations many times before as a journalist. Two sides, neither of them wicked, both trapped by circumstances into opposing the other. But this time he cared about the woman on one side, the woman who was hurt and angry. Hell, he loved Laura so deeply he was still shocked by his own feelings. And never before had he wanted permanency in a relationship, as he did now. Only, he wasn't quite sure how much she cared about him, in spite of their obvious mutual attraction, let alone whether she wanted them to stay together.

When he hesitated at the rear of the chapel, Laura gestured to him to join her, though Deb scowled at him from the other side of her mother. Oh hell, more tangles! But he was damned if he was letting that spoilt brat of a daughter come between him and the woman he wanted to marry.

The service began and he learned how very greatly Ron Cleaton had been loved and respected as several people stood up and offered a short tribute to the man, sharing a special memory of him, often relating how he had helped them through a bad patch. It was a pity, Kit thought, that Laura's father wasn't here to mediate in this family dilemma. He sounded to have been just the sort of man to do that successfully.

Through it all, Laura's mother sat staring blankly ahead of her. At one point she began rocking backwards and forwards, then she became still again. It was the saddest sight he'd ever seen, her indifference to her own husband's funeral.

After the final words of prayer, a curtain was drawn round the coffin and there was a moment's silence as people looked at one another. Then Trev stood up and went to the front. 'We'd be happy to see any of you who want to join us at Gaskell's. We'll just let Mrs Cleaton go out first, if you don't mind.'

Angie and Rick led Pat out to where a car was parked. Two women stood beside it, the carer who had come in to give Ron breaks from his wife, and a social worker. Trev had arranged for them to pick up his mother-in-law, because he hadn't been at all sure how Sue would cope if she had to take her mother to the home, and of course, Pat still got agitated when Laura got too close.

He led Pat across and helped seat her in the car, because she didn't seem to know how to get in herself any more. 'You'll be all right?' he asked the carer.

'Oh, yes. She always behaves when she's out in the car.'

'You can come and visit her any time, you know,' the social worker said quietly.

'We will. Probably tomorrow. At least, I will. My wife will if she's well enough. And thanks for all you've done, Mrs Nash.'

'It was a pleasure to help Mr Cleaton. He was a lovely man. And Mrs Cleaton's a lot less trouble than some.'

As they watched the car drive away, Sue turned to her

husband. 'Thanks. I couldn't have faced another institution yet.'

'I know.'

'Wasn't it wonderful what people said about Dad? They were both good parents. I haven't been nearly as good with Angie.'

'It's what your dad used to say: you did your best. No one can do more. People forget that and try to achieve the impossible. Come on, let's go and greet our guests.'

Gaskell's was a large building, formerly a private residence, with a popular restaurant at the front and signs in gold lettering pointing round the side to *Functions*. More discreet signs just inside the building guided the mourners to *In Memoriam: Ron Cleaton, Suite 3*.

Laura and Sue stood together near the door, thanking people for coming and shaking hands till their own hands ached. Deb ostentatiously avoided Kit.

Ryan found a chair for Caitlin and watched over her anxiously. She was, if anything, even paler than before. 'Are you sure you're all right?'

'Just tired.'

When most of the mourners had left, Trev gathered the family together and asked them to join him in a side room. 'There's a letter from your father. He wanted it read out to all the family, *just* the family, after the funeral.'

Ryan glanced anxiously at Caitlin, so Kit moved across. 'I'll stay with her if you like. I'm not family either.'

Ryan gave him a very direct look. 'But you're involved with my mother, I'm told.'

'I hope so. But this has hardly been the time to make sure of that.' He held his hand out to Caitlin. 'Kit Mallinder. I'm pleased to meet you.'

Across the room, Laura glared at him before swinging round and marching into the side room.

Trev waited till they were all seated, then produced an envelope and opened it. 'I've not seen the letter before, but I promised I'd read it out to you. He wrote it quite recently.

My very dear ones,

I feel my time is very short now, so I wanted to say goodbye to you all in my own words.

I've had a happy marriage, have always provided for my family, and my two girls have been a joy to me ever since they were born. What more can a man of my generation hope for? We weren't brought up to ask for the moon.

I want to offer you all a few words of advice, if you don't mind, because I can see things are not going smoothly for some of you, and because it's the last thing I can do for you.

Laura, love, let go of your anger. It will only hurt you and do no good to anyone. You're a grand woman, I've never seen anyone design a prettier home than you, and your cooking is a delight. It meant a lot to me that you came to try to help me, my dear girl.

Sue, love, don't feel guilty because you couldn't help with your mother. How can you be guilty for being what you are? No one can do more than their best. You're a wonderful homemaker, you have a lovely husband and you've borne a grand lass. You can be so proud of your family, my dear girl.

Ryan, Deb and Angie, my three bonny grandchildren, I wish you a long and happy life, though I can't begin to imagine what the world will bring you. But if you help others, as well as making a life for yourselves, you won't go far wrong.

Trev, you've been the very best son-in-law a man could have, and a good husband too. Look after that lass of mine and don't change a bit.

I don't need to ask you all to look after Pat if I go first. I know you will.

Don't grieve for me. I'm ready to go. I'm so tired now.

I love you all very much.

Ron Cleaton.

When Trev had finished reading, there wasn't a dry eye in the room. Laura reached out for her sister's hand and Sue clung to her, sobbing. The three grandchildren were sitting close together, and without consciously thinking about it, they held hands with one another.

'I think,' Trev said quietly, 'Ron was a wonderful man and we were lucky to have had him as a father and grandfather. I'm not particularly religious, but I'd like to pray for his soul—wherever it is.' He bent his head and the others followed suit.

After a few quiet moments, Trev cleared his throat. 'He left everything equally to his daughters, because he knew it would mean nothing to Pat now. We can see the solicitor and sort out what to do with things later.'

He went to Sue and offered her first his handkerchief, then his hand, before leading the way back into the other room.

Laura remained where she was, sitting staring down at her clasped hands. She became aware that someone was standing next to her and looked up to see Ryan gazing at her anxiously.

'Are you all right, Mum?'

She nodded. 'Just give me a minute or two.'

In the other room, Ryan walked across to Caitlin, warmed by the smile that lit her face at the sight of him. 'How are you feeling?'

'Just a little under the weather. I'll be all right.'

Kit stood up. 'Why don't you two come back with me to my place? I think you need to talk to Laura in private, and there's plenty of room there.'

'Will Mother mind?' Ryan asked.

'I'll ask her.' Kit limped across to the doorway into the side room and disappeared through it.

Caitlin looked up at Ryan. 'I like him. And I think he's very much in love with your mother, from the look on his face when he speaks of her. What did your uncle want?'

259

He sat down beside her. 'To read a letter from my grandfather, such a warm, loving letter. I'm going to ask him for a copy and keep it. I do wish you could have met Pop.'

'So do I.'

Deb came to join them. 'Am I interrupting something?'

Ryan smiled at her and tugged her to sit beside him. 'No, of course not. Kit's just invited us all back to his house so that Caitlin and I can explain about Dad and everything. You will come too, won't you?'

She nodded.

Laura and Kit came out of the small room and joined them.

'I gather we're all going back to Kit's,' she said with careful self-restraint, avoiding looking at Caitlin.

'I'll drive back with Ryan and show them the way,' Deb offered.

On the way, Laura said very little.

'You're still keeping me at a distance,' Kit chided mildly.

'It's better that way, don't you think?'

'Nope. Not when I don't know what I've done to upset you. But you need to sort out your family problems before you and I have our talk, though I'm not going to wait much longer for that.'

She didn't say anything.

At the house, she got out of the car with a feeling of dread. She didn't know how she was going to cope with this confrontation—no, not confrontation, *meeting*. It was all right her father saying to get rid of her anger, but you couldn't just decide to do that. It was still there inside her, hot and ready to rise up at the slightest provocation. Damn Craig! And damn that woman, too!

Once inside the house, she automatically went into the kitchen and put the coffee machine on.

Kit followed her. 'Want me to be there when they explain—or not? Up to you.'

She paused to stare abstractedly out of the window. 'No. Yes. I can't think straight.'

'I love you, you know.'

She turned to stare at him, but just as she was opening

her mouth to tell him not to say things he didn't mean, the doorbell rang.

'I'll get it.'

She watched Kit go to open the door and lead everyone into the living room, and realized that he was limping badly. He'd done too much today. But how would she have coped without him?

In the sitting room, Caitlin sat down with a sigh and pressed one hand to her forehead.

Ryan watched her anxiously.

Deb stared at Kit, trying to see him without anger. Her grandfather's letter had shaken her to the core, reminding her of the time he'd stopped her and Angie from quarrelling. 'Do you love my mother?' she asked suddenly.

His whole face brightened. 'Oh, yes. Very much. Do you mind?'

'I'm trying not to.'

He grinned at this equivocal answer. 'Keep trying, please, because I'm not going to stop.'

Laura came in, carrying a tray with the coffee pot on it. 'I thought we'd have some proper coffee. Um—would you mind if Kit stayed with us?' In the kitchen, she'd tried to nerve herself to go through this on her own, and had found she couldn't. She wanted Kit with her, even if he was two-timing her, because he was basically a kind man and would support her as much as he could. But after this was through, she'd tell him they had to return to an employer-employee footing, because nothing could come of this. She couldn't face another man being unfaithful to her, just couldn't.

When they were all supplied with mugs of coffee, Ryan took charge, explaining simply and concisely Caitlin's background and the reason she'd gone to live with his father.

'Some of those fringe religious sects can make life very difficult for those who try to opt out,' Kit said quietly.

Caitlin looked up. 'And it's difficult to move away, because they brainwash you from birth. I didn't want that for my child.' After a moment's hesitation, she added in a low voice, 'I didn't love Craig, but I was fond of him and

261

I think I made him happy. I—um—think it was the thought of the child that pleased him most about our relationship. We were chalk and cheese in so many ways. If I hadn't been feeling so unwell . . .'

She glanced pleadingly at Laura, who managed a nod.

'Craig hated growing older, and he loved the children he already had. I'm sorry I hurt you, Laura, more sorry than you can know. If I'd felt your marriage had any hope, I'd not have gone to live with him, but—'

'It was over long before he met you,' Laura said in a tight, harsh voice. 'We just hadn't got round to doing anything about it. I think he was waiting for me to finish decorating the house, actually. And I was a coward, not able to walk away.'

Kit sent her a warm, approving glance.

Ryan was watching Caitlin.

'I want to give you the money back now, Laura,' she went on. 'I don't need it and I never really deserved it, but I was frightened for my child, you see. I had to be able to keep it safe from my family. I couldn't have borne it to lead a life like mine.'

Deb had been looking from one to the other, listening carefully, and when Caitlin fell silent, she said suddenly, 'He was the best of fathers, though. Like Pop was to you, Mum.'

And Laura was at least able to grant Craig that. 'Yes. I know, love. It was just that his way of fathering got between me and you two, and that hurt. And he was unfaithful quite a bit towards the end. That hurt too.'

Deb stared at her very solemnly, then nodded. 'Well, maybe you and I will be better friends now. I think Pop would want that.'

'I hope so.'

'Mind you, I'll probably drive you mad at times. I'm not the most tactful of people.'

Laura leaned across to hug her. 'Doesn't matter. I'm not either.' Then she looked at Caitlin. 'I'd like the house money back, because I feel I earned it, but you can do what you want with the insurance money. I don't want to profit from his death.'

Ryan put his arm round Caitlin. 'And what about us two, Mum? Can you cope with that?'

There was a long silence, then, 'I'll—do my best. That's all I can promise. I'm still not happy about the—the relationship. So, we'll have to see how it goes.'

Ryan stood up and scowled at her. 'That's as grudging an acceptance as I've ever heard.'

Caitlin stood up and tugged at his arm. 'Don't!'

He turned to her. 'Don't what?'

'Don't say anything else. Let's all just—try.'

He opened his mouth, his expression angry.

Kit judged it time to intervene, because Laura was looking shocked by Ryan's anger. 'I agree with Caitlin. Don't say any more just now, Ryan. Everyone's feelings are too raw. Laura's lost her father. Give her time to get over that.'

'I don't have all that much time! We have to get back to Australia. I've a job waiting for me there.'

'Ryan, please—' Suddenly Caitlin's eyes rolled up and she crumpled to the floor, lying at Laura's feet like a broken blossom.

Everyone stared down at her in shock for a moment, then Laura pushed Ryan out of the way and knelt to take her pulse. 'Give us some room.'

'Mum's done first-aid courses,' Deb murmured to Kit.

'She's full of hidden surprises. I like that.'

Caitlin gradually came to, but Laura was worried about her pallor. There wasn't a vestige of colour in her face. 'I think we need to take you to hospital just to make sure of things. Did you have a D&C after the miscarriage?'

'No.'

'You may have retained some small part of the placenta and have an infection. A friend of mine did years ago. It should be quite simple to clear up.'

'It won't—stop me having other children?'

'Of course not.'

'I hate hospitals.'

Caitlin was clinging to her hand, and Laura suddenly realized how terrified the younger woman was. 'So do I. But you won't be on your own.'

'You'll come too?'

Laura nodded.

'Even though you still hate me?'

'I don't hate you any more, just the situation. That's different. Look, least said soonest mended now that we all know the full story. We'll get through this, I'm sure. As long as you make my Ryan happy.'

The glow of love that suddenly lit up Caitlin's eyes helped Laura to come to terms with the situation more than anything else had. There was no mistaking such love. It was what she'd always wanted for her children. And he was looking at Caitlin the same way. Why hadn't she let herself accept that before? 'Come on, then. Let's get it over with.'

She turned to Kit and studied him. 'You're looking tired, and I noticed your limp was worse. You've done far too much today, but I'm grateful. I needed you. We'll take Caitlin to hospital, then I'll catch a taxi back.'

He nodded. She was right. His leg was aching furiously and he needed to lie with it up for a while. Besides, it might be better if she was the one they turned to for help.

'Thanks for everything.' She kissed his cheek, saw his wry smile as he pulled her to him and kissed her on the lips. She could feel herself flushing as she walked away, knowing her children had watched this exchange with great interest.

What she couldn't understand was why he'd made such a point of kissing her like that in public.

They were lucky to find accident and emergency having a lull. Within the hour, Caitlin was whisked up to an operating theatre by a cheerful nurse, who told her how lucky it was she hadn't had anything to eat that day.

Ryan sat down to wait, as he'd sat in the hospital in Melbourne. Only, this time he wouldn't have Barry pestering him, and this time he was sure Caitlin wanted him there.

'I'll wait with you, shall I?' Deb offered. 'Angie and Aunt Sue were going back to the house to clear Gran's things out. They don't need me for that.'

'Thanks. I'd appreciate that.' He looked at his mother. 'Kit's not the only one who's tired. You look exhausted too. Why don't you get a taxi back now? I'll ring and let you know as soon as we're sure what's happening here.'

And suddenly Laura could struggle on no longer. She did feel exhausted, as if every bone was made of rubber. She let Ryan walk her to the door and give her one of his hugs.

'Thanks, Mum—for everything.'

She patted his cheek. 'Let me know how she is.'

In the taxi, she leaned back against the seat as it pulled away. I'm trying, Dad, she thought. I did all right there, I think. I'm not as angry as I was, because they do love one another, but I still feel upset inside.

She could almost hear his voice telling her to take it one step at a time.

But now she had a confrontation looming with Kit, because he would insist on knowing what had upset her. She couldn't bear even to try to build a relationship with a man who'd betray her. Just couldn't.

But could she bear to leave him?

Thirty-Two

When Laura got back, Kit was sitting on the sofa with his leg up and his hands clasped round yet another mug of coffee. The crutches were propped beside him, which told her his leg was aching.

'The coffee's still hot. Get yourself a cup.'

'It's a wonder you can sleep at night, the amount you drink,' she said by way of a greeting.

'It's not the coffee that's keeping me awake.'

'Kit, please don't—'

'Please don't what? Please don't even talk to one another?' He grabbed her hand as she tried to move past him, and drew her down on the edge of the sofa. 'We have to sit down and talk.'

'Now isn't the time. I need to start thinking about meals, so if you'd—'

'Go into my office?'

'Yes.'

'Well, I won't.' His voice rose in emphasis. 'I'm not going anywhere until we've *talked*. How many times do I have to say it to get through to you?'

She took a shaky breath, trying to keep her voice steady, but failed. 'I can't do it now, Kit. I need to rest. Please. I promise we'll talk tomorrow, but today I'm totally exhausted.'

He sighed. 'Don't you think you'd rest more easily if we cleared the air?'

She shook her head. She knew it was cowardly, but she wanted to delay the confrontation.

He spread his arms in a defeated gesture. 'All right. I

give you one more day, then we talk. And don't bother getting any food ready. I'm not hungry.'

She got up quickly. 'Thanks for your help today, Kit.' Not waiting for his answer, she hurried out of the room.

The trouble was, she thought as she started to climb the stairs, she didn't know whether she was relieved or sorry that he hadn't insisted. Maybe she should have stayed and had it out with him.

You're a fool, Laura Wells, she told herself. *You always fall for the wrong type of man.*

Kit followed her out into the hall, intending to go across to his office, but something drew his gaze towards the stairs. She was walking slowly, as if reluctant to go to her room. When she switched the stairs light off, he didn't move, just stood there in the darkness and listened as she went into the bathroom. A short time later there was the sound of water flushing, then slow footsteps going across the landing into her bedroom above his head. She sounded weary.

He tried to make himself move away and couldn't, so tried instead to work out what was wrong with him. Then suddenly his instincts took over from his reasoning, that feeling of knowing exactly what to do, which had never let him down before. Hell, he'd been superhumanly patient with her. 'Dammit, I'm not taking no for an answer,' he muttered. 'It's a misunderstanding, it's got to be, and the longer it continues the further apart we'll drift.'

His left leg was aching furiously, so he went up the stairs even more slowly than she had done, making no attempt to keep quiet and pausing every few steps to rub the stiff place near his knee.

Her voice floated down from just above his head and he looked up to see her leaning over the banisters, silhouetted against the light from her bedroom. 'What do you think you're doing? You need to rest.'

'I've decided we have to have that talk now.'

'Kit, I told you: I'm too tired for confrontations. Please go back.'

'Nope.' He set off again.

'Well, you'll be facing a locked door.' She whisked back into her bedroom and slammed the door shut, turning the old-fashioned key in the lock.

He continued to the top and leaned on the banisters for a minute, grinning at her last words. All the bedroom keys matched. He never had been able to figure out why. They were useless for locking people out—or in.

On the way to her bedroom, he collected the key from the next door. He stopped outside her room and knocked to get her attention. 'Are you going to open this?'

'No.'

Very quickly he inserted the key into the hole, pushing sharply to knock the key on the other side out, a trick he'd perfected in his boyhood. He'd never thought it'd be so useful. Turning the key, he flung the door wide open.

She was standing at the foot of the bed, panting a little as if she'd been running, still dressed, her hair tumbled, her face flushed. To him she looked very sexy and he could feel his breathing deepen. She didn't say anything as he moved slowly across the room, but she didn't move away either, though she could easily have tried to push past him.

At the last minute his foot caught on the bedside rug and his weak leg gave way. With a yell he pitched forward. But she was there, catching him, steadying him. So he grabbed tight hold of her and pulled them both down on to the bed, kissing her just as she opened her mouth to protest.

Her lips were soft under his. He'd been wanting to kiss her properly for days. She wasn't fighting now, and after a shocked gasp, she suddenly began kissing him back.

He groaned as the inevitable reaction hit him, then thought what the hell? She's seen a man with the hots for a woman before.

'They call this sexual harassment,' she muttered.

'No, they don't. They call it love, lust, desire, all sorts of words, but not sexual harassment.' He stared into her eyes and demanded, 'What the hell have I done for you to give me the cold shoulder, Laura? And why did you run away tonight instead of talking about it?'

She tried to roll away from him, but kicked him on the shin by mistake.

He couldn't hold back a gasp of pain.

'I'm sorry. Kit, *please* let me go.'

He clung on and repeated, 'Not till you tell me what's wrong.'

She could feel herself sag against him. 'All right. But let me sit up.'

They righted themselves and she tutted as he winced. 'Let me make you more comfortable.' She turned the pillow round to prop him up against the bedhead, then did the same on her side.

He took hold of her hand. 'Well, Laura?'

'I heard you that last morning your friends were here. You and Jules. In your bedroom, really early. You must have been there all night.'

'Ah. So that's it.' He closed his eyes and shook his head slowly from side to side as the implications sank in. 'You think I'm bed-hopping. Thanks for the vote of confidence!'

She shrugged. 'Men do it.'

'Your husband may have done; I don't.' He caught her hand. 'Look at me, Laura. Jules and I were *not* sleeping together. I woke up during the night and had trouble getting to sleep again. Too much coffee and stimulating chat, I think. She heard me moving around downstairs—she's an insomniac from way back—and came down for a chat.'

'Oh?'

Her tone was disbelieving and he snapped, 'Yes. A chat. *I* was happy to chat, but it turned out she wanted more. Jules and I lived together for a couple of years, as you may have gathered—as much as two people *can* live together when both of them have to keep rushing off on assignments. If we'd been together full-time, it'd have broken up much sooner, I'm sure. When we were home, there were good times and bad. Increasingly there were quarrels because I was getting better assignments. In the end, *she* left *me*,

269

saying it was damaging her career to be seen in a settled relationship. But if she hadn't gone, I would have done the deed. We just weren't suited. We make better friends than lovers. That morning you heard us, she intimated she'd be happy to start the relationship again. I told her I wouldn't.'

'Oh?'

'*Yes, damn you!* Just so you know the score, I've had three relationships over the years.' He began ticking them off on his fingers. 'One was with a journo—Jules. Before her, an actress—Kate. Before that, a radio presenter—Lee-Anne. I never cheated on any of them, though Kate cheated on me.' His voice softened. 'That's what you're afraid of, isn't it? That I'd be unfaithful to you?'

She nodded.

'Because of Craig.' It wasn't a question. He'd already guessed the legacy of self-doubt that sod had left her with. He could see how her eyes were shadowed with memories and sadness. 'Damn the man! He's left you all screwed up about relationships.' Kit raised her hand to his lips and kissed it, feeling her shiver at his touch. Then he pulled the hand so that she had to turn round and face him. With his mouth a few inches from hers, he asked, 'Do you believe me?'

She looked at him, then slowly nodded.

He couldn't hold back a groan of relief.

'Is your leg hurting again?'

'What? Oh, a little, but it wasn't that. I was just relieved that you believe me. What you think matters so very much.' He wriggled away from her. 'And now I think I'd better return to my bedchamber, Laura my love. My body has come to life again with a vengeance, and this isn't the time to make love to you.'

'Why isn't it?'

He stilled and stared at her. 'Because of your father, of course.'

'I think Dad would understand more than anyone. Kit, I'm tired of death and unhappiness. I want you tonight, in my bed, in my body. I want to feel alive again. I haven't for months, you know. You're not the only one whose sex drive's been taking a sabbatical.' She leaned forward and grabbed him, pulling him close and kissing him until they both had to pause for breath. 'I want you.'

'You're sure?'

'Yes. Very sure.'

He cradled her cheek for a moment with one hand, then smiled ruefully. 'Trouble is, I don't have any protection. I can get something from the chemist's tomorrow, but tonight . . .'

She did a quick calculation. 'I'm at my safe time. As long as you're— clean?'

'Being a foreign correspondent sounds more glamorous than it is, and I've never been one to hop in and out of beds. I like some mental and emotional contact with the women who share my life—and I want even more with you, Laura, because I think you're going to be the most important woman in the rest of my life.'

Her face showed how that shocked her. 'You can't mean that!'

'I can. I always trust my instincts when I get a certain sort of feeling, and I've felt good with you from the start, as if we're right together. I like you *and* love you. I'm hoping desperately that you have similar feelings for me.'

Her smile was glorious, lighting up her whole face and taking his breath away. 'Yes, I do. Though I've tried not to. I love you very much, Kit, and it didn't take long for me, either. Dad noticed, said you were fond of me.'

'He was a wise old guy, your dad, from the sounds of it. I wish I'd known him, but at least I met him once.' He pulled her close and cut off any more conversation by kissing her again, a very long kiss that left them both panting.

When he began to take her clothes off, she let him, smiling slightly and only once staying his hand for a moment to say, 'I've got stretch marks from having the children.'

He promptly kissed her belly. 'Very nice and soft to kiss, stretch marks are.'

271

But when she helped him out of his clothes, he lost his erection and tried to pull away, saying gruffly, 'You get into bed. I'll do this.'

She realized he was trying to hide his leg and held his hands still. 'The leg's part of you, Kit. Don't try to hide it. And don't think it puts me off, because it doesn't.' She slid his trousers down and bent to kiss the livid scar from his last operation, moving her lips slowly along the line of it as she pulled his trousers off.

He lay back, feeling the desire build in him again, marvelling at how easy she made it, then, as she lay down beside him, he began a joyful exploration of her body.

'I'm too fat,' she muttered in his ear.

'For whom? I'm not into making love to stick insects.' He kissed her mouth to stifle further talk. 'Shh. Stop talking and let's enjoy one another. I'd forgotten how wonderfully soft a woman's body can be.' Oblivious now to anything but her, he kissed his way down her neck to her breasts, caressing them until she writhed beneath him.

He wanted so much to make it good for her. Your body didn't forget, but he used his mind to stay in charge of its pulsing desire, keeping their love-making slow and gentle, trying to gauge by her reactions what she liked, stroking her creamy flesh until he could wait no longer.

It wasn't the most spectacular love-making, given the stiffness of his damned leg and their uncertainties about each other, but it was still good—so very, very, good—to know he was a whole man again, able to pleasure the woman he loved.

As soon as his heart had stopped racing, he said it again, 'I love you, Laura.' He kept wanting to say it, needing to say it, to make sure she understood exactly how he felt.

Her eyes were over-bright as she turned to him. 'I love you too, Kit. And—thank you.'

'I enjoyed it too, you know.'

'It's more than that. Thank you for making me feel whole again, desirable, a real woman.'

'It was mutual. I wasn't sure I'd be able to do it.' He

wriggled into a more comfortable position, still keeping his arm round her.

With a happy little murmur, she snuggled against him. 'I'm tired now.'

'Me too.'

He woke in the darkness to find her trying to get out of bed without waking him, so pulled her back. 'What are you doing?' The bedside clock said two in the morning.

Her stomach growled.

He burst out laughing, drew her to him for a quick kiss, then admitted, 'I'm ravenous as well. Did we eat anything yesterday?'

'Not much.' He let her go and she slipped quickly into a dressing gown. 'Omelettes?'

'Perfect.'

'Drinking chocolate?'

'Whatever.'

He followed her slowly down the stairs, smiling all the way and found her humming to herself in the kitchen as she worked.

Thirty-Three

A week after Pop's funeral, Sue arrived at Kit's house in Wardle in the middle of the morning. When Laura opened the door, she found her sister there, looking upset. She drew Sue inside and took her into her little sitting room, a place she hardly used. 'What's wrong?'

'It's Mum. They rang me to say she passed away in her sleep early this morning.'

'What did she die of?'

'They didn't know. She just—died.'

'Oh, no!' Laura sat staring down at their linked hands for a moment, then looked at Sue. 'I've heard it often happens. One partner dies and the other just follows, for no reason that anyone can work out.'

'She never settled at the nursing home, did she?'

'No. And to tell you the truth—and I know it sounds horrible—but I think it's for the best. She wasn't really Mum any more, was she?'

'No. Only, it seems so *final* to lose them both.'

They sat together for a few minutes, then Sue took a deep breath and said, 'Trev and I will organize the funeral, if you like.'

'Another one.' Laura sighed.

'Your third this year, my fifth. It's been a terrible year.'

'It's been good as well. I did get here to say goodbye to Dad. I feel closer to Deb than I have for years, though she's still very touchy about me and Kit—and there's Kit. I feel so lucky to have met him.'

'Trev and I like him. He's a kind man.'

'I'm glad you do.'

'Are you two going to get married?'

Laura shook her head. 'No. He's asked me but how can I? He's six years younger than me and he's not got any children. I should leave him really, only I can't tear myself away.'

'Why on earth should you leave him?'

'Because one day he'll regret not having children, I'm sure he will. He loves them. You should see him talking to the grandson of the woman next door. Tam came round to ask if he could interview Kit for a school project and Kit was so lovely with him. It brought home to me what I'd be depriving him of. I love him too much to do that. Only, when I think of leaving, the mere thought of it tears me apart.'

Sue patted her hand. 'I don't know what to say.'

'Don't say anything. It's my problem. I'll find a way to solve it. You're looking a lot better now.'

'Oh, yes. I'm going back to work in a couple of weeks.' She gave a little chuckle. 'The counsellor says I'm allowed to have the most immaculate house in the street, but no more than that. And I *will* keep taking the pills till they think it's safe for me to stop.'

'Angie and Deb seem settled in Pop's house. Girls need to move away from home when they're that age, I think.'

'Yes. It's nice to see how well they get on. And they may as well pay us rent as anyone else.'

They sat quietly for a few minutes longer, not saying much, then Sue left and Laura went to tell Kit the news, then ring Ryan.

Two months later, Laura slipped out of the house while Kit was taking a shower, leaving a note on the kitchen table saying, 'Gone out. Need to think about something.'

It was a mild day, and without deciding on a destination, she found herself stopping near the park, giving in to the temptation to take her troubles to the wishing well. She was relieved to find herself alone there. She tossed in a coin and stared blankly at it as it sank, because she didn't quite know what to wish for this time.

She went to sit on the nearby bench, staring into space.

She couldn't believe it, but she was pregnant. It must have happened during that first couple of days, but she'd been so sure she was in her safe time, and anyway, at her age your fertility was supposed to drop. For a while it had seemed more likely that it was one of the first signs of menopause to get irregular periods. Kit had taken her word for that and they'd joked about his 'older woman'.

To add to the confusion, during her other two pregnancies, she'd been sick for the first three months, but this time she'd felt wonderful, as if her whole body was singing with health. Which was another reason she'd been reluctant to consider seriously the possibility that she might be expecting a child.

But when two months had passed without a sign of a period, she'd started to worry, really worry. She'd bought a pregnancy kit to set her mind at rest, only, it had done just the opposite.

She didn't know how to tell Kit, what to expect from him—and most of all didn't want him to feel compelled to marry her. He had asked her to marry him early on in their relationship, and still made long-term plans for them, but hadn't actually mentioned marriage again. Did he regret his original offer? Or didn't he care if they were married or not? She cared, now that they were having a child.

Oh, but it was embarrassing to be pregnant at her age. What would Ryan and Deb say? Or her sister?

Laura didn't know how long she stayed there, only that her thoughts were still in a tangle and she couldn't think what to do next.

Suddenly she became aware that someone had sat down on the seat next to her, and looked quickly sideways. You had to be careful in parks. 'How did you find me?'

Kit smiled. 'This is one of your favourite spots when you need to think about something. You'd been here the first day we met, remember?'

She nodded.

'So . . . what is it you needed to consider so urgently?'

She could feel herself blushing, couldn't find the words to tell him.

His voice was gentle, and he took her hand as he said quietly, 'I hope it's what I think it is.'

'You'd—guessed?'

'It had to be a possibility, whatever you said. In real life, men aren't as stupid about these things as the characters in novels. After all, you and I haven't taken any precautions. When you kept going on about the menopause, it seemed to me you were trying to convince yourself as much as me, so I let things ride. And you weren't going anywhere. I made sure of that.' He grinned. 'I pinched your passport.'

She couldn't help smiling. 'I never even noticed. So you're not—annoyed about it?'

'You've done a test, I gather? It *is* certain?'

'Yes. I did two tests, actually. I went and bought another brand for the second one, just in case something was wrong with the first kit.'

He threw back his head and laughed. 'Oh, Laura, don't you know me well enough yet to realize how thrilled I am about it! If we hadn't been able to have children, I'd still want you and only you, but this is the icing on the cake.' He pulled her to him and kissed first one cheek then the other, the tip of her nose and finally her lips.

When he let her go, he pulled her to her feet and held her hands close to his chest. 'If it weren't for my stiff knee, I'd do the thing properly, go down on bended knees to propose. As it is, will you marry me, Laura darling? Because it really will make me the happiest man on earth.'

She smiled through eyes brimming with happy tears. 'Yes please. I'll marry you when and where you like, Kit Mallinder. I can't imagine how I got so lucky as to meet you, but I know when I'm on to a good thing.'

His voice became quieter, reverential almost. 'And we'll soon be three. I can't tell you how much I'm looking forward to that. Though we must make sure you get the very best of care. At your advanced age . . .'

She pretended to thump him and he chuckled, then felt in his pockets and pulled out two coins. 'Here. We'll each throw in a coin and make a wish.'

When the ripples had stopped moving the water, she turned to him. 'I can guess what our wishes were.'

He put one fingertip on her lips. 'Shh. It's bad luck to tell.'

She nibbled the fingertip and he sucked in his breath sharply. 'How do you do that, woman? You have only to touch me and I want you.'

'Then we'd better go home and do something about it. After which, we'll discuss arrangements.'

Hand in hand they left the park.

In the middle of a sunny January morning three weeks later, Deb went to answer the door of the small terraced house. 'Oh, Auntie Sue. You're early.'

Sue smiled at her. 'Can't help it. I always seem to get ready too soon. Trev's waiting in the car. Shall I ask him to come in?'

'I think you'd better. Angie won't be long, I'm sure.'

As she went back out to the car, there were footsteps on the stairs and Angie came running down, followed by Rick. 'Phew! She nearly caught us there.'

'She must know,' Deb said matter-of-factly. 'She's not stupid.'

'Knowing is one thing, seeing for yourself is quite another.'

Trev came in and made himself comfortable on the sofa, his expression for a minute so exactly like Pop's that Deb had to swallow hard.

'You're keeping this place nice, girls,' he said cheerfully. 'Aren't they, Sue?'

She nodded.

Deb smiled. 'Not to your standards, Auntie Sue, but not too bad, eh?'

'I can't imagine better tenants,' Trev said with another of his broad smiles.

'So—what's the occasion for the party today? Have you any idea?' Sue asked. 'Kit certainly does things in style, doesn't he? I'm looking forward to a night at a luxury hotel.'

Deb shook her head. 'I haven't the foggiest idea. But Mum's been a bit strange lately, so I hope this is going to settle it, whatever it is. My guess is they're going to announce that they're getting married and the party will be to celebrate that.'

'Well, she and Kit seem very right together.'

Deb rolled her eyes. 'Yeah. Lovey-dovey all over the place.' She'd got used to that now, but still thought it a bit gross to see her mother kissing someone so passionately.

Angie looked at the clock. 'I suppose we'd better get going. We don't want to be late.'

It took them over an hour to drive to the hotel, which was out on the moors, a former stately home. They were greeted with a flattering amount of fuss at reception and shown up to adjoining suites.

'I could get used to this,' Angie said.

'Who couldn't?' Deb bounced on the bed and went to peep into the other bedroom in their suite, which was allegedly Rick's, but where she knew Angie would be sleeping. She wished she had a guy, but was making one or two friends now that she'd got a job. It wasn't the best of jobs, but staying at home with nothing to fill your time was much overrated, she'd decided. She was thinking seriously of going to university or college—something to give her better employment options.

The phone rang. Kit. 'We'll expect you downstairs in an hour, dressed in your finest, if you please. If you want to order something from room service, go ahead.'

He put down the phone before Deb could demand to know what this was all about.

The girls and Rick went down and were shown into a room with small groups of chairs. Kit was waiting for them, dressed with unusual elegance in the sort of trousers that belong to a suit, and with a silver-grey shirt that could only be real silk. He beamed at them. 'Great. You're on time. Come and sit down. We won't start until everyone's here. You can say hi to the others for me.'

Exchanging puzzled glances, they obeyed, and he vanished through a side door.

Sue and Trev were shown in.

'Kit says to wait here,' Angie announced. 'Something's not going to start till everyone's here.'

The door opened again and Ryan appeared, with Caitlin beside him.

Deb squealed and flung herself into her brother's arms. 'When did you fly in? Why didn't you tell me?'

He hugged her hard. 'Mum and Kit wanted it to be a surprise.'

'Wanted *what* to be a surprise? Do you know what this is about?'

'Sworn to secrecy. They want to tell you themselves.' He held her at arm's length. 'I'm glad you've put a bit more weight on. You look gorgeous.'

She smiled and smoothed out the material of her dress, which she loved to pieces, then turned to Caitlin. 'You're looking a lot better than last time I saw you.'

'I'm feeling better.'

'I'm glad your cousin gave up on dragging you back into the fold.'

'So am I. It was sheer chance that he met a woman who was as religious as himself and decided that the Lord had brought her to him. He phoned up to give me a lecture on reading the Bible and remembering my upbringing.' She sighed and looked sad for a minute or two. 'I haven't heard from my parents, and I don't suppose I will. My father can be very stubborn, but I thought my mother might . . .' Her voice trailed away.

'That sucks.' Deb reached out to squeeze her hand in sympathy.

'Let's not spoil the day with my problems. We want everyone to be happy.'

The sadness Caitlin was trying to banish made Deb suddenly feel like giving her another hug, a proper one. 'Well, you've got us now. We may not be the most wonderful of families, but we're not the worst, either.'

The door opened and Joe and Gil walked in, both smartly

dressed. They were very much a couple these days, Deb thought.

'Do you know what the surprise is?' Joe asked Deb when she went to greet him and his friend.

'I think they're going to announce that they're getting married.'

'About time too.'

Trev walked across to join them. 'Nice to see you, Joe, Gil. Do you know everyone? I don't think you ever met Laura's son Ryan and his partner Caitlin, did you? They had to dash back to Australia after Pop's funeral and they didn't come over for Mum's.'

Everyone shook hands, then sat down, fidgeting and looking at one another, wondering what was going on.

Then the door at the side of the room opened again and Kit came in, with Laura on his arm. He was wearing the jacket to his very elegant suit, and a tie, something no one had seen him in before. She was wearing a deceptively simple dress and jacket in aqua silk, with a pearl and gold brooch. It was the sort of outfit women know instinctively will have cost a fortune.

'Wow, Mum, you look great!' Deb said. 'Now for heaven's sake tell us what the occasion is.'

Ryan got up and went to hug his mother. 'You don't look old enough to be our mother.'

A hot blush stained her cheeks for a moment, and she looked appealingly at Kit, who came forward to take her arm again.

'We have an announcement to make—well, three announcements, actually.' He gave Laura such a loving glance that Deb felt herself soften still further towards him. Her dad had never, ever looked at her mother like that. 'First, Laura has at last done me the honour of agreeing to marry me.'

Silence, then a babble of congratulations and noise.

'What's the second announcement?' Trev asked. 'I'm not sitting down if I have to bounce to my feet again for more congratulations.'

Laura blushed even more brightly and Kit grinned at her.

'Your mother, sister and aunt is a bit embarrassed about this one, but I'm very proud to tell you that she's expecting my child.'

Stunned silence met this news, then more congratulations and kisses.

Laura held Deb in her arms, looking searchingly at her face. 'You're not—angry about this?'

She shook her head. 'I'm just stunned, Mum. I mean, you're nearly forty-five. Is it all right? Will you be OK?'

'Yes. I've had some tests and there are more to come, but they think everything is quite normal.'

'Did you plan it?'

'No. We were careless. But I'm glad now.'

'So am I,' Kit said. 'She kept refusing to marry me before.'

'And the third announcement?' Sue asked.

'We're getting married in fifteen minutes' time—which is the main reason for this gathering today.'

There was almost a riot at this, as people milled around, kissed, hugged and congratulated the two main players.

The next half-hour passed like a dream for Laura. Kit was mostly at her side. All her family had gathered together. Even her anger at Caitlin had died down. What had happened in the past just didn't seem important any longer. She turned to her new husband as he grabbed her hand and pulled her closer to him.

'Silence, please, everyone! I'd like to propose a toast. To my wife, Laura!' Kit raised his glass of champagne.

After everyone had echoed his toast, he called for silence again. 'And I'd also like to drink to my son!' He patted Laura's stomach. 'We just found out it's a he, and we're dying to meet him.'

When that toast was over, Ryan moved forward. 'Unaccustomed as I am to public speaking, I don't feel I can let this occasion pass without saying a few words and—'

His voice was drowned out by jeers and catcalls and it was a while before he could speak. The newlyweds didn't seem to notice that. They were too busy gazing at one another.

Anna Jacobs is always delighted to hear from readers and can be contacted:

By mail

PO Box 628
Mandurah
Western Australia 6210

If you'd like a reply, please enclose a self-addressed, business-size envelope, stamped (from inside Australia) or an international reply coupon (from outside Australia).

Via the Internet

Anna has her own web domain, with details of her books and excerpts, and invites you to visit it at http://www.anna jacobs.com

Anna can be contacted by email at anna@annajacobs.com

If you'd like to receive email news about Anna and her books every month or two, you are cordially invited to join her announcements list. Just email her and ask to be added to the list, or follow the link from her web page.

Readers' Discussion List

A reader has created a web site where readers can meet and discuss Anna's novels. Anna is not involved in the discussions at all, nor is she a member of that list—she's too busy writing new stories. If you're interested in joining, it's at http://groups.msn.com/AnnaJacobsFanClub